Penguin B

The China Governess

Margery Allingham began leaving a lasting mark
on modern fiction in 1928 when, at twenty-three,
she wrote the first of her many Albert Campion
detective novels. At that time her books were
beloved by the few advanced spirits who enjoyed
her gay and distinctive approach to the problems
and pleasures of post-war youth. Since then her
gentle detective and his strong-arm colleagues have
become known and loved by young people of all
ages all over the world. Her novels cover a
broad field. They vary in treatment from the
grave to the frankly satirical, yet each example
contrives to conform to the basic rules of the good
detective tale. She lived for many years on the edge
of the Essex marshes. She died in 1966.

Margery Allingham

The China Governess
A Mystery

Why each atom knows its own,
How in spite of woe and death
Gay is life and sweet is breath.
Robert Bridges

 Penguin Books

in association with Chatto & Windus

Penguin Books Ltd, Harmondsworth,
Middlesex, England
Penguin Books Australia Ltd, Ringwood,
Victoria, Australia

First published by Chatto & Windus 1963
Published in Penguin Books 1965
Reprinted 1967
Copyright © P. & M. Youngman Carter Ltd, 1963

Made and printed in Great Britain by
Cox & Wyman Ltd, London, Reading and Fakenham
Set in Monotype Baskerville

This book is sold subject to the condition that
it shall not, by way of trade or otherwise, be lent,
re-sold, hired out, or otherwise circulated without
the publisher's prior consent in any form of
binding or cover other than that in which it is
published and without a similar condition
including this condition being imposed on the
subsequent purchaser

Contents

None of the characters in this book
is a portrait of a living person

The Turk Street Mile

'It was called the wickedest street in London and the entrance was just here. I imagine the mouth of the road lay between this lamp standard and the second from the next down there.'

In the cold darkness of the early spring night the Chief Detective-Inspector of the area was talking like a guide-book with sly, proprietorial satisfaction. He was a neat, pink man whose name was Munday and he was more like a civil servant than a police officer. His companion, who had just followed him out of the black chauffeur-driven police car drawn up against the kerb, straightened himself and stood looking at the shadowy scene before him without speaking.

They were standing in the midst of the East End on a new pavement flanking a low wall beyond which, apart from a single vast building, there appeared to be a great deal of nothing at all in a half circle perhaps a quarter of a mile across. The great fleece which is London, clotted and matted and black with time and smoke, possesses here and there many similar bald spots. They are cleared war-damage scars in various stages of reclamation. Around the edges of this particular site the network of small streets was bright and the arterial road by which they stood was a gleaming way bathed in orange light, but inside the half circle, despite the lighted windows of the building, it was sufficiently dark for the red glow which always hangs over the city at night to appear very deep in colour.

'The Turk Street Mile has gone now, anyway,' Munday went on. 'A serious trouble spot for three hundred years, wiped out utterly and for ever in a single night by four land-mines and a sprinkling of incendiaries in the first raid on London, twenty years ago.'

The other man was still silent, which was something of a phenomenon. Superintendent Charles Luke was not as a rule at a loss for words. He was very tall but his back and shoulder muscles were so heavy that he appeared shorter and there was a hint of the traditional gangster in his appearance, especially now as he stood with his hands in his trousers pockets, the skirts of his light tweed overcoat bunched behind him and his soft hat pulled down over his dark face. The legacy of the last few years which included promotion, marriage, fatherhood, widowerhood and the Police Medal, had had remarkably little outward effect upon him. His shorn curls were as black as ever and he could still pump out energy like a power station, but there was a new awareness in his sharp eyes which indicated that he had lived and grown.

'I understand that the district was considered a sort of sanctuary,' the Chief was saying. 'An Alsatia like the ancient one behind the Strand, or Saffron Hill before the First World War. They tell me there was a recognized swag-market down here.'

Luke drew a long hand out of his pocket and pointed to a thin spire far away in the rusty sky. 'That's St Botolph's,' he said. 'Take a line from there to the old gasometer on the canal at the back of the cinema over there and you won't be far wrong. The Mile was a narrow winding street and in places the top floors of the buildings almost touched. Right in the middle there was a valley with very steep sides. The road dipped like a wall and went up again. That's why there was no through traffic to clear it. The surface hadn't been altered for generations; round cobbles. It was like walking over cannon balls.' Now that he had recovered from his first astonishment at the sight of the new building which was not what he expected, he was talking with his usual fierce enthusiasm and as usual painting in details with his hands.

'When you turned into The Mile from this end the first thing you saw was the biggest pawnshop you ever clapped eyes on and opposite, all convenient, was the Scimitar. That was a huge gin palace, built on what you might call oriental lines. The street stalls ran down both sides of the way to the hill and every other one of them sported a strictly illegal crown-and-anchor board. The locals played all day. Early in the morning and late at night by naptha flares. Farther on, round the dip, was the residential quarter. I don't know if that's the term. People lived in caves. There's no other word for them. Have you ever seen a beam eaten to a sponge by beetles? Magnify it and dress the beetles in a rag or two and that's about the picture. I went right through it once for a dare when I was about ten. My mother didn't get me completely clean for a month.' He laughed. 'Oh, The Mile was wicked enough in a way, depending on what you mean.' He turned back to the scene before him and the enormous new block of council dwellings. The design was some way after Corbusier but the block was built up on plinths and resembled an Atlantic liner swimming diagonally across the site.

'What the devil have you got there?' he inquired. 'A prehistoric "wot-o-saurus"?'

'It's a remarkable building.' Munday was earnest. 'In daylight it takes your breath away. It's as sleek as a spaceship, there's not a hair out of place on it. It's the reason why I've had to disturb you tonight. Mr Cornish felt Headquarters must be notified at once.'

'Ah, he's the Councillor, is he? The one who's going to get the knighthood for this lot?'

'I don't know about that, sir.' The Chief was wooden. 'I know he's got to raise the money to build five more of these.'

Luke sniffed and surveyed the monster, scored with sun balconies and pitted with neat rows of windows, each one shrouded with pastel colours, blue, pink, lilac, biscuit and lime. A sudden grin spread over his dark cockney face.

'Got the original families in there, Chief Inspector?' he inquired.

Munday gave him a steady glance.

'Not exactly, sir. That's some of tonight's story. I'm given to understand that although it's the primary object of all these big improvement schemes to rehouse the portion of the populace which has been rendered homeless by enemy action, twenty years is a very long time. The new buildings have had to be financed in the ordinary way and the outlay has got to be recovered, so the tendency has been to allot these very exceptional new apartments – they really are quite impressive, Superintendent – to those people who have proved themselves first-class tenants in the temporary accommodation which was rustled up for them just after the war, prefabs and suchlike.'

He came to an uneasy pause and Luke burst out laughing.

'I shan't be asking any questions in Parliament, Chief. You don't have to explain anything away to me. You've got a handpicked lot here, have you? And that's why this present spot of bother which is only "wilful damage" has so upset the dovecotes? I see. Come on.'

They set off together down the partially constructed concrete ramp. 'Some of these local government big boys are remarkably like the old-time squires, feudal old baskets!' he remarked. '"Don't hang your bedding out of the window", "Teach the kids to say please, damn them" and "No Singing except in the Bath". I don't like it in a landlord myself. Someone has got irritated by it perhaps? Eh?'

'I don't know.' Munday shrugged his shoulders. 'My information is that the couple whose home has been wrecked are a sort of show pair. The old boy is finishing his time at the Alandel Branch factory down the road and he's reputed not to have an enemy in the world. The same thing goes for the old lady who is his second wife. I believe there's a temporary lodger, a skilled worker from Alandel's. They got permission to take him in for six weeks' trial and the rent was properly adjusted, so it can't be jealousy on the part of the neighbours. The damage appears to be remarkable and the feeling is that it may be directed against the building itself, the Council that is, and not the tenants at all.'

'Could be. Who have you got out here?'

'A good man, Sergeant Stockwell. I was speaking to him on the phone just before we came out. He thinks it must be the work of a small gang. Possibly juveniles. He doesn't like the look of it but he doesn't see what can be done before morning.

However, Mr Cornish – ' He let the rest of the sentence remain unspoken.

'He wants the top brass, does he.' Luke was good tempered but fierce. 'Here it is then. Both of it. We'll go and give him a toot.'

His amused, contemptuous mood persisted as they entered the aluminium-lined passenger elevator which carried them up to the top floor. The convenience and neatness impressed him but the termite-hill architecture made him uneasy.

'It's all very quiet. What's everybody doing behind the fancy drapery?' he muttered, the attempt to muffle his remarkably resonant voice failing disastrously.

'The trouble is on the other side of the building, sir. Top floor. All the doors are on that service side.' Munday sounded defensive. 'It's not quite like a street. A lot can happen without the neighbours knowing.'

Luke opened his mouth to say something acid but at that moment they arrived and he stepped out of the silver box to be confronted by a prospect of his beloved city which he had never seen before.

He stood transfixed before the unaccustomed view of London at night time, a vast panorama which reminded him not so much of the aerial photographs of today but rather of some wood engravings far off and magical, in a printshop in his childhood. They dated from the previous century and were coarsely printed on tinted paper, with tinsel outlining the design. They had been intended as backcloths for toy theatres and were wildly ambitious. The Fall of Rome was included, several battlefields, and even Hell itself complete with steaming lakes and cauldrons of coloured fire. Now to Luke's amazed delight he saw the same glorious jumble of grandeur and mystery spread out below him. He saw the chains and whorls of the street lamps, the ragged silver sash of the river and all the spires and domes and chimney-pots, outlined with a sorcerer's red fire, smudging against the misty sky. It made his heart move in his side.

Munday touched his sleeve. 'This way, Mr Luke.'

He turned his head abruptly and caught sight of a small

crowd at the far end of the balcony. Here again the lighting was dramatic and worthy of the view.

The two open doorways were bright oblongs in the dusk and the shafts from them created a barrier between the crowd and a uniformed man on guard.

As they came forward a square figure in a tight suit advanced to meet them. He stepped delicately like a boxer and everything about him proclaimed that he was Sergeant Stockwell, the inevitable 'good man in charge'. Luke gave him a long experienced stare and moved close to Munday so that he could hear the murmured report. It was made with the mixture of smugness and efficiency he expected but there was an undercurrent of outrage which made him raise his eyebrows.

'The Councillor, that's Mr Cornish, has taken the old boy who owns the wrecked apartment in to the neighbours next door to talk to him,' Stockwell said. 'His name is Len Lucey. He's a fitter and a good old craftsman with nothing known against him. Before the war he lived on the edge of this estate with his first wife who kept a tobacco and confectionery business – very small. She was killed in the big Blitz. He then married a woman from North London and he had to live over there, travelling across the city to work every day, until he was granted this new first-class flat. His second wife has made a little palace of it by all accounts and that's some of the trouble. She had a sort of fit when she came in and saw the damage. There's a neighbour with her but I've sent for an ambulance. I shouldn't be surprised if she never comes right out of it. I don't blame her,' he added gravely. 'The state of the room shook *me*. I thought at first it was one of the local delinquent mobs but now I'm not so sure. There seems to be almost too much work in it for them, if you see what I mean.'

'It's the farther doorway, I take it?' Luke inquired. 'And the Councillor and the old boy are in the nearest one, is that right?'

'Yessir. The first flat belongs to a much younger couple called Headley. He's a master baker and works at the meat pie factory in Munster Street. He and his wife are nothing to do with this business and they've got the wind up. They're not being unfriendly but they don't want a dose of the same medicine. They've already approached me on the quiet to get everybody out if I can.'

'But they don't want to offend the old squire, eh?' Luke was chuckling with his own brand of savagery. 'Well, well. Let's hope for everybody's sake the poor old lady hasn't taken things too hard or we'll all be in the Sunday newspapers and that won't help anybody get a title, will it?'

Munday started to speak but thought better of it. Stepping forward, he led the way past the saluting constable to the first of the open doorways. There he hesitated a moment, took off his hat politely and walked in, Luke behind him.

The tiny white-painted vestibule which was merely a nest of doors, was as neat a pack as an orange. Any addition, even a rolled umbrella would have been an embarrassment. The two large men were, physically speaking, an insufferable intrusion; they were both aware of it as they stood one behind the other peering into the small sitting-room in which there were already four people, two different kinds of wallpaper, a television set with the picture going and the sound turned off, a magnificent indiarubber plant, a very expensive, very well kept lounge-dining-room suite of contemporary furniture of the 'bundle and peg' variety, three large framed flowerprints and a fierce wrought-iron candelabra. So much high-powered professional 'design' had gone into the apartment that there was no place for anything else and the present drama was suffocating.

For once in his life Luke was taken completely out of his stride. The owners of the flat, large pale young people whose acute discomfort was the dominant thing about them, huddled in a corner, she in an arm-chair and he behind it, occupying at least a quarter of the floor space. The dazed Len Lucey, old and shaking, his very thin neck sticking out pathetically from an extremely white collar, sat at the dining-room table on a spidery chair while before him was a person who had made much larger rooms seem small, a living flame of a man, as passionate and fanatical as Luke himself.

At the moment he was trudging up and down the 'contemporary' rug, his grey hair bristling, his gaunt shoulders hunched and his long bony hands working together as he clasped them behind his back. A more unlikely aspirant for Luke's hypothetical knighthood it would have been difficult to imagine. The superintendent perceived his mistake and began to revise his ideas.

'Councillor Cornish?' he inquired. 'I am Superintendent Luke from the Central Office, Scotland Yard. This is a shock, I'm afraid.'

He was aware of acute eyes, shadowed but intelligent, meeting his own questioningly.

'It's a damn bad thing,' said a pleasant, matter-of-fact voice with a touch of pure steel in it. 'You're going to get to the bottom of it very quickly, Superintendent.'

'I hope so, sir.' Luke was brisk and hearty.

'I know so.' The voice was still pleasant but still completely inflexible. 'You're going to uncover everything about it and then you're going to stop it once and for all before a great project is jeopardized. This estate is called a Phoenix. It's not a municipal venture, it's a social rebirth, a statement of a sincere belief that decent conditions make a decent community, and I'm not having failure.'

Assistant Commissioners are said to use this sort of tone sometimes to senior superintendents, but since there is never anybody else present to overhear it, the theory is not proved. Luke regarded the man before him thoughtfully and cocked an eye at Munday, who was looking at the Councillor with an expression of gloomy contemplation.

'Oo-er!' Luke did not say the word aloud but his lips moved and Munday received the message. For the first time in their entire acquaintance Luke scored a bull's-eye and had the satisfaction of seeing the primness punctured by a sudden ill-suppressed grin.

The Councillor stopped trudging up and down. 'Your sergeant has got a statement from Mr Lucey,' he said. 'I'm prepared to vouch for the greater part of it myself. I did not spend this particular evening with him, but I can prove that I had his entire life story checked before he was offered an apartment in this new block and I can answer personally for the unlikelihood of him, or his wife, having an enemy. This is a perfectly ordinary innocent citizen, Superintendent, and in any civilized city his home ought to be inviolate. My God, man! Have you been next door yet?'

'No, sir.' Luke was wooden. 'I'd like to visit the flat in the presence of the householder. That's important, sir. If you don't mind.' It was another voice with metal in it and the gaunt, shabby man with the bristling hair looked at him with fleeting curiosity.

'If it's a necessary precaution,' he was beginning.

'No, sir. Just a regulation.' The steel was still there with plenty of butter on top. 'Shall we go? Perhaps Mr Lucey would lead the way.' Luke flattened himself against the egg-shell-tinted wall and the old man was just able to edge past. His frailty was very apparent and as he went by the two detectives caught something of the bewilderment which engulfed him.

He was so small that they towered over him and as they crossed the second threshold and came into his home it was they, the two senior policemen, who caught the full impact of that first unforgettable scene.

A room which had been a comfortable middle-aged home full of comfortable middle-aged treasures, valuable mainly because of their usefulness and their associations, had been taken apart with a thoroughness that was almost tidy in its devastation. Yet at that first glance the one central picture alone occupied their attention. A very neat old woman, still in her good outdoor coat and best beehive hat, was sitting at a polished mahogany table on whose surface there were several scored scratches so deep that a triangular piece of the veneer had come cleanly away, while in front of her, laid out in a way which struck a deep unpleasant chill to the stomachs of the two experienced men, were the entrails of a pleasant old French clock which lay on its back beside them. They were all there; wheels, springs, hands and the pendulum, each torn and twisted out of shape but all arranged neatly in a pattern of deliberate destruction. The old lady herself was not looking at them. Her face was livid and beaded with sweat, her eyes were closed and her mouth had fallen open. Only her weight was holding her in position. Behind her another, much smaller woman, wearing an apron and bedroom slippers but clutching a handbag, peered up at them piteously through gaily decorated plastic spectacles.

'She's gorn,' she said. 'I felt her go. Just now. Just as you came in. The doctor will be too late – won't he?' She seemed to see the little man in front of them for the first time and a bleak expression spread over her face. 'Oh, you pore chap,' she said. 'Don't look, dear, don't look. It was a seizure you see, she never came round.'

'That's right, Dad, come along out.' Luke's glance rested on the livid face which was changing unmistakably before his eyes. The neighbour was right. She was dead. He had no need to touch her. He slid his arm round the old man and swung him gently out into the vestibule. There, with the wide view of the city framed in the open doorway, they stood for a moment like a pair of pigeons huddling on a window ledge.

'You and she came in together and saw the damage, did you?' he inquired gently, still holding the old man to him as if he were afraid he might fall. 'Anyone else with you?'

'Only Reg Sloan. He lodges with us, see?' The old voice was thin and hollow. The significance of the scene had not yet registered upon him. He was still worrying about small things. 'We was allowed to let the room seeing it was empty; we got permission. I told the sergeant. Mr Cornish knows. Reg got the permit from him. He went to see him – went to see him, I say, called at his house.'

It was like a voice on the wind, something sighing through the rushes. Luke was unnerved by it. 'Take it steady, chum. Get a breath of air,' he said. 'How long has this chap Reg lived here with you?'

'How long? I don't know. Two or three months. Before Christmas he came.'

'I see. Recently. He hasn't been here years?'

'Oh no. He's temporary. He's walking the works and they asked me if I could oblige by putting him up for a few weeks. We got permission, me and Edie did. He got it for us.'

'What do you mean by "walking the works"?' It was Munday. He was half out of the sitting-room door, his hands on the lintels as he leaned forward to speak.

'Well, he was learning the ropes. He came from another firm, you see. It was a business arrangement. He wasn't going to stay.'

'I see.' Luke sounded dubious. 'Where is he now, anyway?'

'I don't know,' The old man looked about him suddenly. 'He went for the police. He went to telephone. We all came in together. We'd been out to have one. Reg liked a chat about old times and we used to go and have a chinwag in the pub. Tonight we all came in together and Edie saw the clock all broken on the table and she's upset because it was her father's. It came from her home. Reg began to swear and went into his room – that's the little one through the kitchen – and he came out almost at once. He said "Stay here, Len. I'll go and ring the police, mate. Gawd, I'm sorry" he said. "I wouldn't have that happen for worlds" he said and he went. Don't you know where he is? Edie likes him. He'll be the only one to pacify her when she realizes her clock's broke.'

'Yes.' Luke glanced sharply at Munday. 'What about the neighbour?' he inquired. 'Could she take him along and make him a cup of tea?'

'Yes.' The woman in the decorated spectacles came round the detective like an escaping cat slipping out. 'Yes. I'll see to him. It's the shock, you see. You come along, Mr Lucey. You'll have a lot to do tonight. A lot of people to see and that. You come and have a sit down and get ready for it.' She put her hand under his arm and eased him away from Luke. 'Make way for us do, there's good people.' Her voice, shrill and consciously preoccupied, floated in above the murmur of the little crowd. 'We want a cup of tea we do. If you want to help there's a woman needed in there. That isn't a thing that ought to wait.'

Luke listened with his head on one side. The brutality made him laugh a little.

'I'm too sensitive altogether for a copper,' he said to Munday, who was looking down his nose. 'It was the lodger's quarrel, then. That's what comes of "walking the works" I suppose. Yet it seems a bit fierce for that sort of industrial dust-up.'

'Fierce? Do you see those chairs?'

The D.D.I. stepped aside to reveal a corner of the room which contained two good dining-chairs whose leather seats had been scored neatly into ribbons with a razor blade. 'Like a joint of pork, isn't it? The carpet's the same. That's no wrecking in the ordinary sense. No joyous smashing up for the hell of it. Just cold bloody mischief.' He spoke with clipped fury and the Superintendent's eyes rested on him curiously.

'I don't like the look of that clock,' Luke said. 'I've got a thing against trick-cyclists and head-shrinkers and all their homework. Let's see the lodger's bedroom. "Off the kitchen," he said. 'Strewth! That used to be an electric cooker, I suppose?'

They passed through the little kitchen where nothing breakable was left whole and yet where nothing had been overturned haphazard, then on through the farther door leading to the architect's pride, a spare or child's room. It had no space for anything save a bed and a dressing-chest but there was no doubt at all in either mind as they paused in the doorway that here was the centre of the storm.

Everything a living animal could do to destroy and to desecrate bed and walls had been done. Scraps of clothing and the relics of a suitcase made an untidy heap on the narrow strip of floor. A canister of flour from the kitchen had been thrown at the looking glass and lay like trampled snow over the remains of a decent blue suit with the lining ripped out which lay on top of the ruin of a plastic wardrobe.

On the mirror's clouded surface there was a message written with a gloved forefinger in the kind of printing sometimes taught in schools instead of handwriting.

There were two lines, completely legible and entirely

unambiguous, and yet sufficiently out of the ordinary in the circumstances to startle the two senior policemen.

'*Let the Dead Past Bury Its Dead.*' The portentous statement stared out at them, educated and shocking amid the filth. Underneath, in the same careful, clerkly script was a second message: '*Go Home, Dick.*'

Munday stared at the messages, his thin pink face bleaker even than usual in his suspicious bewilderment.

'"Bury its dead"?' he demanded. 'What the hell is this! Who was to know she was going to die?'

'No, that's a quotation. A piece I learned at school. Tell me not in mournful numbers, Life is but an empty dream, and the something or other is dead that slumbers and things are not what they seem. Psalm of Life, Henry Longfellow.' Luke was talking absently, his cockney flippancy unintentional and as natural a part of his personality as his tremendously powerful voice which, even when geared down to a murmur as now, was a rumbling growl which set the shreds of the curtains shaking.

'Someone else has been to school, eh? They didn't teach him much except poetry either, by the look of this room. Poetry and thoroughness, and the rest is the same old uncivilized brute. The same old Turk Street special, cropping up like a symptom of a familiar disease. There's no mystery now about "walking the works" anyhow.'

'What do you mean?'

'"Go home Dick".' Luke's dark face was glowing. 'The chap's name was Reg Sloan. What else can it mean except exactly what it says? "Dick," you old private eye, amateur or professional, go home. The past is dead.'

'Good Lord.' Munday stood staring at him. He had changed colour, Luke noted.

'What's on your mind?'

The Chief Inspector stepped backwards into the kitchen.

'I was thinking of the Councillor. If he gets it into his head that this is an echo from Turk Street long ago, something pre-war, and if he decides that a detective has been employed by someone unknown to dig up dirt about one of his precious handpicked tenants – any of the three hundred and sixty of them – then I'm going to have a job for life, aren't I?'

'That's right,' Luke said. 'Also he's quite an item, this literary character who is so interested in keeping ancient history quiet. Why is he only interested now? What could he want to hide which has only become important after twenty years?'

Chapter One

The Elopers

In the expectant greyness which was only just less than the night's dark a cock crowed twice. Instantly, from the rise behind the wayside station a second rooster answered him, and with this unearthly sound, the whole ritual of daybreak began.

In the red sports-car which was pulled up on the lane's verge below the station drive, the two young people who were asleep in each other's arms moved drowsily. The girl's lips were still against the cheek of the young man beside her and she completed the kiss which sheer weariness had interrupted before she opened her eyes. 'Oh no,' she protested sleepily. '*No*. Not morning yet, surely?'

'Julia!' The boy was all over awake at once, his eyes bright as the lids flickered open. He returned her kiss joyfully and glanced down at the watch on his wrist; his forehead crumpled and he sat up. 'So much for our careful planning! We've slept for two solid hours and the train will be here in fifteen minutes. Oh hell! You'll have to go down to the Keep alone. Do you mind?'

'I feel as if I shall never mind anything ever. It may wear off but it hasn't yet,' she said blithely. She was kneeling up on the seat and he put his arms round her waist and hugged her. 'But if I'm to get your car under cover by daylight I'd better go now, which is a bit heart-rending . . . you're sure Nanny Broome really is a hundred per cent on our side?'

'Completely.' His voice was muffled as he rubbed his face against her chest with weary longing. 'I telephoned before I collected you. Anyhow, she's almost my foster-mum. She's always on my side.' He sat up to look at her seriously. 'I gave her the full details. I told her what we had in mind.'

She met his eyes squarely, her own round and grave.

'Was she scandalized?'

'Lord no. She was thrilled to bits.' He shivered slightly. 'And so am I.'

'Me too.' Julia was just visible in the cold light. She was a very pretty girl: not very tall, but slender, with fine bones and hair so dark as to be almost black. Her skin was thick and white and unpainted and her bright blue eyes and determined mouth echoed her father's considerable personality. He was Anthony Laurell, head of the Laurell light engineering empire and youngest self-made tycoon in Britain, and one of the most interesting characters in industry. Julia was just eighteen, warm and gay as a lamb, and every detail of her cared-for, well-dressed appearance acknowledged that she was somebody's very precious only child. At the moment she was absorbed, peering down into the shadowed face raised to her own.

'Your smile is like lace,' she said.

'Lace?' He was hardly flattered.

'Decorative.' She was entirely serious. 'It sort of trims you up and makes you glorious.'

'You're idiotic,' he muttered through his kiss. 'Sweet and certifiable and I love you, I love you. God! I love you. Darling, I've got to catch this dreary train back to London but tonight . . .' His voice broke with a disarming helplessness which pinked them both like a sword. 'Tonight I'll come back and find you and damn everybody else in the world.' He pushed her firmly away and climbed out of the car.

'Timothy.'

'Hello?' He swung round in the fast growing light and she saw him for the first time all over again. He had a rangy body, a distinctive, characterful face, grey arrogant eyes and a wide thin mouth whose lines could curl and broaden like copperplate handwriting. He was twenty-two and all the panoply of masculine physical charm which had earned him a host of admiring contemporaries, even in the Oxford where they both were students, was at its freshest and best. To see all this giddy power and splendour helpless before her was a part of the enchantment which bound her and she caught her breath before it.

'I don't want you to go back to London!'

'Nor do I, lady! But I've got to. I've got to see your old man and have it out with him. His trip to Ireland made it possible for me to get you away and safe here while I talk, but we can't just clear out into the blue.'

'Why not?' She was coaxing. 'Honestly, I don't care any more about anything in the world except being with you. Two months ago I'd rather have committed suicide than upset Daddy or get in the newspapers. Now I just can't care.'

The young man put his hands on either side of her face and looked down at her like a child with a treasure.

'You go on thinking just like that and leave the rest to me,' he said earnestly. 'But I can't face the thought of you and me being turned into a nice Sunday "read" for half-wits. It was foolhardy and inconsiderate of your old man to call the whole thing off suddenly, just when his own invitations to the engagement "do" were out, and he must have known that the gossip hounds would be down on us like a blight. I must talk to him. He can't have so much against me.'

'He hasn't. I told you I don't know why he suddenly vetoed the marriage, but he liked you and he liked your background and was impressed by the degree and the sports record and . . .'

'Then why? For God's sake?'

'It was something to do with a letter he got from Miss Kinnit.'

'From Aunt Alison?' He was staring at her. 'Do you know what was in it?'

'No, or I'd have told you. I only knew it came. I didn't mean to mention it.' The dusky colour appeared in her cheeks. 'She was so nice to me. I thought she approved.'

'She does. She's a funny, cold old thing but terribly kind – after all she and Eustace are my only family and she was delighted about you. They keep teasing me about you being the deb of the year. This must be some completely idiotic misunderstanding. I'll go and put it right. Wait at the Keep and love me.'

From the embankment above there was a clatter as the signal fell and her arms closed round him possessively.

'I'd still rather you didn't go. I'll hold you. I'll make you miss the train.'

He released himself gently. 'Please don't,' he said gravely but with great sweetness, his lips close to her ear. 'You hurt too much. Too much altogether.' And turning from her he ran up the slope into the half-light which was already throbbing with the noise of the train.

Julia sat listening until the engine had shrieked away into the fields once more and then with a sense of desolation she let in the clutch and drove away through the back roads to where the village of Angevin lay hidden in the Suffolk folds.

She avoided the turning to the single main street of cottages and took, instead, the upper road which wound through the fields to a pair of neglected iron gates which led into a park so thickly wooded with enormous elms as to be completely dark although their leaves were scarcely a green mist amid the massive branches.

The trees grew near to the house, so close in fact that they obscured it from the north side and she had to use the headlights to find the squat Tudor arch which led into the paved yard. As she passed it a yellow-lit doorway suddenly appeared in the shadowy masonry and the angular figure of a woman stood silhouetted within it. She came running out to the car.

'Mr Tim?'

'No.' Julia was apologetic. 'It's only me I'm afraid, Mrs Broome. We got held up and I left him at the station. You knew he was going back to London, didn't you?'

'Yes. Until tonight.'

There was an indescribable note of satisfaction in the brisk voice which startled Julia as well as reassuring her, and the newcomer went on talking. 'He told me all about it on the telephone and what he didn't tell me I was able to put together. There isn't much Mr Tim hides from me.'

It was a strange greeting, neither hostile nor effusive, but possessive and feminine and tremendously authoritative. Julia was only just sufficiently sophisticated not to be irritated. 'What about the car? I don't think it ought to stand out where it can be seen, do you?'

'No, miss, I certainly don't and I've given my mind to that, all night nearly. I think it should go down to the little piggy brick house. I'll show you where.'

She stepped into the empty seat and pointed to an opening on the farther side of the yard.

As she settled down beside her, Julia noticed that she was trembling with excitement, and her round face turned suddenly towards her showed patchy red and white. Margaret Broome was a woman of perhaps fifty, but her coarse hair was still fair and her light brown eyes were bright and shiny as pebbles in a brook. Her gay green cardigan was buttoned tightly across her chest and she folded her arms against the cold.

'It's all overgrown but if you drive slowly you'll make it'.' she hurried on. 'I slipped down last evening to make sure we could get in. It's the old summer-house at the end of the View. We used to call it the piggy house when Tim was a baby, after the little pig's house that was built of brick you know.' She was unselfconscious in her nursery talk, matter of fact rather. 'Nobody goes there now. It's too far for anyone in the house but right in front of the windows, so no one's going to hop in there courting from the village. Here we are. See, I propped the doors open. You drive straight in.'

It was a little ornamental temple with a tessellated floor and pillars, designed perhaps as a music-room in some far off Victorian age of extravagance.

The panelled double doors had lost much of their paint but they were still stout and the car lights revealed the usual summer-house miscellany piled in spider-infested confusion against the far wall.

'There,' said Nanny Broome, hopping out with the agility of a girl, 'now we'll shut and lock the doors on it and no one will be a penny the wiser. We must hurry though, because it's nearly light. Come along, miss, stir your stumps.'

The nursery way of speaking flowed over Julia, amusing and reassuring her without her realizing that she was receiving a treatment whose technique was as ancient as history. She hurried obediently, helped to close the doors and then followed the angular figure round the side of the building to the broad, terraced path which led up the slope to the front of the Keep. As she looked up and saw it for the first time from this vantage-point she paused abruptly, and the older woman who was watching her exploded in a delighted giggle. In the pink light of dawn, with the long shafts of sunrise cutting through the mist towards it, the Keep at Angevin was something to see.

At that moment it was a piece of pure visual romance, inspired and timeless. Much of its triumph lay in the fact that it was an unfinished thing. The original family who had begun to build a palace to outrival Nonesuch had died out before they had put up little more than the gateway, so that the actual structure which had come down to posterity retained the secret magic of a promise rather than the overpowering splendour of a great architectural achievement.

Two slender towers of narrow rose-pink brick, fretted with mullioned windows, were flanked by three-storeyed wings of the same period, all very carefully restored and remarkably little spoiled by the Victorian architect who had chosen to build the summer-house at this magnificent point of vantage.

'How staggering it looks from here!' Julia was almost laughing. 'When I came to the house-party at Christmas we didn't get as far as this so I never saw it from this angle. I know why Timothy calls it his castle.'

'It is his castle.' Again the satisfied and possessive warning note jarred on the younger woman. 'When he was a tiny boy in the war, he and I used to sneak out here in the very early morning mushrooming, and I used to tell him about the knights riding in the courtyard, jousting and saving ladies and killing dragons and so on. He loved it. All the kids have it now on telly,' she added as an afterthought. 'Do you ever see it? *Ivanhoe.*'

'That was a bit earlier, I think. You're a few hundred years out. When was this building begun? Henry the Eighth's reign I suppose?'

'Henry the Eighth! He was nobody to tell a child about!' Mrs Broome appeared to be annoyed by a fancied criticism. She strode up the path, the patches on her round face brighter, and her eyes as hard and obstinate as stone. 'I'm afraid I wanted my young Mr Timmy to grow up to be a chivalrous gentleman with a proper attitude towards women,' she said acidly. 'I hope you've discovered that he has one, miss?'

She turned her head as she spoke and made it a direct question. Julia regarded her blankly. 'I love him very much,' she said stiffly.

'Well, I thought you did, miss, or you'd hardly be here now would you?' The country voice was ruthless. 'What I was meaning to say was I hope you've always found him what you'd wish, you having been brought up as I hope you have?'

It only dawned upon Julia very slowly that she was being asked outright whether or no she was a virgin, and her youthful poise wilted under the unexpected probe. The colour rose up her throat and poured over her face, making the very roots of her hair tingle.

'I . . .' she was beginning but once again Nanny Broome had the advantage. Reassured on a point which had clearly been exercising her, she became kindness itself and almost more devastating.

'I see you have,' she said, patting the visitor's arm. 'Of course young people are the same in every generation. There's always the "do's" and the "don'ts" and it's only a fashion which seems to put one or the other lot in the front rank for the time being.' And, as if to emphasize her wholehearted cooperation in an enterprise of which she had once been doubtful, she seized the girl's little suitcase and hurried on with it, still talking. 'Sometimes children get funny ideas, but I brought up Mr Timmy myself, and I didn't think the schools could have done him much harm after that. It's a scientific fact, isn't it, that if you have a child until he's six it doesn't matter who has him afterwards.' Again she gave the little laugh that would have been arch had it not been for the alarming quality of complete faith which pervaded it.

The girl glanced at her sharply under her lashes, and the blurred youthfulness of her face stiffened a little.

'I hope you won't mind me calling you Nanny Broome but that's how I think of you. I've heard it so often from Timothy,' she began, taking the initiative. 'Did you look after him from the time he was born?'

'Very nearly. He was just over the two days, I suppose, and the ugliest little monkey you ever saw. Great big mouth and ears and his eyes all squitted up like a changeling in the fairy tales.' She laughed delightedly and her face became radiant and naïve. 'I've looked forward to saying that to the girl he was going to marry for over twenty-one years.'

Julia's intelligent mouth twitched despite herself. 'And is it true?' she ventured. 'I mean, was he really? Or can't you remember now?'

The elder woman blinked like a child caught out romancing. It was a completely sincere reaction and utterly disarming. 'Well, I remember he was very sweet,' she said, thoughtfully. 'I loved every little tiny scrap of him, that's all I know. He was my baby. I'd lost my own, you see, and he crept right into my heart.' She used the *cliché* as if she had coined it, and the essential side of her nature, which was warm, unselfish and mindless as a flower bud, opened before the girl. 'You see I'd been a nurse in the Paget family over at St Bede's and I was just on thirty when I met Mr Broome, who was the head gardener, caretaker and everything else here. He was a widower with five lovely grown-up children and when he asked me I couldn't resist them and all this lovely place to bring them to. So I married him, and my own little boy was on the way when there was all that business before the war – Munich time. The doctors had me in hospital at Ipswich but it was no good. Baby didn't live and I came back knowing I wouldn't have another. So when I was given Timmy to look after you can guess, I expect, young though you are, how I felt. And hasn't he grown up a darling? And now you've come to take him away.' The final phrase was spoken solely for effect and its falseness did not convince even Mrs Broome herself, apparently, for she laughed at it even while she uttered it and there was no trace of resentment in tone or smile. 'You'll never take him right away,' she added with a grin of pure feminine satisfaction. 'He'll always be my little Prince Tim of the Rose-red Castle in one little corner of his heart. You can see that's true because where did he bring you? He brought you to *me* to hide you. Now you come along and I'll give you a cup of tea.'

They had reached the last terrace as she finished speaking and only a lawn separated them from the tall graceful façade, whose blank windows looked out sightlessly to the estuary two miles away.

'It's all locked up except for my little door.' She took her visitor's elbow and guided her over the damp grass to the narrow entrance from which she had first appeared.

Julia was aware of a small service hall with the stone painted walls and varnished woodwork of the more solid variety of Victorian Gothic mansion, and found herself ushered into a long, narrow room with a very high ceiling. It was yet warm and remarkably comfortable despite a double row of painted waterpipes round the cornice.

'Since the children went and Miss Alison wanted Broome and me to live in the house, we gave up our cottage and I've made us a little flat out here.' Her guide led her over to the window where a modern dining unit complete with pews and a gay blue and yellow plastic-topped table had been installed. 'The big kitchen is neary forty feet long so there was no point in poor old Broome and me rattling about in it alone. I use the scullery as my kitchen and the butler's pantry has made me a lovely double bedroom and you'd never guess that this was the still-room before the First World War, would you? It's my lounge now and I love it. Excuse me a moment while I see to the kettle.'

She bustled out of the room, arch, affected, enjoying the romantic situation to the full and yet, despite it all, strangely genuine at heart. Julia looked about her curiously. The room reflected its owner to the point of giving itself away. A pile of weekly magazines whose bright covers promised the latest in patterns and notions stood on the old-fashioned dresser, which itself had been treated with white paint. The walls under the festooning waterpipes were hung with a rose-strewn paper and the sky-blue curtains matched the table-top and the washable upholstery of the chair-seats. Home-made black wool rugs broke up the glare of black and yellow linoleum tiles but the 'contemporary' effect was not so much enhanced as debunked by a peculiarly individual type of ornament. The room was full of toys which had been mended and repainted and which stood about in places where knick-knacks would have been more usual. A wooden engine, for instance, enamelled scarlet over its scars, occupied the place of honour in the centre of the dresser, while all over the place there were little newly-dressed dolls and animals, as well as china wheelbarrows and boots holding cut flowers or little ferns.

Julia's white leather coat and silk scarf appeared remarkably sophisticated in this artless setting and Mrs Broome, returning with a painted tin tray set with multi-coloured china, eyed her with open admiration.

'You look just like what the paper said of you – the one that forecast the engagement,' she announced. '"The leading fashionable young lady of the year", I was so happy I cried when I read that. "A princess" I said. That's what I always promised Mr Timmy when he was a little tiny boy.'

Julia sat down abruptly, trying not to look dismayed. 'Oh dear,' she said. 'You explain quite a lot about Timothy, Nanny Broome.'

'Quite likely, but not *all*.' The woman spoke with unexpected shrewdness. 'There's nothing like a British Public School and Oxford to mould the clay. Mr Eustace Kinnit said that when he insisted on sending the poor little chap away to Totham preparatory school. He was only eight and a bit; he *did* look a baby.'

She was talking fast and pouring out at the same time, but as she picked up a steaming cup to hand it to her guest she paused and fixed her hard brown stare on her.

'Tell me, miss, what exactly has your father got against

young Timmy? I should have thought my boy had every mortal thing a gentleman could want for his daughter. Looks, lots of money, wonderful brains and education, a place all ready for him in a business which will be his one day, and lovely manners, though I say it myself who taught him. I don't understand your Dad because if we'd been preparing the lad for it all his life he couldn't have been more suitable for you, or that's my view!'

Julia hesitated, and Mrs Broome nodded her approval without letting up in any way.

'Did something happen to put your father off?' she inquired. 'He seemed willing enough at first, didn't he? He was going to give you a dance to announce it or so *Probe Parker* said in my paper. Then, quite suddenly, he changed his mind and was dead set against it and the column wanted to know why. Quite frankly, Miss, so do I, and I'm the one who would know if there was anything real to object to.'

The dark and elegant girl in the beautiful clothes sat looking at her thoughtfully and Mrs Broome watched her.

'You were thinking that too, weren't you, my poppet?' she said with her eyes but she did not venture the question aloud and Julia came to a decision.

'Did you ever meet Timothy's parents, Mrs Broome?'

'No, miss, I didn't.' She spoke with decision but there was a faintly satisfied, 'just as I thought' expression in the voice. 'I heard Mr Eustace's and Miss Alison's younger brother had been killed in Spain, of course, but I didn't see much of the family the first year I was married. It was only when I came home from the hospital after losing my baby that I found the family had moved down here because the war was just about to start. When I first married Broome the house was kept as it is now, partly as a show place and partly as a store. The Family owns a gallery of antiques besides having an interest in the big auction rooms. And a lot of the important pieces were very often kept here, as they are still.'

'Yes, I knew that.' Julia was anxious not to intrude. 'I only wondered if you'd ever seen Timothy's mother.'

'No, miss, I only saw the girl who brought him down

because London might be bombed. She wasn't a uniformed nurse and not really safe with him, which was why I took over. I always understood that his Mummy had died in childbirth, but with eighty babies in the house you can understand I was too busy to hear much.'

'So many?' Julia's dark eyes widened. 'Miss Kinnit told me at Christmas about the evacuees. On the first day of the war this house was invaded. It was a sort of clearing station, wasn't it, for the district? You must have had a time!'

An expression of such intense happiness that it could almost have been called a radiance transfigured Nanny Broome suddenly.

'Oh! It was wonderful,' she said, fervently. 'I never had a second to think of my own trouble, and then having Timmy without his mother it saved my life it did really!' She paused. 'Your father's very old-fashioned, I suppose?' she said abruptly.

'Father? No, I should have said the opposite.' The girl was out of touch with the trend the conversation was taking. 'Why?'

'I went to the adoption when Mr Eustace made Timmy his own little son,' said Mrs Broome without explanation. 'We all went up to the Law Courts in London and into the judges' secret room and it was summer and Timmy was in his first white sailor suit with long trousers although he was only five.'

'*Secret* room?' Julia appeared fascinated.

'Or it may have been "private", I forget.' The romantically-minded lady was unabashed. 'Anyway it was hidden away in the panelling, and all the gowns and wigs and waterbottles and things were about, and I sat in the passage while the business was done. Timmy was wonderfully good so the lawyer told me. We used to play "Judges" after that. I had an old white fur shaped stole that looked just like a wig when you put it round your face. Now, miss, Broome will be up in a minute, so I'm going to take you up to your room. I've been getting it ready every since I heard a rumour Timmy had got a young lady. I knew he'd bring you here honeymooning. He always promise dme that. "I will bring my bride, Nan, and you shall look after us. "' She imitated the small boy with such fidelity that for a second he stood before them, an arrogant pygmy, packed with authority in a washable white sailor suit.

She picked up Julia's suitcase and turned a smiling face towards her.

'You'd better get some sleep,' she said. 'You won't get much once you're on the run from the reporters. They'll be on to you like ravening wolves, your father appealing for you on the telly like he did last night.'

It took a moment or so for the astonishing statement to register on Julia.

'But that's impossible,' she said at last. 'He doesn't know.'

'Oh yes, he does.' Mrs Broome was remarkably cheerful about it. 'Parents always know a lot more than children think. They've got an instinct you know, here' – she patted her lean chest delicately. 'Anyway I know it's true because I saw it myself when I was sitting up waiting for you. Just after the last news they caught him getting on to an aeroplane to go and look for you. "I wish she was safe at home in bed," he said, and his poor old face was all wizened with worry. I was quite sorry for him even if he has taken a silly dislike to Timmy. "You've made a rod for your back and you'll suffer for it", I said to him and I switched him off.'

The girl rose slowly to her feet. 'My father was coming *home* on an aeroplane last night from a business trip to Ireland . . .' she began.

'Oh, that may have been it.' Mrs Broome made it clear that she did not care. 'I know I thought that he could go flying to Gretna Green in Scotland, but he wouldn't find you and Timmy because you'd be here, safe in the Bride's Room. Come along, miss, it's quite a way, up on the nursery floor, but it's this side of the turrets.'

She led the way out of the service quarter into the vast house itself. Julia followed her, struck again as she had been on her first visit by the enormous size of the corridors, the endless acres of dark oak ply-wood panelling all looking perfectly new, and the stone staircases which spiralled from floor to floor. Only the windows, whose glazing bars were as finely carved and delicate as if they had been in wood, seemed to belong to the palace which she had seen from the summer-house.

'Wouldn't it have made a lovely school?' said Nanny Broome, only the least bit breathless as they arrived at last in a gallery as long as a skittle alley and looked at the line of mahogany doors all splendidly furnished with brass and cut glass.

'I always call this the Nursery Suite, and there was one time when Timmy was about six and very noisy that we used it for that, but it was always a long way up and lonely. We've never been able to get proper help here, you see, not in my time. It must have been wonderful in Mr Eustace's grandfather's day. Twenty-three people in the servants' hall and then they thought they were understaffed, or so Broome says. He can just remember the old gentleman. "Like God in tweeds, he was." Broome always says that, though I shouldn't repeat it. Well, this is the room, my dear. We always used to call it the Bride's Room, Timmy and me. We had our own names for all the rooms, but the others were nearly always kept empty except when they were needed to show off a great suite of furniture or some tapestries or something. We had his things brought up to the room at the end there but they were all taken back when Timmy went to school. However, the Bride's Room was always here and kept like this under dust sheets. I've got it all out and pressed all the covers; they're not even yellow, they've kept so well.'

Her hand was on the door knob when she glanced at the visitor. Julia was standing in the long, empty corridor, the clear morning light falling on her from the high windows. There was something about her which was peculiarly lonely and which reduced the cosy chatter to the status of an old wives' tale. A scared look passed over Mrs Broome's face as she glimpsed reality's fleeting skirt but her resilience was indefatigable and in a moment she was talking away again as happy as a child uncovering a surprise. She opened the door and stood back to let the visitor pass.

'Look, miss!'

There was a long pause as they stood together surveying the scene. 'You can see why we gave it its name? Yet it was made, I believe, for one of Queen Victoria's daughters who didn't get married – or perhaps Mr Eustace was joking when he told me that. He says some silly things: you never know how to take him. Anyway it's a princess's set of furniture all right, isn't it?'

Julia was silent. The huge square box, parquet-floored and high-ceilinged, had been arranged to display a suite of bedroom furniture designed and made in the halcyon days of the last quarter of the nineteenth century, when modish taste was just due to go clean out of fashion for the best part of the next hundred years.

The half-dozen pieces, all of which were very large indeed, were painted white and carved with festoons of flowers, birds and cupids. To display them the walls had been tinted a vivid blue which had now faded, but the carpet, which had evidently been stored and recently relaid, retained its original turquoise. The bed was the most extravagant piece. Its graceful cane halftester rose high towards the cornice and was so festooned in carved white wood that the effect was positively insecure, as if the great couch were trimmed with icing sugar. A magnificent spread of fine Irish crochet over a blue lining completed a picture of chill grandeur, chaste to the point of being suspect.

'Bridal and pure and oh, I hope you'll be so happy!' Nanny Broome spoke straight from a heart which was coy and warm and unaware of the dismay she was producing. Even when she turned and caught sight of the frozen young face staring from the monstrous edifice in front of her to the horrific intimacy of the double washstand with the green marble top and the waterlily shaped toiletware, she did not comprehend.

'Oh, miss! Don't you like it?' There was reproach as well as astonishment in the question.

'It's very beautiful. Thank you very much for taking so much trouble but the whole room makes me feel rather cold. I don't think I'll stay here now if you don't mind. Is there somewhere else I could change and lie down for an hour or so?'

Julia sounded as if she was aware of being ungracious but had decided she could not help it. Mrs Broome remained disappointed and deeply mystified. 'It's not *the* room, you know, miss,' she said suddenly. 'This isn't the one the tale is about. That one is on the other floor and right the other side of the house, and even that is not the true one either, because it happened in another house. I wouldn't give you *that*, even though I'd take my dying oath it's never been haunted. There's no ghosts anywhere in the Keep, thank God.' She spoke with tremendous fervency but the chill remained and her round eyes were watchful. 'You've heard all about it, I suppose?'

'No.' Julia was already turning towards the door and the nurse made a move as if to intercept her. Her expression was fearful yet naughty, disapproving yet dying to tell.

'Do you know about Miss Thyrza's chair?' She made the murmured phrase sound comically sinister, like a child trying out a suspectedly wicked word.

Julia heard her but without interest. She had reached the doorway and was almost running towards the stairhead. On reaching it, however, she paused and turned back, re-entering the room just as Mrs Broome was coming out. Hurrying across the blue carpet, she climbed on to the stone sill and threw open the window pushing back the casements until they were at their widest so that the morning air poured into the room.

'Why, Miss, whatever are you doing? There'll be leaves from the tree-tops, birds and I don't know what flying in. That spread alone is worth a small fortune.'

'Very likely.' There was unexpected firmness in the young voice. 'But I don't think we'll worry about that. Please leave the room like this to air. I may come back here later but just now I should like to lie down somewhere else.'

Mrs Broome opened her mouth to protest but thought better of it. She was trained to recognize authority when she met it and presently she led the way downstairs again, for the first time looking a little dubious.

Chapter Two

Dangerous Lady

A remarkably ill-tempered-looking old man, as aggressively pink and clean as a baby, wheeled a new barrow slowly across the gravel drive.

As Julia looked down on him from the window of the small sitting-room on the ground floor, the hot midday sun winked off the bright paint of the bodywork and she grinned.

This was Broome himself and his unmistakable resemblance to a Walt Disney dwarf could hardly be entirely unintentional. She wondered if he knew.

Now that she was rested and had fed from the luncheon tray Mrs Broome had just removed, she had reverted to her normal gaiety. She looked cool in a grey tailored cotton dress with a terracotta scarf and shoes and her hair a black silk helmet. She sat on the edge of the table, her small hands, blue-veined at the wrists, folded in her lap. She was very much in love, her mind quite made up.

The morning paper which had been brought to her in triumph with her meal had been folded back by Nanny Broome into a harlequin's wand so that no other news of war or peace should detract from the main story. There was a snapshot of Sir Anthony Laurell across two news columns. He was shown descending from a plane and smiling all over his face, above the caption: 'Tired but On Top; Flying Chairman Settles Strike Threat Yet Again.' The story was a purely industrial one concerning labour disputes in Northern Ireland but it finished with a brief report of the little incident which was all that had mattered to Nanny Broome. 'As he paused to pose for reporters, weary but well satisfied and smiling hugely, one daring correspondent asked Sir Anthony if he knew where his daughter was. This was a reference to the rumour that the engagement expected between Julia Laurell,

Sir Anthony's only child, and twenty-two-year-old Timothy Kinnit, heir to the famous Kinnit's Salerooms in Dover Street, will not now be announced. Gossips are blaming Sir Anthony for the broken romance and are predicting much heart-burning from the young people. In reply to the question last night Sir Anthony's smile broadened. "Safe in her bed, I hope to goodness," he said heartily and strode off to his car.'

Julia had explained the significance of the report in some detail as soon as her hostess returned to collect the tray, but without any noticeable success. She was not very surprised therefore when there was a series of furtive little knocks at the door and the good lady arrived in a flurry.

'I told you you were wrong,' she said, her pebble eyes showing white all the way round but her irrepressible smile escaping through the drama. 'They're here!'

Julia slid off the table and took a step towards the window. 'Who?'

'Newspapers, like I told you and you said was so unlikely. Oh, not out *there*.' Mrs Broome appeared to resent so literal an interpretation. 'Amy Beadle has just telephoned from the Goat and Boot – she's the licensee in her own right and a great friend of mine – she says two different London papers rang up to ask if you or Mr Timothy had been seen in the village. She told them "no" and then she wondered if I knew anything.'

'What did you tell her?' Julia was developing a very firm way of speaking, coupled with unusually clear enunciation when talking to Mrs Broome.

'Oh, I was very careful.' An unexpected shrewdness appeared in the shining face. 'I know Amy. If something isn't there she'll make it up . There's only one thing to do with Amy and that's to look her straight in the face and lie. I said I didn't know why in the world they should want to ring *her*, and if it was anybody's place to know a thing like that it would be mine. I hadn't heard a whisper from London, I said – our exchange is automatic you see, so there wouldn't be a leak there – and I was on the *qui vive* to hear something, but I expected Mr Tim would take you to Scotland or if they've stopped Gretna Green, to Paris or somewhere like that.'

Julia looked very young again. 'You were very thorough.'

'You have to be with Amy. Which reminds me, miss, if you should see anybody arriving in the drive – I don't suppose you will but you never know – nip straight down this passage here on the left and go into the big door at the end. It looks like an ordinary lock but it isn't quite, there's a little brass catch underneath. Pull that sideways and you'll get into the big drawing-room. I call it the Treasure Room. That's where all the valuables are kept and that's the room I never take strangers into when they call, as they do to see the old historic building and so on. The lock closes behind you and there's the same arrangement inside so you can always get out. It's just a safety precaution. You know the room, it's the one the dance was held in at Christmas.' She paused for breath and was silent for a moment thinking. Presently she took a step forward, laid a shining red hand on the girl's shoulder and spoke with a seriousness all the more impressive because it came from so far beneath the surface.

'I've been thinking about you all the time I've been working about the house this morning, and I do hope you'll understand what I'm going to say,' she began. 'It's very easy to take offence at such time I know, but, miss, why don't you have a betrothal? I know Mr Timmy and I think I'm beginning to know you. You'd both be much happier. You want to be happy on a performance like this because there's a lot of little things to worry about.'

There was no doubt at all about what she meant or the genuineness of her concern.

'Mr Lingley, the parson, the Rev-Ben they call him, has known Mr Timmy for fifteen years and I know he'd like to help.'

Julia was sitting on the table again, her black eyes narrowed and her intelligent face looking so young that its defencelessness was a responsibility.

'I don't quite know what you mean by "a betrothal",' she

said at last. 'It sounds perfect but what is it? Some sort of ceremony?'

'Oh, I think so, miss. You'd have to leave all that to the parson, of course, but you read about it in all the stories don't you? There's an exchange of rings I know. You've got your engagement ring and I can find one for Timmy. There's a lovely big one in the cabinet in the drawing-room – it came from Pompeii, I believe.' It was only the faint upward note, on the final word, an infinitesimal lack of decision in the enthusiastic rush, which conveyed to Julia that there was no real guarantee that Mrs Broome had any clear idea what she was talking about. In many ways it was a pathetic situation, the treasures at stake priceless and delicate and both women aware of all the facts without comprehending them.

Mrs Broome was hovering, her eyes hopeful and inquiring.

'I think it's done in church and it's just a prayer and a promise, but the papers aren't signed because you have to have a licence if they are and you're under age, aren't you, miss? What I feel is that it would be a good thing to do be-cause, although it wouldn't be legally binding in a court of law, it *would* be to you two, you being the kind of children you are, and that would make you both much more comfortable. Let me ring up Mr Lingley and ask him if he'd slip round. I won't tell him why but I know he'll come. He's a very good man. Very kind and conscientious.' She was within a hair's breadth of being convincing in her nursery authority, but at her next step the thin ice cracked. 'Long, long ago the man knelt praying before a sword all night and nowadays they just call it a wedding rehearsal in the newspapers,' she said devastatingly.

Julia caught her breath and laughed until the tears in her eyes were reasonable.

'You're thinking of a *vigil*,' she said. 'I'm afraid that's something quite different. No I don't think I'll talk to Mr Lingley. Thank you for thinking of it.'

'But he's a good man, miss. A homely practical chap too, even if he does wear a cassock all day. He'd help if he could.'

'I'm sure he would. I did meet him you know, at Christmas. No, let's leave it to Timothy. I'll tell him what you suggest.'

'Ah!' said Mrs Broome. 'Now I *know* you'll make Timmy a good wife because he's very proud and headstrong and has to be led. I shall hold you to that, miss. You tell him. I'll have a nice supper for him and then you tell him to telephone the Rev-Ben and I'll be bridesmaid.' A sizzling noise from the gravel outside silenced her in mid-stream and they both looked out of the window. A Jaguar had just driven through the arch on to the drive and two men were dismounting almost under the window in front of them.

Nanny Broome took one look at the shorter and darker of the two and flushed scarlet with vexation.

'Oh heck!' she said unexpectedly and managed to make the absurd word shocking. 'Mr Basil! That's torn it. He *would* come rolling in just when nobody wants him! It's Mr Basil Toberman. I expect you've heard of him. He's the other side of the business, the black sheep if you ask me. He drinks like a sponge and thinks he's something an angel's brought in. I don't know who that is he's got with him.'

'I do.' Julia was looking apprehensively at a tall thin man who was climbing out of the passenger seat. 'That's Albert Campion. I don't think he *could* be looking for me already, but I think I'd better get out of the way.'

'What is he? A lawyer?' Nanny Broome had drawn the girl back but was still craning her own neck.

'I don't think so. People tell you all sorts of things about him, what he is and what he isn't. You call him in when you're in a flap. Go and head them off while I get under cover.'

Chapter Three

Miss Thyrza's Chair

The brass lock on the drawing-room door was easy enough to negotiate once one knew its secret and Julia had the satisfaction of hearing the catch spring home as she closed it behind her and entered an immensely tall, gracious room with a polished wood floor dotted with fine, well-worn rugs.

Here the stripped panelling was warmly gold and the pictures, mostly of the English school, were mellow and gentle in the afternoon light. Sepia Delft tiles surrounded the fireplace, their crudely drawn Biblical scenes in faded cyclamen blending with the pinkish pine, while above them, instead of a mantelshelf, there was an archway high enough to form a balcony with slender balusters and a tapestry-hung wall behind. As usual Nanny Broome's pet name for it was extremely apt; there were treasures everywhere including a pair of cabinets in Italian marquetry, huge and splendid things, whose long serpentine glass shelves were covered with porcelain. The general effect was elegant and informed. Glass-topped specimen tables of various periods were scattered among velvet chairs and needlework covered settees and here and there a collector's item, a tiny walnut harpsichord as graceful as a skiff, or a box in stumpwork old as the building itself. The whole place smelled of cedar, probably furniture polish, but pleasant and peppery and very evocative in the slightly airless silence. Through the windows the leaves dancing in the sunlight looked as if they must be making a noise, it was so quiet and still indoors.

The tiles attracted Julia, who had just reached them when she heard the door catch move again and recollected with a shock that at least one of the visitors must know the house quite as well as did Mrs Broome. There was only one hiding-place and she took it promptly, mounting the enclosed stairs which led up behind the panelling to the balcony. A curtain hung over the arched entrance, hiding her, and she sat down on the second step to wait until they left.

'But the Victorians were tough and very interested in crime.'

She did not recognize the voice and presumed that it was Toberman's. 'Here you are. These are the Staffordshire Murder Cottages and their incumbents. All this collection on the centre shelf.' The aggressive, thrusting voice was not so much loud as penetrating. It reached her so clearly that the hidden girl assumed he must be within a few feet of her. Yet Mr Campion's laugh, which she recognized at once, seemed much farther away and she guessed that the two men were standing before the china cabinet on the far side of the room.

'Extraordinary,' Mr Campion said and sounded sincere. She could imagine his expression of innocent bewilderment, his pale eyes smiling lazily. He was not a particularly handsome man as she recalled him but a very attractive one with a strong streak of sensitive interest in his fellow men.

'When you first mentioned the Murder Houses to me the other day I looked them up. It seemed such a macabre idea that I didn't believe you,' he went on frankly. 'To my amazement there they were, illustrated in the text-books; pottery figures representing famous criminals of the nineteenth century and the houses they lived in. I was rather startled in my old-ladyish way. My hat! Imagine looking up from one's fireside to see a replica of George Christie and Rillington Place on the mantelshelf.'

Toberman laughed. 'Perhaps not. But you'd rather like to see Maigret and his pipe, Poirot with a forefinger to his grey cells, or Nero Wolf with an orchid. Taste is swinging that way again. You ought to study this collection, Campion. Eustace will never part with it while he's alive but one day it'll be famous. There's every Staffordshire crime-piece ever made in this cabinet, and that's unique. The Van Hoyer Museum in New York hasn't that very rare second version of Maria

Marten's Red Barn over there, nor the little Frederick George Manning – he was the criminal Dickens saw hanged on the roof of the gaol in Horsemonger Lane, by the way – '

'Yet they have Miss Thyrza and her chair?'

'That's right.' He seemed rather pleased about it. 'The only other copy in the world. Eustace's great grandfather, Terence Kinnit, bought up the moulds and destroyed the whole edition to prevent the perpetuation of the scandal of his murdering governess, but he couldn't resist saving two copies, one for his own collection and one to grow into money to recover what the suppression cost him. As usual his judgement was sound. Miss Thyrza was forgotten and his grandson, that was the present Eustace's father, sold the second copy to the Van Hoyer for the highest price ever paid for a single piece of Stafford.'

'Really?' The quiet man was gratifyingly impressed. 'And the crime happened in this house, did it?'

'The murder? Oh no. Terence moved here *because* of the murder. His restoration of this house took the minds of his neighbours off the other smaller building at the back of the village where the trouble took place. It was pulled down later. Here the lady is, Campion. Drooping over the fatal chair back. How do you like her?'

Tucked away behind the curtain on the staircase, Julia could not see the speaker but she heard the faint twang of the thin glass as the cabinet's doors were opened.

On the other side of the room Mr Campion was looking over Toberman's shoulder as he took the portrait group from the shelf. It was a typical product of the factory, heavily glazed, brightly coloured and sincerely but ingenuously modelled, so that the overall effect was slightly comic. The chair was a cosy half-cylinder, quilted inside and coloured a fierce pink. The lady, in a long royal blue gown very tight in the waist and low over the shoulders, was draped beside it, her long black hair hanging across her face and breast. At her feet, two indeterminate shapes, possibly children, huddled together on a footstool.

'It has very few flaws and that's unusual for Stafford to begin with,' Toberman said, turning the piece over in his short hands. He was a blue-chinned man in the thirties with wet eyes and a very full, dark-red mouth which suggested somehow that he was on the verge of tears. 'It has a refreshingly direct, modern feeling, don't you think? See the packing needle?'

He pointed to a spot inside the chair's curve where there was a small protuberance. Mr Campion had taken it for a fault in the glazing but now that he came to examine it he saw the grey blade painted upon it. He glanced up in startled astonishment.

'A packing needle! Was that the weapon? What a horribly practical and homely item. She simply wedged it, sticking out of the upholstery, I suppose? How very nasty.'

'It worked,' said Toberman cheerfully.

'I imagine it would.' Mr Campion spoke dryly. 'The chair must have become a Victorian version of the medieval "maiden".'

'You could call it that. But the "maiden" was an iron coffin lined with spikes, wasn't it? The victim was pushed inside and the lid shut on him. In this instance there was only one spike, arranged to catch a man just below the left shoulderblade. The needle would be slightly thicker than a hatpin but made of steel and as strong as a stiletto. Either she pushed the fellow on to it from the front, or she went round the back of the chair as he was about to sit down, put her arms round his neck and pulled hard. That was what the prosecution suggested, as a matter of fact.'

'When *was* this fruity little crime?' Mr Campion continued to be astonished. 'I can't think how but I seem to have missed it altogether.'

'You don't surprise me.' Toberman was disparaging without being actually offensive. 'Experts always develop pockets of ignorance. I notice it all the time. You've got an excuse here, though, because Terence Kinnit was an influential man and was able to hush the business up. There were two or three other sensational crimes in the same year – 1849 – also the young woman wasn't hanged. The jury acquitted her but she committed suicide, so it was assumed that she was guilty after all and the public lost interest.'

Mr Campion made no comment and there was silence for a moment in the cedar-scented room. Presently Toberman put the group back and his guest stood looking at it through the glass.

'Who are the little creatures in the foreground?' he inquired.

'Those are the cousins. Miss Haidée, Terence's daughter, and Miss Emma, his sister's child. Thyrza was their governess. They were much older than they're shown there; the artist made them small to emphasize their unimportance. Emma was the eldest; she was just on sixteen. Haidée was a year or so younger. Thyrza herself was only twenty. The victim was the music master. He used to ride out from the town once a week and there was an affair. Little Haidée found some letters, nosey little beast. She showed them to her cousin Emma who gave them back to Thyrza. Thyrza got the wind up in case the kid told her mother and tried to get the chap sacked, but without success. All this came out at the trial. The music master had fancied himself as a rural Don Juan and had talked about his conquests, so Miss Thyrza was practically forced to get rid of him or lose both her job and any hope of marrying well. Being an ingenious young woman she set about repairing the upholstery in the visitors' chair with a nine-inch packing needle.'

'Why did the jury acquit her?' Mr Campion appeared to be fascinated by the far-off crime.

'Oh, I imagine she was young and beautiful and intelligent in the box, you know,' Toberman said. 'She insisted that the thing was an accident and of course, if it hadn't been for the letters and the motive the man had given her by his boasting, it could easily have been one. What a splendidly unhealthy atmosphere there must have been in that schoolroom, eh Campion?'

'Fearful. Why did she kill herself?'

'No future.' Toberman's shrug lent a chill to the statement. 'She came out of the assize court, drifted down the high road, found she had nowhere to go and pitched herself in a horse-pond. There was nothing left for her at all, you see. The Victorians didn't waste time and money getting discredited people to write newspaper confessions, and as an ex-employer old Terence Kinnit wouldn't have stirred a finger. Kinnit philanthropy always has an end product.'

The bitterness of the sneer in the hitherto casual voice was so unexpected that it sounded like a snarl in the quiet room. Mr Campion stared at the speaker through his round spectacles. Toberman laughed, his full mouth disconcertingly unsteady and reproachful.

'I'm the first of my family not to be grateful,' he announced. 'I used to be an angry young man and now I'm a moaning middle-aged one. I'm the last of the Tobermans and the first of them to see the Kinnits for what they must have been all the time – a bunch of natural sharks masquerading as patronizing amateurs.' He broke off abruptly. 'What I need is a drink,' he said. 'Whenever I get unpleasantly sober I clamber up on this boring old hobby horse. The Kinnits are a depressing family. Old Terence must have been typical. He got my great-grandfather out of his particular spot of bother. They used to spell bankrupt b . . . . . . t in those days and he lent his name and a great deal of his money to our Auction Rooms. We remained the auctioneers and the Kinnits kept their amateur status as connoisseurs who did a spot of genteel dealing on the side. That's the Kinnit method; take in lame ducks, don't ask too much about them but make devoted slaves of them ever after. Old Terence hadn't asked for any reference when he took Thyrza on; that too emerged at the trial. She asked very little and he was sorry for her. You can hear every Kinnit who ever lived in that little phrase.'

Mr Campion turned away idly from the china cabinet and allowed his attention to be caught by a collection of enamelled buttons displayed in a glass-topped table little bigger than a dinner plate. When he spoke his tone was casual but the listening Julia, who had only his voice to go upon, realized that he had at last perceived the opening for which he had been waiting.

'Which gets under your skin most? The patronage or the amateurism?' he inquired with misleading fatuity.

'The ruddy wealth!' said Toberman, speaking the truth and being amused by it. 'Terence Kinnit spent a fortune ruining this place in the biggest possible way – he panelled quite two square miles of wall space with pseudo-Tudor plywood for one thing – but it didn't break him as it ought to have done, because he was able to pay for the lot by instructing us to auction off just a portion of the magnificent stuff he found and recognized in the ruins. The original builders had not only imported their skilled labour from Italy but their "garden ornaments" as well. Classic marbles, old boy, which are now in half the museums in Europe. No one recognized them but Terence. I've never forgiven his ghost for that!' He took a deep breath and his dark eyes were briefly ingenuous. 'And why did he do it in the first place?' he demanded. 'All because some silly little bit he'd taken into his house "out of generosity because she was cheap" had got him into a scandal which had to be smoke-screened. He bought the local folly and turned it into a palace to give the neighbours something else to talk about!' He grinned and his sophistication returned. 'You think I've got a chip on my shoulder don't you? Well, so I have, and let me tell you I've got a cracking great right to it.'

Mr Campion coughed apologetically. 'I do beg your pardon,' he said hastily. 'I had no idea you felt so strongly. I imagined that as you spent so much time at the Well House that you. . . .'

'Thought myself one of them?' Toberman sounded both irritated and ashamed. 'I do, I suppose, when I'm *not* thinking. I like old Eustace. I ought to. The man has behaved like a rich uncle to me ever since I remember. Both he and Alison treat me as if I were a nephew and I use the Town house whenever I want to. Why shouldn't I? Everybody else has. They've got a South African relation there now. . . . a humourless woman cousin and her female help. I've been "taken-in-and-done-for" like the rest of the outfit and I happen to resent it whilst being too darn lazy to do anything about it.

Yet the whole thing is a paradox, because if anyone has a right to inherit from the Kinnits I have. At least I'm not a stray.' Again the bitterness behind the contradictory outburst was quite remarkable. He noticed it himself for he flushed and smiled disarmingly.

'Do I talk too much because I drink too much or the other way round ? I never know,' he said hastily. 'We'll go and hunt up some liquor in a moment. There usually is some alcohol concealed upon the premises if one organizes a search. Forgive me Campion, but I'm still reeling under the shock of a discovery I ought to have made twenty years ago. When it came to me the other day I was knocked out, not by its staggering obviousness, but by the fact that I of all people was the one person who knew about it and yet hadn't recognized it in all that time. Hang it all, I saw it happen!'

It was obvious, both to Mr Campion and to Julia still concealed upon the other side of the room, that he was about to make a confidence and also that it was one he had become in the habit of making recently.

'It was when the rumour first broke that young Timothy had landed the Laurell girl,' he announced devastatingly. 'I don't know why, but that got me down in a very big way. Why should a man who is darn lucky to inherit one fortune suddenly have the nerve to marry another? I was thinking about the unfairness of it all when the blinding truth about that young man suddenly hit me between the eyes. Tell me, Campion, you're a knowledgeable chap, who do you think he is ?'

'Eustace Kinnit's adopted son.' Mr Campion spoke cautiously, but Julia could hear that he was interested.

'Everybody knows that, but you assumed he was also his own natural son, didn't you ? Either his own or his brother's, the original Timothy's ? Everybody has always thought that.'

Mr Campion said nothing.

'Well, he wasn't,' said Toberman. 'That's what Eustace let everyone believe, the romantic old so-and-so! That was the view of the whole of London and probably of the boy himself. Certainly that is what my old father thought. He told me about it before he died, as if it was some dreadful family secret and I believed him, that was the extraordinary thing. I believed him although I was one who knew the truth if I'd been old enough to understand it then.' The expression on his highly coloured face was wondering. 'Imagine that!' he said.

The thin man's pale eyes were misleadingly blank as he turned towards the speaker.

'You suddenly remembered something about Tim Kinnit when you heard of the proposed engagement?' he inquired, leading him gently back to the main subject.

'Yes.' The miraculous enlightenment of the moment of discovery was still fresh to Toberman. 'I was having a drink with someone, Eckermann of the Brink Gallery as a matter of fact. He mentioned the engagement and referred to the adoption and asked me which of the Kinnit brothers the boy really belonged to. I said "Oh, the younger one, the Timothy who was killed in Spain" and Eckermann said "Then young Timothy must be considerably over twenty-two mustn't he?" This foxed me because I knew he wasn't, and for the first time I worked it out and I realized that Timothy must have been born just about the beginning of the world war, long after the Spanish affair. And then I *was* puzzled because I could recall that year preceding the outbreak. I was ten and my people had the wind up after the Munich fiasco and I was pushed out of London and into the country down here. Eustace was ill. He was in hospital for seven or eight months and then he came down to recuperate. I remember him and I remember the war preparations here, the fire drill and the gas masks and the reception station for evacuees from the East End of London. Alison was in the thick of it – she would be! Eustace, being an invalid, pottered about in the library doing the paperwork and blubbing over the newspapers while I ran loose like a tolerated mongrel pup round his feet. As I was talking to Eckermann the other day I remembered an incident which had meant nothing to me as a child but which was, suddenly, utterly enlightening to my adult mind. The truth hit me like a bullet and I *knew* how young master Timothy, darling of all the Kinnits, Totham, Oxford, heiress-hunter and Success Boy came into the family. He was abandoned here by some slut of a slum mother, Campion. Eustace just scooped him up in a typically arrogant Kinnit way and gave him the name which happened to be uppermost in his mind – "Timothy Kinnit", after his young brother killed in the Spanish war. After all it cost him nothing, and since the whole world was in flames at the time and no one's chances of survival were worth a damn he didn't appear to be risking very much.' All the jealousy and resentment of a lifetime flickered in the small brown eyes as he confronted the other man with the statement.

Mr Campion's little laugh sounded scandalized.

'Did you actually *say* this to Eckermann?' he inquired.

'I did and I've no doubt he repeated it.' Toberman was defiant. 'I may have told one or two other people as well, and I'm telling *you* now, aren't I? It probably is a silly thing to do but the whole idea has shaken me. I've known it, you understand, I've known it without knowing it all my life. Besides,' he added with an abrupt descent to the practical, 'I don't envisage anybody serving me with a writ for slander, do you? It's true.'

'Wouldn't you have a lot of difficulty proving it?'

'I don't think so.' He was quietly obstinate. 'The fact which misled everybody – the people like my father, for instance – was that the kid had a ration book and an identity card in the name "Timothy Kinnit" long before Eustace adopted him. I remember father commenting on it to Mama, and I remember not being able to understand what the hell they were getting at. It was only when I was talking to Eckermann that I suddenly remembered the incident which explains all that. One day just after the war started I was in the library across the corridor here, sitting on the floor looking at some back numbers of the *Sphere* I'd found, and Eustace was at the desk filling in what must have been the famous "Householder" form of 1939. It was the first census of its kind and it was on the information gathered by it that the identity cards were issued. Once you were on that form you had a right to live in Britain and it was made pretty clear that the converse applied. You were in the services, no doubt, but I wasn't. I remember it vividly.'

Mr Campion nodded. He seemed afraid of breaking the flow but there was little chance of that.

'Each householder in the entire country had to put down the name of every living soul who slept under his roof on a certain night,' Toberman said. 'That was how the census was taken at such tremendous speed. Eustace had the devil of a job because not only was the place crammed with staff from the London office and their families, but also with official and unofficial evacuees from the East End, the residue of three or four hundred of them who'd been hurried out in the first panic – they nearly all went back afterwards but in those first months the countryside was packed with townfolk all camping in other people's houses. Old Eustace made very heavy weather of the form and insisted that each person should appear before him. They had to come in batches of twelve and he'd stop and explain to each lot how important it all was. It took all day. The evacuee mothers with children came last and when he thought it was all done Mrs Broome came trotting in with a bundle saying "Don't forget Baby, sir!" And Eustace didn't look up but said "What's its name?" and she said "I don't know, sir. The young lady has gone back to London to get some of her things and I'm minding him. I just call him Baby."'

He paused and laughed. 'I remember that particularly. It was a catch phrase with me after that. "I just call him 'Baby'." Eustace was so wild with her too. He wanted to get the work done. If the child spent the night in the house he'd have to be entered, he said, and "If he hasn't got a name by tomorrow Mrs Broome, we'll have to give him one."' Toberman's voice died away in the strange timeless quiet of the insulated room and he turned away to look out of the window at the dancing leaves.

'That was it, you see,' he said presently. 'The mother didn't return. Knowing that the kid had got to have papers, Eustace gave him a name to go on with and after that I suppose one thing led to another. I don't remember him after that until he was adopted and going to a prep school. My father was scared of the East coast and packed Mother and me off to Wales.'

Mr Campion did not speak at once.

'They were exaggerated times,' he said at last. 'Confusing too, especially to a child, but you've got no evidence of this little fantasy, you know. It's not a very. . . . well, a very *good* story do you think? To tell, I mean.'

'I shall tell it if I feel like it.' Toberman's truculence was unabashed. 'One of the enormous advantages of not being a Kinnit is that I can be as "off-white" as I like. I've no code to live up to. I think young Tim is a bore and I think he's had a good deal more than his share of the gravy, so why shouldn't I tell the facts about his origin if it gives me any satisfaction? Everything else has come to him gold-lined and free! The father of that girl of his must be worth a million. A *million*. And she's the one and only child.'

'But you've no proof at all of this tale about him!'

'Ah, but Truth has a way of emerging.' Toberman was ponderous in a besotted fashion. 'Eustace probably won't talk and Alison will back him up, but you can bet your life that Ma Broome would chatter if a newspaper offered her enough money. She must know all about it. There's a rumour that the girl's father has stopped Tim's engagement already. That means that there's a Press story there, and if I go on telling my little anecdote some gossip writer will arrive at the big idea all by himself and come beetling down here with a cheque book. Then we shall get the human angle. *Foundling and Heiress. Who Abandoned Tiny Tim?*' He chuckled at his own joke.

'You're going to hand me the one about it not mattering to anyone in these enlightened times where in hell he came from or who his parents were,' he remarked. 'You may be right, but in my opinion the news is going to shake up the wonderboy himself considerably, and that's the angle which interests me.' He met the other man's eyes and shook his head. 'He's had it too easy,' he added, as if he were passing a fair judgement with reluctance. 'Far too easy altogether.'

Mrs Broome burst into the room so suddenly that there could be no doubt that she had been listening at the door. She was in a highly explosive state. Her cheeks were bright with anger and her eyes were wet. She came forward across the rugs, moving very swiftly but taking very short steps, and she glanced round her for the hidden girl with no subterfuge at all so that both men looked about them also. Julia, who could not see her, did not move and the furious woman turned to Toberman.

'Do you want any tea . . . Sir?' she said without hood-winking anybody.

Toberman stood looking at her. He was giggling slightly and wore the sorry anxious expression of one caught red-handed.

'I did say they'd have to offer a lot of money before you'd talk, Broomie,' he said feebly.

Mrs Broome began to cry and whatever Mr Campion had envisaged it was not this. Everything he had ever heard about his sex's terror of feminine tears rushed back into his mind in sudden justification. Mrs Broome was a woman who wept like a baby, noisily, wetly and with complete abandon. The noise was fantastic.

'Be quiet!' said Toberman flapping a hand at her idiotic-ally. 'Be quiet! Be quiet!'

'I wouldn't sell Timmie!' Her extraordinary statement was mercifully incoherent. Her handkerchief was already sodden. 'You ought not to say such things, you ought not to tell such lies, you're jealous of him, you always were. He was lovely and you were always an ugly little thing, and you had that tiresome weakness and I was thankful when you went to Wales.' The incredible words came churning out of the wide-open, quivering mouth in a mass of water and misery. Tober-man threw up his hands in terror.

'Shut up!' he shouted at her. 'Shut up! I'm sorry, I didn't mean it.'

Mrs Broome continued to weep but not quite so loudly. As a spectacle she was unnerving, her face and her drowned eyes red as blood. Both men stood before her temporarily helpless.

'You said yourself that Mr Eustace didn't look at me.' The words were clear but incomprehensible.

'What the hell are you talking about?' Toberman was near panic and his roughness produced another burst of sobbing.

'You said it yourself!' Mrs Broome bawled in her rage and grief. 'Of course I was listening! I had a right to if you were going to tell lies about me. You said it yourself, I heard you. Mr Eustace didn't look at me.'

'When, for God's sake?'

'When I brought Timmy in to him and he asked his name.'

Toberman stared at her stained face. Incredulity and delight were concentrated in his eyes.

'Do you hear that Campion?' he demanded. 'Do you hear what she says? It *was* Timothy! I was right on the bull's-eye.' He seemed astounded by his good fortune. 'She's admitted it. The mother went off and left him and Eustace gave him the first name that came into his head.'

'Oh no, no! That's not what I said. You're putting words in my mouth. Mr Eustace didn't *look* at me. That was how I knew.' The last word rose to a wail which could not be ignored.

'What did you know?' Mr Campion's soft authoritative voice penetrated the protective blanket of noise with which she had surrounded herself. Her tears vanished like an infant's and she turned to him with some of her normal gossipiness.

'I knew Baby was either Mr Eustace's poor dead brother's or his own little son, being slipped home quietly under cover of all the other kiddiewinkies in the house,' she announced, meeting his eyes with a stare of such earnest romanticism that he was set back on his heels by it. 'It was a very terrible *time*, sir, and people were frightened. It stands to reason that if he'd got to give a home from the bombs to all those other children, naturally he'd think of his own flesh and blood.' She sighed, and a shrewder expression appeared upon her tear-stained face. 'I dare say it suited him. He may not have known how his sister was going to take to the idea of a baby. Maiden ladies are maiden ladies, you know, some more than others. They're not like us married girls. I knew at once, of course, because he didn't look at me when he asked who Baby was. People never look at you when they're telling fibs, do they?'

She delivered the final remark as if it were a statement of scientific fact. Mr Campion considered her thoughtfully. She believed it, he saw, literally and obstinately, and always had. Therefore, since she could never have kept completely silent about anything, this version must be the one upon which young Timothy Kinnit had been brought up. He found he was becoming very sorry for the young man.

Toberman was laughing. 'So the next day when you told Eustace that the mother hadn't returned he filled in the name on the form and Timothy got his ration book and identity card. That's your story, is it?'

'No it isn't!' Mrs Broome began to roar again. 'I don't talk, Mr Basil. I was trained as a children's nurse and nurses have to learn to keep little secrets. Where would *you* be if they didn't? Embarrassed every day of your life! You think you've made me say something but you haven't! Times have changed let me tell you. As long as a boy has a home behind him no one's going to ask what church his mother and father got married at. Besides, you're quite wrong about one thing. It wasn't Timmy's mummie who brought him down here!'

'How could you possibly tell that?' said Toberman airily. The man was elated, Campion noted; above himself with gratification.

'A young girl with a new baby. Well of course I could!' An angry blush added to the conflagration already burning in the tear-wet face and Toberman had the grace to appear disconcerted.

'What was her name, anyway?'

Mrs Broome threw up her hands at his obtuseness. 'If anyone had been able to remember *that* it would have saved a lot of trouble when we came to getting him adopted properly for Totham School,' she said with a tartness which hinted at considerable argument at some time in the past. 'No one who wasn't there at the start of the war seems to be able to re-member what that panic was like before the bombing began. *Hundreds* of mothers and babies had been crying through the house. They were all supposed to be labelled but half the tickets had been lost and the babies had sucked the writing off the ones that *were* still fastened. Nine out of ten of the girls wouldn't give their names in case they were asked to pay some-thing, and we were all frightened out of our wits anyhow.' She paused and her devastating streak of commonsense re-appeared like a flash of sunlight in the rainstorm. 'If you ask me, it's a miracle dozens of kiddiwiddies weren't left all over the place!' she said. 'But they weren't. Mothers love their babies whatever you may think, Mr Basil, and so do fathers too. Mr Eustace knew what he was doing all right but I guessed he didn't want the subject brought up, and nor it was until Miss Alison discovered that the baby I was minding at our cottage wasn't any relative of mine or Mr Broome's. After that there was a lot of talk in the family.' She dropped her eyes modestly. 'It wasn't my place to know what went on but I believe Miss Alison caused a lot of inquiries to be made. But she came round in the end and little Timmy softened her heart. Of course there wasn't much else she could do,' she added with the now familiar change of mood. 'The raids had started by that time and the whole London district had gone completely. Only dust and litter left, they said. Not a wall standing. They never knew how many hundreds were killed.'

'They found the road he came from?' Toberman pounced on the admission.

Mrs Broome gave him a warning glance. 'They found the district where the buses which brought the evacuees were *supposed* to start from,' she said stiffly, 'but because of the up-set at the time some of them went off early from their garages and never went to the street at all. They just picked up Mum-mies and babies on the way. Of course I never thought Timmy came in a bus at all. He and his nanna came in a car, I expect, and just mingled with the others, as one might say. That's my idea.'

'It would be! Complete fanciful idiocy! Where was this district? Somewhere in the East End?'

'Hush!' Mrs Broome glanced round her involuntarily and Toberman suddenly comprehended the situation.

'What *is* all this? Who's here?' He stepped out into the room and looked about him for a hiding place. 'Come on,' he said loudly. 'Come out whoever you are!'

'No, no! Be quiet Mr Basil. Mind your own business, do. Come along to the other room and I'll tell you . . . I'll tell you what you want to know.'

'Who is it? This is damn silly! Come out!' Toberman was advancing towards the long window curtains.

Mrs Broome, who suspected the same hiding place, threw in her ace card to delay him.

'It was Turk Street, Ebbfield . . . but when they came to inquire about Timmy it was all gone.' She was too late. The man had ceased to listen to her. He had investigated one set of hangings and was advancing upon another.

On the far side of the room Julia slid quietly to her feet and came out from the fireplace alcove.

'Here I am,' she said. 'I'm sorry, but I was trying to get away from you. Does it matter? Hello, Mr Campion.'

Toberman stopped in his tracks. His smile broadened and his eyes began to dance.

'The little lady herself! You're very like your photographs, Miss Laurell. Well, this is fascinating! It's going to be a better Press story than I thought!'

Chapter Four

'Above at a Window'

'Julia? Me.'

Over the telephone Timothy's voice sounded older, more male and somehow more rough than when there was the rest of him present to soften the effect. 'You got the message and you're quite alone?'

'Quite. Completely by myself. What is it? What's happened?' Julia was frightened and the medium did not help her to conceal it. 'You can say anything you like. As soon as you told Mrs Broome what you wanted she plugged the phone in up here and I think she's sitting on the stairs in the hall keeping guard. What is it, Tim? Is it that you won't be able to get down here tonight?'

He was silent for a moment before he said abruptly: 'Where exactly are you? Where has she put you? What room?'

'Oh I'm not in that white *bedchamber*.' Laughter flickered briefly through the anxiety in her voice. 'I'm in the one your Uncle Eustace has when he comes down on business. It's the little one facing east with the heavenly ceiling and the wall of books behind the couch with eagles' feet. It's utterly secret; we can say anything. The light is out and there's a moon like a new penny pouring in over the fruit trees. I'm on the hearth-rug in front of a special fire Mrs Broome made for us. It's a green wood and it's burning blue.'

'Oh.' She thought he laughed. '"Ash when's green is fire for the Queen." She told you the rest of the rhyme I suppose!'

'"*Ash in its pride, Ash for the bride*"? Yes, she did. She's relentless, isn't she? And very sweet. So gloriously enthusiastic. I think she must have put me in here because of the nightingales. Can you hear them? They're bellowing.

Listen. "Eternal passion, eternal pain". . . . Oh darling, darling. What has happened? Tim, you haven't let Daddy talk you out of anything? Tell me. Tell me quickly before I'm sick.'

'I'm trying to.' He was unnaturally controlled. 'Listen. I'm not coming down. Listen Julia. Listen to me before you say anything. First of all, and this isn't the important thing, Fleet Street seems to be on to us. Three papers have telephoned since tea-time. Eustace has had calls too and I've just heard from him that somebody turned up at Well House asking questions. They want to know if it's true that you are at Angevin and if I'm joining you, and if the wedding is on or if we're eloping.'

'Where are you?'

'At your father's house, locked in his study. The key's on my side of course!'

'I see.'

'You don't, you know. It isn't anywhere near as simple as that.' He sounded grimly helpless. 'The newspapers don't matter much. As long as we're apart there's nothing they *can* say. I don't know who gave us away and I don't see why it should be of the faintest interest to anyone, except that everything to do with your father is news. However, that isn't the real point. I've got something more important to say and that's why I'm making all this hooey about the call.'

'You're not making a hooey!' She was fighting with tears. 'If you hadn't telephoned I'd be *dead*. That beastly little man Basil Toberman gave us away. He arrived here this afternoon and found me. He practically told me he was going to tell on us, and the man who was with him, who is a vague, pleasant sort of person called Campion, took him away hastily but I expect he escaped. That's how the newspapers know. I could kill him.'

'Basil? He didn't mean it. He's not worth hanging for. He's just a silly old drunk.' Timothy was uninterested rather than unconvinced. 'He may have let something out. It's a pity he saw you but he wouldn't have the essential drive to become an informer.'

'But Tim . . .' Her voice broke. 'I've been so afraid of something like this happening. I'll get into the car at once and come to London. I think I'll suffocate unless I see you soon. It's looking forward to you so much, I suppose.'

'Be quiet, darling.'

'Why, for Heaven's sake? It's only to be expected. All the books warn one about that.'

'Sweetie! Be quiet. I can't bear it. Be quiet and listen to me. I've something to tell you that's important to me. I've learnt something today which has shattered me. If I know you, you won't care about it one way or the other but I do.'

She could not help interrupting his shaking voice. The snapping fire, the dreaming light streaming in through the window, and the reckless outpouring from the birds, had created an atmosphere which was overpowering.

'You should be here! You should be talking here!'

'I can't! That's what I'm trying to tell you. This thing makes a hell of a difference. You've got to try to understand me, Julia.'

'Are you talking about you being brought here as a baby by some evacuees?' The statement was out before she realized its danger and she went on, clumsily cruel in her helplessness. 'Because if so you're being idiotic. Suppose it was true. What would it matter or what difference could it make to anybody? And if it isn't –'

'*Where* did you hear this?'

The entirely new note in his voice threw her into panic. She was crying as she answered obediently.

'Basil Toberman was telling Mr Campion and they didn't know I was listening. He seems to have been telling everybody because the penny only just appears to have dropped with him. He's jealous of you marrying someone who might inherit some money. But you mustn't let it matter, you mustn't let anything matter. It's you and me, Tim, tonight and always. You and me.'

'Old Basil! So that's where it's coming from! Your father says he got it from his club a week ago. He wrote Alison and she replied. That's how it happened.' For a moment Timothy

63

had forgotten Julia. The practical mechanism of the betrayal absorbed his attention until dismay overcame him once more. 'I can't believe it of Basil. If he knew, why didn't he tell me years and years ago? We've known each other always.' There was a pause and then he said briefly: 'I'm sorry you should have heard it from him.'

'I didn't exactly.' She was trying to save him. 'It was Nanny Broome who supplied the actual information.'

'Oh God!' The cry came over the telephone. 'It really is true then.'

'Oh, don't worry about it. It happened twenty years ago at least.'

'Does she say it *is* so?'

'Well, she isn't very clear. She never is, is she? But it's obvious.' Julia took hold of herself and began to think again but it was too late. The chemistry by which love kept waiting is distilled to acid had produced its poison on her tongue and touched him. She heard his sigh.

'It was never obvious to me. I just thought I was a bastard.' He spoke lightly and the words were as brittle as icicles.

'Oh don't. Don't. I didn't mean it like that. If I could only see you and hold you. This is like talking to you out of a window. I'll come to London now. Where shall I find you? Tell me, tell me quickly.'

Julia was trying to smother him into warmth again. She was speaking on a single note and the tears were hot in her eyes. 'Wait for me.'

'No. Stay where you are.'

In spite of the discouraging words she was comforted. At least there was contact between them again.

'Are you coming down here tomorrow?'

'No.'

There was silence. 'All right,' she said at last.

'Look darling.' She could hear that he had moved closer to the instrument. 'Julia. Understand darling. Try. It isn't that I've given my word to your father or let him come between us or anything like that, but I've had a hell of a shock and for my *own* sake I can't make any move, or do anything –

anything irrevocable until I've found out. It's breaking my heart but I can't, can I? You do understand, don't you?'

'Found out what?' She was appalled to find herself so lonely and out of touch.

'Who I am.' He seemed to find her stupidity extraordinary. 'Isn't it natural? I've been thinking I'm a Kinnit ever since I've thought at all and now suddenly I find I'm not. Naturally I want to know who I am?'

'Does it matter?' Fortunately she was too choked to say the words aloud. When she could articulate she said pathetically: 'To me you're only you.'

'Bless you!' His laugh was unsteady. 'It may take a little time, I'm afraid, but your father and dear old Eustace, who is reproaching himself like someone out of the Old Testament, are joining forces and helping me to get the thing cleared up once and for all. We're all three completely in the picture and they're both on our side. They want us to be happy.'

'Do they?'

'I'm certain of it.' She could hear from his brisk confidence that the thing she had dreaded without recognizing it had happened, and that the energy which she had been promised and for which she was living that night had been diverted from her to meet this new demand.

'And that's why,' he went on quickly, 'I shouldn't mention Basil Toberman to either of them until you're sure he meant it.'

'But I *am* sure. I heard him. He hates you. He wants to do you harm. He's spreading the story about, hoping it'll get in the newspapers.'

'That just can't be true.'

'He said so. I heard him.'

There was a long pause before Timothy said. 'Well, I'd hate Eustace to know that at this moment. He can't imagine why or how the story has got about suddenly like this. He's fond of Basil and doesn't realize what a drunk he is, and if he found out he was spreading it it would hurt him like anything. He'd be ashamed for him too. Leave Basil to me.'

'Very well.' She spoke softly. 'Timothy?'

'Yes?'

'Look, I'm beginning to understand why this matters so much to you but I don't see why my father took the line he did. After all, as everybody knows, he came of pretty homely stock himself and even when mother was alive with all her grand relations he never tried to hide it.'

'Oh, it's not the homeliness! I never met a more democratic man in all my life. He's a great chap. I hope I can have him for an in-law . . .'

'But there's no doubt of that. I'll be of age eventually. Then we can marry anyway.'

'Can we?'

'Oh, Tim . . .' She was panic-stricken. 'But we love each other! Separated we'd be different people. It means all my life. *All my life.*'

'I know.' He sounded as though he did. 'Mine too. There's no question about that. Your father knows it as well as we do but I see his point of view. While you're in his care he's got to be reassured about essentials. After that it's up to *me* to be reassured. He told me about his sister.'

'Aunt Meg's husband was a nut.'

'He was a hysteric. It wasn't apparent until he was over thirty, but his father and grandfather had finished under restraint. Meanwhile the wretched woman was made miserable until she died.'

'But that couldn't be true of you!'

'Couldn't it?'

'No, it couldn't. Don't be absurd. You don't believe it for a moment.'

'Naturally I don't, but I don't expect your uncle did either when he was my age. That isn't the only thing. There are other diseases one doesn't want in a parent. Hideous things that only come out in the kids. And there's other things as well. Tendencies, weaknesses. They may none of them matter, but golly! One wants to know what they are. You do agree to that? You do see, darling, don't you?'

'I see that between them all they've implanted a great

doubt in your mind,' she said bitterly. 'I see you've got to know *now*. That's what Basil Toberman's done for you.'

'That's what poor old Eustace thinks he has done for me out of sheer kindliness and romanticism, and it's driving him round the bend. You've got to help, Julia. We've got to keep apart until the chatter's died down and the papers lose interest. Your father is insistent on that and he's right. I see he's right. You do too, don't you?'

The appeal produced sudden physical pain in her chest and she gulped like a child.

'Tim. Tim, listen. This may strike you as being absolutely crazy but it's an idea Nanny Broome had when . . . when she thought we were going to spend the night here. I know it's ridiculous and naïve and all that but it would comfort me now. I'd like it. She suggested we went to the old Rev-Ben and got betrothed – more than engaged, somehow. It wouldn't mean anything except to us. Then I'd know that we really were going to marry some day.'

'Oh darling!' His exasperation came over the wire more vividly than any other emotion. 'You haven't understood a word I've said. That's the whole point. Something may emerge which may prevent me from marrying you or anybody. The chances are remote but I've got to be sure.'

'But whatever you discover, if I still want you – ?'

'Then it will be up to me to decide whether I can let you take the risk. We'll have to wait until we get there. We owe that to everybody concerned.'

'Everybody concerned!' Her physical disappointment lent her tone savagery. 'You're thinking of everybody. Your silly uncle and my father and even Mr Toberman, but you're not thinking about me. You're forgetting *me*!'

'My God, girl, don't you see I'm trying to!' His cry was as old as civilization. 'You may have been disappointed but what the hell do you think it's been like for me? Don't be silly, darling. And for God's sake shut up and stay away until I'm human again.'

Julia hung up involuntarily. The movement was as spontaneous as if she had merely turned her back. The sudden breaking of the link between them was so violent that around her the room sang and tingled with shock.

She took off the receiver at once but only the continuous throb of the empty wire greeted her.

Chapter Five

Off the Record

'This place is yet another example of modern jokesmanship,'
Mr Campion remarked as he steered Julia across the splendid
marble floor to the dining-room of Harper's Club in Davies
Street.

'It's rather like a beautiful Inverness cloak one has inherited. Much too good to hide away, so one wears it instead
of an overcoat and pretends it's an amusing new fashion.' He
pushed open the mellow mahogany door and they entered a
vast Georgian room with a cornice like a wedding cake. 'This
was the late Lord Boat's town house,' he went on. 'He had a
butler called Harper who was with him for forty years. When
old Boat died the title became extinct and Alf Pianissimo, the
caterer, bought up the property and rights in Harper. He
pensioned him and even had the old man about the place for
a while until he drove the waiters up the wall and got Alf in
trouble with the Union. At the moment it's very pleasant
and quiet and as good a place for luncheon as anywhere.
I chose it today because Charles Luke likes it and I particularly wanted to get him here so that he meets you and
gets interested in our problem.'

His pleasant voice flowed on as he conducted her to an
alcove on the far side of the room where a round table was set
for three.

'A superintendent C.I.D. of the Metropolitan Police can
find out almost anything on earth if he wants to,' he went on,
stowing his long legs under the table and smiling at her, 'but
he's hemmed in by protocol. If we go to him officially he
has to proceed officially and we don't really want that,
do we? – so I thought we might tap discreetly on the back
door.'

He was watching her while he spoke and it went through

his mind that she was genuinely beautiful with her black silk hair and eyes like blue glass, and that, more rarely still, she was elegant in a puppyish way, naturally graceful and packed with promise. She was uncomfortably young, of course. Still at that most alarming stage when sophistication and naïveté appeared to take turns so that there was no telling what might offend her unbearably or what else, much more difficult, she might take in her stride. He noticed her pretty blue-veined hands. Their short nails were innocent of varnish and she was wearing a ring on her engagement finger. It was a small signet, a schoolgirl's ring. He could see the habitual impression of it on another finger on the other hand. The naïve hopefulness of such a move touched him and reminded him for some reason of something he ought to tell her about Luke.

'He's a rather recent widower, by the way,' he observed. 'It's one of those dreadful stories. His wife made a complete fiasco of having a child. She didn't call for help, and died. The baby girl lived and is being cared for by his old mother who looks after him too. I mention it because it's as well to know these things in case one drops bricks.'

'Of course.' She was looking at him in horror. 'What an extraordinary woman. She was old, I suppose.'

'Prunella? Oh no, not old at all.' Campion was frowning as if he was visualizing someone who had worried him. 'She was in the twenties. The last of the Scoop-Dory's. She had that family's face: high round forehead and hooded eyes like something in a gothic cathedral. I can't imagine how she could have been both so idiotic and so stoic. She didn't want to be a nuisance I suppose, and there was no one there to tell her not to be so silly.'

Julia's youthful eyes were faintly amused by his exasperation.

'Poor girl, anyway,' she said gently. 'Not an awfully suitable wife for a policeman.'

'We all thought not.' Mr Campion was trying to be noncommital and sounding like every disapproving family friend who had ever existed. 'Charles was in love with her, though. Her death hit him like a bullet.'

There was silence for a moment and the girl shivered suddenly.

Mr Campion was contrite and he began to chatter.

'You'll like him,' he said. 'He talks like a dynamo and does a sort of hand-jive all the time by way of added emphasis, but he's tremendously sound. He's a great natural judge of quality in anything, too. That seems to be a gift all on its own.'

'Oh I know,' she said quickly, grateful for the change of subject. 'Timothy's Uncle Eustace is like that. He's a connoisseur of eighteenth-century pictures, books and silver, but he also seems to know by instinct, or so Timothy says, about modern stuff which isn't really in his province at all and which one might expect he'd rather hate. Do you know him?'

'Not very well. We've met.'

'Have you been to the Well House where they all live?' There was colour in her voice when she spoke about Timothy Kinnit, even remotely. 'It's in Scribbenfields, just not quite in the City. I suppose it was one of the first of the London suburbs and it's frightfully ancient. You'd never expect to find a lovely old dwelling like that in the midst of all those warehouses. I believe there was a medicinal well there once and the head is bricked over in one of the cellars.'

Mr Campion appeared suitably impressed and she warmed to him. He was very easy to talk to with those long clown lines in his pale face, a natural goon, born rather too early she suspected.

'It was very good of you to agree to help me,' she said abruptly.

'My dear girl, let's only hope I can!' he interpolated hastily. 'Scribbenfields? Yes indeed. The whole place was a noted spa at one time. Jacobean citizens used to ride out the two or three miles from Whitehall to drink the waters and I fancy people still have a vague idea that it's a healthy district. I had a demented client once, I remember, who actually paid a deposit on a small Epsom Salts mine situated, as he believed, under a disused tram terminus in Sheepen Road. An error, it emerged, which was how I came into it!

Tell me. When you say "they all live there" whom do you mean? Alison Kinnit, her brother Eustace, young Timothy and sometimes Basil Toberman? Is there a resident staff?'

'No. Not as a rule. Several people come in daily but just at the moment Nanny Broome has had to be sent for from the country to cope. There's a niece of the Kinnits and a help, all staying. They're from South Africa and tremendously wealthy. A child is ill in hospital and they've come to London to see doctors. You remember Mrs Broome, do you?'

'The woman who wept? Shall I ever forget her?' Mr Campion said fervently. 'It was the first time I ever saw the Picasso painting actually appearing in the very flesh before my bulging eyes. My goodness she was furious with Toberman!'

'Nearly as angry as I was! A beastly, beastly man!'

The loathing in the young voice was savage and Charles Luke, coming up behind her at that moment, caught the full flavour of it.

'Not me, I hope?' he said laughing, as Campion performed the introductions. 'Some other poor fellow.'

Julia regarded him with quick interest. She had expected the size and the heartiness and a certain masculine splendour, but Luke's own peculiar personality, which was catlike, was a surprise to her. He was a proud, lonely animal for all his force and liveliness.

A waiter brought his aperitif, which was a small scotch and soda, and as he sipped it gratefully he sighed.

'Civilized,' he said to Mr Campion. 'Humanizing.' He described a floating motion with his long hands. 'Cigars and summer days and women in big hats with swansdown face-powder, that's what it reminds me of.' He was entirely unselfconscious and his dark face glowed with energy and pleasure at the picture. It was suddenly understandable how a man with such an unlikely job should take it into his head to marry into the Scoop-Dorys, or indeed any other family on earth if the fever took him.

'I like this pub of yours. I'd like to live here for a couple of weeks every other year.' Although he was grinning he was not entirely joking and his narrow black eyes, which had brows like circumflex accents, were serious as he glanced across at Julia. Something about her had made him gloomy, she was surprised to see.

'And how is the teenage world?' he inquired abruptly, revealing his train of thought. 'All dreams and dance dresses I hope. That's how it ought to be. Something with a future if it's only disillusion. Mine is more homely country and that's in the American sense.' He glanced at Campion. 'Some of the young thugs we're getting in nowadays are dreaming up weapons which would have been thought offside by the Saints and Martyrs!' he remarked and returned to Julia. 'This beastly man you were talking about when I came in? Is this the stern father who won't let you marry the boy friend?'

'Of course not.' She seemed shocked and he smiled at her, amused. 'How much did Mr Campion tell you on the telephone?' she inquired.

'Almost all, a brilliant *précis*,' murmured Campion modestly. 'What I omitted was the part played by Basil Toberman in resurrecting the tale at this particular time.'

'Do you know he did it deliberately to harm Timothy? He *said* he had.' Julia spoke as though she expected Luke to find the statement incredible and he sat listening to her, his head a little on one side. 'I actually heard him say it to Mr Campion.'

'How extraordinary!' His lips curled despite himself. 'I'm glad he's the "beastly" bloke, though. I'm sensitive about daughters who don't revere their Dads. My own young woman isn't exactly respectful but she's only eighteen months old.' He was losing his suspicion of Julia, Mr Campion noted with relief, and his eyes were friendly as they rested on her serious face. 'Well, now,' he said. 'What do you want to know about young Mr Kinnit's birth? Where his family came from or what has happened to it now?'

'Oh, we know he came from Turk Street, Ebbfield, but the place just isn't there any more. It was bombed to the ground.'

'Turk Street?' Luke glanced at Campion. 'You didn't tell me that.'

'No.' The man in the spectacles was apologetic. 'The information came from what one might perhaps call "other than concrete sources". You haven't met Mrs Broome the nurse, Charles. She's a delightful woman but as a witness she's a treat of a very special kind. The buses which brought the evacuees from London were thought to have come from the Turk Street area but there's no proof that the boy came from there. Turk Street had a colourful reputation at one time and I thought we'd break all this to you when we saw you.'

Julia glanced from one man to the other.

'I didn't know there was anything awful about Turk Street,' she said quickly. 'Mrs Broome didn't either. She just remembered the curious name. How awful was it? Vice or crime or what?'

Luke continued to watch her; he was not unreservedly on her side yet.

'It was low class,' he said using the old-fashioned phrase to see if it irritated her. 'Why do you want to know about the young man's family?'

'I don't. Personally, I don't care if they were T.B. infested orang-outangs. Timothy is Timothy to me and nothing and nobody else. It's Tim who seems to have become completely insane on the subject. Father wants to know about the family but Timothy is *mad* to know.'

Luke grunted. 'Why aren't you leaving it to them? You can't hope to suppress anything and if it's there they'll find it as soon as you do.'

She met his thrusting stare steadily. 'I know that, but I want to be prepared and I want to be in it.'

The superintendent seemed satisfied for he nodded.

'Fair enough. He's cooled a little, has he? It happens,' he added apologetically, for the colour had come into her face and a new shininess to her eyes. 'He was all set to elope, poor lad, and got shunted on to a new track suddenly.'

'I know.' Her voice broke, yet she had not looked away. 'But so was I, and *I* wasn't.'

Mr Campion, who was sitting opposite Luke and following the conversation with some misgiving, was unprepared for his reaction. A spasm of pure pain flickered over his face before he smiled faintly.

'Touché,' he said. 'Well, in that case we'll have to do something about it.' He gave her a wide, disarming grin. 'And it wouldn't hurt us to get a move on instead of asking damn silly questions, would it?'

It was an unusually definite promise from anyone as punctilious as the superintendent, so Mr Campion led the talk into other channels and the meal ended happily. He was not astonished to receive a telephone call from Luke three or four days later.

'That twenty-year-old inquiry in the Turk Street area,' the superintendent began, the microphone blurring and vibrating under the strain of his voice. 'I haven't discovered very much, but, as I thought, I recollected something fairly recent which might tie up and at last I've had a moment to study the file. You don't read the *Ebbfield Observer*, I suppose?'

'Supposition sustained, chum.'

'All right. Don't let it worry you. There was a paragraph in it a few issues ago which might have interested you and, since it appeared in print, I don't feel I'm divulging any departmental secrets by calling it to your notice. The headline reads "Model Dwelling Outrage. Lodger Identified. Man Understood to Have Left Country". Got that?'

'Yes.' Mr Campion sounded mystified. 'Model Dwelling refers to that Utility Pile down there, does it?'

'Yes. The idea is to build five more in the same enclosure – they put them on legs like that in the hope they'll make room for each other. About five weeks ago there was trouble there on the top floor. An old couple had their home broken into one night while they were down at the local with their lodger. The place was wrecked in a very big way. When they came in the lodger took one look at the mess and fled after notifying the police by telephone, and the poor old lady had a stroke and died, thereby complicating the issue considerably from our point of view.'

'Oh!' Mr Campion was interested. 'The "indirect responsibility" question?'

'Is that what it's called?' Luke was not enthusiastic. 'All I know is that the legal bosses have suddenly got excited about any case where the original wicked action produces some extraneous consequence besides the one intended. In this business there was talk of a charge of murder or manslaughter. To me it just means more homework. However, there was considerable pressure put on our D.D.I. He is a Scot called Munday – and he had a local demon on his shoulder as well, in the shape of a Councillor who has to raise the cash to complete the building scheme. This lad wanted everything made sweet just a little quicker than soon. Munday worked like a fiend and finally discovered that the missing lodger was one of the Stalkeys.'

'Really!' Mr Campion was gratifyingly astonished. 'The detective agency? Is that terrible old gentleman J. B. Stalkey still alive?'

'Talky the Stalker or Stalky the Talker!' Luke's grunt was amused. 'No. He's gone. The angels got him at last – still pontificating no doubt. Joe, the middle son, reigns in his stead and the other two, Ron and Reg, do the footslogging. Reg was the mysterious lodger. He seems to have taken one look at the damage and scarpered. It must have shaken him, because he went right out of the country. He's looking up family connexions in Ontario now, according to Joe.'

'What was he doing in Ebbfield?'

'Munday would like to know. He'll be waiting for him at the airport to ask him when he comes home. All we know is that he went round from pub to pub raising the subject of Turk Street in the old days and appeared particularly interested in any family who was evacuated from there to the country in the war. When I saw that in the report I wondered if he was on the same track as yourself.'

'It has a likely smell. What does brother Joe say?'

'Nothing. Joe isn't talking. He's the same old sea-lawyer his father was and he knows his rights. We've got no power over him. He's an ordinary citizen. English tecs aren't licensed, as you know. He says he doesn't know what Reg was doing. He's protecting his client, of course.' He paused. 'There's only one other point which might be of interest and that is, that as soon as the Councillor gathered that the crime might have been committed in protest against an inquiry made by a private investigator he shut down on the whole thing like a piano lid and didn't want to hear any more about it. That was after he'd been badgering Munday on the telephone every half hour.'

'Odd.' Mr Campion said slowly. 'Has the D.D.I. any theory to explain it?'

'No. But the Councillor has a home and a wife. He may just not want a visit from the same gang of thugs. But if that's it, I'm surprised. He didn't strike me as that sort of bloke. He was more the fanatical sort. The I'll-do-you-good-if-it-kills-us-both type of social worker.' He laughed. 'Well there it is,' he said. 'All I can do at the moment, I'm afraid. I liked the girl. They've got great charm when they're honest, haven't they?'

If he was talking of womankind in general or a type in particular did not appear. He rang off and after a while Mr Campion took his hat and went down to the East Central District, where in a dusty cul-de-sac there was an unobtrusive door whose small plate announced modestly: 'J. B. Stalkey and Sons, Inquiry Agents. Established 1902.'

He found Joe Stalkey sitting in his father's old chair in an office which had remained carefully unchanged since the founder of the firm had first conceived the idea of a private detective agency having the standing of a firm of family solicitors.

The small room contained one magnificent period bookcase, glazed above and panelled below. It took up all one wall and against its mellow and elegant background Stalkey the Talker had posed and impressed clients for nearly fifty years.

Joe Stalkey had not the old man's florid presence. The slightly harassed expression and deprecating smile so typical of the child of an over-forceful parent had robbed him of authority. He remained a gangling, middle-aged man whose broad features were a little out of alignment, as if they had been drawn by someone with an astigmatism. When Campion came in he looked at him in open astonishment.

'This is a bit of an honour, isn't it?' he demanded, his smile leering. 'I don't think you've been in here in twenty years, have you, Mr Campion? What can we do for you? Any little chore however small will be welcome, I assure you. Don't hesitate to mention it. As long as it's legal and the money is safe we're not choosey. We can't afford it. We haven't had quite the advantages of some people. Do sit down, won't you? I have at least ten minutes before a client–'

' – Who must be nameless, steps out of a brougham with a coronet on the door,' murmured Mr Campion with such complete seriousness that he might just have meant it as a compliment. 'You're very obliging. I don't think your father would have been so kind. He never appreciated my style, I felt.'

The man behind the desk was regarding him cautiously. He did not understand him and never had. He suspected bitterly that his incomprehensible success was due to something basically unfair, such as class or education, but was begrudgingly gratified to see him in the office all the same.

'Help yourself,' he said. 'It's all yours.'

Mr Campion seated himself in the client's chair and crossed his long legs. His hat, his gloves and his folded *Times* newspaper he held upon his knee. 'I wanted to see Reginald,' he said. 'But I hear he's in Canada. I wondered if he could tell me anything about Turk Street twenty years ago.'

The man behind the desk had large cold eyes and their glance became fixed upon his visitor. It rested upon the narrow folded newspaper which Campion held, with an intensity which was noticeable. It was as if he were reading the small type of the advertisements on the outside page.

'Well?' There was nothing even impatient in Mr Campion's inquiry and he was astonished to see Stalkey's tongue moisten his lips. He had changed colour too, and his fist, which was unusually large-boned, was not completely steady where it lay on the desk-top.

'I'll hand it to you, you've got on to it very quickly.' He spoke without meeting Campion's eyes, letting the words slide out regretfully. 'Ron lost his temper,' he said.

Mr Campion had no idea what he was talking about but it appeared to be promising.

'Did he?' he murmured. 'That's always dangerous.'

'There's no real harm done.' Joe Stalkey spoke irritably, 'but of course Ron is a big man. He's heavier than I am and ten years younger. The kid put up an astonishing fight but he hadn't an earthly chance and he is in a bit of a mess, I admit it.' His eyes narrowed suddenly. 'Am I making a monkey of myself, by any chance?'

His visitor grinned.

'We appear to have travelled somewhat quicker than sound, if that's what you mean,' he admitted. 'Let me explain myself. I am interested in anything I can discover about a woman and a very young baby who were evacuated from Turk Street to an address in Suffolk on the day war broke out in 1939. I heard today that your elder brother Reg was making the same sort of inquiry just before he went to Canada, and I wondered if we were all working on the same problem and, if so, whether we could pool our resources. For an adequate consideration of course.'

'Damn!' Joe Stalkey was very angry with himself. He had coloured and his hands were nervous.

'You chaps build such a legend about yourselves that one believes it!' he said with unreasonable reproach. 'I didn't see how you could have got on to this morning's shindig, but because it was fresh in my mind I assumed you must have done as soon as you mentioned Turk Street. You're the reason the Central Branch have suddenly got interested again, I suppose? You've stirred them up and they've stirred up the police down there and some wretched detective constable went and leaked to the kid. That's about it. Otherwise it wouldn't have all happened together, would it? A coincidence like that couldn't have occurred otherwise. You coming in here in the afternoon just when Ron had been tackled by the kid in the morning. I was justified in making that mistake.'

The thin man in the hornrims leaned back.

'I'll come clean,' he said. 'I'm not with you at all. Ron is your younger brother, isn't he? He is carrying on Reg's inquiries I suppose?'

'Like hell he is!' Joe Stalkey showed evidence of having a temper himself. 'That isn't our sort of business at all, Mr Campion. You've no idea what the state of that flat was after the wrecking. I saw Reg before he left for Canada and he was shocked, I tell you. There the message was, you know, written right across a mirror: *Dick, go home!* Like an American film. I don't know what the younger generation is coming to. Stalkey & Sons isn't that kind of concern. Nice neat evidence, clear reports, and if necessary a discreet and creditable appearance in court, that's all we contract for. As soon as we saw what we were on to we walked out and stayed out. Our sort of clients aren't the class to get involved in *violence*!' The final word was invested with unspeakable disgust and Mr Campion noted the return of an old snobbery new in his time. He was still very much at sea, however, and was debating how to remedy it without being too outspoken when Joe Stalkey went on.

'He says he didn't do it, of course, and he pretends he doesn't know who did. It's gang stuff pure and simple. I think the world is damned; modern youth is quite openly against civilization. Higher education just makes them worse.'

Mr Campion raised his eyebrows but ventured no comment. Instead he put a cautious question.

'If Stalkey & Sons washed its hands of Turk Street when the flat was wrecked and Reg went to Canada, how did Ron get into the business?'

The flush on Joe Stalkey's unsymmetrical face deepened and his deprecating smile appeared briefly. 'The ass went to get Reg's shoes, can you beat it? As you probably would not know, East End repairers charge a quarter of what one has to pay elsewhere and the work is often much better. When

Reg was down there he left a couple of favourite pairs of shoes with some little one-man outfit and told Ron to pick them up for him when he had a moment. Ron is a careful chap and it's just what he would remember, being hard on shoe leather himself. This morning he was going that way so he telephoned to ask if the shoes were ready, found they were, went down there. Of course the kid had been tipped off and was waiting for him.'

Mr Campion took a long breath.

'When you say "the kid",' he began, 'who?'

'You know quite well who I mean. I mean young Kinnit,' Joe said. 'There's no point in beating about that bush in my opinion. We were acting for his legal guardians. The aunt and father by adoption. Alison and Eustace Kinnit. Actually we dealt with the woman. We were employed by the family before, you see, when they were first trying to trace the kid's identity about fifteen or sixteen years ago. Father handled it on that occasion but it was hopeless from the start. It was just after the war ended and the whole area was still a shambles, records lost and everything. Pa satisfied the court that every avenue had been explored without result and the adoption or guardianship or whatever it was went through and that was that.'

Mr Campion continued to be dubious.

'You are telling me seriously that young Kinnit was responsible for wrecking the council flat? Have you any proof of this at all?'

'I don't want any. I don't want anything to do with it, and don't forget anything I'm telling you now is off the record.'

Joe Stalkey's face, unattractive to start with, was not improved by an expression of obstinate prejudice. 'Of course he is. Ron reports that he is babbling about having been locked in his college at Oxford at the hour in question, but that only proves he has some useful friends or enough money to employ a few hooligans. What one might be able to prove is one thing but what we know must be the truth is another. Be your age, Campion. Who are you working for? The little lad himself?'

'No. I belong to the other side of the family. I am protecting the interests of the girl friend.'

'Are you indeed? Quite a client!' He was openly envious. 'There's gold in them thar quarters. Oh well, good luck to you. You're welcome to everything we've got – at the right price, of course. Happy to oblige you. But in this particular case we don't want to work with you. We've come out and we're staying out, especially after this morning's performance. That kind is decadent and dangerous. It never pays to take a youngster out of his normal environment and bring him up in something plushy.'

'Do we know what his normal environment was? I thought that was the object of the exercise.'

'We know he came from a vicious slum.'

'Do you? Is that established?'

Joe began to look sulky and his father's mantle showed as far too large for him. The old man had built this busines on fact and proof and not on this type of sophistry.

'He went to Angevin by bus with a lot of other people from Turk Street and he was abandoned, which is a Turk Street trick if ever there was one. He's a violent young brute, anyhow.'

Mr Campion rose. 'I still don't see why you connect him with the wrecking?' he observed mildly.

'You don't think.' Joe was didactic. 'You don't use your headpiece. I'm sorry, but look at it. Who else stands to gain? Who else *cares* if Reg uncovered something about the foundling? As soon as I heard about that message on the looking-glass telling Reg to get out I saw it must be the kid himself. It was obvious.'

'Is that really all you've got to go on?' Mr Campion sounded relieved.

'It's enough for me.' The head of Stalkey & Sons was adamant. 'I don't go in for fancy stuff as you do, Campion. I just see the obvious when it sticks out a mile and I get by all right. Today when the lout set on Ron I was proved pretty right, I think.'

'I see.' Mr Campion appeared to have no other comment.

'I shall receive a modest account from you, I suppose? Trade rates, I take it?'

Joe began to laugh. 'You've got something,' he conceded. 'The grand manner, isn't it? I'll tell you what. I've been thinking. We might come to something sort of reciprocal in this. You wouldn't like to take the boy off our hands now?'

Mr Campion stared at him.

'Where is he?'

Joe looked uncomfortable. 'Downstairs in the washroom as a matter of fact. Don't get excited. He's all right but he needed cleaning up of course, and we couldn't very well send him home. There's a funeral there this afternoon, isn't there?'

'A *funeral*?'

Joe Stalkey shrugged his loose shoulders.

'It's in your *Times*, in the deaths there. I thought you were holding it like that to remind me. It's not one of the family, but he felt he couldn't turn up with two black eyes and a cut lip. It's someone employed there. There it is: "SAXON ... whilst visiting this country with her bereft friend and employer, Geraldine Telpher. Interment today in Harold Dene Cemetery, etc.' A governess, I think the boy said she was.'

Chapter Six

Justifiably Angry Young Man

The washroom under the old building where Stalkey & Sons had their offices had been converted somewhat casually from what might well have been an air-raid shelter and was in fact a wine vault, relic of more spacious days. The ceiling was low and arched, the floor stone-flagged, and the ventilation unsuccessful. The row of wash-basins, installed about 1913, managed to look strikingly modern in the grim surroundings.

There was a rug-covered camp-bed at one end of the cavern and when Mr Campion entered, Timothy Kinnit was seated upon it, clad only in singlet and shorts. His bloodsoaked shirt was lying on the stones before him and when the visitor appeared he raised his battered face in which only the fierce grey eyes were still splendid.

'Hello,' he said. 'I know you. You're Albert Campion. Surely you're not a part of this outfit of lunatics? Where's that damn fool with my clothes?' He was speaking painfully because of the swelling of his lips but he was not sparing himself. His mood came across to Campion in a wave. He was so angry he was out of himself altogether.

Mr Campion glanced behind him. 'I appear to be alone,' he said pleasantly. 'Joseph Stalkey has paused to speak to his brother, who is undergoing repairs in the annex. If it's any comfort to you he too has a few souvenirs of the encounter. He was armed, I take it? May I look?'

The young man got up unsteadily. 'My face'll clear up,' he said, reeling slightly as he bent towards a looking-glass. 'But I don't know if there's an actual hole in my skull. It's at the back here, rather low down. Can you see?'

'Yes. Dear me. Wait a minute. Turn to the light, can you?'

The examination was nearing completion when Joe Stalkey came in. Nervousness had increased his restless

84

clumsiness. His big feet splayed awkwardly and his hands and huge wrists were prominent as he walked.

'He's all right,' he said, making it sound as convincing as he could to himself. 'He's all right. That's all superficial stuff. There's nothing to worry about there. These things do happen.'

The man in the hornrimmed spectacles raised his eyebrows. 'I'm not surprised to hear it if your brother does the family's errands wearing a knuckleduster and armed with a tyre-lever,' he observed mildly.

'It's not a tyre-lever. Just an ordinary, old-fashioned life preserver; we all carry one.' Joe conveyed that the fact made it respectable. 'Be reasonable. A man must have some means of defending himself. Ron expected trouble this morning; don't forget that. He was going back into the area. He realized that the young thugs who would wreck an old people's flat in that peculiarly brutal way merely to warn Reg off an inquiry, would be on the look-out for any return. That's why, when the attack did come, he was ready for it.'

'But there was no attack!' Timothy's explosion was due as much to fury at crass stupidity as to pain and outrage. 'I simply walked out from behind the counter where I was waiting, talking to the cobbler, and asked the man if he was the chap who was making the inquiries about Turk Street just before the war, and if so who was employing him. He went for me with a cosh like a lunatic, and naturally I defended myself.'

'But how did you get here?' Mr Campion demanded.

'I don't know. I went out like a light – I suppose from this wallop on my head.'

'Ron brought him along in his car,' Joe Stalkey said, avoiding Mr Campion's eyes. 'He intended to turn him over to the police, naturally, but as it turned out – '

Mr Campion coughed. 'A wallet happened to slip out of his pocket, spilling an old envelope with his name upon it, no doubt?'

Joe's big washed-out eyes met his own reproachfully.

'Well, things like that do occur, as you must know as well

as anybody,' he said testily. 'Anyhow, you can't blame Ron for being nervous. Reg had simply seen the quality of that damage to the flat, and he threw up the case and cleared out to Canada for a rest, remember. So this morning when an attack was made on Ron he was prepared for it. You'll never shake him on that.'

Mr Campion shook his head. 'No, I don't suppose one ever could,' he admitted. 'What's the matter with Ron? Flatulence? Never mind. Where are Mr Kinnit's clothes?'

'In the next room. He had a bit of a nose-bleed and they got smothered. Ron took them to discover if anything could be done about tidying them up. So Mr Kinnit could go home in them, you see?'

Mr Campion's lips twitched. 'Only too well. The error becomes more apparent at every turn. Ron has my sincere sympathy.'

'I wish you'd all stop blethering and just get me a pair of trousers,' Timothy said wearily. There was something of the helpless dignity of the sick child or the very old man in his appeal. His colour was bad and he was still very unsteady. He stood looking at Joe for a moment, debating his next statement.

'I've nothing against your brother,' he said at last. 'I shan't make any complaint. But I want the answer to my original question. Who was employing you all? Who is trying to find out about me?'

Mr Campion took the young man by the arm and lowered him gently on to the bed again, and Joe came a step nearer.

'So you knew you came from Turk Street?'

'No. I knew that some evacuees went to Angevin from there. I don't know now that I was one of them. Who was employing your brother?'

Joe Stalkey still hesitated and it occured to Mr Campion that he was showing uncharacteristic delicacy. 'You're asking us to divulge the name of a client, you know,' Joe protested at last.

Timothy sighed. 'Then there is a client.' He sounded oddly resigned. 'I went to look for Turk Street because my old nurse mentioned that name in front of my fiancée and I got the story out of her. I found a young bobby down there and chummed up with him and he told me a private detective had been chased out of the district for making inquiries. He put me on to the old man who had had the detective as a lodger and *he* put me on to the cobbler. You say the detective was your brother, so you can tell me what I want to know. Who is employing your family?'

Joe passed one ungainly hand over his chin.

'Well, I don't suppose it'll do any harm, because we're not working for them now,' he said. 'We're turning the whole thing in. It's not our sort of business at all, thank you. As a matter of fact my brother Reg was working for Miss Alison Kinnit and Mr Eustace Kinnit. They approached us just before Christmas.'

The battered face of the young man on the bed grew slowly dusky red and as slowly drained again. He was sitting forward, his head raised towards Joe's. His eyes were very dark.

'Are you sure Eustace was in it?'

'Of course. I saw him myself. It was my duty to warn them that there was very little chance of us having much success. My father undertook the original inquiry in 1944 or 1945 when the question of regularizing the position of Mr Kinnit's guardianship arose. My father had to confess failure then and I have to do it again now. I don't think you've got much to worry about, young man.'

The sneer passed clean over Timothy's head. He seemed completely shattered.

'Twice!' he said. 'Get me some clothes for Heaven's sake, there's a good chap, and let me get out of here.'

He got up and staggered dangerously. Mr Campion caught him.

'I really think you'd better come along with me,' he said. 'There's only one expert I know of who'll get you presentable in a reasonable time. Joe, send your secretary for a taxi and lend us a raincoat.'

They went to Mr Campion's old flat in Bottle Street. The Police Station which used to be next door had gone and time and rebuilding had changed most of the other landmarks, but the pleasant shabby four-room hide-out remained much as it had always been.

Timothy sat in a faded wing chair before a gas fire, Joe Stalkey's trench coat still covering his bloodstained clothes, and glanced dully round walls cluttered with souvenirs. Although the apartment was only just off Piccadilly, it was astonishingly quiet and somehow remote and even secret in the afternoon.

The sound of a key in the lock of the door was unexpected and Mr Campion put his head out of the kitchen, kettle in hand.

'Lugg?'

''Ullo?' There was an upheaval in the narrow hall and the panelled wall shuddered. The newcomer was breathless and his accent London at its thickest.

'We have a customer.'

'Reely?' The sitting-room door opened at once and a huge old man whose personality was as definite and obtrusive as an odour appeared in the opening. Even in an era when individuality in dress is a cult, his clothes were noticeable. He was wearing a hard hat of the low round kind favoured by hunting men, and with it a black duffle-coat lined with white. His large pale face and heavy moustache were alive with interest and curiosity. He glanced at Timothy twice; once casually, and then with a long hard stare from small, unexpectedly shrewd eyes.

'I thought you'd bin fightin' at first,' he remarked. 'Knuckle-dusters, eh? Where you been, son?'

Mr Campion came in and gave him a brief explanation.

'Stalkey!' Lugg was contemptuous. 'It was only 'is name give 'im the idea of being a detective at all. It was a cheap ad for 'im and 'e wouldn't waste it. Any family more kack'anded in their trade you couldn't find. The ole man was nothing but a jaw-fountain and all the children go orf 'alf cock!' He appealed to Timothy. 'Wot a way to treat a client's nevvy. You could 'ave died and then where would they be? Standin' wiv the bill in their 'ands, not knowing where to send it.'

His scorn was magnificent but Timothy did not respond. He sat like a sack, his eyes still dark and shocked. It occurred to Mr Campion, who was watching him, that eccentrics must be a commonplace in his young life. It was an off-beat age into which he had been born and absurdity as an escape-mechanism had been in fashion for some time now. The youngster's condition worried him a little. He was more shaken than his physical injuries warranted. Suddenly, as if in answer to his unspoken question, the young man glanced up at him and spoke abruptly.

'And who are *you* working for?' he demanded. The question came out brashly and he flushed. 'I'm sorry,' he said. 'I'm not trying to be offensive and I'm helplessly grateful to you. But why are you interested in this tatty old business of my paternity?'

The bitterness in his tone was unmistakable and the older man responded to it involuntarily.

'My dear fellow, don't take it like that!' he protested. 'I'll tell you all I know, which is little enough, in a minute or two as soon as we've got you patched up a bit. Meanwhile, what's all this Joe Stalkey told me about you being due at a funeral this afternoon?'

The sudden flicker of emotion, irritation, or perhaps even unease in the battered face took Mr Campion by surprise; in an instant it was wooden again.

'No, I'm not due at it,' Timothy said. 'I don't imagine anyone expected me to attend. I said I thought I ought not to turn up to the house in the middle of it looking like this, though, and Stalkey agreed with me.'

'As well 'e might!' Mr Lugg, who had removed his coat, now took off his hat and thrust it at his patient. 'See that? The idea of this is to pertect yer 'ead from an 'orse's 'oof. If you're goin' to keep stickin' your bonce into trouble you ought to buy yerself one. I'll give yer the name of the place. Now let's see this 'ere depressed area of yours. Keep still.'

He made a long and careful exploration of the damage and finally sighed. 'Yes, well,' he said. 'Ron Stalkey can say 'is prayers. 'E's lucky 'e's not up before the beak for that lot.'

'How bad is it?' Mr Campion made it clear he was consulting an expert.

'I seen wuss; and in this room. 'E'll live ter break someone's 'eart. Come on into the barfroom mate and we'll start the beauty treatment.'

An hour later he was still talking. Timothy, who was looking much more like himself, was wrapped in a bathrobe of his host's while Lugg considered his ruined clothes.

'No,' he said regretfully, turning over the torn and blood-soaked flannel trousers. 'Not reely. Not for a funeral. It would be 'eartless and not quite the article. 'Oose is it? Someone yer know?'

'Hardly at all. She was a stranger. Just an elderly woman staying in the house.'

The young man appeared to be defending himself and Mr Lugg's bright eyes narrowed.

'Yus?' he encouraged. 'Wot's 'er name?'

'Miss Saxon. I hardly knew her, I'm afraid, but the funeral was announced in *The Times* this morning. Joe Stalkey pointed it out to me. Eustace must have made the arrangements and put the advertisement in automatically. It's just what he would do, of course, although no one knew her over here. She came from South Africa with our – or rather Eustace's – relative, Mrs Telpher. She was helping her with the child, you see.'

Mr Lugg managed to convey without offence that he did not see at all and his patient was forced to elaborate.

'Mrs Telpher brought her child to England for medical treatment. It's in hospital now and Miss Saxon came with them to help. They've been staying in the Well House for about six weeks. I had no idea the old lady had heart trouble.'

The fat man stood looking at him, his large head held slightly on one side.

'She died sudden, did she?'

'Yes. In her sleep last Sunday night. I've been down in Ebbfield most of the time since then.'

'Persooin' your private investigations?'

'Well, yes. You could call it that, I suppose.'

Mr Campion, who was sitting at a bureau desk in the far corner of the room, heard the interrogation going on mercilessly, and marvelled at his old friend and knave. He pulled no punches in his social skirmishes.

''Ow sudden was it?' he was inquiring with disarming interest. 'Did yer 'ave a ninquest?'

'No. She'd been under the doctor since she came here. Eustace Kinnit called him at once and he gave a certificate.'

'Any reason why 'e shouldn't, son?'

'No. No, of course not. Can I have my shirt?'

Campion felt it was time to intervene. He turned round in his chair and his pleasant high voice cut into the conversation.

'I hope you don't mind,' he said. 'But I telephoned Mrs Broome at the Well House about half an hour ago and asked her to bring you a change. She should be here at any moment.' He was unprepared for the effect of the words in his visitor. His brows came down and the dusky colour shot over his face. Campion regarded him in astonishment. 'I thought it would be the easiest way,' he said defensively.

Timothy was controlling himself with a visible effort. 'What *is* all this? What do you know about Mrs Broome? You're very kind, but just who has invited you into this? Aunt Alison I suppose! My God! Who else is involved?'

Mr Campion leant back and crossed his legs.

'I do apologize,' he said. 'I told you I'd tell you all I know; here it is. I have an old friend whom you know. His name is Anthony Laurell.'

'Julia's father? Oh! I'm sorry. He didn't tell me. I thought he was being perfectly frank with me.'

'I think he was.' The man in the spectacles hastened to prevent any further damage. 'He spoke to me about you quite a long time ago when you and Julia were first going around together. He and I have been friends since we were both up at Cambridge, so it's quite natural for us to gossip about our various interests when we run into each other. He asked me if I'd heard a spiteful little tale which was going the rounds and I had not, but I was interested and so when I received an invitation to Angevin to see some ceramics I accepted. It was there I encountered Mrs Broome.'

'I see. I'm sorry. How did you know she was at the Well House now?'

'Julia told me.'

'Julia!' His voice quivered. 'Is she pulling strings too?'

'You can hardly expect the poor girl not to be interested.' Mr Campion spoke with asperity. 'Don't be a fathead. She's in love with you and she's left at the starting post, so to speak. Naturally she's desperate.'

'Do you think I don't know that? And do you think I'm not desperate myself?' The violence of the young man's protest was unexpected. There was a raw force about him which was completely hidden and unsuspected in the normal way. It startled Mr Campion, since it seemed out of character in one whom he had assumed to be a typical young Oxford success-type.

'The point your old college chum doesn't seem to have confided to you,' the boy continued bitterly, 'is that he has extracted a promise from me not to see or speak to Julia until all this has been cleared up. Moreover he hasn't explained that fact to her yet. Because he knows she wouldn't wear it, I suppose!'

'Why do you?'

'Wear it?'

'Yes.'

Timothy blinked.

'Do you know, I don't know,' he said at last. 'I've been wondering. It's just that in my heart I believe the old buzzard is right, I imagine. I've never believed in heredity consciously before and I don't know that I do now, but I certainly like to know what *is* behind me. Probably I've always been too much aware of everything I thought was there. Now that it's – well, that it's all been altered, I feel like an untethered balloon. I'm afraid that's Mrs Broome's contribution.'

'Ah.' Mr Campion perceived the position. 'She need only just hand your bag in. If you don't want to see her, Lugg can simply take it from her in the passage. There's someone coming up now, I fancy. You hear everything in these old build-ings.'

'A fac' which 'as bin useful in its time,' said Mr Lugg as he lumbered out into the narrow hallway, closing the door be-hind him.

As in many old London houses, the dividing walls were thin, and made of pine panelling, and as the outer door opened the murmur of protesting voices was very audible.

Timothy stood up abruptly. 'That's Julia!'

He pulled the door open and Mr Lugg, for once completely put out, stepped back to admit two women.

Julia appeared first, looking smartly casual as usual, in a loose grey woollen coat and a heavy multi-coloured silk head-scarf. Mrs Broome followed her, neat in tweeds and beret and tightly buttoned cape gloves. They came sweeping in, feminine and possessive and upset, and filled the whole apartment so that both Lugg and Campion were dis-possessed in a matter of seconds and Timothy, his bath-robe wrapped round him like a toga, met the full force of the invasion.

'Oh, *what* has happened to you?' Julia would have flung her arms about his neck but he repulsed her gently. He was relaxed but very much aloof.

'Nothing much. I'm all right. I had a dust up with a bigger boy. That's all.' He turned to Mrs Broome. 'Did you bring me some clothes?' He gave her no name but added 'Please' as an afterthought.

Mrs Broome did not look at him. She was more than twice his age but her mood was unmistakable. They were in the midst of a serious quarrel.

'They're in the case,' she said without raising her eyes, her lashes looking long against her weatherbeaten cheeks. 'Everything you could possibly want lugged right across London at a moment's notice by me and the sweetest, pret-tiest little princess of a girl who's much too good for you and I don't care who I say it in front of.' She flashed a defiant stare at the nearest stranger, who happened to be Mr Lugg. He was regarding her in pious horror and now stepped back

involuntarily. The appealing glance he shot at his
employer stirred Mr Campion to action.

'It is most kind of you, Mrs Broome,' he said firmly. 'Could
I ask you to unpack them in the bedroom?'

'In a minute, sir.' The tremendous authority of the nursery met him like physical resistance. 'There's just something
I ought to say first. I'm responsible for bringing Miss Julia.
In fact I made her come with me. Before you rang she came to
the Well House looking for Mr Timothy to tell him something. As soon as I heard what it was – I got it out of her, she
didn't want to tell me – I said at once that she'd better come
up here with me. Some things are serious. Some tales are
dangerous and must be stopped. "We'll go and thresh it out
once and for all", I said. "And then perhaps he'll stand up
for himself and not go condoning every cock-and-bull story
told about him. At least he'll know *this* isn't right", I said.
I was there and the only thing he did was to open the door and
in she fell. . . .'

The final words meant nothing to Mr Campion and Lugg
but their effect on Timothy Kinnit was considerable.

His face grew with fury and he turned on her. 'Nan! Go
home at once. I'll talk to you later. Hurry!'

'I won't, you know. Mr Timmy, Mr Timmy! It's im . . .
*por*tant!'

There was an ominous gulp on the final word and all three
men saw to their dismay the dreadful signs of disintegration:
the swimming eyes, the reddening nose, the mouth opening
raggedly like a sodden paper bag. Mrs Broome was about to
cry.

Mr Campion and his henchman stood helpless but Timothy
was experienced in such emergencies. He took a step towards
the suitcase and inquired softly: 'Did you bring my brown
shoes?'

She could only just hear him and the little effort which she
had to make in order to catch the words distracted her attention. It was as if they saw the tears actually receding.

'Brown shoes? You don't want *brown* shoes. I brought your
blue suit. Black shoes with blue cloth, you know that.'

He did not argue but continued to look disappointed, consolidating the position.

Mrs Broome's happy, self-assured little smile reappeared like sunshine. 'Only b.o.u.n.d.e.r.s. wear brown shoes with a blue lounge suit, or that is what I was always told,' she said gaily, one eye on the audience. 'Perhaps I'm old-fashioned but it's very nice to have *some* little rules.' And having reduced one school of snobbery to absurdity she returned brightly to the task she had come to perform.

'Well now,' she said briskly before Timothy could stop her. 'That Basil Toberman has privileges because he's almost part of the family, but even so he musn't be allowed to go about saying you helped to kill a poor little old lady.'

If she was striving to capture his attention she succeeded. He stood staring at her, his bathrobe festooned about him, his expression blank with horror.

'What the hell is all this?' he demanded, turning to Julia.

The girl had been sitting on the arm of a couch, her head bowed and her long silk legs stretched elegantly. Now she raised her face towards him, her cheeks flushing red and white.

'Of course that's only half true,' she said frankly. 'I really came round because I wanted any excuse to see you, I suppose, but the story is going about and I do think it ought to be stopped. Ralph Quy rang me this morning and told me that out at dinner in Knightsbridge last night he heard that you'd got in a temper with an old lady from South Africa and shaken her or frightened her or something so that she had a heart attack and died, and that Eustace Kinnit had hushed it all up "as usual".'

' "As usual"? What does that mean?'

'I don't know, Tim. Don't be angry with *me*. I just thought it was a story which ought to be scotched pretty quickly.' She struggled on with an explanation which she found distasteful but important. 'It's silly and untrue I know, but it's being linked with the other business. The inference is that you're reverting to type. You know, like a dog or a tiger or something, all right about the house until it becomes adult.'

'When it has to be put in a zoo.' Timothy sat down heavily and put his hands through his hair. 'This is a little much, isn't it? Did old Ralph convey that Basil was definitely responsible for this item?'

'Well, yes he did. That was what he telephoned to tell me. He told me to warn you that we ought to get hold of Basil Toberman and stop him spreading dirt which wasn't funny any more.'

'As far as I'm concerned it never was.' Timothy was irritated but not as angry as he might have been and Mr Campion, who was listening to the exchange with tremendous interest, eyed him curiously. His next remark was unexpected. 'Basil is a peculiar chap,' he said. 'He doesn't mean these things he says. He just talks to reassure himself. He means us no harm.'

It was a patron's point of view and highly mistaken, as Mr Campion knew for a fact. Suddenly he understood that it must be the Kinnit view of all the Tobermans, the grander family's assessment of a 'lesser breed', and for a fleeting moment he caught a glimpse of Basil Toberman's genuine grievance. Meanwhile Timothy was still talking in complete innocence and good faith.

'I'll tackle the old blighter,' he said. 'Don't be too hard on him, Julia. It's just one of those infuriating things. You can't really blame him you see, because in a way it's true.'

'What is?'

'The story. I don't suppose poor old Miss Saxon would have died just then if it hadn't been for me.' He got up abruptly and smiled ruefully at Campion. 'I'll go and dress if you'll forgive me,' he said. 'Nanny Broome will explain all this if you care to hear it. I see I'm not going to stop her.'

Julie was looking at Mr Campion. 'You do agree that it matters, don't you?' she said earnestly. 'You heard Basil Toberman talking about Tim down at Angevin. He wasn't talking for talking's sake. He meant it. Tim won't belive that.'

'And don't try to make him, Miss.' Mrs Broome spoke placidly from the other side of the room. She was sitting on one of the few hard chairs the flat contained, in what was once called a "ladylike attitude", both her feet close together and hard on the ground, her thickly gloved hands folded upon her good leather handbag.

'It would break Mr Tim's heart if he found out that someone really close to him didn't love him,' she continued devastatingly. '"People who really know you always love you if you're lovable". I taught him to believe that when he was the tiniest little boy because I don't like people who are always seeing snakes, do you, sir?' She put the question directly to Campion with a bright smile conveying that she had no doubt of his anwer.

The thin man laughed. 'I'm a little afraid of the people who never see them at all,' he said gently.

'Are you?' She seemed astonished. 'I was always taught that if you didn't pull pussy's tail she wouldn't scratch you, and there's a lot of truth in that whatever they say, but of course there are a few horrible boys like Basil and he really ought to be stopped before he does some real harm, which is why we've come, isn't it Miss Julia? We're not just bearing tales, I mean.'

Julia opened her mouth, caught Mr Campion's eye and ceased to worry quite so much. She returned to Mrs Broome.

'Tell Mr Campion exactly what happened when Miss – what was her name? – Miss Saxon fell. Tell him exactly what you told me.'

'*Did 'e lay a 'and on 'er?*' The question, put with earnest interest by Mr Lugg, who had been forgotten, startled everybody and Mrs Broome turned to him, scandalized.

'Of course not! That's another thing I've ground into Mr Tim. Never never *never* hit a lady!'

'Well then, the tale's all cock,' said Lugg, dismissing it. 'Don't worry and don't repeat it. 'E didn't touch 'er and that's the end. Wot did 'appen to 'er? For the sake of the record.'

Mrs Broome hesitated and he stood watching her, his head on one side, his little eyes very intelligent.

'Start wiv 'oo she was,' he suggested.

Mrs Broome's radiant smile reappeared. 'Well that was very difficult to find out, although I tried hard enough,' she said frankly. 'She didn't want to be called a lady's maid, you see, and she wasn't a governess because the child was too ill for one. When I was a girl she'd have been a mother's help and liked it, except that she'd have been sixteen and not sixty. "I wonder Mrs Telpher didn't feel it was too much of a responsibility bringing you with her," I said. "I mean you're quite as likely to get ill on the journey as the kiddie, aren't you?" She didn't like that but I was right, wasn't I?'

Lugg began to laugh in the high teetering way which only escaped him when he was genuinely amused.

'An' she was the one 'oo got 'erself killed!' he said. 'There's justice for you. That's life that is. She'd come from Souf Africa 'ad she?'

'So she said, and you needn't think we didn't get on. She used to talk to me by the hour. She told me all about the diamonds and everything.'

'Diamonds! Now we're coming to something. Where do they come in?'

'They don't. I never saw them.' She sounded regretful and the childlike streak in her character had never been more apparent. Her face actually saddened. 'But they're there in the safe deposit,' she added, cheering visibly. 'Mrs Telpher put them there because, as she told Miss Saxon it wasn't fair to Mr Eustace to keep them in the house. They're wonderful. Enormous. If you hadn't known how rich she is you'd never credit they were real. Miss Saxon told me that she couldn't think of them without her mouth watering.'

Julia leaned forward.

'Tell them about the kitchen door,' she suggested.

'Yes, well, that is what killed the little lady, dyed black hair, painted face and all.' Mrs Broome permitted herself to be kept to the point. 'Mr Tim and I were in the kitchen having silly words about something which after all did happen over twenty years ago, when he suddenly stopped shouting at me and said, "Nan, there's someone listening outside that blasted door." It's an old stone kitchen.

We live in an antique up here all right. I wonder Miss Alison gets any help at all. . . . Anyhow, he leapt across the matting and wrenched open the heavy old door and there she was leaning against the other side. So down she came, poor silly old thing, right down the two steps on to the stones. Mr Tim and I picked her up at once but we certainly didn't shake her. She only said that afterwards to Mrs Telpher, to take everybody's mind off her listening at the door.'

'She did not die at once, then?' Mr Campion appeared fascinated by the story.

'Oh no, thank goodness! That *would* have frightened Mr Timmy and me! She waited until she got into bed, poor little dear, and then she had a heart attack and died and wasn't found until the morning. The doctor said the fall was quite enough to bring it on with a heart like hers. She ought not to have taken the job,' she added earnestly, 'not when there was a child to be considered. She might have dropped it or frightened it, you never know.'

'When did she tell Mrs Telpher about the shaking?'

'The night before. She went to bed early, with me fussing round. Mrs Telpher was worried, because of course they were in someone else's house and illness and accidents are a trouble however polite the people are. In the morning it was dreadful when we knew she was dead. Mr Tim felt so guilty about pulling the door open and he was worried to death anyhow about the silly evacuee story of Mr Basil's, which really is the stupidest thing I ever heard, that he went off as soon as he knew from the doctor that he wasn't to blame and he has hardly been home since. He's a very sensitive boy.'

Lugg raised a heavy hand as if to put it on her shoulder, thought better of it and lowered it hastily.

'Wot is stoopid about the evac story?' he demanded. 'Why shouldn't the young feller try to find aht abaht 'is family?'

'Because he's got a perfectly nice family of people he's very fond of and knows all about and takes after by this time!' Mrs Broome blazed at him in sudden annoyance. 'Why Miss

Julia's father wants to upset all that I do not know. Besides, suppose Tim did find a family he seemed to have been born into – I don't think he can, mind you, but suppose he did – then what could that do but mystify him completely, poor boy?'

'Mystify 'im?' Lugg was puzzled.

'Of course. You don't know anything about people by seeing them! I remember a lady coming to inspect St Mary's Home where I was brought up and seeing us all in our lovely Elizabethan uniforms we were so proud of, and bursting into tears all over us because "it was wicked to dress us like charity children". We nearly crowned her we were so offended. She saw us but she didn't know us, did she?'

Lugg stepped back from her and permitted himself his little high-pitched laugh again.

'You've got it all sorted out, 'aven't yer?' he said admiringly. '"Mum knows best", that's gointer be my name for you! Your young lordship ought'er be dressed by now. You'll all go 'ome together I expeck.' He shuffled out of the room and Julia got up hastily and looked at Campion.

'I don't want to leave it like this,' she began. 'Basil Toberman is doing Tim active harm. He's got to be stopped. If I thought – '

She was silenced in mid-sentence by the reappearance of Mr Lugg whose face was blank with surprise.

'Gorn.' He announced. 'He went down the fire escape so as not to disturb us. Winder's wide open. Wot's the young feller up to, eh?'

There was a moment of complete silence in the room, broken by Julia's sharp intake of breath. Mrs Broome swung round upon her protectively.

'Don't take it to heart! It's only because he promised your father faithfully not to see you,' she said so quickly that no one was convinced. 'It wasn't very nice of the old gentleman to ask it but everything's fair in love and war, isn't it? You two have got to stand up for yourselves. You and me must get together, young lady!'

Both Lugg and Campion glanced at the girl curiously to see

how she would respond to this somewhat over-direct mothering and they were both surprised. A fleeting curl appeared at one corner of the pale pink mouth and the swimming eyes twinkled.

'Poor Tim,' said Julia.

Chapter Seven

Ebbfield Interlude

The highway to the East Coast which ran through the borough of Ebbfield had always been a main road and even now, despite the vast garages, the pylons and the gaily painted factory glass-houses which had sprung up beside it, there still remained an occasional trace of past cultures.

One of these was a fragment of a terrace of early Victorian middle-class houses of a type which had once lined the broad road for two miles on either side. There were three of them left, tall and dark-bricked, with semi-basement kitchens and once-splendid flights of stone steps leading to square porches and fine front doors. The middle one possessed a cast-iron gate with a patch of bald, sour earth just inside it, and a name plate bearing the number 172 and the words *Waterloo Lodge* welded to its serpentine tracery.

It was raining and dark when Timothy Kinnit found the address at last. He was hatless and the collar of his light raincoat was turned up. He was at a splendid age and although his self-assurance was already shaken he ran up the stone steps and pulled the brass knob which he found beside the door.

There was movement inside the house and a light appeared in the transom above his head. The door opened abruptly and a somewhat brusque feminine voice announced: 'Mrs Cornish.'

Timothy became shyly voluble.

'I'm so sorry to trouble you and I'm afraid you don't know me at all but I was given this address by Tom Tray. He repairs shoes in Carroway Street off the Orient Road. I was hoping that Councillor Cornish could spare me a moment or so?'

His diffidence and pleasant voice appeared to mollify her, for although she did not give ground she turned on the porch light and emerged as a small but stalwart woman in the late

forties, still smart and good-looking with bold eyes and a
fashionable hair-do. For a moment she regarded him with
surprised approval.

'My God, you've spoiled your beauty, haven't you?' she
said at last. 'What have you been doing, fighting? I warn you
we don't approve of boxing. Come in and I'll inquire if Mr
Cornish will see you. What is it? Youth Clubs?'

'No, I'm afraid it's not.' He followed her into a long,
shabby hall which could have belonged to any careless or
overworked professional man at any period during the last
hundred years. Mrs Cornish appeared to become conscious
of its shortcomings for she frowned at him and said accus-
ingly: 'When one works as hard as we do for the public good
one doesn't have time for frills. What did you say you wanted
to see the Councillor about? I don't imagine you're from a
firm, so I assume you're canvassing. You're wasting time, you
know, because every vote the Councillor has on any committee is well thought out *and* discussed, so he's already made
up his mind one way or the other and nothing you can do
will shift him one iota.'

Timothy found her trick of answering her own questions to
the second stage of argument highly disconcerting but he
stuck to his purpose.

'It's nothing like that. I merely want to ask him something
about Turk Street long ago and –'

'Oh, you're a reporter. Not from one of the local papers,
because I know them. Of course! You're the B.B.C. Well, we
shall all try to be as interesting as we can.'

'I'm not!' He was trying not to shout at her. 'I'm here on
my own account. I'm told that your husband knows more
about Ebbfield than anyone else on earth. Some weeks ago a
detective –'

'A *detective*!' She gave him a long, suspicious look which he
found vaguely unpleasant. 'So you're a detective! I ought to
throw you out at once, but you wait in here and if he wants
to see you I shan't stop him.'

She thrust him into an airless dining-room in which no one
had eaten for a very long time, and left him standing by the

large round table which was covered with a faded red serge cloth.

The mahogany sideboard was spread with out-of-date magazines and the pictures on the walls were all of mountains in shabby gilt frames. It was a depressing room and he was still looking about him gloomily when the door shot open once more and the Councillor appeared, his wife behind him.

Timothy was nearly as startled by the man as Superintendent Luke had been on an earlier occasion. He recognized the type at once. His university was full of them; all passionate, dedicated, sometimes wrong-headed men, wedded to an assortment of ideas of which a few were practical. The fire behind his eyes, his long bony wrists and impatient gestures were all peculiarly familiar, but the more disconcerting because he had not expected to find them in the Ebbfield High Road. The other surprising thing about the Councillor was his open dislike of his visitor, who was a complete stranger. Timothy was young enough to be hurt by it. Cornish's nostrils were flexed and when he spoke his tone was contemptuous.

'As I have already told one representative of your firm this morning, the matter is closed,' he said. 'I don't want to hear any more about it. I have the name of your client and that is all I wanted to know when I invited him to call on me.'

Timothy relaxed. 'I'm sorry, sir. You're making a mistake,' he said cheerfully.

'You were directed here by Stalkey & Sons.'

'No, sir. I got your name from the cobbler in Carroway Street.'

'Have you any connexion with the Stalkeys at all? Do you know them? Is the name familiar?' There was more force in the probing than the subject warranted and the younger man hesitated.

'I got myself beaten up by one of the brothers this morning,' he said at last.

'Why was that?'

'I don't know. The man set on me out of the air.'

The Councillor stared at him and presently spoke more

mildly. 'That's a very dangerous accusation unless you're perfectly sure what you mean by it, my boy.' Without his animosity he was revealed as a pleasant person, a little inhuman perhaps but possessing a streak of dry humour.

'I should hardly have thought that man I met would have hung about long enough to beat up anybody,' he remarked, sniffing a little. 'His brother, who he assured me was working down here on an inquiry, made the most indecently hasty departure from trouble which I ever witnessed. He was literally jet-propelled and all the way to Canada, I believe. What's your name?'

'Timothy Kinnit, sir.'

'*Kinnit!*' The word was an explosion and the lined aesthetic face grew rigid. 'What's this about? Eh?' He turned to his wife. 'Marion, leave me with this young man for a minute or two, will you?'

Mrs Cornish sat down obstinately.

'I'll wait,' she was beginning, but as he turned and looked at her the colour came into her face and she got up sulkily and went over to the door. 'I shan't be very far away, anyhow,' she said as she left, but it was not clear if the words were meant as a threat or a reassurance.

The Councillor waited until her footsteps had died away before he leaned across the table in an effort, apparently, to be reasonable at all costs.

'Who sent you?' he demanded.

Timothy's irritation began to return. 'I was given your name by the shoemaker off the Orient Road.'

'And you expect me to believe that?'

'I really can't imagine why you shouldn't.'

The Councillor ignored him.

'I think Miss Alison Kinnit sent you,' he said.

Timothy stared. 'Alison? Why should she?'

'You know her then?' The intelligent eyes were shrewdly inquisitive.

'Of course I do. She and her brother brought me up. I live with them.'

'Oh.' He seemed astonished, even a little put out. 'Then

perhaps you know a woman called Flavia Aicheson?' He put contempt and dislike into the name and Timothy frowned.

'Certainly I know her,' he admitted. 'She's been around all my life. She's a great friend of Aunt Alison's and a very nice old thing. Has she been making trouble on one of your committees?' He saw that he had scored a bull's-eye as soon as the words were out of his mouth. The Councillor was verging towards rage and colour had appeared on his thin cheeks.

'You're very plausible, very smooth,' he began with intentional offence. 'I'm not a fool, you know, even if I have lived a great deal longer than you have. As soon as I heard a private detective had been snooping along certain lines I suspected something of this sort and I was disgusted, I tell you frankly. For a while I washed my hands of the entire affair but on second thoughts I decided to check and I invited the Stalkeys to call on me. One brother came down this morning and was quite ready to talk, but I only wanted one thing from him and that was the name of his client. As soon as he gave me that I knew I was right. Alison Kinnit and Flavia Aicheson, they're virtually the same woman.'

'Oh but they're not!' Timothy was so exasperated that he laughed. 'They may have the same interests and they're certainly very close friends but they're quite different personalities I do assure you.'

'Are they?' Councillor Cornish conveyed that he was unconvinced. 'You go back and tell them,' he said. 'Tell them they may feel that they're serving the Arts but that I serve Humanity and I am not going to have my life's work tampered with. You can also tell them that if they're hoping to use dirty weapons they should consider their own position very carefully. At least,' he hesitated 'at least tell them not to be so damn silly!'

'I do assure you you're making a great mistake.' Timothy's embarrassment was mounting. He had discovered to his dismay that the personal aspect of his quest was becoming more agonizingly personal at every new encounter, while at the same time the Councillor's accusatory style upset him in an emotional way which he felt to be absurd.

'I came here on my own account because I want to know the things that Stalkey was trying to find out and I thought you might help me,' he said lamely.

'What things? Go on, young man. Put them into words, what things?' There was something savage in the force of the older man's question and his visitor shied away from it.

'Certain – certain aspects of social conditions in Turk Street just before the second war, sir,' he muttered and sounded stilted even to himself.

'*Social conditions!*' The phrase seemed to touch a power centre in the Councillor, who let himself go. 'Don't be a pompous ass, boy!' He used the word in the old-fashioned way with a long vowel, making it even more derogatory. 'Turk Street was a London slum. Your generation doesn't know what that means. You call yourselves "sick", don't you? So do I. You couldn't have walked a hundred yards of the Turk Street Mile in the thirties without vomiting. It turned me up myself and I wasn't a spoon-fed university product.'

He leant farther across the table, shaking in his determination to make his point.

'Children crawled over each other like little grey worms in the gutters,' he said. 'The only red things about them were their buttocks and they were raw. Their faces looked as if snails had slimed on them and their mothers were like great sick beasts whose byres had never been cleared. The stink and the noise and the cold and the hatred got into your belly and nothing and no one has ever got it out again as far as I'm concerned. For God's sake go back to those maiden ladies and get it into their idiot heads that an anthill is less offensive than a sewer.'

Timothy hesitated. The man was making an extraordinary mistake, he saw, and he realized that he was probably the best source of information about the vanished Turk Street remaining in London. Yet he also knew that for some inexplicable reason he could not put up with his open animosity any longer.

The Councillor glanced up. 'What are you waiting for?'

'Nothing, sir.' Timothy was very pale and the damage which Ron Stalkey had done to his face stood out in angry colour on his skin. 'Good-bye.' He turned on his heel and walked across the room, out through the front door and down the steps to the street without once looking behind him.

Mrs Cornish, who was hovering in the passage, saw him go and she went in to her husband.

'Why on earth did you do that?' she demanded. 'I could hear you from the kitchen. What did the poor boy say to make you so livid?'

Now that his rage was spent the Councillor was a little shame-faced. 'Oh, I don't know,' he said frowning. 'The "holier-than-thou" attitude of that sort of pup always irritates me. A self-satisfied superior approach to matters of taste is infuriating. Those people like the Kinnits and the Aichesons all do the same thing. They look at something which they know nothing whatever about and presume to judge it solely by the effect which the mere sight of it has had on them.'

'Flavia Aicheson,' said Mrs Cornish. 'That's the mannish old woman who runs the Little Society for the Preservation of the London Skyline isn't it? So that's what he came about. Rather a nice type.'

'I didn't notice it. Those people are up to something. I don't trust them an inch. They're the kind of half-baked intellectuals who never know where to stop. They don't like the look of the new flats. The silhouette is an affront to their blasted eyes, they say. Well, there are alternatives which have offended my eyes . . .'

'Yes dear, not again.' Mrs Cornish exerted her own brand of force. 'You happened to walk down Turk Street one winter afternoon long ago when you first came up from the country to be Dad's apprentice, and it gave you such a shock that you've never got over it. We know. We've heard enough about it. You weren't there quite half an hour and it's dominated your whole life. It may not have been the utter hell you thought. Anyhow, why take it out on the first presentable youngster who's been to the house for years?'

'Pompous ass!' said the Councillor again. 'He kept calling me "sir" as if I were Methusela. That's all I noticed about him. A useless, opinionated, over-sensitive ass!'

'Oh rubbish,' she said. 'You can't say that. You didn't even let him speak. Do you know who he reminded me of? You at that age. No one was more opinionated than you were, or more oversensitive for that matter.'

The Councillor stared at her. For an instant he looked positively alarmed. Then he laughed, regretful, even a little flattered.

'You do say the most damn silly things, Marion,' he said.

Chapter Eight

The Well House

'Seen it before, sir?' The brisk inquiry from the helmeted figure materializing beside Timothy in the half darkness took him by surprise and he blinked. He had been standing perfectly still, gazing across the broad street at the silhouette of the house which had been his home in London ever since he could remember, and it was as new to him as a foreign land.

He had just walked back from Ebbfield. His interview with the Councillor had had a considerable effect upon him for he was behaving as if a skin had peeled from his eyes. Children first home from boarding school often notice the same phenomenon, very familiar things appearing not different in themselves but as if they were being seen by someone new. He knew of no reason why it should have happened. The front of his mind was satisfied that he had merely had an interview with a difficult old man, but behind it, in the vast, blind, computing machine where the mind and the emotions meet and churn, something very odd indeed seemed to have taken place.

It was a muggy London night and the road which was an inferno in the daytime was now a deserted river, gleaming dully in a dark ravine.

The constable was a regular and had recognized him. It was a lonely beat and he was prepared to chat.

'It's an anachronism,' he remarked unexpectedly, jerking his leather-strapped chin towards the Tudor merchant's mansion which lay, top-heavy but graceful as a galleon, between two towering warehouses on the opposite side of the road. The overhanging latticed windows, one floor up, were lighted and warmth shone out faintly through reddish curtains. But at street level the low iron-bound doors and small windows were hidden in the shadows. 'Completely out of place in a modern world, isn't it?' he went on. 'But it's nice to see it. It's even better than that row up in Holborn they tell me. Is it comfortable to live in, sir?'

'Not bad. Plumbing was put in very intelligently at the early part of this century but the kitchens are still a bit archaic.' Timothy spoke as if the facts were fresh to him and the constable laughed. 'Still, you're proud of it I dare say?' he said.

The younger man turned his head in surprise. 'I suppose I was' he said, but the policeman was not listening. The light from one of the old-fashioned street lamps bracketed on the building behind them had fallen on to the speaker's face and he was startled by the damage.

'Blimey sir! What have you done to yourself? Met with an accident?'

'Not exactly. I had a dustup with a lunatic!' The words came out with more bitterness than he had intended and he laughed to cover it. 'Never mind, officer. All's square now. Good night.'

'Good night, sir.' The man went off as if he had been dismissed and Timothy crossed the road and let himself into the Well House.

There was a small wooden draughtbreak just inside the door with a curtained entrance to the main hall, and he heard Basil Toberman's voice as he stepped through it into the warm, black-panelled room with the moulded plaster ceiling and the square staircase rising up through it. The first thing he saw was a funeral wreath, and the scent of lilies hung in the warm air, suffocating and exotic, and remarkably foreign to the familiar house.

The tribute was very big, nearly four feet across, a great cushion of white hothouse flowers, diapered with gold, and made all the more extravagant by the shining plastic wrappings which made it look as if it was under glass. It lay on the oak table which flanked the staircase and at the moment Toberman was bending over it, fiddling with a card half hidden among the blossom. Mrs Broome was hovering beside him in a flurry of protest.

'Oh don't,' she was objecting. 'Mr Basil, don't. It isn't as though it's yours. Don't be so inquisitive, don't!'

'Shut up,' he said without turning round. 'I'm only having a look. The order must have come from South Africa through one of the flower services, I suppose. That's the flaw in these things. There's no way of telling what you're getting for your money.'

'What are you talking about?' she demanded. 'It's beautiful. It must have cost I don't know what!'

'I know. That's what I'm saying. Out there – wherever it is – flowers are probably dear at this time of year. Over here in late spring they cost nothing. I don't suppose anyone, however stinking rich, intended to send to a servant's funeral the sort of wreath which one expects to see the Monarch parking on a War Memorial.'

Nanny Broome sniffed. 'No wonder no one could do anything *with* you,' she observed without animosity. 'Your naughtiness is right in you. Miss Saxon wasn't a servant, and if she had been all the more reason that she should have a nice wreath, even if it did come so late it missed the hearse. I wish I'd had you as a little boy. I'd have scared some of the commoness out of you, my lad. Miss Saxon was a governess and a very intelligent woman with a great sense of humour.'

'How do you know?'

Mrs Broome silenced him. 'Well, she used to laugh at *me*,' she said and seemed so pleased about it that there was nothing to say.

Toberman swung round on his heel and saw Timothy standing in the doorway. He stood for an instant contemplating the scarred face, his eyes wonderfully shrewd and amused, but he made no direct comment.

Instead he returned to the flowers: 'Wonderfully wealthy guests we have,' he remarked. 'This is how the staff is seen off. How does this appeal to the young master?'

It was a casual sneer, obviously one of a long line. There was hatred behind it but of a quiet, chronic type, nothing new or unduly virulent, and he was taken aback by the flicker of amazed incredulity which passed over the younger man's ravaged face. Toberman was disconcerted. 'What's the matter?' he demanded truculently.

'Nothing.' Timothy's eyes wavered and met Mrs Broome's. She was watching him like a mother cat, noting the signs of shock without altogether understanding them. She opened her mouth to speak but he shook his head at her warningly and she closed it again without a sound.

'You look like a lost soul,' Toberman said. 'Where have you been?'

Tim turned away. 'I walked home,' he said briefly. 'I'm tired.'

Nanny Broome could bear it no longer.

'Come down to the kitchen, Mr Tim,' she said. 'I want to talk to you,' and as her glance met his own she formed the word "Julia" with her lips, giving him a clue as she used to do long ago when there was a secret to be told in company and he was a little boy.

Despair passed over the young face and he turned away abruptly.

'Not now, Nan,' he said, looking at Toberman who had found the card he had been seeking amid the lilies and was now transcribing its details into a notebook. He was doing it with that off-hand effrontery which so often passes unnoticed because people cannot bring themselves to credit their own eyes. When a step on the landing above surprised him, he slid the book into his pocket and patted the covering back into place.

'We were saying how beautiful it is,' he remarked blandly as he glanced up the stairwell. Mrs Geraldine Telpher, the Kinnit's visiting niece, was coming down, moving quietly and smoothly as she did everything else. She was a distinguished-looking woman in the late thirties, pleasantly pale with faded old-gold hair and light blue eyes, who radiated authority and that particular brand of faint austerity which is so often associated with money. She was wearing a grey jersey suit with considerable elegance, and the way her jacket sat on her shoulders and the trick she had of settling her cuff straight confirmed her kinship with Eustace and Alison so vividly that the others were made a little uncomfortable. Her method of handling Toberman was also startingly familiar. She laughed at his antics with a mixture of ruefulness and tolerance as if he were a slightly offensive household pet.

'The smell of the lilies is rather powerful,' she said. 'The house is full of it upstairs. Is there somewhere where the wreath could go, Mrs Broome? It's a pity it came so late. Perhaps it could be sent to the grave in the morning?'

'I was going to take it myself, first thing.' In her determination to keep in the limelight Mrs Broome spoke on the spur of the moment and it was evident to everybody that the idea had never entered her head before that instant. 'In a taxi,' she added after the briefest possible pause.

'Perhaps so,' Mrs Telpher agreed gravely. 'They might not let you take it on a bus but you could try. Anyway it's very good of you and I'm sure she would have appreciated it. She had taken a great fancy to you, hadn't she?'

'Well I should think so, she talked enough to me!' Nanny Broome was "giving back as good as she had got" in an instinctive self-preservative fashion which had nothing to do with reason. The Kinnit trick of making people feel slightly inferior without intending to or noticing that it had been done had never been more clearly demonstrated.

Toberman went on chatting in a determined yet deferential way.

'We were thinking that the flowers must have been ordered from abroad by wire,' he was saying with a little inquisitive laugh. 'The whole wreath is very lush – very grand. The card only says "Love dear from Elsa" but there's a box number which suggests either a P.O. box address, as in South Africa, or a florist's reference.'

Geraldine Telpher favoured him with a wide-eyed stare which might have been one of Alison Kinnit's own and shook her head, smiling.

'I imagine it must have come from the family she was with before she came to me,' she said, making it clear that she was humouring him. 'I notified her home and they must have told them. It was the Van der Graffs, I remember. How nice

of them. They're good people. You find its size a little osten-
tatious, do you Basil?'

'Don't make fun of me,' he protested. 'I'm just impressed,
that's all. I like lavishness. It's rare. By the way that name –
Van der Graff – are they anything to do with the Ivory
people?'

'I'm afraid I just wouldn't know.'

'Ah!' he held up a warning hand to her. 'No wicked snobbery. Trade is in fashion. As a matter of fact I was coming to
talk to you about that.' He turned to Mrs Broome and lifted
the wreath into her arms, all but hiding her.

'Run along with that to the scullery, Broomie. I shan't stay
here tonight, by the way, because I've got to get the late plane
to Nice, but I'll be back tomorrow rather late and I'd like to
stay then. The room is ready I expect, so you won't have to
worry about me.' It was a plain dismissal and Mrs Broome
went, but not defeated.

'Me worry about *you*?' she said from the doorway. 'That'll
be the day!'

Toberman laughed and returned to Mrs Telpher. 'They
used to sack them for that sort of remark,' he said. 'I suppose
you do now. How wonderful. Now look, Geraldine my dear,
I don't know if this is of any interest to you at all but I thought
I'd mention it. I'm going to Nice tonight to see a little fourth-
century bronze which Lagusse says is genuine. I've seen a
photograph and it's more than promising. I shall just take
one look and come home, because if it's real the only man
who has both the taste and the money to buy it is in your
country and I've got Philip Zwole flying there on other business and I want to brief him. He'll be overseas for the best part
of a month and he'll spend quite a week in Johannesburg, so
if there's anything you'd like him to take or any message
you'd like to send by him, well, there he is.'

It was a request for introductions and Timothy, who had
moved away, turned back irritably.

'I imagine Geraldine can keep in touch, Basil,' he said.

It was a protest and sounded like one and Toberman
received it with a stare of reproachful amazement while

Mrs Telpher looked at Timothy and laughed a polite rejection of the whole subject.

'It's very kind of him,' she said. 'If I do think of anything I shall certainly remember the offer.'

Toberman snorted. His dark face was swarthy with blood and his round black eyes were furious.

'Don't be damn silly,' he exploded, turning on the other man.

'Geraldine has just had her Miss Saxon die in a strange country. Presumably the woman had some things which ought to be taken to her home. I was merely offering a service. What other reason could I possibly have?'

'None,' intervened Mrs Telpher with all the Kinnit tolerance in her quiet voice. 'I do appreciate it. It really is most kind.'

Toberman appeared mollified and bounced again. 'Well then,' he said, 'when I come in tomorrow evening I'll collect anything you want to send and give it to Zwole when I see him in the morning. I can understand you being windy about the poor old thing's family, Tim. You actually knocked her over, didn't you?'

Mrs Telpher intervened.

'Tell me about the bronze,' she said.

'Why? Are you interested?' His sudden eagerness made her smile and she bowed her long neck. 'I might be,' she conceded.

Timothy left them and went upstairs to the sitting-room whose lighted windows he had seen from the street. It was a civilized, lived-in room, part panelled and part booklined. A vast Turkey carpet with a faded tomato-soup coloured background hid much of the black oak floor, and the remarkable collection of upholstered furniture which had comfort alone in common was welded into harmony by plain covers in the same yellowish pink.

Miss Alison Kinnit and her friend Miss Aicheson were sitting where they always did, Alison on one of the angular couches with her feet tucked up beside her and Flavia in a big rounded arm-chair with a back like a sail on the opposite side of the hearth. There was no fire and the wide brick recess housed a collection of cacti, none of them doing very well because of the shade and the draught.

The likeness between Alison Kinnit and her niece Mrs Telpher was considerable but the twenty years between their ages was not entirely responsible for the main difference, which was one of delicacy. Mrs Telpher was a pale, graceful woman but Alison's pallor and fragility were remarkable. Her skin was almost translucent without being actually unhealthy and her bones were as slender as a bird's. She had always had an interesting face but had never been beautiful and now there was something a little frightening in the greyeyed intelligence with which she confronted the world. Miss Flavia on the other hand was a more familiar type. She was one of those heavy ugly women with kind faces and apologetic, old-gentlemanly manners who all look as if they were John Bull's own daughters taking strongly after their father, poor dears. She was older than Alison, sixty perhaps, and happy in the way that some elderly men who have had great trials and overcome them are happy: quiet-eyed, amused and not utterly intolerant.

It was obvious that they had been talking about Timothy; not because they seemed guilty when he came in but because they were so interested and so clear about who he was and what was happening to him. In the normal way they were apt to be completely absorbed by their own affairs of the moment and these might be literary, charitable or political – one never knew which. The fact that Miss Flavia had stuck to her romantic name all her life said much for her character. Now she turned slowly in her chair and looked at Tim through her glasses.

'Certainly battle-scarred but I hope not woebegone,' she said in her fluting, county voice. 'What does the other fellow look like? Come and sit down and tell us all about it. Shall I get him a drink, Alison?'

'Would you like one, dear?' Alison nodded at him, screwing up her face with mimic pain at the damage to his face. 'We won't. But it's there in the cupboard if you'd like it. Mrs

Broome told us you'd been in the wars. Where have you been? You look awfully distrait.' Her own voice was clipped and academic, and friendly without warmth.

'Down to Ebbfield again,' he said as casually as he could as he seated himself on the edge of the round ottoman which took up a huge amount of space in the fairway between the fireplace and the door. 'I saw a man called Councillor Cornish: he seemed to think that you or Aich must have sent me.'

'And did we?' Alison glanced inquiringly at her friend.

'I don't recall it.' Miss Aicheson's nice eyes regarded him innocently. 'Yet the name is familiar. Is he an Ebbfield councillor?'

'I imagine so. He's responsible for building a block of flats.'

'Oh, of course. The skyline committee, Alison. He's the poor wretched man with the dreadful temper. I remember.' Miss Flavia was delighted. Her charitableness had never been more marked. 'I can imagine him remembering me but I can't think why he should suppose I should have sent you to him. People with chips on their shoulders do get wild ideas, of course. Well, did he help you? What did you ask him?'

Timothy appeared to be wondering and Alison, mistaking his reaction, intervened tactfully.

'Aich is on top of the world. She's had a letter from the Minister.'

Miss Aicheson's red face was suffused with shy pleasure. 'Oh, it's nothing. Only an acknowledgement, really,' she said, 'but it's from White's, not the House, and it's signed, and there's even a little postscript in his own hand thanking me for my "lucid exposition". I'm very bucked. I admit it.'

Timothy frowned. His young body was tense and as he sat with his long legs crossed he tapped on his knee with nervous fingers.

'Is that the Minister of Housing? Is this the Ebbfield business?'

Alison's laugh silenced him.

'Oh, no my dear, Ebbfield is very small beer. This is the Plan for Trafalgar Square.'

Miss Aicheson made a happy succession of little grunting

noises. 'Ra-ther a different caper!' she announced with satis-faction. 'I expect the over-earnest little men will get their own way at Ebbfield and it can't be helped because that part of London is spoiled already. One just does what one can in a case like that and doesn't break one's heart if one fails.'

'Cornish didn't strike me as being a *little* man.' Tim appeared astonished at his own vehemence and Alison turned her wide grey eyes upon him, surprised also.

Flavia Aicheson waved the protest away with a large mas-culine hand. 'Very likely not,' she agreed. 'I can't visualize him at all. I only remember how angry he was and how nearly rude, so that all the rest of the conference was on edge with embarrassment. He was over-earnest, though, wasn't he? These dear chaps remember some picture from their child-hood, some little injustice or ugliness, and let it grow into a great emotional boil far, far more painful than the original wound . . . Don't let them influence you, dear boy.'

She and Alison exchanged glances and suddenly became utterly embarrassed themselves.

Miss Aicheson made an effort, her face scarlet and her voice unsteady with nervousness.

'This inquiry into your birth is a very difficult and awk-ward experience for you, Timothy, and Alison and I both feel (although of course we haven't been discussing you, don't think that!) the real danger is of you losing your sense of proportion and swinging violently either one way or the other. Left or Right.'

She was as uncomfortable as a young girl and, since the problem was emotional, quite as inexperienced. The boy got up.

'That's all right Aich,' he said kindly. 'I shan't go Red or Fascist.'

The two ladies sighed with relief. 'Of course you won't,' Miss Flavia said heartily. 'You're far too sensible. Well now, about the investigation; any progress?' She hesitated and a little wistful smile, as feminine and pathetic as any Nanny Broome could muster, suddenly crept over her homely face. 'Don't forget that in one way it could be very romantic and exciting, Timothy,' she murmured. 'I mean – one never knows.'

Alison burst out laughing. Her grey eyes were as hard but also as innocent as pebbles in a stream.

'Dear Aich!' she said. 'Isn't she wonderful, Timothy? She's thinking: "Even the Minister must have been young in 1939!"'

Miss Flavia's colour increased to danger point and she shook her head warningly.

'That's not funny, Alison,' she said. 'Vulgar and not funny at all.'

At once Alison Kinnit lost her poise and became contrite.

'Sorry, Aich,' she said, hanging her head like a delicate child. 'Really truly.'

Timothy went out of the room without them noticing that he had gone.

Chapter Nine

The Stranger

Eustace Kinnit was the author of many books and pamphlets
on various aspects of the china collector's art as well as being
an enthusiastic correspondent on the subject. The small study
where he did his endless writing was at the far end of the gallery which ran round the staircase-well on the same floor as
the sitting-room. There was a sliver of light under the door as
Timothy approached after leaving Miss Alison and her
friend, and he stood outside for a moment, hesitating, with an
anxious expression in his eyes which was new there. Any sort
of nervousness was foreign to his temperament and he bore
it awkwardly. Presently he pushed his hand over his hair,
stiffened his shoulders, and walked in more abruptly than he
would have done at any other time in his life.

Eustace was sitting at his desk in a bright circle of light
from the shaded lamp, his pen squeaking softly as it ran
swiftly over the page. Timothy, who had seen him in exactly
the same position so often and who loved him so well that he
had, as it were, never seen him at all, observed him objec-
tively for the first time.

He was a spare, tidy man of sixty or so with a sharp white
beard, and a sweep of white hair above a fine forehead. His
eyes were like his sister's but more blue and infinitely more
kindly and the lines at their sides radiated in a quarter circle.
As he wrote his knee jogged all the time. It was a ceaseless
tremor which made a little draught in the otherwise still and
muffled room. He took no notice of the newcomer until he
had finished his paragraph, putting in the final stop with care.
Then he put down his pen, lifted his head and removed his
spectacles. These were in white gold, made to his own austere
design, and were one of his few personal vanities. As they lay
on the page they were as typical of him as his signature.

'Hello,' he said happily. 'There you are. It went off very well. Nothing too barbaric but respectably splendid and decent. I think she was pleased.'

'The funeral?'

'Eh? Oh my goodness, yes! What did you think? I meant Geraldine, too. There's no way of telling what the other poor woman felt about it!' His laugh was schoolboyish and charming. 'Are you all right? I can't see you very well over there. Turn the light on will you? Good Heavens, boy! What have you done?'

Timothy had touched the switch by the door obediently and as the light fell on his face Eustace's horrified reaction to the damage was so completely out of proportion to it that the younger man was irritated.

'It's nothing,' he protested, shying away. 'Only a scratch or two.'

'Not a road accident?' Eustace was speaking of something he was always dreading and fear flared in his voice embarrassingly.

'No, of course not. I merely got a hiding from one of those damn detectives of yours. What on earth made you pick them, or was it Alison?'

'The Stalkeys? I heard something of the sort from the women.' Eustace opened his eyes very wide. 'I can't believe it.'

He spoke gravely, meaning the words literally, and managed to look both so hurt and so completely incredulous that the exasperated colour poured into the boy's face, hiding some of the injuries in a general conflagration. Eustace sighed as if somehow he had been reassured. 'That's much better,' he said unreasonably. 'But you shouldn't make sweeping statements like that. If you attacked the man I suppose he defended himself. They're a very old established firm and excellent people or we shouldn't have employed them for the second time. Even so I don't know if it was wise. We're only trying to help you, Tim, you know that.'

It was a transparent mixture of prejudice, obstinacy and

genuine dismay, and so like him that the young man could have wept.

'Oh scrub it!' he exploded, and suddenly blurted out the one bald question that he had made up his mind never to ask outright.

'Uncle, had no one *really* any idea whatever where I came from?'

Eustace gaped at him in amazement. When his urbanity dropped away from him, as now, he had an innocence of expression which was almost infantile. It was as if the world had never touched him at all.

'But I told you,' he said earnestly. 'I told you, Tim. I confessed it.' The young man watched him helplessly. There was no hope that he was lying. The chill truth shone from him as only truth does shine. 'It was absurd and unrealistic of me perhaps,' he went on, betraying that he was still not entirely convinced of the fact. 'I can see something of that now, but then . . .! My goodness! What a time that was! The world was cracking up all round us, you see. Civilization, Beauty, Law and Order, all crumbling like the pillars of a city. You were just a little bundle of helpless jelly, so very vulnerable and appealing. It didn't seem very important what I did. I thought I'd provide for you as long as I could, you know, and there was that thwarted, childless woman so delighted to be able to mother you. I felt I did right afterwards because Alison and I both became so fond of you. I've said I'm sorry, Tim.'

'Don't . . .' the boy put out his hand. 'I'm not ungrateful, you know that. It's only that – I mean, you are absolutely dead sure that I can't possibly be a Kinnit?'

Eustace appeared to consider the remoter possibilities for the first time.

'How could you be?' he inquired.

The utter reasonableness of the question struck Timothy with the impact of a pail of cold water. The final shreds of his romantic swaddling-clothes were washed away and he stood quivering and ashamed of himself for ever clinging to them. It was a moment of enormous danger which anyone in

Eustace's position who had a reasonable degree of emotional imagination or experience must have found terrifying, but his protection was almost complete. He reacted in his own way and changed the subject.

'I'm getting on,' he announced, nodding at the written page. 'But it's not easy. There's very little data about Chandler's first factory at Bristol. Oh well, it must wait for the moment. I'm very glad you came in, Tim. I wanted to have a word with you about poor Basil. He *drinks* these days, doesn't he?'

The young man stood looking at him. In his eyes was the half-horrified, half-amused expression with which so many people meet the solution of a lifelong enigma. Eustace the father-figure had turned into Eustace the dear old fuss-pot.

'Basil? Oh, he takes his noggin,' Timothy said. 'It's not serious.'

'Ah, but I understand it makes him *talk*.' Eustace's glance had become frosty and the aesthetic lines in his face were very marked; he had also coloured a little as he always did when he was embarrassed. 'Alison came in here an hour ago,' he said. 'She'd been talking to Nanny Broome – that woman is only up here for a few days and we learned things about each other of which we've been happily ignorant for years! I don't take her too seriously but one thing she is reported to have said worries me very much.' He lowered his voice to a confidential murmur. 'Have you heard an extraordinary story about Basil actually saying – when drunk of course – that you had been *rough* with that poor old woman who died here?'

Timothy frowned in irritation. 'I heard something of the sort.'

'Tim. It's not true?'

'Of course not! Don't be silly, Nunk.' The old endearment from his childhood slipped out without him noticing. 'Even if no one has faced this birth business until now, you can't suddenly decide you don't know me at all! Miss Saxon happened to be listening outside the kitchen door when I pulled it open. She fell into the room and on to the stones.

Nan and I picked her up and dusted her down and she went off quite happy, but afterwards she told Geraldine that I had shaken her.'

'And you hadn't?' The anxiety in the tone was wounding.

'No! She was only creating a diversion; she'd been caught listening at a door! Do put it out of your head, it's so unimportant.'

'I don't think so,' Eustace got up from his chair and walked up and down the small room. Something had frightened him. Timothy found that he recognized the signs but was no longer made afraid himself by them. Eustace was pale and excited and the knuckles of his hands grasping the lapels of his jacket were white.

'It could be most damaging. Most. He's got to be stopped, Tim. He's got to be stopped at once. Where is the silly fellow?'

'He's in the house. He's flying to Nice in the dawn and coming back here to sleep tomorrow night. Don't bother with him. He does chatter and nobody takes any notice of him. Really it doesn't matter.'

'You're wrong. She's dead you see. It makes it very awkward. Very dangerous.' Eustace paused in the midst of his walk and was thinking, his eyes narrowed and his lips moving. 'I'll speak to him,' he said at last. 'Don't you say anything. It's my responsibility. Leave it to me. He must give up alcohol if he can't trust his tongue.'

The younger man turned away wearily. 'I don't care a damn what he says!'

'That's nothing to do with it my boy. Don't you see? I gave Dr Gross my word that there could be no possible need for a post-mortem.'

'That was a bit god-like of you, wasn't it?'

'Wasn't it?' Eustace's gentle laugh escaped him. 'Something warned me at the time that I was being presumptuous. However, I did it. Gross came over as soon as I telephoned and when he found that she was dead he came in here to me and said something about mentioning the death to the Coroner. Well, I've known him for years, as you know, and rightly or wrongly I dissuaded him. I pointed out that he had attended her so he was behaving quite properly in giving a certificate if he was certain nothing abnormal had occurred, and I took it on myself to guarantee that nothing had. After a certain amount of humming and haa-ing he agreed.'

'Why did you go to all that trouble? Because Geraldine is so rich?'

Eustace looked hurt. 'Tim, that was a sneer!' He shook his head and added with disarming frankness, 'I don't know why one does go out of one's way to oblige Money. It's a funny thing and very wrong but everybody does it. Yet, you know, it wasn't quite that. I think I wanted to save us all embarrassment. Geraldine has trouble enough on her hands with that poor child in hospital.'

He paused and alarm appeared in his kindly eyes again.

'Basil must hold his tongue though. What a stupid man he is! It could be particularly awkward, since the woman was a governess. I noticed that at once.'

Tim looked at him blankly for a moment before he laughed.

'On the principle that the Kinnit family is governess prone?'

'Don't be a fool, my boy!' Eustace actually stamped his foot. 'Use your imagination. Nothing colours a new scandal like an old crime story. In the last century the Kinnits were involved in a Coroner's inquest and a trial which concerned a governess, Thyrza Caleb. The name is not forgotten after a hundred years. It would certainly cause comment if we appeared in a new one now which also concerned a governess. It's obvious. That was why I wrote the announcement for the newspapers myself. I was very careful not to let the name Kinnit appear. "Kinnit" and "governess" are not good words together. We live in an age of mischievous publicity; it's stupid to ignore the fact. Basil must stop drinking and be quiet. I'll see to it myself.' He sat down at the desk again and took up his pen. 'You go and have a good sleep,' he said. 'You're not like yourself tonight.' Tim turned to the door.

'I'm not like anybody, that's the trouble.'

'What's that?' Eustace was looking over his glasses. 'Turn that light down will you as you go. I like just the one lamp on the page. What did you say just now?'

'Nothing of any interest. Good night.'

'Good night, Tim.' He was already writing. 'Don't brood,' he said without looking up. 'And don't forget, not a word to Basil. I'll do that.'

Timothy went out into the passage again and walked round the staircase-well to the other side of the house. The door of the sitting-room was closed but he heard Toberman's unmistakable laugh and Miss Aicheson's high hollow voice as he passed it. The rest of the building was as quiet as only London's night-time deserted areas can be quiet. From every side the roar was still audible, but now it came from far away and in the middle there was stillness and the grateful pandemonium quelled.

His own room possessed a staircase of its own which ran up from the end of the right wing where Eustace, Alison and any guests staying the night had bed and bathrooms. It had always been his room and as a child he had been thrilled by the sense of importance and security which the staircase gave him. One entered it through a small door which one could pretend was secret and the stair wound up in a full half turn to the big low room with the uneven oak floor and the tiny washroom and shower built in an oversized cupboard, the panelled bed and the bookshelves filling the wall beside it.

He was so anxious to get to this sanctuary, to shut the door and clear his mind, that he did not notice Nanny Broome who was standing by the passage window, her dark dress mingling with the heavy curtains.

'Mr Tim?' The voice, almost in his ear as he passed, surprised him and he shied away from her. 'Mr Tim. I've got to tell you something.'

'Not now, Nan, for God's sake!' The words came out more savagely than he meant and she responded in her own particular fashion. Her eyes flashed and her lips hardened. 'Oh well then, you must find it out for yourself and I shan't take the blame!' she said tartly. 'I'm sorry I wasted my time waiting for you.'

She was not really put out; he could tell that from her voice. She was in one of her slightly naughty and entirely feminine moods, excited and truculent. The threat might mean anything; in his present loneliness he did not care.

He left her without speaking, shut the door of the staircase carefully behind him, turned on the switch which lit the bedroom above and ran up into it, to come to a sudden halt on the threshold. Someone was there, lying on the bed, the shadows of the high foot-board hiding her face. He knew who it was before he went over and looked down.

Julia was lying on her back, her hands behind her head, her eyes wide open and very dark. There was no expression whatever on her face and he got the impression that she was not breathing. She watched him silently, only her grave eyes, dark with exhaustion from the emotional struggle she had lost, flickering to show that she was alive.

Timothy stood looking a moment and then made as if to turn away from her, his face working, and she put up her arms and pulled him down.

For a little while he let the tide of relief and peace close over him but as the surge rose up in his blood he took hold of himself and pushed her away as he struggled to get up.

'No. Stop it,' he whispered fiercely. 'Not here I tell you. Not in this hole and corner. I won't let you. You're mine as well as your own. We've got something to lose. "With my body I thee worship" and don't forget it, my – my *holy* one.'

'I don't care.' She was shaking and her face was wet against his cheek. 'I was promised. I was *promised*. I can't go on. I can't. Not any more.'

'Be quiet!' He took her shoulders and forced her away from him back against the pillows. 'Listen and for God's sake try to understand. I've just been involved in a sort of . . . *birth*. It has been happening to me all day. I feel that until today I've been in a . . . an eggshell. But all through today I've been breaking out of it. Everything I've ever taken for granted has come apart in my hand. Do you know that even until tonight I secretly believed that somehow it would turn out in the end that Alison *was* my aunt and Eustace *was* my father? Well, they're not. What is more, it must always have been perfectly obvious that they were not. Eustace is a honey, a sweetie, a charmer, but he couldn't be anybody's father. I saw it quite clearly – almost in an off-hand casual sort of way – when I went in tonight. I've known him all my life and never appreciated before what every adult must have felt about him. Julia, don't you see what this is *doing* to me? I'm altering. I'm coming down to earth. I don't know what I'm going to turn out to be.'

She was rigid and the tears were forcing themselves between her closed lids. 'What about *me*? Oh Timothy. What about me?'

'Understand.' It was the ultimate appeal, as young as childhood and as old as the world. 'I must exist. I can't float about unattached and meaningless. I'm a component part. I'm the continuation of an existing story, as is everybody else. I thought I knew my story but I don't. I have been misinformed in a very thorough way. I've got to go on and find out who I am, or I'm unrecognizable even to myself.'

The girl's eyes opened and her hot little mouth was salty as she pulled him to her.

'I'm here. Don't shut me out. I shan't change. I *can't* change. I love you. I'm all love.'

'How do I know?' He was pulling back from her in terror. It was the last question of all.

There was a long silence and then she sat up, suddenly the stronger of the two. 'Well,' she said with the courage of certainty, 'if the rest of the world has changed for you, have I? Look and see. Love isn't love if it alteration finds. That's how you know, I thought.'

It was a gesture of curious generosity. Its blessing flowed over him cool and comforting. He sat down on the bed and held her hands and looked at her and she met his eyes and presently they began to laugh.

They were so engrossed that the clatter of the staircase door and the flying footsteps took a second or so to break through to them, and Basil Toberman was already on the threshold when they first became aware of anything but each other.

For some moments he stood just inside the room, staring like a scandalized frog. His eyes were bulging and his mouth was very red and wet as usual, while they sat blinking at him.

'Do you know the police are downstairs,' he demanded, fixing his pop-eyed stare on Timothy alone. 'They want you to go to Holborn headquarters with them. Apparently the office of the Stalkey Bros. has gone up in flames. It's been a hell of a fire. Four brigades. They don't know if they're going to revive the night watchman. You'd better come down pretty pronto if you don't want them trooping up here. In my opinion, for what it's worth, they've got "arson" written all over them.'

He turned to Julia, truculent and offensive. 'The ruddy young fool is in plenty of trouble as it is,' he said. 'I should sneak out the back way and slide quietly home if I were you. I've got to dash off and catch a plane or I'd offer to take you. Meanwhile I shall hold my tongue until I get back. So make the most of it, my dear. Come down and placate these chaps, Tim. Never say I didn't mean well.'

Chapter Ten

Conference in the Morning

Superintendent Charles Luke at breakfast in his own home was something to see, Mr Campion reflected as he sat opposite him in the kitchen of his mother's house in Linden Lea, one of the newest north-west suburbs. It was a very bright room, so clean that it might have been made of highly glazed china, and the wide window looked out on a neat bright garden with white stone paths, smooth green grass, and geraniums all in a row.

In this setting Luke appeared larger and more lithe, darker and more vital even than usual. With his chin freshly shaved, his linen freshly laundered, his crisp, upstanding hair newly oiled and his teeth gleaming, he appeared part and parcel of the whole. Old Mrs Luke's lifework, a credit to London, the police and a good woman's one pair of hands.

Despite it he was bearing up pretty well, Mr Campion noticed, wearing the cherishing with good-natured ease, and even now at a quarter past seven in the morning his native cockney exuberance was unimpaired.

'I'm glad you came along,' he said, his eyebrows rising even higher than usual. 'The office is like any other Government Department – not an ideal place to be seen taking an unofficial interest in an old friend's private griefs. It's not a question of the odd snake or so, you understand; just human nature and the requisite spot of common. Here we can say what we like and no harm done. Even Mum is out of earshot.'

Mr Campion glanced behind him. 'I wondered about that,' he said anxiously. 'I hope I'm not keeping her out of here.'

'Don't you worry!' Luke was amused in his own ferocious way. 'You couldn't do that, chum. Not if you were the Pope. Fortunately she's attending to the baby. That young woman is saving my life mopping up some of her energy.' He reached for a piece of toast and attacked it, including his guest in the campaign with a gesture. 'Well now, as soon as you phoned I got on to Inspector Hodge who is my assistant on nights this week – I don't think you know him.' He blew out his cheeks, sketched in a waterfall moustache with three fleeting fingers, and favoured Campion with a slightly rakish leer, producing by the performance a lightning portrait of someone alarmingly real. 'He's a good chap,' he said. 'Old school cop. All beer, brain and bullockheart. Very comforting to have behind you. Thank you for leaving it till 6 a.m. by the way. The young woman was not so considerate, I have no doubt?'

'No. She telephoned at one in the morning.'

'Frightened stiff I suppose?'

'Upset.'

Luke put his shorn head on one side. 'Does she believe her Timothy could have done it?'

Mr Campion sighed and his eyes were carefully expressionless behind his spectacles. 'I don't quite know what has happened yet. All I've been told is that the young man was taken to the Thurstable Inn station where he is said to be "helping the police" in their investigation.'

'Ah.' Luke was satisfied. 'I've got a bit more and the rest will come in in a minute. When I rang, Hodge had only got the preliminary. So far it's the simplest case of arson I've ever heard of. Evil without frills. You were at the place yesterday, I believe?' He was more than usually inquisitive, his narrow eyes watchful. 'I hear there's an ordinary, old-fashioned street-door with a letterbox hole in the middle. The typical square job with an iron surround and a flap but no actual box. The mail falls straight on to the mat as it did in grandpa's day. Is that right?'

'I couldn't tell you. The door stands open during office hours and I imagine the postman comes right in.'

'Very likely.' Luke dismissed the point as unimportant. 'Anyway it's a mean entrance. Bare boards and peeling paint and a short flight of wooden stairs leading to the main staircase, just inside. It's an old building which has undergone several conversions in its time. Am I right so far?'

'Yes I think so. My impression has always been that it was a bit pokey, you know. Dark and over-full of the eternal grained panelling. Horribly inflammable, I should think. Where did the fire start?'

'That's it. Just inside the front door. Someone merely posted three or four packets of household firelighters of the ordinary paraffinwax type, the final one of which was alight.' Luke laughed without amusement. 'Brilliantly simple and purely venal. The stairwell acted as a flue with a draught under the door, and the caretaker brewing up in the basement found he'd got five floors of blazing building over his head before he noticed the smell. The door burned in the end but not immediately and there was enough evidence to point to the firelighters. Actually one empty carton was found in the yard.'

'When was this?' Mr Campion was listening in horror.

'Last night. The alarm went out at eight-thirty-four and the street door would have been closed around six. That's as near as they'd got when Hodge rang. The caretaker is in no condition to talk, but if he followed his normal routine he would have toured the building and wouldn't have gone down to the basement where he was found half suffocated until just before seven. It's too early to say how long a fire like that would take to get the hold it did, but I should say that your lady client's young man must have spent the night telling the boys at the Thurstable Inn station just exactly where he was between seven and eight-thirty.'

The thin man hesitated. 'He was with us in Bottle Street until about a quarter to seven, I suppose,' he said slowly.

'Fair enough.' Luke glanced at a note which he had propped up against a packet of cornflakes beyond his plate.

'Some bright young constable who knows him seems to have leapt forward with the information that he saw him coming home in "a dazed condition" to that house of the Kinnits in Scribbenfields at approximately eight-twenty. He must have been somewhere.'

Mr Campion did not speak. He sat looking into his coffee cup until the Superintendent laughed.

'What does the crystal ball say?'

'Not enough!' Campion set down the cup and smiled at his old friend.

'I suppose we have to thank the Stalkey brothers for the promptness of police action?' he murmured.

'That doesn't surprise me, does it you?' Luke leant back in his chair, gulped discreetly, and produced a packet of cigarettes from his coat pocket. 'Look here,' he said without looking up. 'I've got complete faith in your judgement and I liked the girl, but while we're in lodge, so to speak, are you quite sure we're on the right horse in this business?'

Mr Campion's pale eyes flickered wide open. 'It's not a doubt which had occurred to me,' he said frankly. 'Why?'

Luke hunched his wide shoulders and shook his cropped head from side to side with exaggerated uncertainty.

'There's a sort of awful similarity between this arson story and the original bit of bother out at Ebbfield. Both crimes have a frightening streak of modern efficiency in mischief about them. I shouldn't like to explain what I mean in court.' He raised his long hands absently and sketched in the sweeping lines of a full-bottomed wig. 'It's not evidence at all, but if you'd seen the damage done to that flat you'd know what I mean. There's something young and elemental and damn bad in both crimes.'

'I understood Timothy Kinnit had a very good alibi for the Ebbfield affair,' Mr Campion objected gently.

'So he had,' Luke agreed. '"Police-proof" is how it was described to me. They're very clever, these modern kids. They know how to gang up, too, better even than we did.'

Mr Campion frowned, his kindly face was genuinely puzzled. 'Frankly I don't see your argument,' he said. 'According to Julia he's mad keen to know who he is.'

'Ah, that is what he *says*,' Luke objected patiently. 'That's his story. But it's a new one, isn't it? He's lived over twenty years and he's never tried to find out before, has he? It's the proposed marriage which has set this hare running, don't forget that. As soon as the marriage appears on the horizon – before even the girl's father pops up with his little query – the Kinnits get busy because they know they're going to be asked the awkward question. Detectives are employed, the whole family becomes excited and suddenly the boy makes a move. He does something about it. He makes a secret, rather silly but dramatic action to discourage the searchers.'

Mr Campion made a sound of protest.

'Why?' he demanded. 'Why do you suppose this? An intelligent educated boy with a good record, good at sport, every future prospect excellent! Why should he suddenly start behaving like a lunatic thug?'

Luke leant further back in his chair and there was a disarming touch of colour in his dark cheeks. He was laughing and a little embarrassed.

'You're a dear chap, Campion,' he said. 'I like you and I like your approach. It makes me feel I'm riding in a Rolls; but sometimes I wonder if you're not a bit too nice, if you see what I mean. Look at it from my point of view. Here is a boy – not a specially bred one, conditioned over the generations to withstand a bit of cosseting like a prize dog – but an ordinary tough boy same like I was, packed with his full complement of pride and passion, and he's brought up to believe quite falsely that he's inherited the blessed earth. Money, position, background, servants, prospects. He's got the lot handed to him on a plate all for being his handsome self. He makes an effort and he's successful as well. Finally he gets the girl he's set his heart on. She's an heiress, a beauty and a social cop. For a dizzy fortnight or so he is the topmost, the kingpin, the biggest orange on the whole barrow! And then, at that very moment, what happens? A ruddy great Doubt as big as a house crops up. Security vanishes and there's a hole at his feet. The people he has known all his life as the corner stone of his existence suddenly start employing private detectives – *detectives* – half-baked stuffed owls like Joe Stalkey – to go and find out who he, *he* himself, the sacred one-and-only, who he IS? Blimey! Couldn't that send him bonkers? Couldn't it?'

He finished the little oration with one hand outstretched

and his eyebrows disappearing into his hairline. Mr Campion remained looking at him curiously.

'I see what you suggest,' he said at last. 'I do, Charles. I do indeed.'

'But it hadn't occurred to you before?'

'No, no it hadn't. "Conditioned over the generations to withstand cosseting" is a new conception to me.'

Luke laughed. 'I could be wrong,' he said. 'The kid could be exceptional and tough enough to take the treatment. But also I could be right. It's delicate going. One doesn't know where one is. My advice is play it cautiously and I'm glad we had a chat out here.'

The telephone bell from the shelf behind him cut short his warning and he took the call eagerly. The voice at the other end was a steady rumble and Mr Campion waited, his fingers drumming absently on the brightly printed cloth. When Luke hung up his face was shadowed.

'Hodge has had a word with the D.D.I. and has been at the Thurstable Inn station all night,' he announced. 'The information is that the lad is bloody-minded and won't talk at all, so that's not very promising. He says he was at Ebbfield during the relevant period but won't say why or who he saw there. He merely describes the borough, which is damn silly considering Ron Stalkey had already found him there in the morning. I don't know what he's playing at.'

Mr Campion hesitated. 'He may be just growing very angry,' he ventured.

'Whatever he's growing it's trouble!' said Luke, dryly. 'He's asking for it and the Kinnits are behaving like lunatics. One always finds it with these well-off egg-heads. They must live in spacehelmets in the normal way of things! The moment life touches them on the skin they panic and start plaguing absolutely any eminent bird they happen to know personally to "pull strings"!' He pushed his chair back noisily from the table and stood up, six and a half feet of righteous indignation. 'Hodge says that amongst others Eustace Kinnit has telephoned the President of the London and Home Counties National Bank and the Keeper of the Speight Museum of

Classic Antiquities in his attempt to find someone of influence to help him get the lad released. Neither of them as much use as my poor old Auntie Glad, and just about as unlikely! The kindest thing you could do, Campion, is to go down there right away and tell them gently to stop being so silly, antagonizing the police!' He paused in full flight. 'Oh and by the way, in the middle of all this a thought occurred to me. How did she know?'

'Who?'

'The young woman. The police didn't get round to the Well House after him until close on midnight and they wouldn't have let him do any telephoning. Yet by one she'd got on to you? How come? I thought there was supposed to be no liaison there on father's orders.'

Mr Campion appeared interested. 'Odd,' he said. 'But, yes of course, the nurse. Don't forget the nurse, the ubiquitous Mrs Broome.'

'Ah, very likely.' Luke was satisfied. 'She keeps on cropping up, that woman.'

'That's her way.' Mr Campion got up as he spoke, and smiled briefly. 'I must apologize for my dubious chums. Thank you for the breakfast, Charles, and all the good counsel.'

He became silent. The door had opened and old Mrs Luke, who was a force in her own right, came puffing in. She was carrying a baby of eighteen months or so whose arms were clasped tightly about her neck, so that she peered at him over the infant's shoulder. Her arrival was like a train, full of steam and bustle. She was very small and square, with Luke's own narrow black eyes and a ridiculous hair-do, tight and strained to her head and finished with a knob on top.

'I wondered when you were coming to see her, Mr Campion,' she said reproachfully. 'Men are frightened of babies I know, but she's past that stage now, aren't you, Love?'

The child which, Campion saw, was tall and fair suddenly turned its head and looked at him directly. His heart jolted and dismay crept over him. There it was, just as he had feared, the face again! Prunella Scroop-Dory herself, Luke's lost enchantress, had not had higher arches to her brows nor the promise of a rounder, more medieval forehead.

Mr Campion had not disliked Prunella for her own sake but for Luke's, and now he pulled himself together hastily and said all the right things with the best grace in the world.

'What is her name?'

Luke grinned. 'Hattie,' he said. 'Her Mum, God bless her, wanted her called Atalanta, which is sweet but silly in a daughter of mine. It was after a character who was always being chased. This is the best we can do.'

Old Mrs Luke beamed happily at the visitor.

'My daughter-in-law wasn't chased enough,' she remarked. 'A sweeter woman never drew breath but she didn't think enough of herself, being too well trained. That won't happen to you, Love, will it?'

The baby, appealed to, laughed revealingly as infants often do and the startled Campion found himself confronted by Prunella's aristocratic face with Luke's cockney intelligence blazing out of it like the sun in the morning. He went off feeling chastened and secretly apprehensive. It had occurred to him that in fourteen or fifteen years there might well be a personality of considerable striking force in Linden Lea. He put the thought from him; at the moment he had more immediate trouble to contend with. As soon as he was well out of the district he stopped the car at a kiosk and called Julia.

She answered at once, which told him that she had been waiting at the telephone, and her reaction to his cautious *précis* of the news to date was swift and practical.

'I think we ought to see the family at once,' she said. 'I'll meet you at Scribbenfields in twenty minutes.'

'Very well. But are you going to find that embarrassing? I mean – I thought there was a certain amount of pressure to keep you apart.'

'Oh, I'm past all that.' The tired young voice pulled him up and reminded him of the bright, sharp world of his teens in which all colours were vivid and pain was always acute.

'Of course,' he said. 'I'm sorry. I'll be there.'

With a little manoeuvring they contrived to meet on the doorstep which now, in mid-morning, was in a boiling stream of passers-by, hurrying business-people speeding past in a flurry of fumes and dust in the bright haze. Any apprehension which Campion might have felt about their welcome was dispelled by Eustace who opened the door to them himself. After his first blank stare of non-recognition, his face lit up like a delighted child's.

'Splendid!' he exclaimed unexpectedly. 'Hooray! Just the two minds we want on the problem. This is wonderful. We're all up in the sitting-room putting our heads together you know. Putting our heads together!' It would have been untrue and unkind to have suggested that he was enjoying the emergency, but the unaccustomed crisis was certainly exercising emotions he did not usually experience and there was new colour in his cheeks. He led them to the big room with the pink upholstery and the garden of cacti on the hearth. Alison and Mrs Telpher, the family likeness less acute now that they were together, were talking to a round middle-aged man who wore careful clothes and possessed the solicitor's occupational expression of slight incredulity.

He turned as they appeared and regarded them doubtfully as Eustace made the introductions.

'And this is Mr Woodfall,' Eustace said. 'He has looked after our affairs for years but not, I'm afraid, in this sort of caper. We're having a little difficulty, Campion. Tim won't ask for a legal representative to be present and Woodfall can't very well force himself on the police, he tells me.' There was the faintest hint of inquiry in the words and Campion met the lawyer's eyes with sympathy. Mr Woodfall looked away at once.

Meanwhile Alison turned from the open bureau where she had paused in her restless wandering. A fault in a half-written page lying there had caught her attention and she had stooped to correct it in exactly the same way that another type of woman might have paused in a trying situation to put a picture straight. 'I don't know what's the matter with the boy,' she said, replacing the pen carefully in its tray. 'It's so unlike him to be awkward. You've never found him *awkward*, have you, Julia?'

The query focused everyone's attention on the girl and everybody noticed at the same moment how angry she was. Her face was pale and strained and her eyes were dark with misery. 'I think he may be in a very excited condition,' she said huskily. 'After all, he's had rather a lot to put up with.'

'I suppose he has.' It was Mrs Telpher speaking from her seat in the corner of the long couch. She was an oasis of calm in the room, sitting there in her quiet clothes, aloof and elegant. 'I don't really know him, of course, and he's not terribly like the rest of the family, naturally. Much more dominant in many ways.' She smiled kindly at Julia. 'A man of action. It stands out, you know. But I don't think he'd do anything capricious would he? He must feel he can manage on his own. Am I right?' She glanced at Eustace, who nodded.

'Yes,' he said. 'Very good, Geraldine. Dominant; that is the word. That's a very good word. I don't see why he's being kept there, though, I really don't.'

Mr Campion drifted towards Mr Woodfall, who moved back a little.

'The Stalkey Brothers are being very explicit, I suppose?' Campion murmured the words but Alison heard him from across the room and paused, like some slender bird, her grey eyes penetrating.

'It was I who persuaded Mr Woodfall to let us employ the Stalkeys again,' she remarked. 'In fact I suppose I started the whole wretched business. Eustace was all for letting sleeping dogs lie and now I realize he may have been right, but I expected that we should have an inquiry from Julia's father and I thought we ought to be ready for it to save embarrassment. I had no idea that old Mr Stalkey had died and the sons would prove to be so inferior. My recollection of the old man was that he was rather kind and not really too unintelligent.'

'I assure you they are very reliable people.' If Mr Woodfall had requested her in so many words to cease being indiscreet, he could hardly have made his meaning more clear. He took a fine antique watch from his waistcoat and consulted it and directed a brief smile at the whole company. 'I must go,' he said. 'If the young man should decide to change his mind and answer perfectly proper police questions, don't hesitate to call on me and I shall do the best I can.'

'You're behaving as if you think he did it!' Julia's youth betrayed her and Mr Woodfall shied like a startled pony before the outburst. He became very severe.

'Not I, young lady,' he said. 'You don't either, I hope?'

'No, I know he didn't.'

'Ah. Was he with you?' He pounced on the idea hopefully but relapsed into gloom again when she shook her head.

'I just know he couldn't have done anything so silly.'

'You're very lucky to be able to speak with such conviction for any man.' He laughed as he spoke, not unkindly but with that little edge of superiority which is cynicism's only privilege, and returned to Alison. 'I must go.'

'Must you? I thought you were staying to lunch.' Nevertheless she moved to the door with him as she spoke, and his laughing protest that he had two appointments before then in his office, and could see himself out, floated back to them from the passage.

'That reminds me, Eustace.' Alison spoke as she came hurrying back into the room and took a large, old-fashioned public house menu card from a drawer in the bureau. It was a dog-eared product, the blanks on the printed folder filled with cramped handwriting in violet ink. 'I always forget to do this,' she went on, 'and they do like it early. Let me see. There's oxtail. Will you like that?'

Eustace smiled at the visitors.

'We used to have the most frightful bothers about meals,' he said with the shy charm which was his most attractive attribute. 'With the vanishing of the domestic it seemed to me that food in the home was destined to be a thing of the past for anyone like myself who is purely an intellectual worker, but I might have known my wonderful sister. Now she merely rings up the *Star and Garter* down the road, and lo and behold we have luncheon on our own table as we always did.' He hesitated and his lips, which looked so pink in his beard, twisted wryly. 'The fare is rather nasty, of course, but one can't help that.'

Alison laughed. She was pink and girlish at his praise. 'Is it the food or the china?' she inquired. 'I shall never know. Those very thick, smeary plates with the smudged blue crest are terribly offputting, but one can't very well scrape everything off on to Wedgwood, it would get so messy.'

'And cold!' said Eustace. 'And there would be two lots of washing up for someone. Oh no, I think we do very well. Yes. I'll have the oxtail but not peas. I don't like their plastic peas. I shall stick to onions. They do onions very nicely.'

'Eustace has onions every day of his life and with everything.' Alison was still gay.

'Better be safe than sorry!' said Eustace, sounding as if he thought the phrase was original. 'Now. Who is going to join us? You Geraldine, I know, but how about Julia and Campion?'

'And Aich.' Alison was scribbling on a telephone pad. 'Geraldine, you and I will have the plaice, I expect, and Aich will have the joint whatever it is. A great meat-eater, Aich.'

'Thank you.' Geraldine drew her beautifully shod feet up on to the sofa beside her as she spoke. Her Italian shoes suggested wealth more discreetly than any other single item he had ever seen, Mr Campion reflected. 'What about Mrs Broome?' she inquired wistfully. 'Doesn't she eat?'

'Nanny Broome does her own catering. She's not with us up here all the time, you see. She won't touch anything cooked outside.' It was evident that Alison saw nothing incongruous in the statement. 'I pay her extra money and she fends for herself.'

'Interesting,' Eustace said with apparent seriousness. 'I don't think she's a vegetarian either. Now Julia, my dear, can I tempt you to a dish of oxtail?'

The girl looked at him with flickering disbelief.

'No,' she said firmly. 'Thank you very much but aren't we going to do something about Tim?'

'I agree.' Alison was jotting down the luncheon order as she spoke. 'But of course there are two schools of thought about whether one *should* interfere even if one knew quite *how*. Eustace found the Police most uncooperative when he went down there last night. And then one doesn't know what Tim's own attitude is. At the moment we're relying on Flavia Aicheson. She's gone down to see the Ebbfield Councillor.'

Mr Campion heard the news with dismay. 'I don't think the police react very favourably to high-powered pressure from outside,' he began hesitantly.

'I know! And it's not easy to get it either!' Alison's grey eyes met his own. 'People want to help one but they don't feel they ought to. The Councillor, whose name is Cornish, was quite abrupt with poor Aich this morning when she telephoned him. They're old enemies and Aich took a risk in approaching him, but she regards Tim as a nephew and just put her pride in her pocket and went ahead. When Mr Cornish said he wouldn't go to the Thurstable Inn station to speak for the boy she just hung up the receiver and went down to fetch him.'

'But why?' Julia exploded. 'Why upset the police by getting hold of someone who doesn't even want to worry them?'

Alison remained happily unruffled.

'Of course,' she said kindly. 'You don't know, but Tim went to Ebbfield yesterday and saw this man. He happened to mention it when he came in. We're naturally hoping that they were together at the important time. The only awkward thing seems to be that the boy didn't make it clear to Mr Cornish why he had called on him, and so when this query came up the man immediately wondered if the visit had been made on purpose to manufacture an alibi. He seems to be a difficult person with a highly suspicious mind.'

'Wait!' Eustace spoke from the window where he was standing looking down into the street. 'Here *is* Aich getting out of a cab. Ah yes, she's got the man with her. This must be he. He couldn't be anything but a firebrand councillor could he? Look. Oh! yes, by George! Yes. This is wonderful. Tim is with them. They've got him away. Wait a moment; Mrs Broome may still be out with that extraordinary wreath. I'll go and let them in.'

Chapter Eleven

The Councillor

Miss Aicheson was first into the room. She came striding across the black polished boards which were scattered with fine worn old rugs, and the ancient timbers shook beneath her while the dust motes in the shaft of London sunlight, streaming through diamond panes, danced wildly at her approach. She looked tired but triumphant and she turned to Alison for praise.

'Done it!' she announced. 'Tim is on the stairs now. Councillor Cornish is with us, and by the way, dear, I think *all* the credit ought to go to him.'

'Oh *splendid*! Quite, quite wonderful, Aich.' Alison Kinnit's emphasis was nearly generous but her glance wandered at once to the menu in her hand and she almost mentioned it, only thinking better just in time as the Councillor, with Eustace fussing behind him, appeared in the doorway.

Here in the Well House Councillor Cornish was still a vigorous personality, but this morning there was a new wariness about him and there was caution in the fierce eyes under the shock of grey hair. His astonishment on meeting Alison for the first time was slightly funny. Her thistledown quality appeared to bewilder him, and if he had actually said that he had expected to see a second version of Miss Aicheson he could hardly have made the point more clearly.

The reaction was not new to Miss Kinnit and she became more feminine than ever, twittering and smiling.

'Thank you, thank you. We are all so very relieved.' Her intelligent eyes met his own gratefully. 'I'm just ordering lunch. You will join us, won't you?'

'I? No, really!' He sounded appalled. 'Thank you very much of course, but I only want to have a word with the young man.' He was preparing to explain further when an interruption occurred. Tim had arrived. He glanced round the room, caught sight of Julia and walked over to her, his face dark as a storm.

'*Darling!*' he exploded. 'I did so pray that you'd have the good sense to keep right out of this! Why didn't you do what I told you?' He was on edge and his protest was unreasonably savage.

The colour rushed into Julia's face, Eustace made a deprecating cluck, and everyone was startled by the Councillor, who turned on the speaker.

'*Don't* shut her out when she's backing you up!' he exclaimed violently. Realizing his interference was outrageous, he tried to cover it. He smiled at Julia, rubbed his ear and shot a sidelong, slightly sheepish smile at Timothy.

'I'm sorry,' he said. 'Can I meet the young lady?'

It was a direct apology, and Tim relaxed.

'I do beg your pardon,' he said quickly. 'Yes, of course. I'm afraid I was surprised to see her here. Julia, this is Councillor Cornish but for whom I should be in jug, I suppose.'

'Would you? That's what I wanted to talk to you about. Is there anywhere where we could have a word on our own?'

'Yes, of course,' Timothy looked surprised but acquiescent and the unexpected objection came from Eustace.

He came forward, smiling, so smooth in his old-fashioned way that both the Councillor and Tim appeared clumsy beside it.

'You two mustn't shut any of us out,' he said gently. 'We want to hear all about it. We've been sitting here completely in the dark, consumed by a most natural curiosity. I know a little about the fire because I've read the report in the *Telegraph*, but that's all. Why did you decide to keep so silent, my boy? Our solicitor was most anxious to be present at any interrogation. Why didn't you cooperate?'

Tim shrugged his shoulders. He looked tall and big-boned standing there, his face, which was still scarred, pale and stiff with fatigue. He eyed Eustace and laughed. 'Because I was sulking, I suppose.'

'But was that wise?' Eustace was at his mildest, innocently inquiring without a trace of malice.

'No. It was silly. But they made me absolutely furious.'

'You're talking about the police?'

'Yes.'

Eustace jerked his chin up and his neat beard looked sharp.

'They have a very fine reputation,' he said gravely and his eyes were reproachful rather than severe.

'Well, they got my goat.' Timothy was being factual. 'Probably I was in the wrong, but to drag me out in the middle of the night and keep me in a smelly office while two highpowered thugs told me I must know what I'd done, and would I "come clean", for hours and hours on end seemed high-handed.'

'But you could have told them where you'd been.'

'If they'd been polite about it I should have, but they were excited because it was such a damned awful fire. They knew Ron Stalkey had been right about his beating me up, because they could see my face, and so they assumed that everything else he'd said about me setting light to his blessed office was probably true. The whole inference was so insulting and so *silly*, I'm afraid I just wouldn't play.'

Eustace was both hurt and amazed.

'But Tim,' he said. 'You're a civilized, intelligent young man. The police couldn't have behaved as you represent. Not the *British* police . . .'

The young man opened his mouth and shut it again and a sullen shadow settled over his eyes. At the same time there was a smothered sound from the Councillor, and as everybody turned to look at him it was discovered that he was laughing.

Eustace's glance grew cold.

'You don't agree with me?' he said so charmingly and with such disarming diffidence that the unobservant could have been misled.

'Of course I don't!' The Councillor checked himself. 'I mean I'm afraid I don't. I'm inclined to think that the young man has summed up the position pretty accurately. After all, the police are men. Only a nation which can honestly believe that by putting a boy in a helmet it can turn him into something between a guardian angel and a St Bernard dog overnight could make the British Force what it is today, the worst used, worst paid, most sentimentalized-over body in creation.'

Eustace regarded him with frank amazement.

'Good Heavens!' he said. 'You consider there should be an inquiry do you?'

Something of the same sullenness which Eustace's reactions evoked in Timothy appeared in the Councillor.

'I am not to be drawn,' he said cagily, 'but I feel it might help if this country sometimes ceased to consider the police either through motorists' goggles or rose-coloured spectacles. As it is, ninety-nine per cent of them have chips on their shoulders. Since I don't want my affairs dealt with by chaps who feel like that if I can possibly help it, I keep away from the police as much as I can.' He paused and laughed again. 'If one's forced to talk to them, go to the top. The chaps at the top in the police are all men with something remarkable about them. They've got to be. They're the people who've been through the process without cracking.'

'You amaze me,' Eustace conveyed very nicely that he did not believe a word of it. 'But at the same time I don't see why Timothy *refused to help*. That is the point which mystifies me. I should have said that Timothy was the most courteous and obliging lad in the world. Why Tim? Why didn't you tell them where you had been?'

On the other side of the room Mr Campion, who had been standing quietly by the window effacing himself with his usual success, began to find the conversation painful. This purely mental approach to what was after all a most acutely emotional problem, at least for Timothy, was getting under his skin and he turned to Geraldine Telpher who was sitting listening, her head bent and her gaze fixed on her folded hands.

'How is the child?' he murmured. 'May one ask?'

He was startled by her reaction. She was taken by surprise and the grey Kinnit eyes which met his own were dilated for an instant. 'I'm so sorry,' he said, embarrassed. 'I shouldn't have asked you so suddenly.'

'Not at all.' She became herself again, calm and intelligent. 'It's very kind of you. It's only that sometimes I find I'm not quite as brave as I think I am. Then I panic. She's just the same, thank you. Still unconscious. This is the second year.'

Mr Campion was appalled. 'I had no idea. How old is she?'

'Nine. It's tragic, isn't it?' Her voice was intentionally inexpressive and he felt compelled to continue the conversation until she had recovered.

'Where is she? In hospital?'

'Yes. In St Joseph of Arimathaea's. In a public ward!' Her smile was very wry. 'It's ironic but it can't be helped and she knows nothing. I was told that her only hope was to come to London to be seen by Sir Peter Phyffe. He's one of those dedicated men who won't take private patients and so there she is, poor baby.' She sighed and looked away. 'It was a car accident, her governess was driving.'

Mr Campion murmured his sympathy. 'You're very convenient here for St Joseph's,' he said consolingly.

'I know. Isn't it wonderful. Just behind us. That's why I'm so grateful to Eustace and Alison for asking me to stay. They really are wonderful, aren't they?'

Mr Campion felt himself to be no judge of that point, Alison was still hovering with her alarming looking menu, while on the other side of the room Eustace was quietly persisting in trying to get a rational explanation for Timothy's behaviour.

'You seem to understand the boy rather better than I do, on this occasion at any rate,'' he was saying to the Councillor, a touch of acidity appearing in his voice for the first time. 'I'm very glad you do and we're all eternally grateful to you for coming forward like this – I won't say "to substantiate his story", but anyway to give him a complete alibi.'

The Councillor looked at him without moving his head. As he had been staring at the floor it was a sharp upward glance through his fierce brows, very characteristic and effective. Eustace paused abruptly, colour in his cheeks.

'I take it that you have?' he demanded.

'I was wondering,' the Councillor said frankly. 'That is why I came here to talk to the young man himself. The Police have let him go for the time being but that hardly means that they've lost interest in him. All I've done is to convince them that he was with me in Ebbfield during the period when the crime was almost certain to have been committed. "Almost" is not "quite" though, and arson is a notoriously difficult business to bring home to anybody. Do you see what I mean?'

'No,' said Eustace testily. 'You are simply telling us that it is a question of the time.'

'No, I'm saying it is a question of evidence. The Police naturally want to make out a case. But if their suspect can prove where he was during the *likely* period for the crime to have been committed, they've got to think again haven't they? They've got to widen their times or find another suspect.'

Eustace sighed. 'I can't believe the police, *our* police, work like that,' he said. 'However, I hear what you say. May I know what you want to ask Tim?'

'You want to know if I did it, don't you, sir?'

The young man who had been standing behind Julia's chair put the question wearily. He looked very tired, standing with his hands in his pockets, the dark smudges across his eyes emphasizing their colour. 'Well, I didn't.' He rubbed his hand round the back of his head and pulled his ear and laughed. 'It was such a damn *silly* thing to do!'

'A wicked thing!' Eustace put in quickly. He was prompting openly, rather as if he were prodding a junior at a business conference when the opposition was not too intelligent.

'But also imbecile.' Tim spoke with sudden affection, his warmth noticeable beside the older man's colder personality. 'For one thing, they're forced by law to be fully insured and the building was patently due for an overhaul. The fire may have saved their lives. No, if I had felt that I wanted to get my own back on the Stalkey Bros., and frankly it never occurred to me, I had only to tell the story to everyone I met.

"Fuddy duddy firm of detectives beat up own client in fumbling zeal." It couldn't have done them any good where-ever I mentioned it and they could hardly sue.'

'All right!' Councillor Cornish wiped his eyes with amusement. He appeared to be entertained out of all proportion to the joke. 'I take the point. I'm satisfied. Now I want to hear exactly why you came to see me yesterday.'

'I told you. I got your name from the cobbler in the Orient Road. That was before Ron Stalkey came in and we had the dust-up. I was waiting there talking to him for about an hour I suppose. He's a veteran of the 1914 war – a nice legless little bloke who talks and talks with his mouth full of tacks. Do you know him? I imagine most people in Ebbfield do.'

'Yes, I know him. His name is Tom Tray. Did you meet his sister Dora?'

'I didn't see a soul there until Ronald Stalkey arrived. After we started belting each other there was a crowd, of course. I went back in the evening to square up for any damage we'd done in the shop, but Tray was quite happy about it and reminded me that he'd told me to go and see you. So I did.'

'But that means you can prove that you were in Ebbfield earlier than Mr Cornish here was able to tell the police?' Eustace demanded.

'Yes, I know. I told you. I did not set light to the Stalkey Office.'

'Nevertheless,' Eustace was persisting when the Councillor interrupted him in his own house.

'I've got that,' he said to Tim. 'What I want to know is *why?* How did you think I could help you?'

Miss Aicheson could bear it no longer. 'But I explained all that to you when I was persuading you to come down to the Thurstable Inn police station this morning. Otherwise you wouldn't have come, would you?' She spoke from across the room, her voice more flutelike than ever. The Councillor coloured.

'I'd like to hear it from the boy himself,' he protested, making it a grievance. 'Why did you come to see me, Tim?'

His use of the Christian name jarred on the family and the young man himself did not answer at once but stood hesitating. It was a silent tussle between them. The whole room was aware of it.

'Well?'

Timothy shrugged his shoulders helplessly.

'If you've already discussed the story with Miss Aicheson, do I really have to tell it again?'

'About this belated search for your identity?'

'Yes.'

'I see. Having actually seen the squalor of your beginnings you've become violently ashamed of them. Is that right?'

Cornish was trying to be offensive and succeeding. Eustace bristled and Alison made a little protesting sound.

Tim laughed. It was a chuckle of irreverent amusement at the pomposity of the accusation. His eyes narrowed, his wide mouth turned up, and a rare shaft of gaiety which was not a normal part of his everyday make-up appeared for a flashing instant.

'My heart did not leap up when I beheld the gasworks, sir. Since you ask me, no.'

His reaction was a relief to most people present, but the effect of it upon the Councillor was devastating. The man appeared to freeze. He stood rigid for an instant.

'I'm afraid I can't help you,' he said stiffly. 'I was in the R.A.F. by the end of 1938. All we young apprentices were in the reserve. I didn't get to know Ebbfield very well until the war was over. Surely some public records were saved?'

'None,' said Eustace. 'Naturally we looked into that immediately.'

His mind, which was always unhappy and fumbling when emotions of any kind were involved, seized on the purely factual point gratefully.

'It was a tremendous story. I was fascinated when I went into it. When we first inquired during the war the books – ledgers, registers, or whatever they were – had been evacuated and were unobtainable; when we asked again later we were told they had been returned on the very morning before the first great raid which destroyed half the district, and were completely lost.'

'Yes of course. Yes, I remember now. I've heard that in another connexion.' The Councillor was still subdued. 'I'm sorry,' he said again, speaking to Tim. 'I can't help. What are you going to do? Shall we expect to see you wandering about the district, looking for clues?'

'Probably not.' Eustace spoke blandly before the younger man could reply. He was smiling in his pleasant adult way and seemed disposed to be philosophical.

'But you can understand the boy's interest,' he went on. 'When one is a child one gathers scraps of information about oneself, little pieces of embroidery from nurses and so on, and one weaves perhaps a rather romantic story until the time comes when cool reason demands facts which are dull and even a trifle drab compared with a tale of fancy, all moonshine and romance.'

The Councillor stared at him. 'Romance!' he exploded. 'My God, if you want romance you must go to reality! The things she thinks up take the shine out of any old invention. I'm sorry I can't help you. If the police need me again presumably they'll contact me, or of course I shall be available to any lawyer of yours. That's really all I can do at the moment. Good-bye.'

He would have left without shaking hands had not Eustace put out his own, and Tim would have followed him down to let him out but there was an unexpected development.

Julia got up and came over. She was smiling politely.

'Councillor, I'm going the same way as you are, and I must go now. We'll go together if you don't mind.'

Tim looked at her in amazement and there was a moment when Cornish hesitated and she stood placidly forcing him to think twice about being rude to her.

'Why not?' he said at last. 'Come along.'

They went out of the room with Tim behind them.

Eustace smiled first at his sister and then at the others.

'A funny fellow,' he said mildly. 'In many ways an extraordinary fellow. Did you notice he was so excitable and

emotional he was almost in tears at one point? What a character Julia is, too! She got him out of the room in case he upset Tim any further. I like her, she has special courage. Very
rare these days.'

Alison looked at the menu in her hand.

'Now I really must make my list,' she said, 'or everything
nice will be off. What will Tim have, I wonder?'

Chapter Twelve

The Cobbler's Shop

Councillor Cornish paused at a bus-stop and glanced down at his companion dubiously.

He was hatless and the charcoal-coloured raincoat flapping about his bones echoed the tint and texture of his fierce hair and eyebrows, so that he looked like a grey Irish elkhound slinking along silently beside an elegant child of whom he was privately terrified.

He cleared his throat: 'I get my bus here for Ebbfield,' he said.

'I do too.' Julia did not look at him. There was a reckless obstinacy about her which he was trying not to recognize, it frightened him so.

'What are you going to do in Ebbfield?' He fumbled over the words and she moved as the red monster came bearing down on them and made a gesture to shoo him on to it ahead of her.

'I've got business on the way there,' she said and followed him on to the half-empty lower deck.

As the acceleration jerked them into a seat far up in the front, he spoke grudgingly:

'I hear your father is a man of drive. You take after him I suppose?'

'I suppose so,' she said. 'I want to talk to you about Tim.'

'I've told all I know. I've given a statement to the police. He was at my house from approximately seven-thirty to eight o'clock. I've done all I can.' He was keeping his voice down, for a London bus is no place to shout in, and kept looking at her in a kind of horror. She had trapped him, he saw; even a teashop would not have afforded more restraining conditions. He could not storm out from a vehicle jolting and swaying over the ancient stones of Scribbenfields at forty miles an hour.

Julia turned her head and regarded him with an accusing stare.

'It's not that. You think you know who his family is, don't you?'

'I certainly don't! You're off your head, young woman – '

He did not finish the sentence; the need to keep reasonably quiet was hampering him but even so his reaction was unconvincing to himself. He was silent for a moment and she continued to look at him.

'You do, don't you?'

'What makes you think that?'

'Because it's the same family as yours.'

She spoke hastily, and leaning back suddenly in her seat ran her hand up behind her head and brought it down to pull her ear. It was a curious gesture which was very distinctive yet familiar to him.

'I don't do it very well,' she remarked. 'But you and Tim do it all the time, whenever you're embarrassed. You're doing it now.'

'You're mad!' He pulled his hand down from his ear and sat gaping at her. 'That's the most absurd and dangerous accusation I ever heard in my life. I should advise you – '

She sat frowning, looking at him. 'I don't see why you're so excited,' she said, and her innocence becoming suddenly apparent set the ground quaking under his feet. 'Surely you've got *some* relations? Tim is a very nice person. They might be very glad to know.'

'I can't say anything about that.' He felt as if he were shuffling his feet.

'Of course you can't,' she said with enormous reasonableness. 'That's why I wanted to talk to you alone. Haven't you got brothers or sisters or even cousins? You see, I don't know if you know but family characteristics, gestures particularly, are liable to crop up most unexpectedly. I know my father had a Canadian cousin who came over in the army in the war, They'd never met and their parents hadn't met since they were literally babies, and yet the first thing this man did when he came into the house was to push his hair, which was quite short, back over his ears with both hands. No one had ever seen anyone but Daddy do that. It was quite meaningless too, because neither of them had ever worn their hair long, and –'

'You're sure you're right about young Timothy?' he interrupted her gently. 'About the ear-pulling?'

'Oh yes.' She smiled at him with complete assurance. 'I watch everything Tim does. I've seen him do it hundreds of times and so when you did it too I watched you too. Besides, you may not know it, but you smile the same way and the big planes at the sides of your faces are identical. It wouldn't be so extraordinary if you were distant relatives, would it? You both come from the same place apparently.'

'No, I don't come from Ebbfield,' he said woodenly. 'I was born in Norfolk. I came to London as an apprentice. I can't help you in that way at all. If the police want to put him through it again he can call on me. That's as far as I can go.'

'I see,' she said bleakly and continued to ride beside him in silence. 'It's very good of you,' she ventured at last. 'Please don't feel we're not very grateful.'

He grunted and looked out over her dark head at one of the least beautiful main roads in the world; there was mile upon mile of it, a wide-worn ribbon lined with shabby two-storey shops and shabbier open spaces.

'Have you ever been in love before?' He put the question so reluctantly that it sounded angry.

'No. Not really.' She flushed and shot an apologetic smile at him. 'Not with a real person.'

'I see.' He was smiling despite himself. 'And how long has it lasted so far?'

'Oh, ever since I first saw him. It's an "always and for-ever": one usually knows, I think. Don't you?'

He drew his eyebrows together and sat for a moment framing a question which, when it came, was utterly unexpected.

'You say you watch him all the time?' he began at last. 'Did you happen to be looking at him when he made that damn silly remark about the gasworks? I'd been taking the

mickey out of him and he suddenly spiked me with a certain
kind of flippancy, with a funny sort of grin on his mouth . . .'

'I know. Like a cat laughing.' He saw to his relief that she
had not thought the question in the least extraordinary. 'He
doesn't do it often. It's always when someone is being a bit
pomp – or a bit grand, you know. That's not like your family
surely, is it?'

He laughed briefly. 'No,' he said. 'It's not like my family
or me. Not at all.' Once again he looked out at the dismal
road and there was water suddenly in his fierce eyes. 'Not at
all,' he repeated.

Julia was not listening to him. 'What worries me is that it
must be someone,' she remarked. 'Someone really is doing
these awful things . . .'

'Setting light to office buildings?'

'Or tearing up old people's homes. You know Tim was
asked where he was when that flat down here in the East End
was smashed up? We simply couldn't understand it at the
time. The police were awfully polite and cautious, and since
Tim didn't know then that the Kinnits were employing the
Stalkeys to ferret round Ebbfield the questions sounded insane. We'd never heard of Ebbfield. He soon satisfied the
detective that he hadn't been out of Oxford that week at all
and the man went away.' She paused and sat looking at him
with wide-open eyes. 'It must have been the flat-wrecking
that the police were investigating though, because it happened about then and the Stalkey who was making the
inquiry was staying in it, wasn't he? I only heard about that
last night from Tim's old nurse, Mrs Broome.'

'Where had she heard of it?'

She frowned. 'I don't know. Alison Kinnit, perhaps. But
Tim must have heard it yesterday from the Stalkey brother
who attacked him. I expect that was the real reason why he
was so difficult when the police began to question him again.
Being wrongfully suspected of some crime you don't know
anything about is all very well if it happens once, but it's
rather different if they do it to you twice. It's so frightening.
Suppose they pin something on him?'

'When he's innocent?'

'Of course. That's what I'm trying to tell you. Someone is doing these dreadful things. Who is it?'

'How should I know?'

'But don't you?' Her gentle persistence appalled him. 'Can't you think round and see who it might be? Can't you guess?'

'Why should I? What are you talking about?' His voice rose in panic and the old working man dozing on the seat beyond them opened an eye and regarded him with idle curiosity.

Julia sighed. 'I don't know. I'm just at the end of what I can bear, I think. I was sitting there in that pink room, looking round at all those people and thinking how well they all meant and how useless they all were, and wondering who *was* there who could possibly help us. And I looked at you and I thought that you really were awfully like an older Tim and you'd been dragged into the business by a sort of Act of God anyhow, and I felt suddenly that I could *make* you think of something which could give us a lead.'

'Do you know what you're saying?' He was looking at her in a kind of horror. 'Can you hear yourself?'

Tears came into her eyes. 'Oh *don't*,' she said. 'Don't bully. Just try to help.'

The fact that she was strained to a point beyond reasoning, and was proceeding by intuition's reckless compass alone, came home to him. He remained quiet, watching her warily and she returned his stare, her eyes utterly without guile. At last he became convinced that she was only conscious of making a vague but passionately felt appeal for help and he spoke cautiously.

'You're thinking that because I live down here and know the people I might be able to find out something? Is that it?'

'You've got some authority.'

'Suppose I find some suspect and can't prove anything? What do you expect me to do then?'

He had begun to breathe again and it was a return to his normal manner, just a fraction aggressive and unsure.

'But you know what to do.' The protest was inspired. 'You told everybody less than an hour ago. You said the only thing to do was to avoid the ordinary police and go to the very top flight. That's what I came with you to tell you. I know one of them. He's a Mr Charles Luke, a senior something or other at New Scotland Yard. I've met him and I think you're right and one could tell him anything. He's larger than life but – '

'I know Luke.'

'You do?' She smiled with radiant relief. 'That's miraculous! That's what people mean when they say a thing is "meant". Start thinking who it might be and if it comes to you – and I've got a hunch it will – then you go straight to him. You will, won't you?'

He got up to get away from her and out into the air. There was sweat on his forehead and he stood for a moment swinging on the rail before he bent to take her hand.

'I get off here,' he murmured. 'There's a request stop. Good-bye.'

She held his hand tightly.

'You will try?'

'I will, God help me,' he said and hurried off the bus, leaving her to go on alone to the Ebbfield Market Cross.

It was the next stop; she got down and paused for a moment looking about her. The Old Cross proved to be a Music Hall now used as a box factory, and it lay before her as ornate and derelict as a toy in a dustbin. She was still in that strange mood when hypersensitiveness reaches the point almost of clairvoyance, a direct product of emotional exhaustion in the otherwise healthy. As she pulled her wide blue coat about her, and her eyes, which echoed its colour, wandered over the immediate view, the squalor of the place crept very close.

She was standing in a vast drab circus where five highways met and the heavy transport vehicles rattled and crashed over a patchwork of every known road surface. The filthy pavements were not crowded and many of the shops which lined them were closed, yet the passers-by were all going somewhere, all well fed and gaily dressed but apparently tired out, their eyes dust-rimmed and their skin sallow. It was the lunch hour and the steamy windows of the eating houses, pubs, and coffee bars were like blind eyes. For London's East End it was a singularly uncosy neighbourhood, neither friendly nor even noisy but hurried and dirty and preoccupied.

The name-plate saying *Carroway Street* above the public house on the nearest corner caught her attention and she set out to walk down it. She was looking for the cobbler's shop without any very clear idea of why she wanted to see it. Her business on the way to Ebbfield had been done.

The road was very long and passed through many phases, none of them particularly attractive, and at one point, having walked for what seemed like half a mile beside a twenty-foot hoarding, she almost lost heart; but presently, as so often happens in London, the whole character of the thoroughfare changed abruptly and it became for a hundred yards or so a village High Street which, although decayed was still a definite entity.

All the familiar shops were there, the gay greengrocers, the coal office, the rather horrible butchers, and the forlorn laundrette looking like some unspeakable peepshow. And then, very much in keeping amongst them, the place she was looking for.

Mr T. K. Tray's establishment turned out to be unexpectedly alive. It was a double-fronted shop, with one window devoted to the boot and shoe repair business, and the other to newspapers and magazines with a sprinkling of cheap stationery, tobacco and confectionery. There was a panel of small advertisements beside the door and a notice offering an accommodation address.

At the moment it was besieged. A fast-moving queue of chattering women, most of whom appeared to know each other, was forcing its way into the darkened doorway and every so often one of them squeezed back out again and shot away like a bee from a hive, a brightly-coloured periodical in her hand.

The beginning of the queue was a crowd on the pavement, and Julia, who could not pause outside without joining it,

found herself sucked into the jostling stream. She gathered
that the cause of the excitement was the little polythene
packets of detergent being given away with one of the
women's magazines. They were worth perhaps a penny and
each woman was determined to get her due before the supply
ran out. As soon as Julia realized that escape was impossible
until she had done the round, she began to feel suffocated.
Many of the women were factory workers, their boilersuits
and headscarves lending them the ruthless camaraderie
which paper hats on an outing lend a charabanc load. They
were all in a hurry, all in ferocious good humour, all hot, and
all laughing aloud. The brutal noise, meaningless as a bird
call, reached an intensity which stunned her and she became
swallowed up in a whirlpool of sound in which scraps of intelligible sentences were few and all ugly. The uniformed factory women were imitating their menfolk and swearing as
they never did in the normal way when each was as it were a
private person. The trickle of dirty fantasy threading through
the cackle produced a shocking sound which she had not met
before, and which gave her the illusion that there were no
individuals present, only a single merciless personality.

As the queue fed her relentlessly into the dark shop the
stale, sweaty smell of leather and newsprint met her in a wave,
and as her eyes grew accustomed to the shadow she saw the
counter embedded in a grotto made of magazines. Her impression was that there were two figures in the dark cavern
behind it and that one of them was telephoning at a wall
instrument hanging amid the crowded shelves, whilst the
other, who was little more than a vast stuffed bodice swinging
there, was handing out papers and packets with the speed of a
machine. As she approached the end of the line she caught
sight for the first time of the half-dozen copies of a periodical
which decorated the shelf on the front of the counter.

'*Oracle,*' it said. '*Oracle. Oracle. Oracle.*'

It was as she was actually looking at the word in superstitious astonishment that a single intelligible name suddenly
leapt out of the noise.

'Basil Kinnit!'

She heard the words as clearly as if they had been a phrase in the mother tongue amid a torrent of foreign language.

'*Basil Kinnit!*'

There was no way of telling who had spoken. Either of the two behind the counter could have said it or it could have come from any of the brass-lined throats screaming about her.

'Basil Kinnit' said the oracle.

She threw down a sixpence, received her magazine, and sped out into the air. As she came into the light again the nightmare of the shop receded and reality broke over her like morning.

'But there's no such person,' she said aloud. 'No such person at all.'

Chapter Thirteen

'The Top of the Police'

Councillor Cornish's request for an immediate interview was so unexpected that Superintendent Luke went out of his way to grant it at once and saw his caller in one of the private interrogation rooms. It was a square, austere office where the desk was very wide and very solid. Too wide to lean across, too solid to be turned over. Yet the room was pleasant enough with a view across the grey river.

They had been talking for some minutes and Luke sat prodding the blotting-paper in front of him with a long-suffering pen. He was fascinated and his shorn head was held sideways, his black eyes fixed, and his shoulders, which were so wide in comparison with his narrow hips, hunched as he doodled on the folder.

Councillor Cornish sat back in his chair opposite, his feet together, his hands folded in his lap and his head bowed in the traditional way of resignation. It was not a conscious pose. Luke had been watching him like a cat and had decided that the man was genuine. He was acting under a strong compulsion moving from a sense of duty deeply rooted, and the source of his fanaticism was unveiled. His sense of guilt was temporarily appeased, his truculence gone. He was making his sacrifice completely at peace.

'We shall have to check each point,' Luke said. 'You know that, don't you?'

'I suppose so.' There was no secret complaisance. The policeman was listening for it. 'The wallowing martyr', as he called the type, was one of his private hates. He noticed with relief that Cornish was merely regretful.

'Go as easy as you can with us all,' was his only request.

Luke offered him a cigarette. 'Don't worry about that, sir. We're not quite as hamfisted as we're said to be. At least we try. Well now, you've spent three hours with this boy and you think he could be yours. Is that your first point?'

'Not quite. I should *like* to think he was mine. That's the danger. But whether he is or not isn't my reason for visiting you.'

Luke nodded. 'I appreciate that. You're merely going on his history as you know it, plus certain likenesses?'

'Yes.'

'And you'd never heard that history – in regard to young Timothy Kinnit that is – until today, when it was told you by Miss Flavia Aicheson while she was persuading you to give evidence on his behalf? You don't think she realized that the history might have some significance for you?'

'Oh no. She merely wanted me to tell the police that he had visited me yesterday evening.'

'And he had?'

'Yes.'

'Do you know why?'

'I didn't know at the time, and this afternoon when he gave me an explanation I didn't believe him, but now since a certain idea has occurred to me I think I do. He told me that the cobbler in Carroway Street had sent him to me.'

'And in view of the likeness between you, you think the cobbler might have done so?'

Cornish smiled. 'You're very shrewd Superintendent,' he said, relaxing. 'Tommy Tray was mending shoes in that same shop when I first came to Ebbfield. He'd lost both legs on the Somme in the First World War and when I first knew him I was about the age which Timothy is now. My first wife and I used the newsagent half of his shop, which was and is run by his sister, as an accommodation address for our letters. My wife lived actually in Turk Street with her only relative, an aunt who was an illiterate, suspicious old woman whom we never trusted not to give us away, so we used the shop very frequently and often went there. I imagine that when Timothy went in recently, asking questions, old Tray noticed something about him which made him send him along to me. It's the sort of thing he would do.'

'Your first wife?' Luke murmured, his pen resting on a note he had made. 'Excuse me, sir. Were you in fact married to her?'

'Yes.'

'It can be proved can it? Forgive me, but it's as well to get everything quite clear as we go along.'

'I know. I realize too that there is a gap in all the Ebbfield records of about that time, but although Somerset House, even, may not have the details, I can say that I have reason to believe that at least one copy of the marirage certificate is in existence.'

The odd phrase came out softly in the quiet room and Luke's glance kicked upward as if an elusive quarry he had been seeking had suddenly appeared.

'Good,' he said, making the comment non-committal. 'I have this straight now, then. One year before the Second World War, at the time of the famous Munich crisis, when war almost broke out, you were in Ebbfield finishing your apprenticeship to the small tool-making firm of Boxer & Coombe Ltd, which you now own.'

'My present wife and I own it in equal shares. She was a Miss Boxer, her mother was a Miss Coombe.'

'Ah yes. I see.' Luke's pen was busy again. 'In autumn 1938 – that is at the time of the Munich agreement – you were a member of the Royal Air Force Volunteer reserve and you were called up and drafted to a training camp in Yorkshire. Is that when you married your first wife?'

'No. We married in the first week of July of that year.' Cornish was smiling at the recollection as if he had never thought of the ceremony since it happened. He was remarkably relaxed and the fierce energy which had made him a somewhat uncomfortable companion had disappeared. 'We were "done",' he said, laughing a little, 'in a dusty church in Saracen's Square. I don't suppose you've ever heard of the place. It's all gone now. We turned up very early on the Friday morning just before my summer holiday and we had two witnesses out of the street, a sweep and a milkman. The parson – he sounded as if he had no roof to his mouth, poor chap – had read the banns every Sunday for three weeks, but as he had no congregation no one who knew of us heard him and we got clean away with it without anyone knowing.' His grey eyes were dancing and Timothy, twenty-one and joyous, looked out of them at Luke, who did not recognize him of course. 'Clean away to Southend-on-the-Mud,' Cornish went on. 'A couple of kids, happy as the buds in May.'

'Why did you have to keep it a secret?' Luke was watching him with a half smile.

'The terms of my apprenticeship!' Even at this distance he seemed to find them vitally important. 'Old Fred Boxer, the boss – he was my present wife's father – was more than hot on that sort of thing. Originally he came from my own home village in Norfolk and when my mother was left a widow she sent me up to him to learn the trade. I was bound all right, you never saw such a document!'

'I know. They are tough, those apprenticeship contracts. Did you go into the R.A.F. as unmarried?'

Cornish nodded. 'I had to. Old Fred was backing my papers. Besides, if you remember, nothing like that seemed to matter very much just then. There was no discernible future.'

'How right you are!' Luke's eyes flickered in faint surprise at the recollection. 'Future dubious. That was 1938–9 all right. Funny how one forgets. So you went off to Yorkshire – sent all over the place in the first draught I suppose, as an unmarried man?'

The Councillor continued to smile. 'She followed me whenever she could. She was younger in years than I was, but older in intelligence. A city girl and a country boy, that's what we were. She did the thinking for both of us and I let her.'

'What did she live on? Got jobs I suppose?'

'Yes. Waitress, nursemaid, anything. She was that kind of woman . . . independent, capable and wonderfully gay.' He looked up and made a gesture of resignation which was disarming. 'That's the key to the whole story. That's how it happened and why this boy, Timothy, has knocked me endways. People keep mentioning that he resembles *me*. My God! He not only looks like her but he *is* her. He's treated his own

poor little girl now just as he treated me. He's keeping her
out of it, suffering all alone. I never understood the bit
about honouring one's father and mother so that *one's days
would be long in the land* before today. If one respects one's
parents' fiascos at least one needn't waste time going over
the same ground twice. I didn't know, you see. It never
went through my mind.'

'You didn't know she was having a child, you mean?'
Luke, whose own experiences were still very close to him, was
deeply interested and sympathetic.

'It never entered my head,' Cornish said. 'I was a stupid,
ignorant, idealistic young idiot. Perhaps I never believed it
worked, or something. I don't know. I left everything to her.
As the time must have gone on she wrote instead of coming
but as I'd been moved to Scotland by that time I wasn't surprised. She kept saying she'd see me in October, I remember.
I had letter after letter full of everything but the important
subject.'

Luke's wide mouth twisted. 'Then the balloon went up?'
he suggested.

'On the second of September. We were ordered overseas. I
sent her a telegram to her aunt's address in the Turk Street
Mile and got one back to say she was in St Saviour's Hospital,
Ebbfield. That was the one which got the direct hit from a V2
at the end of the war.'

He moved uneasily in his chair and ran his hand over his
head and ear in the gesture Julia had recognized. 'I had an
hour, I remember. I didn't know what to do and I panicked. I
remember a fatherly old Flight explaining to me patiently
that I was on active service and if I deserted I'd be shot. I
telephoned at last. I had a lot of help – I was that sort of chap.
They got me a line in the end and when I got through to the
hospital I didn't know if she'd gone in as Miss or Mrs and
there was a hell of a flap on down there and they couldn't find
her. Finally I heard them say Maternity Ward and I didn't
understand even then. It meant nothing to me. I was still
thinking of a street accident; that's what hospitals spelt to
me at that time.'

It occurred to Luke that the man had never told the story before; he could see its reality dawning upon him afresh even while he was talking.

'There was an interminable pause, I remember,' he said softly. 'And the wires were full of voices as if one was listening in to the world, and then they asked if I was the husband, and when I told them I was they said they were afraid they had bad news. By this time the lorries were starting and the Flight was pulling my tunic. "How bad?" I said. "I'm sorry," the voice was kind but sweety-sweet if you know what I mean, "she died peacefully ten minutes ago." I just hung up.'

The eyes which met Luke's were still astonished. 'I just hung up,' he repeated. 'I went out with the Flight and we ran for the transports. It never even occurred to me that there might have been a baby until days later when we were in France.'

Luke did not speak at once and the room which had heard many stories of human insufficiency was silent and friendly.

'What did you hear from the aunt?' he inquired at last.

'Nothing. I wrote her but there was no reply, and when at last I got back a very long time later there was no sign of her or the house. You couldn't even see where it had been. I found out that the whole street had been evacuated soon after hostilities began. The authorities were terrified of the tinder-box areas and they emptied them as soon as they could. There were no raids at first, though, and many people had trickled back by the time the bombs fell so the old lady may have gone with her home. She liked it. It wasn't as bad as most in Turk Street.' He shrugged his shoulders, 'Anyway I never got an answer and the hospital merely referred me to her as the next of kin given. It had been cleared for casualties on the outbreak of war and although they confirmed the death of my wife in childbirth there was nothing on the form about the child.' He hesitated awkwardly. 'I didn't persist, you know,' he said, still speaking with surprise at his own inadequacy. 'I accepted the double death and put it out of my mind like . . . like a sight seen in battle. Things were happening to me by then and I suppose I didn't want to know, either. We were sent to Canada and I came back a navigator. I had a most inglorious war. Having cost the country a packet to train I went out on my first raid, got shot down, and went straight into the bag. It took me two years to get away.' He laughed briefly and shook his head. 'So there you are,' he said. 'That old sissy Eustace Kinnit irritated me this morning. He said something about a romantic tale told to the boy by a nurse. My God! No nurse made up a tale like the real one. Well that's it, briefly. You can guess what happened when I got back, at last. I'd had rheumatic fever whilst a P.O.W. and my heart was gippy.'

'Your old boss was doing essential work and could use you.' Luke hardly made it a question. It was the most natural development, the history of thousands of young men who were early casualties in a war of tremendous movement and change. 'Where were the Boxer & Coombe works then?'

'Out at Epsom. We only got back here after old Fred died in 1948. I'd just married his only daughter Marion, a nice girl. I'd always liked her. She knows nothing whatever about this story, by the way.'

Luke ducked his chin. He looked most discreet and intelligent.

'And that,' he said presently, 'is not all, I take it? Now we arrive at the bit which made you come to see me.'

His eyes were friendly but very sophisticated and they filled with surprise at the other man's sudden reaction.

'Neither bigamy nor blackmail, Superintendent,' Cornish said briskly. 'I think I could have met either of those with less embarrassment. My difficulty is that *I have the son of that marriage complete with his birth certificate* and he's a very awkward young customer, but not I think entirely to blame for what he is – and does. The time has come when I feel I've got to clear my mind about him and so I've forced myself to come to you.'

'I see, sir.' Luke had become remarkably cautious. 'How do you mean "you have him"?'

'I know him. I support him. His name is Barry Cornish.'

Luke recognized the mood behind the abrupt words. It was the confessional state of mind, a phenomenon of human behaviour which never ceased to make him nervous.

'Address?' he inquired.

'I don't know it at this moment but I could find him. At any rate he'll appear at the end of the month.'

'Ah, yes.' The superintendent pulled his jotting pad towards him once more and waited. It was all coming. He could feel the man looking for the best place to begin.

'I first heard of Barry at the end of 1947 when the Trays returned to their shop. They'd been in the West Country all through the war.' The Councillor sounded as if he were dictating and Luke coughed.

'I shan't take it down at this moment, sir,' he murmured. 'Just let it come out as it will. We'll sort it out later. Where were you at that time?'

'In Epsom still. My father-in-law was ill and Marion and I were due to inherit the business and the house where we live now. Our premises had escaped and we were moving the works back to London. I had put up for the Council. I was always keen on social work and the state the place was in made me mad to get at it and see if I couldn't get a better deal for people.' He ran out of breath, coloured, and glanced angrily at the policeman. 'I'm not trying to excuse myself for what I did, I'm only explaining it.'

Luke nodded gravely. 'I understand, sir.'

'Then the boy turned up,' Cornish said. 'I was reached through the Trays as soon as the shop opened again. The only thing which existed to lead to me was the envelope of a letter I had written to his mother at that address. It was in a little cardboard writing folder she had had with her in hospital, tucked in the back. The birth certificate was there and so was our marriage certificate and half a letter written to me.' His voice betrayed him and he pulled himself up savagely. 'Still no mention of the child, even though she was dying, silly girl. Only love stuff and wishing I was with her and worrying how *I* was. Dear God, who'd be young, eh?'

The superintendent's eyebrows drew close together.

'I haven't got this,' he said. 'The child didn't come alone, surely?'

'Oh no, of course not. It was the nuns who brought him.' Cornish was peering at him earnestly through his fierce brows. 'I'd have taken an entirely different line if it hadn't been for them. You must believe that. There's a lot in my life that I reproach myself for, but if they hadn't been there to look after him you must believe me that I'd have done something more than merely paying. I'd have told Marion – '

He broke off and Luke leant across the table, a man of his own age and outlook. 'Look sir,' he said, 'don't worry. I believe every word you're saying. There's only one really impossible thing about the truth and that's how to tell it. The nuns brought the child to you, did they? Who were they, Sisters of Mercy?'

'Nuns of the Good Shepherd. They've got a rather poor but very good place in Crusader's Row, almost into Islington. Do you know it?'

Luke waved him on. 'Wonderful people,' he said. 'How long had they had him? Just tell me the story as it comes . . . start from the first interview. Where did it take place?'

'At Tray's shop. Doris Tray wrote me a note at the works asking me to step down there. When I did she told me how some nuns had come round asking if she knew me. We fixed a meeting and two of them turned up and showed me a little cardboard attaché-case. It had this writing compendium in it and a broken comb and a strap. That was all. The sisters were very kind. There had been other items in it, no doubt, they said. But when people were poor and tempted things got used up. That was how they put it. They were sweet unworldly women although they appeared to be living up to the knees in sin and dirt and rubble.'

Luke laughed. 'They have a sort of triple glaze,' he observed, 'and as long as they follow the instructions it never wears off, or that's what they taught me when I was a nipper. Had they got the child with them?'

'No. I saw him later.'

There was a shadow in his tone which made Luke glance

up at him but Cornish went on without elaborating. 'The story they told me was so damn silly I knew it must be true,' he said. 'It struck a dreadful bell inside me, like first hearing the facts of life when you're a kid. Incredible and ridiculous but inescapably, horribly true. There was a woman who was slightly "sub", they said. They didn't call her that but they made it perfectly clear. She had been a casual, part-time ward-maid at St Saviour's, Ebbfield at the outbreak of war. The whole hospital had been in a panic getting ready to be cleared for the expected blitz casualties and she was frightened by all the talk. She heard that mothers of newly born babies had been issued with pink tickets, which entitled them to a seat on a bus to take them to complete safety as soon as the warning came. Because she was terrified she stole the suitcase of a patient who had died in childbirth, went down to the crèche part of the hospital or whatever they call it, presented the other woman's credentials and got the baby. Then she went off to join the bus. That was on the Sunday morning, 3 September.'

Luke sat back in his chair. 'Blow me down!' he said inelegantly.

Cornish met his eyes. 'I know the type of woman, don't you?'

'God yes! A right nit! We breed 'em in the cities. Too little grub, too little air, too much of everything else including noise. The hospital must have accepted her story that she was the next of kin and been pretty relieved to see her if they were clearing the wards for casualties. So she went on the bus with the child and the suitcase?'

'No. Not the suitcase. The little attaché-case I saw had been inside a larger affair containing clothes, I understood. She found this too heavy to carry as well as the child so she left it, if you please, with the porter of the hospital and asked him to have it sent to her own address, which was some digs in Bethnal Green. Are you with me?'

'Utterly.' Luke had given up writing and was in the story himself, on his own ground. 'It's extraordinary how they never vary, that particular type,' he observed. 'Do you know their behaviour is more predictable than a normal person's? They simply move straight on, taking the easiest way every time. That is why they appear to get away with so much. Paths open up before them as they trickle along like water on the ground. The landlady kept the suitcase quite safely, I suppose?'

'She did,' Cornish said. 'That's another amazing part of the story, to my mind. She put it in a cupboard and thought no more about it until five years later when she happened to see the girl again in a bus queue. She'd been in London all the time. The house had stood up to all the raids. Dozens of people had passed through the building. Every sort of commodity was short but still there the bag was, unopened under a pile of junk, exactly as it had been placed when the porter sent it round out of the kindness of his heart. The Nuns of the Good Shepherd reproached me for finding it extraordinary. It was *willed* that the papers should survive, they said.'

Luke was thinking, his brows raised and the long furrows deep on his forehead.

'This evacuees' bus,' he began cautiously, 'where did it go? Suffolk?' The Councillor interrupted him. 'Oh, my dear good chap,' he said, 'don't think that I haven't been wondering about *that* possibility. Ever since that woman Flavia Aicheson – a type I hate on principle – told me the story of Timothy this morning I've been trying to prevent myself regarding it as a revelation.'

'Why?' Luke spoke in astonishment. 'Why prevent yourself? It could so easily be the other half of your story. It's worth exploring, surely?'

'No!' The exclamation was vehement, and at the sound of the tone Luke's experienced ear pricked up and his eyes became wary once more as he recognized the point at which their views were due to separate.

'One could make it fit!' The Councillor said. 'One could want it to fit so much that one could deceive oneself and everybody else. Anyone would rather have a splendid, intelligent, decent, good-looking, honest boy than – well, than what I have.'

The man was lashing himself with a bitterness Luke could just understand but which he was far too old a hand to believe he could cure. 'I haven't told you about Barry yet,' Cornish went on. 'It's the thing I came to tell you and I still haven't brought myself to do it. He's abnormal, Superintendent. It was apparent when he was a child. That was why I felt I couldn't ask Marion to take him into our home and why I left him with the nuns.'

Luke was very serious. The pattern was unfolding before his knowledgeable gaze like the symptoms of a familiar illness before a physician.

'Is he what they call a mongol, sir?' he murmured, his gaze on his notes.

'Not quite. But he's not right. Yet he's not a fool. I wish he were. In some ways he's damnably intelligent. Horribly so.'

Luke sat rubbing his chin. All his training and experience shied at the pitfall which he saw opening before him, and yet his human judgement told him it did not exist and that the man, however misguided, was at least honest.

'Sons tend to take after their mothers,' he began slyly.

'The ward-maid? Agnes Leach? Of course I've thought of that.' Cornish dismissed the inference with a gesture. 'The nuns thought of it. They suspected me and insisted that they brought the woman while they watched us to see if there was recognition there. I could have been lying. All the story of my first wife could have been a fiction. I admit that.'

'No, no sir,' Luke was laughing softly. 'Come. That isn't what *I* was saying at all. There's an old English word which isn't often used nowadays but it's still useful on occasions, and that's "changeling". Mothers have been known to do that before now.'

'No.' Cornish shook his head with a martyr's obstinacy. 'I've thought of that. With longing. It would be a nice, easy, soft way out, wouldn't it? But life isn't like that or I haven't found it so.'

Luke leant back. He knew he was going to waste his time but couldn't help having a shot.

'My official life hasn't exactly been what you might call

sheltered,' he said, 'but I've never found it anywhere near as consistent as the cynics do. "Surprise, surprise!" That's the message of life in my opinion. Look here, sir, what makes you think that your first wife and you would have produced the sort of child you describe to me? No. Don't answer yet. But then tell me what sort of kid you *would* expect this subnormal Agnes Leach to mother?'

The Councillor shook his head. 'You mean very well, Superintendent,' he said. 'I should like to believe you, but aren't you overlooking something? What sort of chance has a child whose mother, my first wife, came from the most dreadful of slums (and believe me, there's nothing in England today to match Turk Street when I was a boy) and was then, almost on the day after he was born, thrown to a half-wit, hysterical girl who dragged him through the countryside in terror? Wouldn't that account for him, whatever he's become?'

'No sir.' Luke spoke briskly. 'Not if he's what you describe.'

'But don't you think so?' There was a masculine naïveté in the man's face and all the passionate ignorance of the unscientific mind on a deeply emotional subject.

'No sir.' Luke was a father too but also a practical man. 'As long as he was properly fed (and he must have been to survive), not dropped on his head, and kept reasonably warm, it wouldn't hurt him at all.'

'I think you are wrong.'

Cornish spoke simply and his weakness was revealed like a man uncovering a wound. 'It was my fault. I ought to have known the child was coming and I ought to have been there to take over when my wife died. It was a duty I failed in. The R.A.F. was reasonable in such matters. Don't you agree?'

'No sir.' Luke was wooden.

Cornish smiled at him and his mouth twisted.

'You think I'm clinging to a cross,' he said.

Luke's sudden grin was disarming.

'Well, if you set it up yourself it's nothing much to cling to, sir, or that's what the Holy Sisters taught me, but I take it we're not having that kind of discussion. What exactly are you trying to tell me about this boy of yours, Mr Cornish? You're thinking of the fire and the flat-wrecking, aren't you?'

Cornish looked up gravely and sighed.

'I don't know anything, mind you. But as soon as I realized that the probable reason for the attack on the flat was an attempt to frighten a private detective off an inquiry into the history of a baby evacuated from Turk Street on the first day of the Second World War, I thought of my son Barry. It's the sort of interference which might make him very excited. Agnes Leach keeps in touch with Ebbfield gossip. He would hear about it from her.'

Luke's glance grew bleaker.

'Who did you think had employed the detective?'

'I knew. The police told me. Alison Kinnit. I associated her with Miss Aicheson and I thought she had done it in an attempt to find out something to discredit me.'

'Really?' Luke sounded amazed and a touch of colour appeared in the Councillor's thin cheeks.

'Now I've met her socially I see that's unlikely,' he admitted. 'But you've no idea what she's like in committee: she gives you the impression she'd fight with no holds barred.'

Luke's smile escaped despite himself, but he made no comment.

'When this boy Barry gets excited, is he liable to do dangerous and even criminal things, sir?' he inquired.

Cornish nodded. It was an admission which he had prepared himself to make but he still found it difficult. 'All his life he has been frighteningly awkward. The Nuns of the Good Shepherd passed him on to the Sisters of St Vincent de Paul who specialize in caring for that sort of case. He became too much for them and he went to some Brothers who wouldn't keep him at all.'

Luke began to understand very clearly. 'Has he got a record?'

'Yes.'

'Oh well,' the superintendent made it sound a relief,

T – G

'don't distress yourself, sir. I'll look him up. We probably know more about him than you do. Does he live alone in the normal way?'

'No. I should have felt more guilty still about him if he had, but this Mrs Leach . . .'

'The ward-maid?'

'The ward-maid, Agnes Leach, has been quite touchingly faithful to him. Through all his vicissitudes she has always been about. Actually I pay his allowance to her, now, so that he keeps it for at least a day or so.'

'And yet you really believe . . . ?' Luke bit back the rest of the sentence. 'She's good to him, anyway,' he said instead and made a note.

The Councillor had risen and now stood looking at him with a stern dignity which was yet homely enough not to appear absurd.

'You know what you're forgetting, Luke,' he said, using the name as if they were friends for the first time. 'You're overlooking the facts, man. The boy *is* my son. He's got written proof. He's got his papers.'

The superintendent was taken aback. It was an aspect of the situation, a purely legal one, which had indeed escaped him entirely in the emotional problem.

'Who is to judge the age of a youngster?' Cornish asked. 'Is a squinting, backward baby four years or three? Or a gangling teenager twenty or nineteen?' He held out his hand. 'Well, there you are,' he said. 'I shall do what I can for him as I always have. You must be prepared for that, but these dreadful acts of destruction must be stopped. I see that. Look up your files and I'm afraid you'll find him, under "Cornish" alias "Leach". He always uses his own name when he's in trouble. He has his papers, you see?'

As soon as Luke got back to his own room he told his clerk to find Mr Campion. 'Wherever he is,' he said, 'and get him on the line. Meanwhile I want details of a youngster called Barry Cornish. There'll be a juvenile record if nothing else.'

Twenty minutes later he was talking over the telephone to his old friend.

'Campion, I want to see you right away. Quicker than soon. It's quite a story and quite a development. I think we've got our delinquent. He has a record like a horror-comic strip. Campion?'

'Wait a minute.' Mr Campion's light voice, which still had its characteristic streak of vagueness, came gently to him over the wires. 'I'm at the Well House. The Kinnit's home you know. There's a bit of a flap on. The nurse I told you about, Mrs Broome, has just come in with the story that she has again met the woman who brought Timothy to Angevin with the other evacuees all those years ago. What? Oh yes. She says she knew her at once. She was in the cemetery snooping round the governess's grave.'

Chapter Fourteen

Kitchen Business

'Come, Miss Julia. You sit in the old basket chair while Mr Tim and I get supper ready. Shall I make you a little fire in the hob-grate and you can pretend you're Cinderella?'

Mrs Broome's ever-young voice tinkled gaily in the low-ceilinged cavern which was the kitchen of the Well House. As a sample of conversation in the world of today it had to be heard to be believed, and Tim and Julia exchanged secret glances. Julia was still slightly emotional and her eyes were wet as she laughed and turned to look at the carefully restored chimneypiece hung about with iron spoons and skillets.

'You're wonderful, Nanny Broome,' she said. 'I don't think that thing is meant to light though, do you? Eustace would be horrified.'

'Very likely, but he'd get over it. If we put up with all his antique bits and bobs he must give way to us sometimes.'

Mrs Broome was making noises rather than talking and her glance was running over the details of the fireplace as she weighed up the difficulties of the project.

'I do like a flare,' she said. 'And there are some wine boxes through there we could break up, but it's warm enough with all these pipes. I just want to make you feel at home, miss. After all, as I said to Mr Tim when you rang up so upset, you've been such a good little girl over all this engagement business we ought to make a fuss of you or he'll lose you.'

'Nan! This will do!' Timothy was embarrassed and, as usual, Mrs Broome bridled dangerously at any reproach from him.

'You still show you've been fighting, especially when you colour up, young man,' she said spitefully. 'Come along: there are four places to be laid on the kitchen table. We'll

180

give Mrs Telpher something down here with us, shall we? Poor thing, she won't want to eat alone even if she is so rich! It was a great shock to her losing that little Miss Saxon and she was worried enough before, what with the kiddiewiddie and being so far from home.'

Julia stirred in the creaking chair. She was laughing but yet grateful for the mothering, which was comforting, however absurd.

'I hope you're right that Miss Alison won't mind me coming to stay,' she said. 'I was dreading the evening at home alone but it seems rather an imposition to move in on you when I live reasonably near.'

'Oh, rubbish! Miss Alison always lets me settle little things like that when I'm here. If Mr Tim wanted to bring a school friend home for a match or the Boat Race he only had to ask me. I do the extra work, you see!'

Mrs Broome was trotting round the kitchen with her little steps swinging her seat and conveying such ecstatic happiness as could alone excuse her. 'One of these days you'll be the mistress and we shall be the poor old things all very glad that you've got something to be grateful to us for.'

Tim put his arm round her and lifted her gently off the floor. 'Shut up!' he said.

Mrs Broome squeaked with delight like a musical-comedy soubrette. 'Giving away secrets, am I?' she inquired contentedly. 'I'm always doing that. Never mind me. We must get a tray for the gentlemen. I shall give them theirs in the study. Then they won't come and bother us down here.'

Tim stood for a moment absently caressing his ear lobe.

'Poor Campion,' he said. 'Eustace has frozen on to him as if he was the only spar in an angry sea. I've got a terrific admiration for your father, darling. This deft introduction of an expert instead of bungling about in it himself is masterly.'

The girl looked up quickly. 'I like Mr Campion, though, don't you?'

'Immensely. I don't know why. He's on our side anyway, perhaps it's that. I'm afraid he's having a depressing day,

Alison gave him some dreadful lunch and now he's going to be asked to share Eustace's boiled milk and bickies.'

'No. I shall make him a nice little omelet and he'll eat it with a glass of wine and a roll and butter and like it.' Mrs Broome was beside herself with happy home-making. 'I shall put a pretty tray cloth on and find a bit of cheese and he'll enjoy it. They're very busy talking about something *I* was able to tell them, Miss Julia.' She was bursting with her news and carefully avoided Timothy's warning glance. 'I happened to go out today and I . . .'

'What about Alison and Aich?' Timothy interrupted her ruthlessly. 'Where are they feeding?'

'Oh, they're going to the Art-Lovers Club.' Mrs Broome was sidetracked. 'They've got to go to this recital in Wigmore Street you see, because they know the gentleman who's giving it. It's a harpsichord he plays and very rare, but afterwards they're slipping over to the Club to have a hot sandwich and they'll be back at once after that, because of course they're as interested in the goings-on here as anyone is. You finish this table, Mr Tim, and I'll slip up to the dining-room pantry and fix the tray and find the wine.' She bustled out of the room but put her head back inside the door immediately afterwards.

'Make him tell you about what I found in the Cemetery, miss,' she said and fled before she saw his reaction.

For once she had misjudged the situation, however, for the instant they were alone they were in each other's arms, too wearily frustrated to care about any mystery save one. Julia lay in the creaking basket chair holding her beloved back from her by his ears.

'Oh God, this is awful,' she said. 'It's like dabbing a burn with cold water, brief peace and then twice as much pain. Look darling, before she comes back, I've got to tell you. I had a sort of extraordinary experience down in Ebbfield at the cobbler's shop.'

'Oh, be quiet.' He pushed his mouth over hers and with his weight upon her edged her back farther into the hard flock cushions sewn into the groaning basket work. The discomfort was a delight to her and the very absurdity of the noise of the chair seemed to add to the pleasure of the sacrifice, but she wriggled away from him at last and struggled on with her story.

'I heard someone say *Basil* Kinnit. Do you think . . . ?'

'Basil Kinnit? There's no such person.' He was momentarily interested.

'I know. That's what I thought. But it couldn't be a coincidence because it's an unusual name and anyway Basil's in it, isn't he?'

'Basil Toberman?'

'Of course.' They were whispering without knowing why. Two conspirators, their heads together, their breath mingling. 'He started it all, didn't he? He hates you – he hates us both.'

He was about to protest but changed his mind and began to kiss her again, pressing his forehead hard into her chest.

'It's ridiculous,' he said, suddenly, his head bobbing up like a child out of a cot. 'We want so little, only a bit of peace and solitude, only for a tiny while . . . It's like dying: you only need your narrow bit of earth. Hush – '

They both paused, listening. Someone was coming down the flight of wooden stairs which led from the ground floor to the half-basement in which the kitchen was built at the end of the entrance yard.

Timothy got up and Mrs Telpher came in quietly and nodded to them. She was aware that she was intruding and regretted it in a mild Kinnit-like way.

'Mrs Broome tells me we are to have a meal down here,' she remarked, looking about her with the impersonal interest which was so very characteristic of the whole family. 'She is still very excited about her encounter. It's quite an extraordinary chance that she should have found the woman there, of all places. Oh – haven't you told Julia about it yet, Timothy?'

The dark colour came slowly into the boy's face.

'Julia's only just arrived,' he said.

'Oh, I see.' She looked from one to the other with the calmly inquisitive stare which was reminiscent of Alison, and then laughed with a touch of hardness which was not Alison at all. 'I think I should tell her if I were you,' she said. 'It's rather her affair.'

There it was again, the hint of superiority, unaware and unselfconscious, which denigrated the other person's importance in an off-hand, unintentional way. Although he had been familiar with the trick all his life, Timothy could still be flustered by it.

He swung round and addressed the girl who was still sitting in the chair.

'Nan went over to Harold Dene Cemetery to take a wreath which arrived too late for Miss Saxon's funeral,' he said. 'While she was there she ran into a woman whom she fancied she recognized, and afterwards she decided it was the person who brought me down to Angevin when I was a baby. Naturally everybody is rather excited because I suppose there's a very good chance that she is my mother.' He hesitated. 'Nan won't have it, because she didn't take to her. She sounds something of a problem Mum!'

Julia received the full message and made no false move.

'That could be very useful and interesting,' she said slowly. 'I suppose people do recognize each other after twenty years?'

Mrs Telpher laughed gently. 'One can see how young you are!' she said. 'Did the other woman recognize Mrs Broome? I shouldn't think she'd changed since the day she was born.'

Timothy looked startled. 'No one seems to have thought of that. I'll ask Nan. She must know.'

Mrs Telpher sat down at the partly laid table where she managed to look remarkably elegant despite a background of white kitchen fittings.

'She may have made it all up,' she said placidly. 'Not intentionally you know, Timothy. But in a bedtime story fashion. Here she comes. I should like to hear it from her.'

'Everybody wants to hear it from me.' Nanny Broome caught the tail end of the sentence and responded happily as she came softly in, her quick light steps pattering on the stones. I should think that Mr Albert Campion – who isn't nearly so gormless as he looks, let me tell you – took me through it a dozen times. Where exactly was the grave?

Where was I? Where was the water tap? Where was the Keeper?'

'The *keeper*?' Julia demanded.

'Well, the man in the peaked cap who was wandering about.' Mrs Broome was on the defensive. 'It's a very modern place, you know. The same idea as the zoo. Graves not quite graves and cages not quite cages but all lovely paths and gardens. Anyway I spoke to him and asked him the way because he looked as if he ought to know, and he did. There it was, covered with all our flowers. Mr Eustace's cushion of roses looked lovely. Naturally I was surprised to see a lady kneeling there because she wasn't one of us.'

'A lady kneeling?' Mrs Telpher's utter astonishment splashed through the chatter like a shower of cold water.

'Well, a person,' said Mrs Broome, reddening. 'She was stooping if she wasn't kneeling.'

Mrs Telpher's shrewd eyes began to laugh and Nanny Broome's blush became sulky. 'I said "kneeling" because it was a grave,' she explained unnecessarily. 'I went up softly and, not liking to disturb her in case she was someone we knew, I put the new wreath up against a headstone behind her and went off to get some water. I thought there must be a tap somewhere and I could see the poor tired flowers could do with a nice fresh sprinkle.'

'Had she seen you?' Timothy inquired.

'I don't think so. Not then. But when I came back with a little jam-pot of water – I found one hidden behind the post the tap was on – she was sitting back on her heels looking at the label on the wreath I'd just brought.'

'You mean the card.' Julia spoke absently.

'No I don't. I mean the label.' Nursery authority was very marked and a certain feline streak, directed at Mrs Telpher, appeared in the narrative. 'I didn't take the wreath out of its wrappings to carry it there, particularly since I was going by bus: so the label was still on it. It was sent "Care of Kinnit" to our address here and there was the name and address of the people who had sent it, too – somewhere in Africa. Well, this lady – I always call people that because it's more polite – was squatting there reading it. I thought "There's cheek if you like!", so I said "Excuse me, please" and took it away.'

'Is that when you recognized her?' There was still faint amusement in Mrs Telpher's face.

'No. I shouldn't have known her from Adam. I kept my eyes down you see. I was annoyed with her and I intended to show it.' Nanny Broome conveyed the scene with complete veracity. One could see her, cross and prissy, waggling her bottom, taking her tiny steps, and keeping her eyes downcast so that the lashes were black on her red cheeks.

'I unpacked the wreath and folded the celophane very carefully for one doesn't want to make litter,' she said virtuously. 'And I set it up in the best place and I said to it "now you lie there and look nice".'

'You actually spoke aloud?' It was Mrs Telpher again. She seemed fascinated.

'Yes, I did. I always talk aloud to things. It helps me to concentrate. Why, there's no harm in it, is there, Madam?'

She was within an ace of impudence, overplaying her part dangerously. Tim interfered hastily.

'What else did you say?' he inquired. 'Did you speak to the label? Did you, Nan?'

'Why should I?' She flushed so brightly that he was answered.

'Because I know you,' he said. 'What did you say?'

'I only spoke to it as I put it with the rest of the rubbish to go into the litter bin. I said "Well, I don't know, but everyone seems interested in *you*. First Mr Basil and then a perfect stranger.' Afterwards I did look at her and I was surprised, because I thought "My goodness! I have seen you before!" But I couldn't think where, until I was nearly home.'

'How did she take your delicate criticism?'

'Don't you laugh at me, young man. I couldn't tell you. I didn't stop to talk. I came away. She wasn't the kind of person to get acquainted with. The years had altered her. She was a silly girl in those days – she had adenoids I shouldn't wonder – but she wasn't downright *awful* like she is now.'

'I've lost the thread of all this,' Mrs Telpher intervened

with sudden irritation. 'What did you mean when you said Mr Toberman was interested in the label on the wreath?'

'Well, he was. He copied it down in his note-book, didn't he? I thought you saw him. You were at the top of the stairs.'

'Really? Was this yesterday evening when it arrived?' She seemed amazed. 'What an extraordinary thing for him to do! I'm afraid I find the whole story amazing. Are you sure you recognized this woman by poor Miss Saxon's grave?'

'Pefectly. Her face came back to me. I told you. I kept thinking about her and then when I was nearly here, "My goodness!" I said. "That's who it was!"'

'Did she know you?'

Nanny Broome seemed to find the question as surprising as everyone else had done. She stood considering and finally made a virtue of necessity, as usual.

'I was always taught it was very wrong to go about wondering what effect one is making on the other person all the time, so I never do. If she did know me she didn't say so, but she did have a silly sly smile on her face, now you come to mention it. It would be funny if she didn't recognize me, wouldn't it? I haven't got any older at all, everybody says that.' She turned away. 'Now I must get on with your meal and hurry. I'm to see the police, Mr Tim. First you and now me.'

She tossed the small grenade lightly into the conversation and busied herself at the sink. 'Mr Campion told me,' she said over her shoulder. 'He and Mr Eustace were full of it when I took the tray up from the pantry. As soon as I've seen to you all down here I'm to slip into a dark coat and go with Mr Campion to see somebody called Superintendent Luke.'

'Officially?' Julia got the question in before Timothy could speak. Mrs Broome turned to look at her reproachfully.

'Not quite,' she admitted regretfully. 'I'm not going to headquarters and I said I'd rather not go to a public house, so I shall meet him out.'

'Why doesn't the superintendent come here?' Tim, fresh from his own experience, was apprehensive.

'He doesn't want to.' Mrs Broome still talked with her back to him. 'I asked Mr Campion that and he explained that it's a question of etiquette. So of course I understood at once.'

She bustled out through a door at the back of the room and Timothy looked at Julia, his eyebrows raised.

'What's your chum playing at, do you know?'

'I don't.' She was wary. 'Superintendent Luke is all right only very high-powered. I'm surprised though. I didn't think he'd interfere unless —'

'Unless what?'

'Unless the Councillor talked to him. He conveyed that he might, but I didn't think he'd do it so soon.'

'The Councillor?' Tim spoke in astonishment but did not continue since Mrs Telpher was watching them with polite interest. Finally, as the silence grew longer she spoke herself.

'Did you want to talk to him or were you just determined to get him out of the house before he drove Eustace out of his mind? I never saw a man so astounded in my life as when you carried him off like that.'

Julia regarded her gravely.

'I liked him,' she said. 'He knows a great deal about Ebbfield. Did you like him, Timothy?'

'I did rather.' He seemed surprised by the admission. 'He's either very human or else he's just a type I happen to know and understand. He annoyed me but I never felt I didn't know what he meant, which is odd because I'm rather slow on the uptake with strangers.'

Julia sat hesitating, her eyes dark with indecision. 'I was wondering,' she began at last and was saved, or perhaps merely interrupted, by a shout from Mrs Broome somewhere in the back of the building.

'What's happened here? Look at this!'

Both young people hurried out to her, entering first a whitewashed passage of a type which still exists in old London houses, and then on to a square room which must once have been an outhouse before the city had closed not merely round but over it. It was lit by a single bulb hanging from a cracked ceiling and still possessed a flagged floor. Nanny Broome was looking up at the outer wall. Just under the ceiling there were three lunette windows, heavily barred and blacked out in the normal way by centuries of grime. Their bases were on a level with the pavement outside, a narrow way which was several feet lower than the road behind the house.

At the moment, however, a draught of cold, soot-laden air was flowing in freely through the centre window.

'See that?' Mrs Broome demanded. 'The glass has come clean out. It's simply gone, unless someone has cut it. Keep away from that Mr Tim, do, or you'll get yourself filthy.'

Tim had swung himself up by two of the bars and now dropped back obediently, dusting his hands.

'There's no sign of it and the wire netting has gone too,' he said. 'They do sweep along there, though. It serves as a fire escape from the basement of the factory beyond the warehouse next door and has to be kept clear. I expect the netting rotted and the glass fell out and broke and both were shovelled up by the scavengers.'

'In that case they must work funny hours,' Mrs Broome said, tartly. 'It was perfectly all right at lunch-time. I'm in and out here in the mornings but this evening I felt the fresh draught as soon as I set foot outside the kitchen door.'

'What an extraordinary place.' Mrs Telpher came in cautiously, as if she were entering a cave, and Mrs Broome frowned.

'It's antique, madam,' she said sharply. 'This is where the famous well was. It's under the floor where that ring is, full of medicine. That's why we can't do anything useful with the room, like making a laundry of it. Someone has been up to mischief with our window, trying to get in, I suppose.'

'Nonsense Nan,' Timothy spoke soothingly.

'No one could get through those bars, they can't be six inches apart.'

'A rat could,' said Mrs Broome. 'Come along out of here at once and we'll shut the door.'

Julia was uneasy. 'Oughtn't we to report it to the police?'

'I'll mention it,' Mrs Broome said grandly. 'But as Mr Tim

says, if those bars are no protection a bit of dirty glass certainly wouldn't be. If anyone was hoping to get in there they've been put off. Now all sit round the table please because I mustn't keep the gentlemen waiting.'

On the whole it was a relief when at last, some little time later, they persuaded her to leave them. She tripped lightly up the stairs, her long purple coat wrapped round her and her eyes as bright as if she were going to an assignation. Tim sighed when at last they heard the front door slam.

'Now we can start again,' he said. 'Geraldine, how about another tin of lovely pink soup?'

'Are you still eating? Splendid! We did hope we'd find you still at it.' Miss Aicheson appearing suddenly in the doorway took them by surprise. She was tired but still game and was fussing a little in an old-gentlemanly way.

'The club was shut,' she said. 'I'd been told, too. Alison was quite right. It had slipped my memory completely. So home we came only to find Mrs Broome on the doorstep being carried off by that pleasant Mr Campion.' Her smile was disarming. 'I feel certain I can open a tin. You must just tell me what to do, Tim. Alison won't mind as long as we steer clear of onions or red pepper.'

Both young people rose to the occasion. Julia cleared a place and Tim gave up his seat.

'Don't worry Aich,' Timothy said. 'How was the concert?'

'Oh, very good indeed. I'm so glad we went to make two more. Poor Henry Ambush hasn't many friends and he's so talented. It's a very exacting instrument, the harpsichord – on the ear, I mean.'

'Is it?' said Mrs Telpher mechanically. She had relapsed into her unforthcoming mood and sat relaxed and withdrawn, as if she were out of the circle altogether.

'So this is where you all are!' Alison came flitting in with Eustace behind her. The Kinnit resemblance both between brother and sister and Geraldine Telpher herself had never appeared more marked. They were all mature people, past the age when the family stamp appeared unmistakably in the bone structure, and they looked to Julia like three little moulds off the same line, only differing superficially where some celestial paintbrush had been at work.

'Don't worry about us,' Alison sat down in Julia's place beside Miss Aicheson and smiled at everybody. 'Eustace has had his sandwiches and I hardly want anything at all. What have you been eating? Soup and cheese? How very nice. What are you doing down there, Eustace?'

'Looking at this fireplace.' He spoke from behind Mrs Telpher. 'I come down here so seldom it always takes me by surprise. It's perfect and just as we uncovered it. Every brick quite perfect. A simple ellipse. It's pure fourteenth century, much older than the house, and must have had a big square chimney, long since gone, of course.' He rose, dusting his knees. 'One day Nanny Broome, or some other silly woman, will try to light a fire in it and smoke everybody out. But it's most interesting; this must have been the original ground level, eight feet or more below the street of today. The same period as the Well in fact. Have they shown you that, Geraldine?'

'I saw the slab over it just now. One of the windows has been broken in there. Julia thought it should be reported to the police.'

'What? A window? Really? Tim, you didn't tell me this? I ought to have been informed at once!' Eustace was already on his way to inspect the trouble, Timothy behind him.

'My dear boy,' his voice came floating back to them, 'we mustn't take any unnecessary risks. These are evil times. There are a lot of unprincipled people about and we have treasures here.'

Alison noticed Mrs Telpher's expression of astonishment and hastened to explain.

'Eustace is thinking of irreplaceable antiques,' she murmured. 'We don't keep money or jewels in the house. That's why we wrote to warn you to put yours in a safe deposit. We feel it's wrong to tempt people. Any burglar who came here would have to know exactly what he was after or he'd be very disappointed.'

'I see.' Geraldine Telpher inclined her head gravely and

everyone was left a little irritated, as if she had disparaged the contents of the house.

'I believe you're right.' Eustace returned to the room wiping his hands on his handkerchief and still talking to Timothy who was behind him. 'The bars are a complete protection but we'll report it in the morning and it must be repaired at once. I can't think it has been done deliberately but – ' An expression of dismay spread over his gentle face as a tremendous rattle and thump directly outside the door leading up into the house shook the whole basement.

In the silence which followed somebody outside used a familiar but ugly four-letter word.

Timothy pulled the door open and put his head out.

'Oh, it's you,' he said. 'What's happened?' There was a pause and he glanced back into the room, trying not to appear amused. 'It's Basil. He's slipped down the stairs. Get up, you ass. Are you all right?'

'Ruddy Kinnits!' The voice which was unquestionably drunken sounded tearful. 'This is just the welcome I should expect. I've already been called Basil once tonight – just outside this inhospitable house. I've been asked by a perfect stranger "Are you Basil Kinnit?" What's the answer? That is the question. The answer is no.'

'All right,' Timothy sounded harassed. 'Don't worry about it, old boy, just get up.'

'But I do worry.' The tears were more evident. 'I hate the ruddy Kinnits and all their damned governesses and let me tell you, Wonderboy, I'm in a position to tell them something they don't all know.'

'So you shall, chum, so you shall.' Timothy was speaking whilst expending considerable exertion. 'Just get up and you shall tell us all anything you like.'

Chapter Fifteen

The Beanspiller

'Public house nothing! This is a hotel.'

Charlie Luke had never appeared a finer animal in harder condition. His suit might have been buttoned tightly over wood, and he perched on the plush-seated chair in the deserted upstairs dining-room of the Eagle Tavern in Scribe Street, E.C.3, glowing at Mrs Broome as if she were a plate of cornflakes and he a greedy child on a poster advertising them. Mr Campion, who was between them, was amused despite his anxiety.

'At lunch-time this room is crowded with solid businessmen but in the evening they've all caught their trains home and it is quiet and comfortable for us to have a chat in, see?' the superintendent was explaining. 'You're being given Royal treatment. I've had them open it up and turn on the lights for us.'

'Not many.' Nanny Broome, smug in her purple coat, glanced up at the spray of bronze wall-lights above the table. They shed a somewhat ghostly glow over the rest of the thickly carpeted room. 'I know it's been used at lunch-time because I can smell spirits and cigars. Still, if Mr Campion says it's all right I don't mind staying.'

'That's handsome of you, Missus.' Luke was a trifle dashed and his eyes were inquisitive. 'I've invited you to come along because I want to ask you one or two very simple questions. You may not be able to tell me anything but there is a chance you could help with an inquiry which is nothing whatever to do with anyone you know.'

'I understand.'

'Do you?' He seemed surprised. 'That's good. I could take you down to the police station and the detectives there could get you to make long, long statements, but I don't want to put you to all that trouble.'

'Why?' She appeared genuinely curious and he caught his breath and let it out in a short explosive laugh.

'Because you're needed at home to do the washing up,' he said and gave Mr Campion a sidelong glance. 'Would you like a cake with that coffee, Mrs Broome? No? I'll have a ham sandwich,' he added to the resident manageress who was serving them herself. 'The others will too. Some of those very expensive ones.'

'That's all right, Mr Luke, don't worry.' The woman, who was tired and motherly for all her spiked heels and diamond ring, set down the coffee tray and waddled off into the darkness.

The superintendent returned to his guest.

'Now I want you to take your time over this so we'll start with something which hasn't very much to do with it,' he began mendaciously. 'Mr Campion here was telling me that you believe you saw the woman who brought Mr Timothy Kinnit down to the country when he was a baby, and that to the best of your belief she was in Harold Dene Cemetery this afternoon. Is that right?'

Mrs Broome smiled at him and presently threw back her head and laughed like a girl.

'I'm not as green as I'm cabbage-looking,' she said. 'You ask me straight questions and I'll give you straight answers. You want to know if Mr Tim's mummie has turned up out of the blue, don't you?'

Luke blinked, exaggerating the reaction and leaning back in his chair.

'I didn't say anything of the sort.'

'No, I know you didn't, but that's what you were thinking.'

'Was I? You're a mind reader, I suppose?'

'No. I don't pretend to be that.' She was cocky and deprecating at the same time. 'But I generally know what lies behind any question I'm asked. Some people do, you know.'

The superintendent sighed and the wrinkles on his forehead deepened as his eyebrows rose.

'Yes,' he said. 'Some people do – and damn dangerous they are, too! Well then, suppose that is what I wanted to know? I'm not saying it was, mind you.'

Mrs Broome touched the sleeve of his coat where his wrist lay on the table beside her.

'You're wasting your time, anyhow. She hasn't,' she said reassuringly. 'I told Mr Toberman that, and Mr Campion here was listening – as he usually is, it seems. That girl was not the mother of Timothy or anybody else when she came down to Angevin.'

Luke leaned over the table. Cosiness and man-to-woman approach glowed from him.

'It's very easy to make mistakes in a matter like this. I've been taken in time after time. Motherhood is like any other natural thing: there are hundreds of variations of condition.'

Mrs Broome shook her head. She was sitting up very straight, her cheeks pink.

'I don't doubt that you're a very clever man and that being in the police you've had to get to know a lot of things that aren't a gentleman's business, but you've never had a baby have you? Not personally, I mean.'

Luke scratched his chin but before he could comment she continued:

'Well, I have. More than that, I had just come back from hospital after losing my baby when this girl turned up with Timmy, who was quite new – still on his stalk. That's a thing no one can disguise. Naturally, although I was run off my feet looking after all the other mummies, she was my chief interest because the baby was so young, and I put her to sleep in my little room where we shared the same bed, and all day I was looking forward to talking to her about her confinement.'

'Oh.' A wave of comprehension passed over the superintendent's expressive face. 'She didn't give the right answers?'

'She didn't know anything at all!' Mrs Broome's contempt and disappointment were as fresh as if she felt them still. 'I spent all the night trying to get some sense out of her and I soon found out she wasn't only a liar but a very ignorant young monkey. Do you know, another woman on the bus had *lent her a bottle* or he would have starved by the time I was there to save him! A wicked, wicked girl!'

'She was pretending to be the mother?'

'Not to me, she wasn't. She soon saw how ridiculous that was. She had had to say she was his mother to account for the pink ticket. She had to have a pink ticket to be allowed on the bus. No. That girl was simply frightened of the bombs. They were her worry, silly little cat! Not a thought for the poor baby. I'd have given her bomb!'

Luke was watching her with the whole of his body.

'After talking to you she ran away?' He could not help anticipating the story.

Mrs Broome raised mutinous eyes.

'Yes, she did. I knew I'd frightened her but I never expected that. The next morning she vanished. I thought she was hiding so I didn't say anything but looked after the baby. I was so busy and so happy with him that I kept putting off mentioning that she'd gone. Then, when Mr Eustace practically owned to him, naming him like that, I didn't bother any more. I made up my mind that she was a maid sent down to bring him to me.' She paused and took a defiant breath. 'If you don't believe me I can't help it. But I'm not a liar.'

'No,' said Luke, grinning at her. 'You're not dull enough! I believe you. What about the kid's clothes? I don't suppose they were anything to write home about, but didn't you keep anything? A bootee or a bit of embroidery or anything at all?'

She shook her head. 'The only thing I kept that Timmy had when he came to me was most unsuitable for a baby,' she said. 'It was a cotton head-scarf tucked under his shawl. It was a lovely pale blue. Blue for a boy. It had little jumping white lambs on it and writing made of daisy-chains. "Happy and Gay" it said. All over it. It was just my meat and I've got it somewhere and I'll show it to you, but it wasn't special. There were hundreds of scarves like it in Woolies that year.'

'If you're certain of that, don't bother.' He shook his head regretfully. 'What's your observation like?' He had taken his worn black wallet from his pocket and was looking for something amid the bursting contents. 'This is a curio in itself,' he said to Campion. 'They wouldn't let me borrow the file of course, but the photographic section got me these in fourteen minutes flat.' He produced two small photographs of a woman, one full face, one profile, and handed them to Mrs Broome who wore the expectant expression of a player awaiting his turn in a quiz game. A single glance, however, wiped everything but dismay from her face.

'Oh, doesn't she look awful!' she said aghast. 'She's not as bad as that, not even now. What are these for? Her passport?'

'You could call it that,' Luke said dryly. 'Is it she?'

'Oh, yes, I can see it's her. They're not as bad as that.'

'Do you remember the name she gave you?'

'She didn't give me any name. If she had I should have remembered it and it would have saved a lot of trouble.'

'Wasn't it on the pink ticket?'

'I had no time for tickets! You have no idea what it was like. We had hundreds of mummies and kiddiewiddies in the house – hundreds! All wanting – my goodness! – all sorts of things.'

'What did you call her?'

'Me?'

'Yes, when you were getting down to the intimate details. "Ducky"?'

'No, I should never have said that. I'm very particular how I talk.' She was thinking, casting her mind back as he was persuading her to. 'I'm not sure, but I think I called her "Agnes". She must have told me that was her name if I did. It's not a favourite of mine.'

'All right, don't worry. Have you ever heard of a Mrs Leach?'

'No. Is that who she says she is?'

The superintendent ignored the question. He was looking at some scribbled notes on a sheet torn from a telephone pad.

'I understand,' he said at last, 'that you told Mr Campion here that you didn't have a chat with her in the cemetery. It was a chance meeting and although you thought you knew her you didn't place her until you were on a bus coming home. Did any word pass between you at all?'

'None.' With the recollection of Mrs Telpher's reaction to her habit of addressing inanimate objects fresh in her mind, Nanny Broome was cautious, sticking carefully to the letter of the truth. 'I might have said "excuse me" as I passed her to put the wreath on the grave, but nothing more.'

He nodded acceptance. 'You say she was kneeling?'

'I might have been wrong. She might have been just bending, looking at the flowers.'

Luke scratched his clipped black curls. 'What was she doing there at all, do you know? Was she just ghouling about among the graves, or pinching flowers, or what? I mean was this an absolutely chance meeting, do you think, or was she interested in that one particular grave?'

'Oh, of course it was our grave she was looking at!' The idea of any other explanation seemed to astound her. 'I thought "Ah, there's somebody whose heard the talk!"'

Mr Campion raised a warning hand but he was too late. Luke had heard.

'What talk?' he demanded, looking from one to the other of them with the same suspicious flicker.

'Miss Saxon fell in the kitchen just before she had her fatal heart attack.' Mr Campion made the explanation carefully. 'She appears to have been listening at a door and when Timothy Kinnit pulled it open suddenly, she fell in. Basil Toberman has been making a point of the incident. He's inordinately jealous of the young man.'

'Oh the tale isn't *true*,' said the irrepressible Mrs Broome airily. 'I was there and I saw what happened so there's no question about that. Mr Eustace hushed it up because she was a governess – not because of Mr Tim.'

'*Hushed it up?*'

'Played it down.' Mr Campion spoke with more firmness than one might have supposed possible in one normally so casual.

'All right,' Luke conceded but he was still interested. 'Why is he cagey about governesses?'

'Because they had one who did a murder.' Mrs Broome was enjoying herself. As soon as Luke noticed it he calmed considerably.

'A hundred and twenty years ago,' murmured Mr Campion testily. 'Miss Thyrza Caleb and her Chair of Death.'

'Oh?' The superintendent was delighted. 'It's the same Kinnit family, is it? We used to have a book of famous trials in the house when I was a kid, illustrated with dreadful old woodcuts. I remember Thyrza with her white face and streaming hair. There was something funny about that story. Wasn't there a postscript?'

'I never heard it,' said Campion. 'I missed the crime entirely. It was new on me when Toberman told me the other day.'

'Oh, no. It's famous in its way.' Luke was still searching his memory. 'She committed suicide, I think.' He shook his head as some of the details remained obstinately shadowy and turned a broadly smiling face to Mrs Broome. 'Well, anyway, you got it in and startled the poor copper,' he said. 'You're old Bean-spilling-Bertha herself, aren't you?'

Nanny Broome was not amused. As usual when the joke was against her she made every effort to get her own back.

'I've got nothing to hide,' she muttered, jerking up her chin. 'Not like some people!'

Luke's interest was captured despite his better judgement. 'Out with it,' he commanded. 'Who are you telling tales on now?'

'No one. I've got none to tell, but Miss Saxon had. Painting her face, dyeing her hair, listening at doors, and over sixty years old if she was a day! What sort of governess was she?'

'Better than no one,' said Luke, flatly. 'You can't catch me with that sort of stuff.'

'But she had a secret. She was always just about to tell it to me. She'd keep leading up to it and then being put off, or Mrs Telpher would call her.' Nanny Broome was labouring her points a little. There was a touch of desperation in her bid for drama. 'She told me herself, only the day before she died: "I'm under a great strain" she said.'

Mr Campion took it upon himself to see that no more harm was done.

'Miss Saxon was driving the car when the accident occurred that resulted in the tragic condition of the child who has been brought over here to hospital,' he said. 'It has been unconscious for two years.'

'Oh Lord!' Luke's sympathetic grimace was lost in Mrs Broome's amazed reception of the news.

'Oh, so that was it! Well! No wonder she wanted to share a feeling of guilt like that, and why she seemed more upset about the poor kiddiewiddie even than its own suffering mother.' She paused and added brightly, 'and why she dyed her hair.'

'Eh?' Luke's eyes were sparkling. 'Go on,' he said. 'I dare you.'

'Because she knew she was too old to have been driving the car, of course,' said Mrs Broome, gathering her gloves and purse. 'And now if you don't need me any longer, sir, I'll be getting back. There'll be some clearing up to do and Miss Julia is staying the night, so I want to pop a nice hot bottle in her bed. Just to comfort her. She's very young and no Mummie.'

Luke got up. 'Very well, be off,' he said. 'Thank you for your help. I don't suppose I shall have to call on you again.'

'Oh, I'm very glad.' Disappointment was evident in every line of her body and her lashes made half circles on her cheeks. 'I shouldn't like to have to give evidence in court.'

'God forbid that indeed!' said Luke, ducking his chin in to his neck. 'Run along, I'll send you a box of chocolates one day.'

She flashed a smile at him which was as gay and provocative as seventeen itself. 'I don't eat them,' she proclaimed, triumphantly. 'I'm slimming.'

The last they saw of her was her seat, wagging as happily as if it carried a tail, as she trotted off into the shadows.

Luke laughed softly. 'It's a crying shame one could never risk her in the witness box,' he observed. 'She's got all the answers. It must have been tremendous fun being brought up by a woman like that. You'd know all the important things about the whole sex before you were seven.'

Mr Campion put out his hand for the photographs and studied them curiously. They showed a bedraggled sprite of a woman with a slack mouth and huge vacant eyes, who yet managed to convey a hint of cunning. She was unusually dishevelled, he suspected, which was what had so shocked Mrs Broome.

'What about Agnes Leach's record?'

Luke shrugged. 'She's a type and she has the usual long silly history. Shoplifting, soliciting, minor fraud. Our welfare people suffer from her. They get her job after job and each time she reforms completely for a couple of weeks until something else catches her attention and – whoops! She's flat on her kisser again.'

'I suppose Mrs Broome did recognize these photographs?'

'I'd take my dying oath she did.' Luke spoke with the conviction of long experience. 'She recognized her in the cemetery and these confirmed it.'

Mr Campion passed them back. 'What was Agnes Leach doing there? Looking for an address?'

'I should think so. "Looking at the flowers on the grave" suggests hunting among them for florists' labels to me. Somehow or other – almost certainly from Miss Tray at the cobbler's shop – she heard that the young man who was making the awkward inquiries was due at the funeral of someone called Saxon, and that there was an advertisement about it in *The Times* newspaper. No address was given in the paper but the place of burial was mentioned so she went there.' He shook his dark head. 'In my experience it's almost impossible to underestimate anything which Agnes and her associates are likely to know for certain. They snap up bits of unrelated information and make a tale of them. They knew the name Stalkey, hence the destruction of the flat and the fire at the office, but apparently they didn't know the name Kinnit.

The chance of Agnes remembering it, if ever she heard it on her brief visit to the country, is remote. She is a simple defective. He, of course, is quite a different caper.'

'Ah,' said Mr Campion, blinking behind his spectacles. 'At last we come to the dark figure in the wood pile, the lighter of fires and smasher up of flats.'

'Slasher of mail bags and dresses in the cinema, burner of bus seats, and at least three knife attacks on girls who ought to have known better than to be out with him.' Luke spoke without venom. 'He's a problem child,' he added unnecessarily.

'Agnes's son?'

The superintendent leaned back, tipping his chair, and prepared to enjoy himself. 'She says not. To prove it he has a birth certificate and the marriage lines of his parents. An almost unheard-of possession in their vicinity! According to Agnes his name is Barry Cornish. Certainly his reputed father appears to have done what he could for him.'

'Stap me!' murmured Mr Campion, who permitted himself unlikely expletives when really shaken. 'So that's it.' He was silent for a moment considering the ramifications of the new position. 'Tell me,' he said at last, 'had Cornish any idea of the true story himself?'

'None at all. He accepted Barry meekly. It was only this morning that Miss Aicheson woke him to tell him a tale about Timothy's arrival at Angevin which was quite obviously the other half of one he had already heard from Agnes's friends about the other boy. Agnes never invents more than she needs, you see. That's the most dangerous thing about her.'

'Yes. It would be. How did Cornish take the discovery that he had been swindled, virtually blackmailed, all these years by some wretched woman who'd pinched his son's papers?'

'He didn't take it,' said Luke slowly. 'He's an honest chap and he realized that Barry was probably behind the violence, so he came to me acting on a moral compulsion. I've got the impression that he's tickled to death with Timothy, who seems to be very like him, but do you know I don't believe he'll ever attempt to own him to disown the other.'

Mr Campion sighed. 'Poor man,' he said. 'He sees his

great sacrifice rejected by the gods and so, no doubt, all the Misses Eumenides let loose again to plague him.'

Luke eyed his friend curiously.

'What a funny chap you are, Campion,' he said. 'I told him that he was clinging to a phoney cross. Also of course he's a perishing official. He can't bring himself to believe that there isn't something sacred about a certificate!'

'Let me get this absolutely straight for the sake of the record.' Mr Campion was diffident as usual. 'Your suggestion is that Agnes Leach left Timothy with Mrs Broome but retained his papers?'

'Only by accident.'

'Oh, I see. She left the mother's possessions in a station cloakroom?'

'Better. She parked the whole suitcase on an honest landlady who kept them until Agnes turned up again four years later. By that time Agnes had become baby-prone herself – after her chat with Mrs Broome perhaps! – and had achieved Barry who was then about three years old. I imagine she dressed him up in anything she could find in the other woman's bag and thought the certificates might fit him since nothing else did, if she called him four instead of three. He was backward, wasn't he? So he could pass for a bit worse. It wouldn't worry Agnes.' His eyes began to dance. 'Anyway I'll bet it was the dear good nuns who looked up the father for her in all innocence once she produced the marriage certificate and told the story of rescuing the baby from the bombs. Agnes has that kind of history.'

Mr Campion sighed. 'I believe all this,' he said sadly. 'What about Agnes and Barry now? Have they been pulled in?'

Luke glanced at his watch. 'I dropped the word to Munday, the D.D.I. at Ebbfield, who has probably got the boy by this time. His last known address was somewhere in Wandsworth. Sometimes it takes a few hours to locate a chap like that but there's never any difficulty in picking him up in the end.'

'I suppose not. You have some fingerprints from the arson business, haven't you?'

'Nothing very good. They were being treated in the lab when I left. I wanted to get an identification of Agnes from Mrs Broome off the record, just in case the woman proved to be involved in a criminal charge and so become unavailable for private questioning.' Luke was a little shamefaced about his own consideration and seemed to feel a need to excuse it. 'I never see any point in involving people who have a little front to keep up if it isn't necessary,' he went on. 'I didn't know Mrs Broome would be so convincing. She might have had to meet Agnes again before she could be sure. As it is, everything is plain sailing. You ought to be able to convince little Miss Julia's papa there's nothing worse than obstinate self-sacrifice in the lad's family, and the poor old Councillor can choose his own bed of nails. Aren't you satisfied?'

'No.' Campion was frowning. 'The thing that's worrying me Charles, is why didn't she follow her?'

'Why didn't Agnes follow Nanny Broome?'

'Exactly. The only explanation must be that she had already found the address of the Well House and the name Kinnit, presumably on one of the wreaths. She must also have recognized Mrs Broome. That meeting took place somewhere around early afternoon, leaving plenty of time for Agnes to telephone the news to anyone anywhere. She could have spoken to the cobbler's shop, for instance.'

Luke was listening doubtfully.

'She might,' he said. 'Barry has any intelligence there is between them. He's got a sharp mind in a warped sort of way. You feel he might attack the house because of Timothy?'

'No,' Mr Campion was gently obstinate. 'I think he might be bright enough to see how many beans make five. Surely the only person on earth who can testify that Timothy was the baby left at Angevin by Agnes Leach at the outbreak of war is Nanny Broome?'

Luke sat up. 'Corblimeah!' he said. 'And we've sent her home alone. Let me get on the telephone!'

Chapter Sixteen

Indictment

Once he was seated at the kitchen table with Alison and Miss Aicheson facing him, Mrs Telpher on his left and Eustace on his right, Tim and Julia in the background draped round the basket chair, Basil Toberman passed into a stage of ponderous arrogance.

With his face crimson and his full mouth glistening he achieved a dictator-like appearance, squat, myopic and preternaturally solemn. The Kinnit family were bearing with him in their own peculiar way and sat smiling at him with tolerant superiority, but the rest of the company was suffering.

'The bronze is unquestion – unquestion – unquestionably genuine,' he announced, adding unnecessarily, 'I have said it.'

'So we hear.' Miss Aicheson was almost as red as he was and had never appeared more masculine 'Don't you think, perhaps, all this could wait?'

'Silence!' Basil had apparently decided to treat them as a public meeting. 'I have just been half across Europe and have flown through the sky with one of the greatest experts the world has ever known. I speak of Leofric Paulfrey of the Museum.'

'Professor Paulfrey!' Eustace was delighted; his face lit up with pleasure. 'Oh splendid. Now that's an opinion which is really worth having. Does he say it's fourth century?'

'*I* say it's absolutely genuine.' Toberman was frowning with the effort of articulation. 'It is a fellow to the Boy Jockey of the Artimisian wreck; in better condition. I am prepared to guarantee that it's by the same man.'

'Are you though!' It was Eustace who spoke but both Alison and Geraldine Telpher looked up with exactly the same twinkling smile of good-tempered derision.

'Laugh! Go on, laugh!' Toberman's thick hand shot out in a gesture which would have been a little oversize in a Pagliaccio 'Laugh your heads off. You can do it today but it'll be for the last time, because I've heard the truth about you and I never keep my mouth shut, do I?'

'My dear fellow, if you've only got the truth about the Bronze it'll be enough for one evening!' Eustace turned the attack gracefully and shot an apologetic glance towards Julia. It was most discreetly done, but Toberman was in the state of over-awareness typical of certain toxic conditions and he pounced upon the girl, noticing her presence for the first time, apparently.

'This is fitting,' he declared with thick theatricality. 'This is Rich. This is Justice. Bride of the Wonderboy meets Family Skeleton.'

'I should hardly call yourself that, Toby.' Tim was juggling with the situation. 'What about a bit of beautiful shut-eye? Shall we go up to bed?'

'No. Certainly and absolutely not. I am not as canned as that.' Toberman began to laugh a little himself. 'I've got something to tell you, Timothy, and when I do you're going to know I'm right just as I knew old Paulfrey was right when he told me. The man was afraid of flying, Timothy. I saw it. I saw it in his eyes and because I was queasy myself, as I always am in the air, I suggested we behaved like reasonable men and drank ourselves out of it and that's how he came to tell me. Otherwise I don't suppose he'd have brought himself to talk to me at all. The man was afraid. He was funky. He sweated. I saw it. To save his face he had to babble out something and because my name reminded him of the Kinnits he babbled out this glorious story.'

'Which was that the Bronze was genuine,' said Mrs Telpher briskly.

'God!' Toberman regarded her with overdrawn contempt. 'You're a Kinnit and that's typical. That's the first, last and only thing you'd think of. Don't worry, Geraldine, you won't be left out. Professor Paulfrey was very interested to hear that you were staying with your relatives. He knew your late husband by repute, he said, and he knows the Van der Graffs very well indeed. He's been staying with them. But it was your governess he was interested in and so was I, my God, when he told me.' He lurched round to peer at the basket chair. 'Timothy? Do you know what was the really interesting thing about the original Kinnit governess?'

'Basil, you're becoming an abominable bore!' There was an unfamiliar edge to Eustace's voice which jarred warningly on every ear in the room except, apparently, Toberman's own.

He swayed a little but was still remarkably articulate.

'Don't you believe it you silly old Kinnit,' he declared. 'Pay attention my little man. I have news for you. The family secret is out. Miss Thyrza is vindicated. She wasn't guilty, Timothy. She didn't kill the boy friend. It was her pupil, the thwarted fifteen-year-old Miss Haidée Kinnit whose immature advances he'd rejected, who prepared the trap for him. She did the murder and planted the blame, with sweet Kinnitty cunning, squarely upon her more successful rival, the unimportant and defenceless governess. Moreover, there is a very strong supposition that the family knew.'

'Basil! Be quiet! Stop him somebody. Eustace, make him be quiet.' An unexpectedly passionate protest from Alison wiped away any possible doubt of the truth of the story.

Evidently the ancient tale was taken very seriously by the present-day Kinnits. Eustace was shaking with anger, every trace of his normal urbanity gone. Alison was on the verge of tears and for once even Geraldine Telpher seemed startled out of her natural calm. Her face was grey and rigid.

Toberman was enjoying himself.

'Now I can understand why old Terence Kinnit made such a business of hushing up the crime. Why he bought the Staffordshire moulds and moved house and all the rest of it,' he said happily. 'If his daughter was the murderess the whole thing hangs together and holds water. They'd driven the poor governess to suicide, you see, between them. I don't suppose that worried them. They'd done her a service by taking her in without references, hadn't they? So it was her duty to repay them with her life if necessary. That would be their attitude.'

'Will you hold your tongue, sir?' Eustace when angry was quietly formidable and some of it got through. Toberman began to complain.

'I don't see why you should victimize me,' he grumbled. 'It all came out in a book; Paulfrey told me so. At the turn of the century a book was published which blew the whole gaff. He told me its name. I've forgotten it but it'll come back. *Ten Trials of Yester Year* I think he said. Something corny like that. You'd know, Eustace.'

'Toberman, you're drunk! Oblige me by going to bed immediately.'

'Don't you dare to talk to me like that, old man. Your great grandfather did mine a favour but you haven't bought us body and soul! We're not lackeys!'

'Good Heavens, boy! What utter nonsense. You must be out of your mind. Pull yourself together.'

'I am perfectly sober and I am talking to Timothy. Professor Paulfrey told me that this book which he remembered well was written by a parson who had known Miss Haidée when she was an old woman. When she died she left him a letter confessing the whole thing. He didn't do anything about it but put it in a book when he was pretty ancient himself. He was a damn dull writer and nobody was very interested in Miss Thyrza at that time, but somebody bought up most of the copies of the only edition. I wonder who that was. Your father, Eustace?'

'That will do!'

'Anyway, no one appears to have read the book but a few kids, one of whom was Paulfrey, and the publication passed without comment in the press.' Basil leant back in his chair and began to laugh.

'There's no question that it's true, is there?' he jeered, addressing Miss Aicheson and the two young people. 'Look at them all. Kinnits we have loved. We're all in the same boat, you and me. We're all lame ducks taken in and enslaved by Kinnits because we were cheap. And we all hang about ready to take the buck when it's passed to us.'

Miss Aicheson put a large hand over Alison's slender wrist. 'I shall go up now, dear,' she murmured. 'I can't stand much more of this.'

At the same moment Eustace turned to Tim. The old man was very white and there was a helplessness about him which was embarrassing. 'It's not true,' he said but without conviction.

'Of course it isn't!' Tim's response, which was furious, swept the accusation into perspective. 'It's half true, like all Basil's lies. He's a silly inferior ass and he's tight as a tick. Come on, Basil. Come to bed, you ape. No more damn nonsense. Up you get. Come along.'

He left the arm of the basket chair which creaked protestingly, strode across the room and picked up Toberman in a fireman's lift. The green strength of his body emerged as an unexpected deliverer and Toberman made no attempt to resist. They caught a glimpse of his puffy face and round stupid eyes, solemn and owlish with his head hanging upside-down, as he was borne away through the doorway.

The abrupt departure left a tingling silence behind it. Miss Aicheson settled down again but did not release Alison's arm. 'I shall wait for a moment or two until he's got him settled,' she murmured.

'Very sensible, Aich.' Eustace smiled at her vaguely and taking out his handkerchief passed it over his forehead.

'What a silly fellow,' he said. 'How tiring. An asinine line to take.' He glanced towards his sister who was looking down at her plate, her delicate face pale and expressionless. Opposite him Geraldine Telpher was in much the same mood. She had withdrawn into herself and appeared preoccupied. The light was unkind to her. Beyond her he suddenly saw Julia sitting quiet in the basket chair, and a frown flickered over his face.

'My dear child,' he said. 'I'd quite forgotten you were here. I'm so sorry you should have had to listen to all this unpleasant nonsense. Tim will be down in a moment and he shall take you home.'

Julia was young enough to blush scarlet. 'I'm staying, I think.'

'Really?' Eustace was the last person to be impolite but he was irritated and surprised. 'Alison? I thought we promised – I mean I thought that there was an understanding with Julia's father that the youngsters shouldn't meet just now?'

Alison lifted her head and looked at him blankly. She had been roused out of deep thought and took some time to surface. 'Perhaps there was,' she said vaguely. 'Don't fuss, Eustace.' She turned to Julia. 'Do you know where your room is?'

'No. I'm afraid I don't.' Julia was uncomfortable and the situation was saved by the unexpected appearance of Nanny Broome, pink and pleased with herself and still wrapped in her purple coat. She came dancing in, smiling at them all and talking as usual.

'I just got in the door when the phone went,' she announced, addressing them collectively. 'It was my nice policeman asking if I'd got home safely! I think he felt a little bit guilty that he hadn't minded his manners and sent someone with me if he couldn't bring me himself. Oh, they're terribly busy those two. Talking nineteen to the dozen when I left. Well now, have you all had some nice supper? Where's Mr Timmy?' She was stripping off her thin leather gloves as she spoke and paused to pull them out and straighten them before she stowed them away carefully in the side compartment of her good handbag.

Eustace scowled at her.

'Miss Alison tells me that Miss Laurell is proposing to stay here tonight . . . ?' he was beginning when Mrs Broome sailed in to the rescue like a hen defending her chick.

'Miss Julia's been asked to stay here sir,' she said firmly. 'Her father's away and it's a big house right across London, so Miss Alison and I put our heads together – didn't we madam?' The interpolation was a warning. 'And we decided the best thing for her to do was to have the little room beyond Miss Aicheson's. It's all aired and ready and I'll just slip a bottle in the bed and she won't know she isn't at home.'

'But I thought we'd promised Anthony Laurell – '

'I'm sure I don't know about that,' Mrs Broome interrupted him shamelessly. 'All I know is that if Sir Anthony is a proper father, as I'm sure he is or he wouldn't be fussing so, he couldn't care for his daughter to go home through a neighbourhood like this at night. I'm an old woman and I'm nothing to look at – ' she seemed a little hurt to hear no cries of protest and her tone became a trifle sharper – 'but even I had quite a little run for it outside here tonight. There are a lot of dark shadows and people coming out of dark corners where there aren't any lamp-posts and pushing against one and whispering things.'

'What things? You silly woman, what are you talking about?' Eustace was testy and exasperated. 'You do talk a lot of rubbish!'

'Ah, but I make you all very comfortable. There's a nip in the air tonight. What about a nice hot toddy?'

'No. We've had quite enough alcohol in this room this evening.'

'Really? I thought I smelled it. Mister Basil I suppose?' She was uncovering the situation with the speed of light. 'Mr Tim's putting him to bed, no doubt? It's very bad for him, all this drinking. He'll go just like his father, *bang*, one day. Well, we'll all have some nice malted milk. Would you like that, madam?' She addressed Alison, who shook her head without speaking, but Geraldine Telpher looked up.

'I would like a Scotch and soda,' she said. 'May I get myself one out of the dining-room as I go up, Eustace?'

'My dear girl, I'll come and see to it. I'm so sorry. You're so much one of us that I forget you don't know all about our little difficulties. You must have found Basil very upsetting.' Eustace was still flustered and Mrs Telpher waved him back into his seat.

'I'm sure I can manage,' she said with her faintly commiserating smile. 'He didn't worry me at all. In my life my trials have been rather more specific and he isn't my affair. Poor man, if it's inherited we should be sorry for him I suppose. Good night, everybody.'

'Good night, Geraldine.' Eustace waited until the door had closed and the murmured blessings ended before he turned on Mrs Broome.

'You really mustn't say things like that,' he began testily. 'Poor old Ben Toberman may have enjoyed his glass at the end of his days but in his time he was a most intelligent, sensitive, perhaps over-sensitive person.'

Mrs Broome behaved as she always did when reproved by authority. Her eyes opened very wide and she looked a picture of amazed innocence.

'I didn't know. I always undertsood he drank like a fishie,' she said earnestly. 'Delirium tremens and everything and everybody talking. Of course I didn't know him at all well. You didn't like him coming down to the country, did you?'

Alison roused herself. 'That'll do, Mrs Broome. Take Miss Laurell up to her room please. We'll make your excuses to Tim when he comes down, Julia. He may be rather a long time. It's sometimes very hard to get Basil to settle. He's one of those excitable alcoholics. He just won't lie down and go to sleep. Such a bore and so tiring. I'm so sorry this should have happened, my dear.'

It was the most ruthless dismissal a guest could have received. Miss Aicheson tried to soften it with a smile which would not quite come and Eustace held out both his hands in a gesture which was more like an appeal for help than a reassurance of goodwill.

Nanny Broome slipped an arm round Julia's waist and drew her firmly and swiftly out of the doorway so that she was still saying 'good night' as the wood closed behind them.

'Mr Basil always gets them in a state when he does this.' Mrs Broome made the confidence as they walked up the broad stairs together to the hall. 'He's so rude and open and that's the thing they can't put up with. They're very civilized sort of people, very covered up.'

It was not the easiest statement on which to comment and

Julia did not try. Her own brand of politeness was of the rare long-suffering kind which is at least one parent of serenity. Instead she said simply, 'I don't think I shall want a hot-water bottle. It's very good of you to think of it but I never have one at home.'

'Very well, you can kick it out but you won't go to bed yet, surely?' Nanny Broome paused at the foot of the main flight to look at her in astonishment. 'Poor Mr Tim hasn't had a chance to see you at all. What with Mrs Telpher and the ladies he can't have had you to himself for a second, poor boy.'

Julia laughed. 'What had you in mind?' she inquired.

'Eh? Oh, don't you worry about the oldsters.' Mrs Broome clearly considered herself an evergreen. 'We all have to jolly them along because when they get excited they get tired, and when they get tired they feel poorly and that makes them cross. So I tell you what we'll do.' She broke off abruptly and stood aside to permit Mrs Telpher, who had emerged from the dining-room, to pass them. She was carrying a glass and smiled at them before she went her placid way up the stairs.

'I shall get you some milky-drink,' said Nanny Broome loudly to her protégé, adding more softly, 'you sip it in your room and brush your hair, and then when they've all gone to bed, which won't be very long, you and Mr Tim can have half an hour in the kitchen in the warm.'

'If you think it's all right,' Julia was beginning, but Mrs Broome was not listening to her. She was looking up the stair-case, a thoughtful expression upon her face.

'That was a very dark whisky, wasn't it?' she said. 'Did you see it? I suppose it couldn't have been neat? It was over half a tumblerful. I wonder now?' She shook her head and answered her own question. 'No, I don't think so. I should have said she's too much one of *them* to do anything like that. Perhaps she doesn't pour it out herself as a rule and has just overdone it. Yet of course you never can tell. Well, come along miss. I'll lead the way, shall I?'

For the first time she turned her back on the guest and put out her hand to take the baluster rail. The folds of the good purple coat rearranged themselves and the girl stared at them and put out her hand to touch.

'You've torn your coat.'

'I can't have done, it's perfectly new. Where is it?' She turned her head to look over her shoulder and swept her skirts round her, craning her neck to find the damage.

'It's not like that.' Julia sounded frightened. 'Look. Take it off.'

She lifted the soft woollen garment off Mrs Broome's shoulders and swung it round to face her. The featherweight velour which looked brown in the subdued artificial light had been scored like the crackling on a joint of roast pork. Five two-inch-wide slashes had been made from between the shoulderblades to the hips and the cloth hung like ribbons, showing the silk lining beneath.

Nanny Broome stared at the damage and for once in her life words deserted her. Her face, which was never in repose in the ordinary way, was frozen into a weatherbeaten mask on which her discreet powdering stood out distinctly. The silence in the house was noticeable and the warm family atmosphere had chilled.

'You said someone pushed against you as you came home. Is that where you felt it? On the back, here?' Julia was wide-eyed but still very practical. 'You said someone whispered? What was it? Did you hear?'

'Not really. I thought it was a swear word so I didn't listen. It was a sort of hiss, that's all. Oh miss! This'll upset everybody. We shan't get them to sleep tonight.'

'All the same, we ought to tell the police.'

'Not tonight. I wouldn't go out there again for a fortune. And I wouldn't like anyone else to. My poor best coat! I bought it in Ipswich, I don't know what Mr Broome's going to say.'

Julia was persistent. 'There's no need to go out to the police station. We'll telephone.'

'Not tonight.' There was an unfamiliar undertone in Mrs Broome's voice which Julia recognized. The woman was deeply frightened and not particularly by the physical attack.

She had perceived that the true danger came from something more serious still, an unclean shadow falling across her bright nursery world.

'I'll telephone tomorrow when it's light,' she said earnestly. 'Tonight we'll just say our prayers and go to sleep. If we get hold of the police now they'll only come round thumping about and upsetting the whole house, which is edgy enough as it is with Mr Basil drunk. He's still saying awful things about Mr Tim, I expect.' She glanced round the dark raftered hall and lowered her voice in confidence. 'Tim really didn't touch Miss Saxon, you know, miss. I was there. She died of a sort of fit. I saw her afterwards and I thought "You look as if you've suffocated, you poor old girlie." The blood rushed to her head and smothered her. That's what I'm always frightened of with Mr Eustace. He looked terrible tonight, I thought. Mr Basil ought to be muzzled.'

'I could ring Mr Campion.'

'Do it tomorrow. He'd only tell my nice Superintendent and *he'd* have the place upside down. I know his sort. No one better when you feel like it, but very tiring when you want to go to bed. Oh, my goodness! Now what?'

They both started violently as a commotion occurred suddenly at the top of the stairs.

Basil Toberman, bare-footed and in pyjamas, had appeared on the landing with Tim, looking grey and furious, behind him.

'I am going to get myself a snifter. Go away, Wonderboy. I want a drink. Don't I make myself plain?' Below the bogus authority there was the thin high note of delirium which rings a danger signal in every human ear. Tim seized him and began to heave him back to his room.

'You're not going to drink any more tonight.' His voice, breathless with exertion and lowered in an attempt not to disturb the house, floated down to them in the warm air. 'Oh, for holy Moses' sake, man, come back to your bed like a good little bloke. You'll start seeing things if you don't look out. Have a heart, Basil. You're driving me round the bend.'

Another scuffle followed and then a door slammed. Mrs Broome sighed.

'Poor Mr Tim! It is a shame just when he particularly wants to get him quiet so that he can come down to talk to you. Mr Basil is bad tonight. Just like his papa whatever Mr Eustace says. He couldn't have meant all that, you know. He just likes to hear himself saying generous things. That's all that is.'

'How long will it take Tim to get the man to sleep?'

'Oh, until Mr Basil's exhausted, I'm afraid.' Mrs Broome made the pronouncement casually. 'He's had a very long day so he may drop off presently, but I have known him play up for a couple of hours wearing everybody clean out. It's a very long-suffering family you're marrying into, miss.'

'Why on earth do they put up with him?'

Mrs Broome laughed. 'Oh, it's not only with him, my dear. They put up with the most extraordinary people. They gather them. It's only because they like to be tolerant. I never heard that the older generations were like it but the way Eustace and Miss Alison go on you'd think they were trying to work off some sort of sin they'd committed.'

The thought flitted out of her head and she gave the little self-consicous wriggle which was so characteristic of her.

'Now I'm not like that at all,' she said happily. 'If I love somebody I'll forgive them, but if I don't I certainly won't. If you put up with people who are awful and you don't even love them then you're encouraging awfulness and nothing more. Well, I mean to say, aren't you? Never mind. Come along and I'll tell you all about my Mr Luke. He was ever so interested in Mr Tim and it will be nicer thinking of that than crying out over my poor mauve coatie.'

Chapter Seventeen

The Boy in the Corner

The kitchen smelled warm and airless and the only light came from the small glowing rope across the bright shield of the electric heater which Mrs Broome had put in the mock fireplace to make it look 'like home' for the sweethearts.

The door into the house opened cautiously and Tim put his head in. 'Julia?'

'I'm here in the chair.' They were both whispering and he came round the table, feeling his way cautiously.

'Is he quiet now?' she murmured as he bent over the chair.

'I think so. He keeps dropping off, snoring like a donkey-engine and waking himself up again. Then he thinks he'll go and find a short one for his dry throat! However, forget him. I think he's about had it tonight. Where are you? Oh my God, my darling, where are you?'

'Here. Come on, there's plenty of room.'

He scrambled into the protesting basket, wriggling his shoulder under her and pulling her head into the hollow of his neck.

'Damn this chair! What a thing to make love in! How like Nan to expect us to.' Julia was laughing, shaking the noisy contraption, and he joined her.

'She's keeping the party light,' she gasped.

He began to titter. 'We might as well try to go to bed in an accordion! Don't laugh, don't laugh. "It'll end in tears." I want to kiss you. I want to kiss you. Where's your mouth, woman?'

Julia stiffened. 'Listen.'

The boy craned his neck and they held their breath.

All round them the house creaked and breathed but was an oasis of partial quiet amid the vast city's endless noise. Yet the only recognizable sounds which came in to them were far-off ones, tugs hooting on the river, the rumble of hidden trains.

'I'm sorry,' Julia whispered. 'I thought I heard him on the stairs.'

'He wouldn't come down here. If he is up again he's streaked off to the dining-room tantalus, in which case there'll be an almighty crash in a minute as he falls flat on his face. He only needs another shot to put him out cold. He's got me down this time. Put him out of your mind.' Timothy settled himself again but the moment had passed, and although he was holding her possessively, rubbing his lips against her ear, she could feel that his thought had wandered from her. She controlled the thrill of panic but it was not easy and she shivered.

'What's the matter now?'

'Nothing. It was only a sort of feeling. Don't you get them? You feel you're waiting, watching for the exact moment when something new is about to begin.'

'Here?'

'No, I wasn't thinking about us for once.' Her cheek was hot on his own. 'I didn't mean an act so much as a turn in the road. You feel that one curl of the pattern is nearly finished and another is just about to spring out of it, and all the people involved are converging to the right spot whether they like it or not. Don't you know what I mean?'

'No,' he said honestly. 'No I don't dig that sort of thing myself but I don't mind you doing it. In fact I rather like it. I'm a bit shaken tonight, though. All that stuff of Basil's in here just now. That was new, you know.'

'About Miss Thyrza? I wondered.'

He moved restlessly. 'It was true, you see.' The whispering seemed to lend importance to the confidence. 'We all recognized it as soon as he said it. Did you notice? It was like suddenly seeing something awful and unmistakable, like blood on the road. The penny simply dropped. Everything one had ever heard or noticed fitted in. I remembered at once, for instance, that there was some mystery long ago about a book being suppressed. A master at school referred to it with an odd inflection in his voice but I never heard the story and it had remained a mystery all my life.'

'But does it matter? Miss Thyrza died well over a hundred years ago.'

'Oh, we shan't have the police in because of Basil's discovery! Now it's you being obtuse, my little muggins. It's rather worse than that, in my opinion, because one spots the basic living sin which the original crime exposed. The Kinnit family *is* what Basil said it was. They do tend to capitalize their charitable acts since they do them for the wrong purpose. They don't keep helping folk for the warm silly reason that they like the people concerned, but for the cold practical one that they hope to see themselves as nice people doing kind things. Alison and Eustace are particularly unfortunate. They know all about this and don't like themselves very much because of it. Basil hurt them horribly. They know they're missing something by being so cold but they don't know what it is. The rest of us recognized that suddenly. Blast Basil.'

'But Eustace is fond of you. Really fond.'

'He is, isn't he?' It was an eager whisper. 'I was thinking that. He's a cold old fish but there is a warmish patch there.' He turned his head and kissed her ear. 'Thank God for you, Lovely. This has been a night of revelation for me. I should have hated it alone.'

'I don't think it's over yet,' she said, creeping yet closer to him. 'Anyone who is loved as much as Eustace is by you must be thawed a bit.' She heard her own jealousy and hurried to disarm it. 'If you're responsible for the thawing you mustn't ever stop. You know that, don't you?'

'Yes,' he said. 'I know that.' She could feel his heart beating under her cheek and her thought followed his own.

'You owe *her* a lot.'

'Nan? Twice as much as everything! She's balmy. She goes through the world like an old butterfly clinging to its wings in a bombardment. They're all she's got so you can't blame her. I say, did you see her coat? She showed it to me just now up on the landing.'

'I noticed it first. It's terrifying. I didn't realize this district was as tough as that. She wouldn't let me telephone the police.'

'I know. She told me. She was still playing the whole thing down just now upstairs on the landing. That means she takes it very seriously indeed. If Nan thinks something is merely naughty she points to it and screams the place down, but once she perceives what she feels is Evil, she hides. She's a type and they drive some people round the bend, but I remember as a kid thinking that God must be fond of her because she took such inordinate delight in "His Minor Works".'

'She's very taken with Superintendent Luke just now.'

'So I gathered. How does he come into the picture? Does that mean underground assistance from your influential Papa?'

'No. I'm afraid that was me. I told Councillor Cornish that if he had any idea who had started the Stalkey fire he ought to tell Mr Luke and I think he may have done so, but from what Mrs Broome reports of her interview they don't seem to have talked entirely about the fire. Tim? I've been thinking about Councillor Cornish.'

'So have I, sweetie. That's my true old man, isn't it?'

'Do you think so?' She turned her head quickly, her voice sibilant in the darkness. 'I'm sure you belong to the same family.'

'I think it's a bit more than that. So does he.'

They were silent for a while, lying close in the chair, their heads together and their breath mingling.

'When did you decide about this?'

'I didn't decide at all. It's been sort of seeping into certainty all day. The cobbler was the first person to put the thought into my head. As soon as he heard that I had been evacuated from Ebbfield as a baby he became vehement that I should go to see Cornish. He didn't commit himself but he was extraordinarily insistent. "Let Cornish have a look at yer," he kept saying. "Go and let him 'ave a look!"' He hesitated. 'The likeness really is phenomenal, I suppose? I saw Aich eyeing us very oddly this morning.'

'It's pretty strong. It lies in movements and personal tricks of behaviour as much as in anything else. When you're nervous you clutch your ear in the way he does.'

He caught his breath. 'Do you know I noticed that! He did it when I first saw him and it made me furious. This is horribly dangerous emotional ground, I feel, don't you? I don't like it very much.'

'Are you going to mind if it does turn out to be him?'

'No, I don't think so.' Here in the dark their intimate communion had the quality of complete honesty. 'I'll be rather relieved, I think. I mean I *am* rather relieved. He's the sort of person I know best, anyway. He's an intellectual trying to be practical. He could easily have been a don or a boffin if his training had turned that way. As it is, a lot of that drive of his is being spent on being indignant. I feel I know him frightfully well which is what I resent about him.'

'You're anoyed that you are like him?'

'No. Of course not. I'm very grateful. I do want to belong to someone's line.'

'Why?'

'I told you. When at last I realized that I really was not a Kinnit I felt utterly lost. I felt I didn't know what was coming next and that when it did I might be entirely unable to cope. It wasn't ordinary windiness at all but something subterranean.'

'But you had *me*.'

'Bless you! Of course I had and thank God for it, but this wasn't loneliness. You can see what I mean if you think of this latest business of Eustace and Alison and poor Miss Thyrza. That story has taken over a hundred years already and they aren't at the end of it yet. Our days appear to be "longer in the land" than we are – that's about the essence of it.' He was silent for a time. 'I don't know how *he's* going to react,' he said at last. 'He has a new wife who is not my Mum. It may be that.'

'Which makes him so determined that it shan't be true?'

'Hell! Why did you say that?'

'I don't know. I just thought that he did have some reason.'

But I don't think it's a low one. It's something he feels rather tragic about.'

'What an extraordinary thing to say! How do you know?'

'Because you sometimes have very strong reasons for not doing something you want to do very much, and when you have you feel tragic about them, and when that happens you look and act as he did today.'

'Poppycock! Sorry darling, but that's nonsense. I never feel tragic. Shut up. You're talking rubbish.'

'My arm has gone to sleep.'

'Oh, my dear, I'm sorry! Is that better? Darling? Julia? What's the matter?'

She had become rigid at his side and he caught her alarm and copied her so that there was no sound at all save the thumping of their hearts.

'A light.' She formed the words with her lips and breathed so softly that they came to him like ghosts.

'On the stairs?'

'No. The other way. Look.'

'What?' It was a moment of superstitious alarm for there was no through way on that side, only the narrow passage and the cellar where the well was.

Julia was holding Timothy, restraining him, her eyes held by the shadows which were black round the inner door. As they waited, their bodies stiff, their necks craned, a clear thin angle of light, wide under the door and narrow as it slid past the ill-fitting jamb, stabbed across the floor, wavered, and vanished.

'It's a bobby who's found the broken window and is shining his torch in,' he said softly. 'I'll go and have a word with him or he may come round to the front and ring. You wait here.'

'No: the light was too near for that. The torch was just outside the door.'

'Impossible. Stay there.'

He stepped softly across the room, opened the inner door a few inches, and stood looking in. Now that the shaft of light was wider it appeared less strong but it still fluctuated, weaving backwards and forwards. There was still no sound whatever.

Timothy remained motionless and after a while an odd quality in his stillness conjured sudden panic in Julia.

She rose to her feet very quietly but the chair creaked and a whisper which was so strained that she hardly recognized it came back to her across the dark. 'Keep still.'

Timothy was too late. She had come up beside him and together they stood staring down the short passage to the open cellar door.

Something black and sinuous was moving above a torch beam directed downwards on the stone with the iron ring in it which marked the well. The figure itself was rooted to a single spot but the pool of light ran round the crevice busily, probing, darting, resting, moving again, while, thrown by the diffused upward glow, a writhing shadow reared across the white wall and ceiling.

As an unexpected confrontation it was shocking because the mind registered it as an impossibility, something appearing in an empty room without an entrance. Julia's little gulp deep in her throat jerked Timothy out of his frozen astonishment. The light switches for the passage and the Well cellar were on the wall just outside the door and he brushed his hand over them.

The cellar was lit by a single swinging bulb which gave a hard yellow light and now the full scene sprang into sight.

There was a harsh slither of rubber on the gritty stone and a soft high whimpering noise, very thin and brief, as the figure scurried back under the high window through which he must have entered. He stood there facing them, still swinging on his strangely rooted feet. Even in full light he was horrific, and that despite his own terror which came across to them like an odour. He was tall and phenomenally slender but bent now like a foetus, seated in the air, knees and one forearm raised very slightly and the whole of him swaying as if he were threaded on wires. He was dressed in black from head to foot in jacket and jeans so tight that they did not permit a wrinkle, let alone a fold, and also – an item which gave him a deliberate element of nightmare – his head and face were covered with a tight black nylon stocking which flattened his features out of human likeness without hiding them altogether. The other factor which was dismaying was that even at a distance he appeared deeply and evenly dirty, his entire surface covered with that dull iridescence which old black cloth lying about in city gutters alone appears to achieve.

Timothy recovered himself first and reacted in the only way left to this century's youth, which has had its fill of terrors. He proceeded to laugh it off. He pointed to the well-head with an expressive gesture, rather as if he did not expect the newcomer to understand words.

'Are you going down or coming up?'

The figure giggled. It was a little snuffling sound, very soft and ingratiating. Also he relaxed and straightened so that the horrible bent quality induced by his sudden alarm was almost lost. He remained on wires however, still rooted to the single spot under the window, still swinging.

'Do you know what's down there? Have you ever had it open?'

It was a soft, lisping voice, very quiet indeed and by no means ill-educated but muffled by the nylon mask. Neither Julia nor Timothy spoke and their silence appeared to worry him. His black stocking mask was open at the top and now he pulled it down, using his left hand. His right was either useless or hidden behind him.

The face which emerged was not reassuring. It was blunt and grey, the nose springing thick and flat from high on the frontal bone of the forehead, whilst his eyes were narrow slits of dark in a tight bandage of tissue. He was not a mongol but there was deficiency of a sort there, and it was not made more pretty by a latter-day hair cut which involved eccentrically long elf-locks and oiled black curls.

Experimentally, his right hand still behind him, he edged forward until he reached the well-stone again and presently he touched it with a long shoe; it appeared to fascinate him.

'There could be thousands of pounds down there. Treasure and stuff like that.' The soft little voice was still off-hand.

He was boasting, but in an uncertain way which made the statement half a question.

'What makes you think that?' Tim spoke cautiously, aware of Julia behind him. He could feel her shaking and guessed that the narrowness of the bars across the window above the intruder was causing most of her horror. The fact that the visitor must have squeezed between them was obtrusive and unnerving since it underlined his reptilian quality, which was deliberately accentuated anyway, to a degree which was unbearable.

'It's old, you see?' The lisping, toothsucking accent was very slight but the arrogance was there. 'The house is called after it. I mean to say, that's the ad-dress, isn't it? The Well House. That means it's old, and old wells in the City have been used for more things than water and not only for what you'd think. There's been plagues, you know, and people have been put down quickly with no time to go over them properly. Everything rots but metal. I see you don't read, yourself.'

Elementary academic snobbery was the last thing his listeners expected and it almost touched off hysteria.

'Do you?' Tim asked. He had not smiled but the newcomer took offence. His sensitivity was psychopathetically acute and was almost telepathy.

'Do you mind?' he inquired, rearing backwards but without moving his feet. 'I do as a matter of fact and I've had access to some very remarkable books. You'd be surprised what you can find out in a library. If you've got all the time in the world.' There was no mistaking his meaning or his pride in it and again they were silent and out of their depth. He looked them over consideringly.

'You two work here I suppose, waiting on them upstairs. I should have thought in a house like this they'd make you wear uniforms but that's old-fashioned, isn't it? "Au pair", that's what you are now. That's what they call you. Well, shut up and you won't come to any harm I think. I want to see Basil and I want to see him alone.'

'Who?'

225

'Basil. You know who I mean. I know he's here. I saw him come in. He's drunk but that won't matter. He'll understand what I've got to say to him if he's paralysed. The girl can slip me up to his room and I shan't touch either of you two. Basil Kinnit. That's who I want.'

'But there's no such person!' The words escaped Julia for the second time that day and the superstitious element surrounding them flared suddenly in her mind, and she put her hand over her mouth because she was afraid of screaming.

Her alarm seemed to reach the newcomer physically as if he had heard or smelled it, for he retreated a yard or so and stood swaying again, not quite weaving but horribly near it. He was also angry.

'You're lying, you're in love with him, you're hiding him.'

He was spitting and whispering and the short syllables were like grit in the fluff of sound.

'Nonsense.' Tim took over. He was puzzled, curious rather than frightened, and his tone was soothing. 'Who is it exactly that you want? Let's get it quite clear. There is no Basil Kinnit. Are you sure you have the name right?'

'Well, yes. As a matter of fact I am.' The newcomer relaxed again and the confidential lisp, soft and ingratiating, returned to his voice. 'I've known his name was Kinnit for a long time, see? But I only got the Basil today. I had to wait for a telephone call.' He conveyed that he considered the use of the instrument to be important and romantic. 'I put a friend of mine on to find out and she telephoned from outside the cemetery and left a message for me at a shop we use for that sort of thing. "His name is Mr Basil and the address is The Well House." That was the message I got. When I heard that, well, I mean to say it was waiting for me, wasn't it? There was no point in me messing about any longer. So I came round right away.'

'But you must have been here some time. When did you take the glass out of the window?'

He seemed to have no objection to answering questions. His answers were glib and at least partially truthful.

'This afternoon. I've been round here all the time. There's

a lot of perching places round here, see. It's made for it and you don't see a bogie. I smoked twenty sitting in a ventilator next door.' Twenty. It was a boast. 'Twenty in an afternoon.'

'Why did you wait so long?'

'I always wait. I like to look round. I like to know who comes in and out. It's my business. I'm interested, see? Mr Basil Kinnit, that's who I want to talk to.'

'What do you want to say to him?'

'I want to warn him to lay off me. I want to teach him not to interfere, see? I don't like private dicks making inquiries into my birth, see? I'm not having no prying, see? And nor is Ag. I've given his bloodhounds a warning and now I'm going to warn him. And you two can keep your mouths shut or you'll learn the same song. . . . Words *and* music.' The final phrase had no meaning but was a threatening series of sounds only, and he repeated them with satisfaction. 'Words *and* music!'

'Why should he want to know about your birth?' Tim's quiet question was yet so forceful that it captured his wayward intelligence and held it on course.

'Because he wants to stop Ag getting the money, see? My Dad slips her a bit, see? As soon as Ag heard about this Kinnit lark it came to her what it was about, see? Ag's not a great intelligence. She's got no mind. She's not with it, really, but she's bright enough over money. She knew what he was after and so she came to me and told me and of course I took it up. Tonight will put a stop to his mucking about round us.'

'Is Ag your mother?'

'No, she's not. She's not. She's not. She never said so and she isn't. She's a friend; she's interested. She does what I say. Like today. She went to the graveyard, see? I told her she'd find the address on a wreath when we couldn't find it in the paper but she went right away. Then she used the telephone.'

'All right. I understand.'

'You don't. You don't understand. You've got no idea. I'm not ordinary, see? Ag rescued me when I was born. I wasn't born normally, see? A lot of famous people aren't as a matter of fact, if you read history and all that. I wasn't quite in the world when a bomb hit the hospital I was in. On the first day of war this was, and my Mum was killed and Ag rushed in and picked me up like a kitten and carried me off all bloody to the rescue buses. Then she had to look after me, she was months going round the camps, until she found my papers and the nuns took over for her and found my Dad.'

'But there were no bombs on the first day of the war. There were no bombs for a year.' Julia made the protest and got the full repercussion.

'That's a lie!'

It was an objection which he appeared to have heard before.

'People say anything but they're wrong and I'm here to prove it anyway, aren't I? I'm not ordinary. I've got certificates. I'm legal. I've got rights. My Dad and Mum were legally married. In a mucking church. It was a white wedding. Five hundred guests, I believe. Fancy spending all that on a do. It's amazing!'

'What is your name?' Tim was trying to distract his attention from Julia.

'You've got a nerve! What's my name? I'm not sure I shan't pay you for that. That's cheek, that is. That's what they call it in the posh schools. Cheek. What's my name. Do me a favour! You must think I'm bonkers.'

'Is it Cornish?' Julia spoke as Timothy thrust her behind him.

He was just in time. The figure made a dart at her and for the first time brought out his right hand. The sight of it sent them both back on their heels and their reaction satisfied him. He paused to enjoy the sensation he was making. Up to the elbow his arm was a paw furnished with mighty bloodstained talons, a fantastic and improbable horror familiar to connoisseurs of certain comic strips and films.

Its realism as far as construction and fit were concerned was quite remarkable and as convincing as moulded and painted rubber, inset with a certain amount of genuine monkey fur, could make it. Only the distinctive convention in which the original designer had worked lent it a merciful artificiality.

Timothy began to laugh. 'We had some of those last term,' he said. 'Did you get it from the joke shop in Tugwell Street?'

The newcomer forgot his anger and smirked himself. He sat back in the air again, but intentionally this time, and let his forearms swing upwards from the elbows, his hands flapping.

'Child of the Fall-out,' he said and laughed.

The offbeat joke which to any other generation must be indescribably shocking amused them all, albeit a little guiltily, but it was very shortlived. Flushed with his triumph over them, he turned his right hand in its ridiculous glove palm uppermost. The five razor-blades appearing through the rubber caught the hard light.

Tim leapt straight for him, caught his upper arm and jerked it backwards. It was a purely instinctive movement so prompt and thorough that it came as a complete surprise. The stranger's reaction, which was equally spontaneous, almost over-balanced them both. He began to scream in a terrifying, hoarse, but not very loud voice and every joint in his body sagged limply to the ground, so that Tim was left holding his full weight. He let him drop and put his foot on his shoulder while he stripped off the glove. The razor-blades were stitched into a webbing bandage inside it and its removal was a major operation with the quivering, yelping creature writhing round his feet on the stones. When he stopped screaming he began to swear and the stream of filth, in the soft lisping voice, had a quality of nastiness which was out of their experience. Tim turned a furious face on Julia.

'Take these damn things out of the way and put them somewhere safe. Don't cut yourself, for God's sake. You'll get tetanus, they're dirty enough.'

She obeyed him silently, taking both glove and bandage, and disappeared into the dark kitchen.

Left to himself Tim stood back and wiped his hands.

'Shut up and get up,' he said.

The speed with which the creature on the floor leapt to the window high in the wall was as sudden as Tim's own leap at his arm had been, and had the same instinctive precision.

Only the bars prevented him from getting away. Their close spacing, which had required a certain amount of negotiation even from one so slender, effectively prevented him from bolting through and he fell back and lay against the wall, hanging limply, a black streak against the grey.

'Get down and turn round.'

The newcomer obeyed. His subservience was more distasteful than his arrogance. He shuffled into a corner and stood in it, letting it support him. His dirty hands hung limp in front of him. His face was wet with sweat and blubber and he smelled like a sewer.

'What is your name?'

'Barry Leach, sixty-three Cremorne Street, The Viaduct, E.'

He gave the information in a stream, clearly the result of long experience, and then paused. A new idea passed over his face as visibly as if he were an infant. 'That's the name I arrange with Ag to give. It's her name. She's Mrs Leach. We don't give my Dad's name until we have to. It's part of Ag's arrangement, see? We keep him quiet and he pays up. It's Ag's address too. I live with her when I live anywhere, but you know my real name that's on my papers so it's no use hiding it from you. Ag's got my papers. She doesn't show them but she's got them and I read them when I feel like it.'

'Do you ever see your father?'

Timothy was concentrating and much of the youthfulness had left his face so that he looked tired and absorbed. He made a good looking but worried young man, very much a product of the age. 'Does he talk to you?'

'Sometimes.'

'How often?'

'Not as often as he wants. Can't take him, see?'

'Why's that?'

'Well, he's old – we're not the same generation, see. We don't see things the same way. He's got no sense of humour. You've got more humour than he has. It's age, see?'

'But he gives you money?'

'He gives Ag money for me.'

'Why?'

'Well, I don't keep it a day, see. I spend it. I take taxis when I have any money.'

'Taxis? Where to?'

'Oh, I don't know. Anywhere. I like taxis, they make me feel I'm who I am. . . . educated and legitimate and that.'

'I see. Have you ever lived with your father?'

'No. I never wanted to. Ag's right when she's against that. Your soul wouldn't be your own, not with him. He's very rich but he doesn't spend it. He's a do-gooder. It's because he thinks I ought to be living with him, and he doesn't want it because he's got a new wife, that he keeps giving Ag money for me. If you read you keep learning about men like that. Guilty, that's what he is. It suits me.'

'Where do you do your reading?'

'Inside. I get a job in the library, see, because I'm edu-cated. The screws can't read at all. They don't know half the books they've got in those libraries. It makes me laugh and it would you too. You're about my age, aren't you? The old generation is responsible for the next. That's what they think. But it's not true. It's your own generation that lives with you, isn't it? Blaming the bloody old fools doesn't help. I didn't read that, you know. I thought it. I think sometimes. What are you going to do with me?'

'When?'

'Do me a favour! Now, of course. Have you gone soft or something? Push me out, that's what you'd better do. Push me out. You might lose your job if they found us together. I might say anything and you couldn't deny it. I've got a say same as you have. I'm legal. I've got papers, you can't take those away. Can you?'

'Something is happening upstairs.' Julia's voice came in to them from the passage. 'Tim! Somebody is screaming up-stairs.'

'No, I don't think I want to.' Tim was answering the boy in the corner. He turned and spoke to Julia.

'The house is aroused, is it? I think we'd better take him with us. He's our pidgin.'

Chapter Eighteen

Night-cap

'Very nice,' said Luke, settling back in Mr Campion's most comfortable chair. A glass was in his hand, the telephone was on his knee to save him having to get up when it should ring again, and his feet were on the fender. 'This is how I like waiting. We'll give them another half-hour. O.K.?'

His host glanced up from the message he was reading. He had found it on his desk when they had come in to the Bottle Street flat some little time before, and his anxiety to see if it had arrived had been one of the reasons why he had asked Luke in for a night-cap instead of being persuaded to go elsewhere after they had left the dining-room of the Eagle Tavern. It was a long dispatch, written in Mr Lugg's schoolboyish hand, and had been taken down from the telephone which in England is now so often used for the relaying of telegrams. Mr Campion had read it without astonishment and now there was a curiously regretful smile on his pale face as he put it into his pocket.

Luke cocked an eye at him. 'Secrets?' he suggested. 'You don't tell us more than you have to, do you, you old sinner? I don't blame you, we've got no finer feelings. Lugg has gone to bed on principle, I suppose? What does he do, a forty-hour week?'

'He says it's nearer a hundred and forty and that if he had a union he'd complain to it, ruin me, and be deprived of the little bit of comfort he *has* got. I could hardly help overhearing you on the telephone just now. They've got Mrs Leach, then?'

Luke's grin appeared widely, as it only did when he was truly amused. His eyes shone with tears of laughter and his mouth looked like a cat's. 'I don't know why these gormless habituals tickle me so,' he said. 'It's not a nice trait. They do, though. Do you know where she was all the time? In custody at the Harold Dene nick.'

'The cemetery Harold Dene?'

He nodded. 'On a charge of pinching flowers and trying to sell them to the little shop opposite the main gates. The startled proprietor had only just handed an expensive and distinctive sheaf of Arum lilies to a regular customer, who hadn't left the shop above fifteen minutes so he could hardly ignore it, when she brought them in. He asked Agnes to wait while he got some money and nipped out of the back door to find a policeman. While he was away she helped herself to a telephone call and was just hanging up as he returned with a copper. We find 'em, don't we!' He was silent for a moment and sat sipping his drink and looking into the gas fire as if he saw castles there.

'That boy Timothy was lucky,' he observed at last. 'That was his Mum's last throw turned that number up. Some guardian angel looked after him all right.'

He appeared to be very serious, the long waving lines deep on his forehead. 'Remember that tale we heard tonight about the head-scarf? I thought at the time it had the true outlandish ring about it. Little white lambs dancing on a blue field and "Happy and Gay" – *Happy and Gay!* – written all over it in flowers. I ask you, Campion! Think of that poor girl, dying in a hospital which everyone confidently expected to be bombed in a couple of hours. She was married to a nervy, over-conscientious nut who didn't even know he was a father and was away on active service anyhow. Her only relative was helpless and there was no one to mother the baby. So what did she do? She caused the kid to be wrapped in a shawl marked "Happy and Gay" and then dropped off uncomplaining into Eternity. What happened? What you'd think? Not on your nellie! A bird turned up out of the air, a wayward nit, who scooped up the kid as a pink ticket to safety and flapped off with it, to drop it neatly into the empty cradle of the one kind of woman who wouldn't see anything extraordinary about its arrival and who found the message perfectly comprehensible. There you are, a straight answer to a straight prayer.'

Mr Campion regarded his friend dubiously.

'It's one way of looking at it,' he said. 'There are others.'

'Not if you take her viewpoint.' Luke was unrepentant. 'Locate the true protagonist of each story and straight away you're living in an age of miracles. That's my serious and considered opinion. I see no other reasonable explanation for the stuff I come across.' He laughed and dismissed the whole stupendous subject. 'Munday is wild, I understand,' he remarked. 'There'll be some ruffled plumage to be smoothed down there, I shouldn't wonder.'

'Hadn't he realized that Barry Leach was anything to do with Cornish?'

'He didn't know Barry Leach or Barry Cornish existed. Why should he?' Luke was midlly ferocious. 'One Charles Luke, Superintendent, might have pulled a finger out and recollected something about a small-time problem brat in a totally different manor when the flat-wrecking case first came up, but did he? No, of course he didn't. He'd never heard of the silly twit until this afternoon when he put a query through to records. It's my fault. Cornish is somebody in Munday's area. It might have helped him had he known about this skeleton in his cupboard before. Munday has a grievance.'

'Will he show it?'

'I don't know. It'll be interesting to see, won't it?' As if in answer to his question the telephone upon his knee began to ring and he lifted the receiver.

'Luke,' he said, and brightened visibly. 'Ah. Hello. Your name was on my lips, Chief. How goes it? What? Here? Why not? Mr Campion won't mind, he may even give you a drink. Right away then. O.K.'

He hung up and made one of his comic faces.

'He'd like to have a direct word with me, *if* I don't mind. Very proper and correct. That'll teach me!'

He was still mildly apprehensive when Munday appeared ten minutes later; and when Mr Campion, who had not met him before, let him in the thin man was surprised by the newcomer's attitude, which was not at all what he had been led to expect. The correct pink-faced official was neither reproachful towards Luke nor packed with secret satisfaction at the new advantage he had suddenly acquired over the Councillor. Instead he came in with the unmistakable air of a man determined to put a delicate piece of tactics across. His light eyes were cautious and his prim mouth smiling.

'I must apologize for intruding on your hospitality at this time of night, Mr Campion', he said, with an effusiveness which was obviously foreign to him. 'I've always hoped to meet you but this is an imposition.'

Luke, who listened to him with astonishment, relaxed openly.

'He won't mind,' he said cheerfully. 'Even if he won't tell me what's in his telegram. Now then Chief, what's happening? Have you got the boy?'

'Not yet, Superintendent. But he was noticed by a uniformed man in Scribbenfields this afternoon before the call went out, so he's about there as you supposed. He hasn't been seen since it got dark but the building is being watched and I've had a word myself with the woman Leach.' He shook his fair head. 'A poor type,' he said. 'Not imbecilic you understand, but a distressingly poor type. She admits telephoning the cobbler's shop and leaving a message for Barry Leach with Miss Tray. Just the name and address of the person she thinks was responsible for hiring the Stalkeys, that's all.'

'Did she say how she got it?'

'She got the surname and the address from a label on a wreath, and the first name she learned from something said by a woman she saw by the grave, and whom she thought she recognized as someone she'd met years ago in the country, she doesn't know where.'

'Ah,' said Luke. 'So Mrs B. did speak. I thought that story of uncharacteristic silence was too good to be true.'

'Probably she spoke to herself, don't you think?' ventured Mr Campion, who had appreciated Mrs Broome in his own way. 'Having picked up the habit from *Alice in Wonderland*, no doubt.'

'Alice? That's just about what she is!' Luke was hearty. 'Classic and intended for children. What about this watch on the Well House, Bob? We don't want any more tricks with firelighters; that place is full of antique curiosities.'

'So I understand. Some of them human.' Munday could have been joking but his expression of complete seriousness was unchanged. 'I don't think there's any fear of that. I have two good men on it and the uniformed branch is cooperating. We haven't alarmed the occupants yet.' He hesitated and they realized that he was coming to the purpose of his visit. 'I've taken an unusual step which I hope you will approve, Superintendent.'

'Oh yes, what is it?' Luke was highly intrigued by the entire approach. 'What's the matter with you, Munday?'

'Nothing, sir, but I don't know if you quite appreciate the peculiar position of a fellow like Councillor Cornish in a place like Ebbfield.' He took the bull by the horns. 'I've taken the liberty of informing him and he'll be present when we make the arrest. I'd like it. I'd be happier.'

'Do what you like, old boy. It's your baby.'

Luke was sitting up like a cat, his eyes bright as jet bugles. 'I didn't know the local governments had such powers. He can make you a lot of trouble if not buttered, can he?'

For the first time Munday smiled, his thin lips parted in a frosty smirk.

'It's not that,' he said. 'But he has a position to keep up, you understand, and he's at a great disadvantage in being a man of remarkable conscience. Such people are more common in Scotland than they are here.'

'I don't get this at all,' said Luke frankly, 'but it fascinates me. What are you frightened of?'

Munday sighed. 'Well,' he said, 'let me put it to you this way. Suppose he comes to his son's rescue as he has before, understand, and he sees him in custody with one or two abrasions on him, perhaps.'

Luke ducked his chin. 'I like "abrasions",' he murmured. 'Then what?'

'Then the father has a great fight with his terrible conscience,' said Munday with granite seriousness. 'Should he make a row with the police, who may have done their duty a little over-conscientiously, thereby calling attention to himself? Or should he say nothing about it and condone brutality for fear of appearing in the newspapers?' He paused. 'I know him. In the ordinary way I have dealings with him once or twice a week. He's an awful nuisance but a good man. Every devil in Hell would drive him to sacrifice himself and we'd all be smeared over the London Press, let alone the local journal, when we could save ourselves a scandal in a nice suburb with a splendid building estate.'

Charles Luke thrust a long hand through his hair.

'I haven't fully appreciated you all these years, Chief,' he said. 'I didn't know you had it in you. So he's coming to see the arrest? That's very sensible. That'll do it, will it?'

'Very possibly.' Munday was wooden-faced. 'But to make perfectly certain of the desired effect I have suggested to him that he brings the probation officer with whom he's had dealings once or twice before, and I myself have taken the precaution of borrowing a C.I.D. sergeant from over on the Essex side. He's a man who knows Barry Leach well and has, in fact, arrested him on two previous occasions.'

'Without abrasions?'

'Without abrasions.'

Luke leant back, his dark face alight with amusement.

'Carry on. It's all in your safe hands, Chief. We'll stay here and leave it to you. It's been a long day!' The telephone bell interrupted him once more and he took up the receiver. 'Luke here.'

He sat listening while the voice at the other end chattered like a starling just out of earshot. Gradually his face grew more grave and there was an unnatural stiffness about his wide shoulders.

'Right,' he said at last. 'The Chief Inspector's here. I'll tell him and we'll come along. Good-bye.'

He hung up, pushed the instrument across the table and rose to his feet.

'Come along, chaps,' he said. 'The balloon has gone up at the Well House. There's no fire but they seem to have had a murder. I'm afraid, Chief, you're going to get publicity after all.'

Chapter Nineteen

Meeting Point

When Timothy and Julia hurried up the staircase to the bed-room floor, where a considerable commotion was taking place, Tim took Barry Leach with him. He had him gripped firmly by the arm, since he felt that it was not safe to let him loose, and he had no immediate idea what to do with him. The captive made no resistance and came not only quietly but in a series of eager little rushes like a timid dog on a choke chain.

The only lights left on in the house were two of the lamps in the candelabra which hung in the stairwell, so that all round them the building seemed ghostly and enormous, a great creaking barn, as they stumbled up the shallow steps among its shadows. Besides the noise from above there was a terrific draught and the night air of the city swept down upon them in a tide.

'It's Nanny Broome,' Julia said breathlessly. 'Shouting out of a window I think. What on earth is happening?'

Eustace asked the same question as he appeared suddenly at his door, the first in the passage down the right wing. He was wrapped in a splendid silk robe and had paused to brush his hair, so that he loomed up neat and pink in the gloom.

'What is all this?' he demanded. 'Is someone ill? Tim, what are you doing?' He caught sight of Barry Leach. 'Good Heavens! Who is that?'

A sudden gust of violent protest in a deep yet unexpectedly familiar voice reached them from the open doorway of a room on the opposite side of the corridor. It was Miss Aicheson. She sounded frightened.

'Be quiet, Mrs Broome! Hold your damned tongue, woman, and come and help me with him. He's dead, I think.'

'Isn't that Basil's room?' Eustace did not move but spoke to Timothy. 'Isn't it?'

'Of course it is. *Shut up!*' The final admonition was addressed to his captive, who had reared up suddenly like a frightened animal. 'Keep quiet!'

Julia was the first to reach the doorway and she turned on the light switch just inside the room. It had been in partial darkness, only the small bedside reading lamp alight. It was the main spare room and a big one, furnished with Tudor elegance, but now the wall tapestries and the long silk curtains were blowing out across the room like banners, and Nanny Broome, fully dressed but white faced and dishevelled, drew her head in through the window.

'They're coming. I'd been watching them, so I called. The police are coming.'

'Good God, woman, that's no good!' Miss Aicheson was struggling to lift something in the bed, her clumsy hands plucking at it ineffectually. 'Look at this! Come here, somebody. Somebody come at once.'

The new arrivals swept forward in a group and for a dizzy moment stood staring uncomprehendingly.

Something huge and shining lay among the pillows. It was a pool of glistening colour, pink and blue and iridescent in the newly blazing light. At least half of those who came upon it so suddenly were reminded absurdly of flowers, a parcelled bouquet freshly delivered from a florist, until in another instance the evidence of their eyes could be denied no longer and the appalling truth came home to them. They were looking at Basil Toberman's face, flushed pinkish purple and with froth upon his lips, lying inside a plastic bag.

Miss Aicheson was both frantic and embarrassed and for the first time appeared an old maid. She had been trying to tear the bag and now, giving up the struggle suddenly, she pulled down the bed-clothes and threw them aside. The heavy polythene sack designed to store a long dress had been pulled down over Toberman's head. The surplus length, bunched into folds, had been tucked tightly about his neck and shoulders and covered by the blankets. Although he had rolled over, and his knees were drawn up, he was still held securely.

Julia reacted instantly with Timothy a quarter second behind her.

'He's not breathing!' she said. 'Quick.'

He leapt forward and struggled to get an arm behind the heavy shoulders. 'I'll lift him. You pull the bag.'

In the emergency he forgot his captive completely and as his grip on the leather sleeve loosened the stranger slid away like a shadow. He made no sudden rush but melted through the little group and shot out into the passage. No one noticed him go; the entire attention of everybody present was focused on the bed. It was proving a little difficult to get Toberman out. The damp plastic over his mouth and nostrils tended to cling and the material was exasperatingly strong and would not tear. It was several seconds before they had him freed.

'I want to get him on the floor,' Tim said, exerting all his strength to lift the limp figure out on to the carpet. 'If I get above him I can work on his arms. He's got to be made to breathe somehow.'

His authoritative tone pulled Nanny Broome together. Her dramatics ceased and she dropped on to the floor, to help turn the heavy body. Tim took off his own coat and prepared to give artificial respiration. Both she and Timothy were sitting on their heels and the light which hung from the centre of the ceiling shone down directly on the flushed face of the man between them. Presently she bent forward to look at him more closely and, putting out her hand, pulled the lower eyelid down for a moment.

'He's just like she was,' she said to Timothy, but speaking distinctly and clearly enough for everyone to hear. 'I mean that Miss Saxon. She looked just like this but without that froth.'

'My God, woman, what will you say next!' Eustace's voice rose in horror and then ceased abruptly, as from just outside the door and very close to them there was a scream, apparently of pain. At the same moment they all became aware of heavy footsteps flying up the staircase, while from somewhere far below an unfamiliar male voice was shouting instructions.

Meanwhile Miss Aicheson had recognized the voice.

'Alison!' She scrambled round the bed and went blundering across the room to the doorway while everyone else save Tim, who was fully occupied, turned to watch her.

Alison reeled into the room and collapsed in her friend's clumsy arms. She was clad in a little-girl dressing-gown splattered with pink roses, and with her hands held over her face and her sleek silver head bowed she looked pathetic.

'He hit me!' Although her voice was tearful her tone was principally astounded. 'He hit me, Aich! I was just coming out of my room and there he was before me in the passage. I said, "Who are you?" and he hit me and ran away.'

'Who dear, who?'

'Tim! He's got away!' The words escaped Julia, and Eustace, who was dithering midway between both casualties seized on them.

'Who? Who?' he demanded. 'Who was that man in here? What is going on? How did you all get here fully dressed? What is all this about and who – Good Heavens! Who are you, sir?'

The final question was addressed to a square man in a tight suit who had just stepped daintily into the room.

Sergeant Stockwell gave the scene a single comprehensive glance. He was delighted with himself and confidence oozed from him. He was also sufficiently human to be rather excited.

'I'm the police, sir,' he said to Eustace. 'The lady called to us out of the window. It's all right, we've got him. Somebody called out up here just as we came in and he came streaking down right into our arms. It's all right, he's in custody.'

'Who? Who are you talking about? A burglar?' Eustace was roaring suddenly. His smooth face was damp and he was trembling.

'His name is Leach, sir. At least that is what he's called. But it's all right. You just sit down for a minute while I see the damage.' He thrust Eustace firmly into the arm-chair under the window, turned towards the group on the floor, and dropped down gingerly on one knee. 'That's good work, son,' he said. 'Carry on. I'll get you some relief first thing.' He looked at Julia. 'I wonder if you'd mind, miss? Slip along and tell the uniformed man that he's needed up here urgently. Is there a telephone on this floor?'

'Yes, in my bedroom, just here.' Eustace bounced up again and seized the sergeant by the arm. 'I want an explanation. This is my house and I haven't the faintest idea what is going on. I want information from you.'

'Yes, sir.' Stockwell was experienced. His manner though gentle was remarkably firm. 'But what you want most, you know, whether you realize it or not, is a doctor, and if I can catch our police surgeon before he goes to bed he'll be here in a couple of minutes or so. He only lives round the corner. We must do everything we can, mustn't we? Even if it doesn't look very hopeful. Just lead the way to the telephone sir, please.'

As soon as Julia returned with a constable, Timothy, who was on the point of exhaustion, prepared to give over to him gratefully. The newcomer turned out to be a powerful youngster, fully trained and eager to help, and he stripped off his tunic at once. Meanwhile Nanny Broome was recovering from her initial panic and now seemed anxious to make up for any kudos she might have lost, by exerting her personality to the utmost. She took the policeman's helmet and placed it on a chair, and unfolded his tunic to shake it and fold it up again for him.

'It was lack of air, that's what did it for him poor man,' she said unnecessarily. 'As soon as I saw him I threw up the window and shouted to you. I'd been watching you all from the landing. You were on my mind.'

The constable was not listening to her. One look at the patient had convinced him of the seriousness of the situation and now he went round behind Tim, rolling up his sleeves, and set about making a careful take-over without upsetting the rhythm.

Tim extricated himself and got up wearily, to stand holding on to the bedpost. He was grey with mingled fatigue and dismay and his forehead was wrinkled like a hound's. 'He's like a log,' he said, glancing over at Julia who was watching them helplessly. 'How did he do it?' He bent down and touched the limp body and drew back again. 'Someone has sent for a doctor, I suppose?'

'I think so. They were telephoning from Eustace's room as I came past.' She paused for a moment and the room was quiet save for the steady pumping. 'It's that dreadful colour. It's not quite like anything I've ever seen.'

'He's poisoned himself with his own breath, I think. Something like that. Keep at it for a minute or two, Constable. I'll take over when you want me to.' The constable nodded and continued his exercise, forcing the air in and out of the clogged lungs. Basil Toberman had ceased to be a person. His body had a new and terrible personality of its own, filling the room with its oppressive presence.

The night air streaming through the wide window brought all the far-off street noises which they had not noticed before, and its chill was mixed with a different cold which was settling into them as the first shock passed and they began to think again.

'It's not possible,' Julia was beginning and was interrupted by Miss Aicheson who spoke with sudden petulance from the other side of the room.

'Mrs Broome, do come here a moment. Miss Alison's face is marked, see? Can you help me to take her to her room so we can at least bathe it?'

The new emergency seemed to have driven Basil Toberman completely out of her mind and she was both tenderly maternal and yet hopelessly shy and ineffectual in her concern for Alison, who might have been mortally wounded she was making such a fuss. The realization that she had no idea that anyone else was hurt occurred to both the young people as Nanny Broome bustled over to help her. She herself had recovered, almost, and her consequential little wriggle as she walked had returned. On the other hand Miss Aicheson appeared to be on the verge of going to pieces; she was at the stage of having to explain.

'I was passing the door on my way to Alison's room with her book when I heard you shouting,' she said hoarsely as Mrs Broome came up. 'Why did you do that? Why did you call out of the window instead of trying to get the wretched man out of his damned bag?'

Mrs Broome stared at her and they could see the question presenting itself for the first time. Her answer was spontaneous and clearly perfectly true.

'I didn't know it was a bag,' she said frankly. 'I didn't know what it was. There wasn't a lot of light and I wasn't wearing glasses because I don't need them except for reading, and I thought he'd somehow gone like that after all that drink. All liquid and awful.'

It was one of those frank statements of a familiar if idiotic state of mind. 'He didn't look human and I lost my head and screamed the place down. I knew there were police outside and they were real so I called them.'

Julia ceased to listen to her and turned abruptly to Timothy. Her face was pale and her eyes enormous.

'Somebody must have done it to him,' she said. 'I've only just realized it. He couldn't have tucked the bed-clothes round his own neck after –' She left the rest of the sentence in the air.

'It's all right, miss. The man has been taken. We got him downstairs.' The constable spoke without relaxing his steady work. He was breathless and the words came out explosively.

Timothy and Julia exchanged startled glances and Timothy protested.

'If you mean that chap we brought up here with us, that's utterly impossible.' The constable said nothing but he smiled, and Timothy looked blank.

'I suppose they'll assume he did it,' he began.

'If they do we can alibi him.' Julia dismissed the suggestion. 'Tim! Basil mustn't *die*!'

The young man did not speak at once but looked down at the limp bundle and away again.

'My God, I hope not,' he said earnestly. 'Now we'll know.'

Sergeant Stockwell had returned bringing the doctor, who proved to be a slight man who was remarkably self-important.

He walked over to the group on the floor and after a

cursory glance went over to the dressing-table to find a suitable resting place for his splendid leather box.

'Very well,' he said over his shoulder as he unlocked it. 'Now I want everybody out of the room at once please, except the constable. I don't care *where* you go, madam.' He threw the information at Miss Aicheson, who had opened her mouth but not yet spoken and had been about to ask him to look at Alison. 'Downstairs, upstairs, wherever you like as long as it's out of here. I want to try to save this man's life and what I need is space and air. You too!' he added to Julia, who was waiting her turn to move. 'Outside everybody. As quickly as you can. Send me up another man Sergeant, please, and when your inspector arrives tell him where I am.'

'Yes sir.' Stockwell glanced at Timothy and his left eyelid flickered. 'I'd like everybody to come downstairs to the big room on the floor below this one. You lead the way, miss.' They trooped out and the doctor called after them. 'Don't forget my second constable, Sergeant. This man is nearly all in.'

'Very well, sir.' Stockwell spoke heartily, adding under his breath as they reached the passage, 'I'll take one out of the box. They come in dozens.'

'Alison must have her face bathed. He hit her, you see.'

Miss Aicheson turned in her path to appeal to authority and Nanny Broome, who was supporting Miss Kinnit, paused hopefully.

Stockwell was interested and as Tim and Julia went on alone they heard him talking eagerly behind them.

'You mean the man who broke in? He went for her, did he? Did he actually touch her?'

'He did, dear, didn't he?'

'Oh yes Aich, of course, I told you. He saw me and hit out. He was frightened, I think.'

'I expect you were frightened too, miss.' The sergeant aimed to comfort. 'He's an ugly young brute. Just show me where you were and tell me exactly what he did.'

Tim and Julia passed out of earshot. The drawing-room

door stood open and the pink light streamed out into the gloom.

'Are you worrying about him?' Julia drew the boy aside for a moment and they stood close together whispering, leaning over the heavy oak balustrade which ran round the stairwell.

'No, but they can't charge him for something he hasn't done. He's broken in and he's almost certainly responsible for Nan's coat and for socking Alison, but they can't say that he's to blame for poor old Basil's condition. Whatever that may be.'

'No, of course not. I wasn't accusing you. I was just asking.'

'Oh! Blast everybody.' He turned and kissed her ear, pressing his face for a moment into her warm soft hair. 'What did you do with that horror glove?'

'Hid it. It's in the oven at the back of the mock fireplace. Aren't you going to tell them about it?'

'I'm not going to rush at them with it.'

'Tim! Oh darling! You *can't* feel responsible for him.'

'Why not? He's our age and I caught him.'

'I see.' She was silent for a moment or two and then turned to face him. 'Did you hear Nanny Broome say that Miss Saxon looked like Basil does?'

'Yes I did.'

'What are we going to do?'

'What can we do? Nothing. We're not in that at all. The Basil business appears to be entirely the older generation's headache. That's the only thing we do know about it. Come along, Sweetie.'

They went on into the drawing-room to find Eustace standing on the hearthrug before the cacti collection. Councillor Cornish was in a chair on the opposite side of the room, his back was bent, and his long arms were drooping. He still wore his hideous raincoat and his black hat was on the floor beside him.

Eustace hailed Tim with relief. 'Oh, there you are, my boy!' he said heartily. 'How is Basil? It's not as bad as it looks, is it? He'll come round, I mean? Please God! What a frightful accident to happen! Where were you when all this was going on?'

'Julia and I were in the Well-cellar catching that chap who came in through the broken window. He took the glass out this afternoon, apparently.'

Eustace's kindly face became amazed. He had recovered from his initial shock and his wits were about him again.

'Be discreet, Tim,' he murmured and glanced down at the room towards the Councillor, who was rising as Julia crossed over to him. 'I don't think it could have occurred quite like that, you know. No human being could get through those bars for one thing. Doubtless he was about the house before you found him.'

'He wasn't.' Tim was gentle but adamant. 'We were in the kitchen and he couldn't have reached the cellar from the house without disturbing us. He could get through the bars all right. He could get through a keyhole. Have you seen him?'

'Yes, I have. He and a plain-clothes detective and a pleasant young man who seems to be some sort of welfare officer are all in the dining-room.' Eustace hesitated and presently led the younger man into the window alcove. 'It's Cornish's boy, apparently,' he said softly. 'There's been trouble before, I understand.' He sighed. 'An extraordinary coincidence, don't you think? Just after he was able to help us this morning? I don't mind telling you I'm wondering about that fire. Let's go over. I don't know what your little Julia is telling him about the cellar. We don't want to raise his hopes, poor man.'

As they came up to the two they caught the tail end of an earnest and intimate conversation.

'I hoped so hard you'd go to Mr Luke.' Julia's voice was as clear as a bird's. 'I'm so relieved. As soon as I heard he'd sent for Nanny Broome I knew that you must have.'

'My dear, be quiet,' said the Councillor. He was a gaunt figure in agony. There was no mistaking his helpless misery. He turned to Timothy and spoke doggedly.

'You didn't hurt him,' he said. 'I'm most grateful you didn't hurt him. Do I understand that he is responsible for something quite terrible upstairs?'

'No, sir. He has done nothing at all since he got into the house except talk to me.'

With exactly the same doggedness Tim was disregarding Eustace's frantic pressure on his arm. 'Julia and I saw the light from his torch when he got into the Well-cellar and after that we didn't let him out of our sight. When we heard the commotion and came up to investigate I brought him with me. We went into Basil Toberman's room together.'

'Basil Toberman? Is that the man who was murdered?'

As the question escaped the Councillor, Eustace made an ineffectual gesture of rejection and drew a long whistling breath. It was as if he had been listening for the word and when it came he had no resistance to offer. He dropped into the nearest chair and sat there like a sack. 'Is he dead?' he demanded.

'I don't know, Uncle.'

'I didn't realize there was any doubt of that.' Cornish was both apologetic and deeply relieved. 'I was misled by something I heard one plain-clothes man tell the other.'

Eustace looked up at Timothy. 'It'll be the end of us if he does die and there's any sort of mystery about it,' he said gravely. 'That scene at supper tonight and everything the stupid fellow has been saying to God knows who on the aeroplane, it'll all come out. All over the newspapers, everywhere, and that will be a quarter of the damage. Once the old stag goes down, you know, the hounds are on him in a pack! In his mouth the florid simile sounded natural enough but Tim, who was hypersensitive concerning the old man's dignity snapped at him.

'Then we'll have to dig in and live it down, because there's nothing else we can do.'

'My boy, that's easy enough to say.' Eustace was an odd mixture of despair and a sort of relish. 'Wait until you see Julia's father's reaction. Wait until it touches you personally.'

'But how is Tim concerned? What is it to do with him? He's not a Kinnit.'

Julia's intervention cut clean across everybody's private reservation. She made a terrifying picture of innocent

recklessness, interested only in her love. Both older men turned
to her beseechingly but Tim was not sidetracked. He put an
arm round her and jerked her tightly to his side. 'You be
quiet,' he said. 'We can't be bothered with all that any more,
darling. We know all we need to know about me. Consider
all that settled and done with. Now, if your father says you're
to wait until you're twenty-one we'll have to wait and that's
an end of it. We shall marry as soon as we can.'

Councillor Cornish hesitated. He seemed relieved to have
found somebody of his own weight with whom to deal.

'Do I understand that you can give Barry a complete alibi
for the – the happening, whatever it is, upstairs?'

'I am not giving him anything.' Tim had never looked
more exactly a younger edition of the man before him. 'I am
simply confirming that I was with him while he was in this
house tonight. He will confirm that he was with Julia and
me. We alibi each other. On this occasion his word is as good
as mine. He has an identity. He told me so.'

The Councillor's eyes flickered under his fierce brows.

'You know about that, do you? I was wondering what I
was going to say to you and this young lady about that.' He
hesitated. 'Or if I was going to say anything at all.' There was
a pause and presently he spoke with a rush. 'He takes his
papers very seriously,' he said, and it was as if he was speaking
of some strange animal for which he was responsible but
which he could never hope to understand. 'They are the only
aspect of Law and Order for which he seems to have any
respect at all.'

'He takes his identity seriously,' Tim said. 'Naturally. It
appears to be all he has.'

It was an extraordinary piece of conversation, momentous
and completely enlightening to each participant and yet, to
everybody else, almost casual.

Cornish looked at Tim anxiously.

'How about yourself, Son?'

Timothy's glance fell on Julia's sleek head next his shoulder
and wandered over to Eustace still sitting hunched and old
in his chair. At length he met the Councillor's gaze.

'I've got responsibilities,' he said seriously. 'I'm all right.'

'Mr Timothy Kinnit?' Stockwell, appearing in the doorway, put the question sharply. He was excited and his habit of swinging on his light feet had never been more evident.

'Here, Sergeant.'

'I see.' Stockwell appraised him. He was behaving as if he felt the situation was a little too good to be true. 'I have the Superintendent and my Chief Inspector coming along. They'll be here in a moment. Meanwhile I wonder if I could ask you to clear up a little question which has come up. I understand from my constable upstairs that you admitted in his presence that it was you who took the man Leach into Mr Toberman's room?'

'That's right. My fiancée and I took him upstairs with us when we heard the rumpus. We didn't know what else to do with him.'

'I see, sir.' Stockwell was approaching a conclusion as it were on tiptoe. 'Then when you took him into Mr Toberman's room it was the first time he'd been there, in your opinion.'

'Of course. Doesn't he say so?'

'That's exactly what he does say.'

Tim stood looking at the broad face with the half-triumphant grin on it.

'What's the matter?' he demanded. 'What are you getting at?'

'You've given yourself away, young man, haven't you?' Stockwell, still a little disbelieving at such good fortune, took the plunge squarely, nevertheless. 'It was you who put Mr Toberman to bed, wasn't it? When he was too drunk to get there himself, let alone into a bag? That's the truth, isn't it?'

The inference, so direct and simple that its enormity became a matter for complicated investigation and endless legal argument before their very eyes, burst in the room like a bomb.

There was a long moment of appalled silence, broken in the end by a voice from the doorway behind the sergeant.

'Oh well, if you're going to be silly and imagine Mr Tim

did it,' said Nanny Broome, irritably, 'I suppose *I* shall have to tell the truth.'

As the sergeant turned slowly round to stare at her, Superintendent Luke's voice speaking to the constable on duty at the front door floated up to them from the hall below.

Chapter Twenty

Eye Witness

The reading-lamp on the desk in Eustace's study cast a small bright pool of light on the polished wood, and the reflected glow struck upwards on the faces of the earnest men who stood round it looking down at Mrs Broome, who sat in the writing chair.

Luke was there and Campion, Munday, and Stockwell, a solid bunch of human heads intent and silent save for the occasional murmur of assent.

For once Nanny Broome had no illusions. She was frightened and completely in the picture. She had no time to be self-conscious.

'We were nearly an hour I should think, me and Mr Tim, getting him off.' Her voice was very quiet, almost a whisper, but she was keeping to the point remarkably well and they were all too experienced to distract her. 'He'd been up and down, up and down, until he drove you crazy. But he dropped off at last and we tiptoed out into the passage and Mr Tim went off downstairs to his young lady, and I waited about for a bit in case Mr Basil woke again. I did one or two little jobs. I turned Mr Tim's bed down and looked in on Mr Eustace to see if he'd got everything, He was reading; he always does. Miss Alison had finished her bath; I could hear the waste running. And so I went across the hall to the other three rooms and saw Miss Julia's bed was all right. Mrs Telpher wanted me to help her close her window which was stuck, and I did that and went next door to Miss Aich but I didn't go in.'

'Did you attempt to?' Luke's tone was carefully lowered to match her own so that there was no physical interruption, as it were, to the flow of her thought.

'Not really. I knocked and she said "All right, all right" in her way, so I thought, "very well". And I didn't disturb her.

Then I came back and listened at Mr Basil's door. He was snoring quite regularly so I went and sat down on the window-bench at the end of the passage and looked out into the street. I sat there for a long time. I often do. It's my seat. I'm not in the way because I'm behind the velvet curtains and the light is up the other end of the passage and doesn't really reach to where I am. I sat looking out at the police for a long time. I thought the plain-clothes chaps were just ordinary men hanging about for a while but presently, when they kept speaking to the copper in uniform and looking about as if they weren't doing it, I guessed who they were and I wondered if Miss Julia could have telephoned them after all.'

'Why should she?'

'Because I'd had my coat cut when I came in after seeing you, Mr Luke. I told her we'd report it in the morning.'

'Very well.' Luke was holding himself on a tight rein. 'Then what happened?'

'Nothing for a long time. I was wondering if I dare go to bed and leave those two young monkeys up downstairs. You can't really trust anybody at that age. It's not right to ask it of them. Then I heard someone and I peeked out through the curtains and saw a woman come along and go into Mr Basil's room. I was so angry I could have smacked her because we'd only just got him to sleep, but there was no noise and after quite a few minutes she came out again and went back to her room, and I sat listening with my heart in my mouth because, I thought, "Well, if he's going to start all his tricks again it will be now that he'll begin." There was no sound, though, and presently I got up and listened at his door and he was snoring.'

'Did you go in?'

'No. I only opened the door a foot and put my head in. The street lamps shine into that room. I could see him. He was all right. Sleeping like a great grampus. Poor, poor chap.'

'Don't think of that now. What did you do?'

'I went back to my seat and watched the detectives fidgeting about across the road. A police car came crawling by and one of them went off after it down the side street. To make his report I expect. There was no one else at all about. We don't have many people pass at night although it's so crowded in the daytime. I might easily have gone to bed then but I didn't. I waited to see the detective come back and that was why I was still there when the person came again. I could hardly believe it when I saw her, but she went straight into Mr Basil's room and she was there five or six minutes. Then she came out again.'

'The same woman as before?'

'Oh, yes.'

'Are you sure you could identify her?' In his effort to keep his voice level and in tone Luke exerted so much strength he set the entire group trembling.

'Well, one never is absolutely sure, not at night, is one? I wasn't sure who it was. I had to satisfy myself. That was why I spoke to her.'

Munday made a little strangled sound deep in his throat and turned it into a cough whilst everybody else held his breath.

'I said, "Is he all right?" I couldn't think of anything else to say. She didn't jump, she just turned round and came up to me. "There are lights on downstairs" she said. I said "I know: it's all right. How is Mr Basil?"' Miraculously Mrs Broome's urgent whisper had never faltered but, now, remembered indignation interfered with her clear picture. 'She said "I never went in". The cheek of it! "Tim put him to bed", she said. "I never went in." Of course I didn't know then what she'd been up to or I'd have given her something to go on with! . . .'

'Wait.' Luke dropped a hand on her shoulder. 'Take a deep breath.' He was treating her as he treated child witnesses and she responded, obeying him literally.

'I've done that.'

'Right. Now go back. You spoke to her. She answered you. You were sure who it was. When she said she had not been in, what did you do?'

'I stared. "I thought you had", I said. "Good night." Then I sat down again and looked out of the window. She

255

stood there waiting for a second and I thought she was going to explain, but she didn't. She just turned round and went straight back to her room and I stayed where I was, never dreaming he was in that thing.'

'How long before you looked at him?'

'Several minutes.' It was an appalled whisper. 'I sat behind the curtains getting warmer and warmer. My mind was easy, you see. She hadn't woken him the first time and I didn't expect her to do it on the second. I sat wondering why she'd gone in and why she'd been so silly as to try to pretend she hadn't with me actually sitting there, and I almost dozed!'

'Never mind. Keep on the ball. When did you look?'

'After about ten minutes. I'd meant to go down and call the children because they're only young and enough is enough. When I got up I listened at Mr Basil's door and I couldn't hear him. It was as silent as the grave in there. I didn't think much about it but it did strike me as extraordinary and I wondered if he was lying awake. I opened the door very softly and looked in. The reading lamp was on and there he was, shining like a great pool of water in the bed. I told one of you, didn't I? I lost my head and began to scream and because I knew you were all there outside the window I shouted to you.'

'Because you thought it was a crime?'

'No. Because I wanted help. I don't think of policemen as always having to do with crime.'

'The trusting public,' murmured Mr Campion under his breath as Luke spoke.

'You'll have to give us her name,' Luke said gently. 'Loyalty and long service and the respectability of the house, all those things are important, but not important enough at this point. Who was it Mrs Broome? Just the name?'

'It was that old girl who was shouting when I came into the bedroom, wasn't it?' Stockwell could contain himself no longer. 'What's her name? Aicheson? She's pretending to be absorbed by the attack on the old sister of the householder.'

Nanny Broome stared at him.

'Oh no,' she said. 'Miss Aich wouldn't hurt a fly and couldn't without it getting away! No. It was Mrs Telpher. I should have guessed that without seeing her, once I'd noticed the likeness between Mr Basil's colour and Miss Saxon's.'

'Mrs Telpher? Who's she? I haven't even heard of her!' Stockwell was already half-way to the door and Mrs Broome's unnaturally quiet voice arrested him.

'When you first came over the road who let you in, young man?' she demanded. 'I've been wondering that ever since I came in here. There wasn't anybody else. She must have been going out as you came in. She's bolted. As soon as I spoke she knew she was found out, see? Even if she had been able to get back for the bag before I found him I'd have known she was to blame in the morning when it came out he was dead!'

In the moment of silence while her meaning became clear, there was an abrupt tap on the door and the little doctor came hurrying in, brusque and important.

'I've an announcement,' he said to nobody in particular. 'He'll do. He's just spoken. I don't think the brain is impaired. The last thing he remembers is Miss Alison Kinnit bringing him a drink in bed.'

There was a long silence broken by a deep intake of breath by the Chief Inspector.

Luke shrugged his shoulders. 'That has torn it every which way,' he said. 'Now what? I'm glad he's alive but I wish he'd stopped talking.'

'But it *was* Mrs Telpher who gave him the drink. That was the first thing I noticed.' Nanny Broome was so excited that she was on the verge of incoherence. 'Miss Julia was with me when we saw her bring the glass upstairs and I mentioned it. I said "She must have half a tumbler of neat spirit there".' She paused and turned to Luke again with one of the sudden outbursts of utter frankness which were her most alarming characteristic. 'That was the real reason why I went to her room when she called me to help with the window. She was taking a long woolly dress out of a plastic bag then. I wanted to see if she really had drunk all that stuff. It's not only that

I'm inquisitive, but if I'm to look after the house I must know what's going on.'

'And she hadn't?' Luke pounced on the thread before it got away.

'No. There it was untouched on the dressing-table. She'd put a tissue over it but you couldn't miss it, it was smelling the place out. Later on, when I saw her taking it in to Mr Basil, I guessed what she was up to. "You're going to make sure he passes right out so there won't be any more disturbances to-night" I thought. "You selfish thing! Serve you right if he gets delirium and the whole place turns into a mad-house." I remember his Papa, you see.'

Luke ignored the historical reference.

'Can you swear on oath it was Mrs Telpher you saw in the passage and not Miss Alison Kinnit? They're very alike.'

'Of course they're alike! That's what muddled Mr Basil in the state he was in. All the Kinnits are alike; the family flavour is very strong. Their natures are alike. When she tried to put the whole thing on to Mr Tim she was exactly like any other Kinnit. I thought that at the time.'

'*When?*' Luke leapt on the flaw. 'When you were speaking to Mrs Telpher in the passage you didn't know that anything had happened to Mr Toberman.'

Nanny Broome's innate honesty shone through the clouds of wool.

'No, but as soon as I saw Mr Basil all glistening like that I realized that whatever had happened to him it must be Mrs Telpher who'd done it, and that she'd clearly meant to put the blame on Tim. *That's why I screamed and called the police.* I'm not very easily upset, you know. I don't scream for nothing. I usually know what I'm doing. Where would Tim and I be now, let me ask you, if I hadn't screamed and you weren't all here but it had been left to the family to decide what story to tell? I knew she'd have to run because I had spoken to her and she knew I knew who'd been into Mr Basil's room. She's got away. Good riddance! I've been thinking she would if I gave her time enough.'

'You be careful what you're saying, Missus!' Munday

intervened despite himself. 'The lady hasn't a chance of getting far. Meanwhile, have you ever heard of an Accessory after the Fact?'

'Only in tales,' said Mrs Broome contemptuously. 'Catch her if you think you can, but don't bring her here near my kiddiewinkies!'

'Who are they?' Munday was beginning with interest, but Luke signalled to him hastily.

'Forget it,' he muttered.'We've only got one life. Sergeant Stockwell, you ought to have noticed the lady at the door. You put out the call. Wait a minute. She has a child at St Joseph's. You might try there first. I think we can take it that she's not normal. It's the old psychiatric stuff. There'll be no very definite motive I mean, and. . . .'

'I rather think there is, you know.' Mr Campion, who had taken no part in the proceedings and who had been forgotten by everybody, now ventured to intervene a trifle apologetically.

'She was the only person who had sufficient motive, or so it seemed to me. Fear is the only adequate spur for that sort of semi-impulsive act, don't you think? Fear of loss. Fear of trouble. Fear of unbearable discovery. Especially when backed by the glimpse of definite gain.'

Luke stared at him.

'"Oh my prophetic soul", your telegram!' he said. 'I might have known! She is not Mrs Telpher, I suppose?'

'Oh but she is.' Mr Campion appeared unhappy. 'That is her true name and she is the Kinnit niece. The telegram was a reply to a routine inquiry I made about her through the Petersen agency in Jo'burg.' He paused, looking awkward. 'It's one of those sad, silly, *ordinary*, explanations which lie behind most criminal acts,' he went on at last. 'I suppose her secret is the most usual one in the world and she hid it successfully from everybody except Basil Toberman, who is the kind of man who spends his life making sure he is not deceived on that particular point.'

Luke's eyebrows rose to peaks.

'Money?'

Mr Campion nodded. 'I'm afraid so. She simply isn't rich. It is as easy as that. She isn't even badly off, hard up or in straightened circumstances. She is simply not rich. She never has been rich. The deceased Telpher was an accountant but not a financier.'

'But the Kinnit family must have known this?'

'Why should they? There are people who make a habit of keeping an eye on the financial positions of their various relatives, but with others, you know, complete ignorance on the subject is almost a cult. Mrs Telpher was a distant relative. Distant in miles. The Kinnits were aware of her but not at all curious about her. How the idea that she was extremely wealthy was implanted in their minds originally I do not know. It may have started with some trifling mistake, or be based merely on the simple fact that they are extremely wealthy and she had never let them know that she was not. At any rate, when she had to come to London she found it very easy to make use of them. Her success lay in the fact that she understood them so well. They are all alike. Cold, incurious, comfort-loving and deeply respectful towards money, and yet in an odd inhuman way hospitable and aware of the duties of hospitality.'

'That woman only lives for one thing and that's cash,' said Mrs Broome unexpectedly. 'If she hasn't got a fortune already her main reason for coming here was to make sure of an inheritance when the time came. You can be sure of that! Don't forget she's the only Kinnit relative except for Mr Tim and she probably thought he ought not to count, being merely adopted. Her idea was to oust him, take it from me. Meantime, here she got her living free, and Miss Saxon's.'

This prosaic thought, which had been in the minds of everybody present, passed entirely without comment.

Luke was still waiting for Mr Campion, who finished his interrupted statement.

'The one great risk she took never materialized,' he said. 'No one insisted on visiting the child. Knowing the family she did not think they would.'

'I insisted and was soon told where I got off!' the irrepressible Mrs Broome put in tartly. 'The poor little mite was "far too ill to see strangers! Doctors' orders." As if a visit from me would hurt a kiddie!'

Luke flapped a silencing hand at her and continued to watch his friend. 'Isn't there a child?'

'Oh, yes, there's a child,' Mr Campion spoke sadly. 'And its condition is just as she said – silent, incurable, unconscious. A heartrending sight, too terrible for anyone very close to sit and watch for long. Mrs Telpher is not very close. She is the governess. She was driving when the accident occurred. She was sent by her employers to London with the child and her nurse, Miss Saxon, when every other hope of cure had failed. The child's name is Maria Van der Graff. She is registered under it at the hospital. Anyone could have discovered it had they thought to ask.'

The story struck the depressingly familiar note with which true stories ring in the tried ears of experienced policemen. No one queried it. It was in the classic pattern of human weakness, mean and embarrassing and sad. The second note, the high alarum, not so familiar and always important since it indicates the paramount sin in Man's private calendar, took most of them by surprise although they had been well prepared.

'Attempted murder,' said Luke. 'She did it to avoid discovery and the failure of her plans, and when she saw she was caught she made a definite attempt to incriminate the young man who stood between her and an inheritance. That covers the present charge.' He hesitated and they waited, the same thought in every mind.

Mrs Broome's eyes met Luke's.

'If Miss Saxon was the nursie, that was why she was so fond of the kiddie and why she tried to tell me about the diamonds.'

'The *diamonds*?' He was as amazed as if she had attempted to introduce elephants.

'The diamonds in the Safe Deposit,' said Mrs Broome placidly. 'In the beginning, when Mr Eustace wrote in his fussy way and told Mrs Telpher not to bring a lot of jewellery to the house but to put it in a safe deposit, he put an idea in her head. She invented some diamonds because she saw that he expected her to have some with her, and pretended she'd put them under lock and key. When she mentioned them in front of me Miss Saxon told me – in front of her – that they were so big that she wouldn't have believed they were real if she hadn't known. Well, she did know, didn't she? If they were in service together she'd have known Mrs Telpher wasn't wealthy. She knew the diamonds weren't real and probably weren't even there. She was on the verge of telling me the joke. We were getting far too friendly, Miss Saxon and me; that was why *she* had to have her head put in a bag! It was aspirin, not drink, that was used *that* time I expect!'

'Quiet!' Luke's big hand thumping on the desk silenced her. 'You open your mouth once more, my girl, and it's you and no one else who'll be inside! Doctor, suppose the gentleman upstairs had died, what would the autopsy have shown?'

The doctor glanced over at him in astonishment.

'Oh, I don't think there would have been any need for an autopsy, Superintendent. It was perfectly clear what had happened to him.'

'Yes, I know, sir. It's a hypothetical question. What would have been the finding if the man had died and the bag been removed and hidden?'

'If I hadn't known? If I had simply been presented with the corpse and not told about the bag?'

'That's it, sir.'

The little man hesitated. 'Well, I don't know,' he said irritably. 'How can I know? There might be any sort of condition which could account for death. We're a bit more complex inside even than a television set, Superintendent. I certainly shouldn't be able to tell that he had suffocated, if that's what you mean.'

'You wouldn't?'

'No. There might be a slight increase in the carbon dioxide in the blood but – no, I couldn't be expected to diagnose suffocation. There'd be no foreign matter in the mouth or windpipe, no bruising, no marks of any kind. No, I should not have thought of suffocation. Fortunately it doesn't arise.'

'Exactly,' said Luke and scowled at Mrs Broome. 'And it mustn't', he said, 'or we'll all be in the bag! Don't you forget it! Chief Inspector, has your sergeant gone to put out that call? Where will you take Leach?'

'Ebbfield, I think,' Munday said seriously. 'We'll sort out the charges down there on the home ground, don't you agree?'

Luke's reply was forestalled by a knock on the door, and the Chief Inspector, who was nearest it, pulled it open to reveal a sleepy-eyed, yet harassed looking young man whom he welcomed with relief. There was a hasty conference on the mat whilst the noises from the excited house swept into them from the well of the staircase. After a moment or so the Chief Inspector turned back into the room and leant across the table to Luke.

'There's a question of a glove which Leach was thought to have with him. It's missing.'

The doctor snorted with impatience but the superintendent was very interested. He turned to Mrs Broome.

'You said you had your coat cut tonight. What did you mean?'

She caught her breath. 'Oh, I wasn't going to think about that until the morning!'

Luke's bright teeth flashed in his dark face and the look he gave her was positively affectionate.

'In case you got frightened of the dark, I suppose? You'll do. Run along with the gentleman at the door. He's not a policeman, he's a probation officer. Tell him everything he wants to know. He's trying to help someone before they break his heart for him, poor chap.'

Mrs Broome had the final word. She was bustling to the doorway when it occurred to her and she looked back.

'You could have a very nice nature if you weren't so cheeky,' she said and went out, Munday after her.

Charlie Luke, reduced to half-pint size, flushed and turned sharply on the doctor, who was making noises. 'Now, sir?'

'I want to get that man in a nursing home.' The statement was aggressive. 'He won't die now but he's still ill. He's still confused. Some of it may be alcohol, you understand. Professional nursing at this stage is essential.'

Luke stepped back.

'Excellent idea,' he said briskly. 'As soon as possible. You make the arrangements and as soon as the Chief Inspector returns he will make provision for a preliminary statement. Nothing detailed. Just enough to take us through the next phase. We've got to charge the lady when we find her, you see.'

'Of course.' The doctor was satisfied and busy. 'Fortunately there's a telephone in Mr Eustace Kinnit's bedroom.'

Luke smiled at him without irony. 'Fortunate indeed, sir,' he said cheerfully and turned to Mr Campion as the man hurried off leaving the door open.

'It could be a long trial, you know,' he said presently. 'She might get away with it on the medico's evidence of Toberman's first waking words. I can just hear Sir Cunningham cross-examining Mrs Broome about what she saw on the landing, can't you? That'll be murder if you like!'

Mr Campion was still standing by the table, looking into the limpid mahogany.

'The world is certainly going to hear about the Kinnit family and their governesses, alas!' he said at last. 'No one on earth can prevent that now, I'm afraid. There'll be no more hushing up Miss Thyrza. She's out of the grave. She wins after all.'

'Murder doesn't hush,' Luke had moved over to the doorway. 'My old copy-book was dead right. *Murder will out.* There's something damn funny about it. The desire to pinpoint the blame gets out of the intellect and into the blood. I've known murderers give themselves away rather than leave it a mystery!'

Mr Campion was thinking along other lines.

'It's very odd how the word "governess" is a guilty one in this particular history,' he remarked. 'Just before we came in here I had an account from Julia of the row in the kitchen tonight. Apparently Eustace Kinnit's father tried to suppress the truth about a governess. Eustace himself went to considerable lengths to prevent the word Kinnit and the word Governess appearing together. Mrs Telpher was responsible for a fearful accident whilst acting as a governess and she came over here, deceiving her relatives and bringing an assistant whom she said, quite unnecessarily, was a governess. To the Kinnits it has become an evil word which is always accompanied by trouble. Miss Thyrza is not so much a ghost as their minds playing the goat.'

Luke laughed briefly. 'I know which one frightens me the most!' he said. 'Mr Eustace and Miss Alison are going to need their adopted boy's support. It's a merciful thing he has a sound young woman.'

He went out into the corridor and when Mr Campion joined him he was standing in the shadow by the balustrade.

They paused together, looking down at the curious scene which the old house presented with its open doors and lighted alcoves. It was strongly reminiscent of one of the early Netherlandish mystery paintings; little bright unrelated groups were set about in the dark and tortuous background of the carved staircase, and its several stages and galleries.

From where they stood they had a foreshortened view of a knot of men below in the hall. Munday was speaking to a constable and a plain-clothes man down there while a dejected black wand, bent like a question mark, wavered between them like some spineless overgrown plant.

On the next floor, through the open doorway of the drawing-room, they could see Julia talking to Eustace. She appeared to be comforting or reassuring him, for he was leaning back in one of the pink sofas looking up at her while she talked, emphasizing her words with little gestures. It was a very clear scene, the colours as vivid as if they were painted on glass.

On the upper floor, in the corridor to their right, Mrs Broome was showing her coat to the probation officer. She had carried it to the baluster rail to catch the light from the candelabra, and the purple folds gleamed rich and warm out of the shadow. Miss Aicheson, wearing a plaid dressing-gown and carrying a tray with a white jug and a cup upon it, was coming up the kitchen staircase. And opposite them, across the well, the doctor, stepping out of Eustace's bedroom, paused a moment to look across at Luke and give an affirmative sign.

Mr Campion was comforted. It was a picture of beginnings, he thought. Half a dozen startings: new chapters, new ties, new associations. They were all springing out of the story he had been following, like a spray of plumes in a renaissance pattern springs up from a complete and apparently final feather.

The murmur of voices from the corridor directly below them caught his attention. Luke was already listening. Councillor Cornish was talking to Timothy.

'It was very good of you and I know how you felt,' he was saying earnestly. 'But if you do happen to know where this glove weapon is I think we'd better go and pick it up and let the police have it. We're not the judges, you see. That's one of the very few things I've learned in the last twenty years. We're simply not omniscient. That seems to me to be the whole difficulty. We haven't got all the data, any of us. When we do gang up and make a concerted effort to try to get it, as in a trial of justice, that's the thing which becomes most apparent. As I see it now, anything we suppress may turn out to be the one thing absolutely vital to the lad's safety or salvation. We have absolutely no sure way of telling, that I can see. Life is not predictable.'

'I wasn't trying to hide anything.' Timothy's young voice, which possessed so much the timbre of the other was vehement. 'I was merely not rushing at them with it. I didn't want to be the one who damned him, that was all.'

'Oh, my boy, don't I know!' The older voice was heartfelt. 'That state of mind has dogged me all my life!'

There was a long pause before a laugh, curiously happy, floated up to the two men by the banisters.

'We may not see much of each other,' the Councillor was saying as he and his companion began to move away towards the lower floor, and his voice grew fainter and fainter. 'You're going to have your hands full with your commitments here,

I can see that. But now that we have an opportunity there is just one thing I wanted to say to you. It – er – it concerns my first wife. She was just an ordinary London girl, you know. Very sweet, very brave, very gay, but when she smiled suddenly, when you caught her unawares, she was so *beautiful*. . . .'

The sound faded into a murmur and was lost in the general noises of the busy household.

More about Penguins

If you have enjoyed reading this book you may wish to know that *Penguin Book News* appears every month. It is an attractively illustrated magazine containing a complete list of books published by Penguins and still in print, together with details of the month's new books. A specimen copy will be sent free on request.

Penguin Book News is obtainable from most bookshops; but you may prefer to become a regular subscriber at 3s. for twelve issues. Just write to Dept EP, Penguin Books Ltd, Harmondsworth, Middlesex, enclosing a cheque or postal order, and you will be put on the mailing list.

Some more Penguins by Margery Allingham are described on the following pages.

Note: *Penguin Book News* is not available in the U.S.A., Canada or Australia

Sweet Danger

Margery Allingham

Driving home from Italy, Guffy Randall
passed by the Hotel Beauregard at Mentone,
where, with some surprise, he saw a small
man, armed with a pistol, climbing secretively
out of a ground-floor window. Guffy, who
knew the manager well, stopped to tell
him about the incident, and learnt that
several other suspicious characters were
also in the hotel. After inquiries these turned
out to be Albert Campion and two friends
engaged in a fantastic and fateful pursuit of
a European crown. Again, Guffy described
what he had seen, and the excitement that
followed was so intense that he decided to
stay and follow this sweetly dangerous
adventure to its end.

More Work for the Undertaker

Margery Allingham

'The victim's name is Palinode, and two
vital characters are Jas Bowels and his
son Rowley Boy, the Apron-Street
undertakers, with Harry James,
bank manager, intervening. The "old
and valued clients" to whom *More
Work for the Undertaker* is dedicated will
have guessed the author before I
mention Albert Campion and Stanislaus
Oates: only Margery Allingham's
creations have these impudently
inevitable names' – Christopher Pym
in the *Sunday Times*